THE COLLECTED
SHORT STORIES

THE SHERLOCK HOLMES
AND LUCY JAMES MYSTERIES

The Last Moriarty
The Wilhelm Conspiracy
Remember, Remember
The Crown Jewel Mystery
The Jubilee Problem
Death at the Diogenes Club
The Return of the Ripper
Die Again, Mr. Holmes

THE SHERLOCK HOLMES
AND LUCY JAMES SHORT STORIES

Flynn's Christmas
The Clown on the High Wire
The Cobra in the Monkey Cage
A Fancy-Dress Death
The Sons of Helios
The Vanishing Medium
Christmas at Baskerville Hall

The series page at Amazon:
amzn.to/2s9U2jW

For a FREE copy of
THE CROWN JEWEL MYSTERY – the prequel to the series
please visit sherlockandlucy.com

THE **SHERLOCK HOLMES/ LUCY JAMES** MYSTERIES

THE COLLECTED SHORT STORIES

BY **ANNA ELLIOTT** AND **CHARLES VELEY**

Typesetting by FormattingExperts.com
Cover design by Todd A. Johnson

ISBN: 978-0-9991191-7-4

FLYNN'S
CHRISTMAS

"The stairs were steep, and it was a long way down."

CHAPTER 1

The night was cold and foggy, but up ahead Flynn and his three mates could see the Whitechapel tenement where they expected to sleep. The building was four stories tall, dirty brick, and ugly. Flynn didn't like it. A roof over their heads had become a necessity most nights this December, now that it had gone below freezing, but still, Flynn didn't like it. For one thing, he got the fidgets whenever he was indoors.

Flynn noticed tracks in the frozen slush on the front steps. There was no light above the door, but the dim yellow light of the street lamp showed the imprint of a man's boots. Wide and square-toed.

"We better go around back," Flynn said. "Old Shaw is here."

Lonnie, the baby of the group, gave a groan but quickly stifled it. Lonnie had a broken collarbone that hadn't mended properly. But he wouldn't complain, even though it was past midnight and they were tired.

Bart, the new boy, a bit bigger than Flynn, said, "Maybe he's in with Mrs. Rigsby."

"Then he won't see us," said Tom, the fourth boy. He was Lonnie's older brother, but still younger than Flynn. "And Lonnie won't have to climb up the ladder."

A pack of drunk-looking people staggered along the street, singing, although not the same kind of songs drunks usually sang in this neighborhood. This lot was singing Christmas carols. Now that midnight had come and gone, today was December 24th, which meant tomorrow was Christmas. Not that it meant anything to Flynn and his mates. Christmas was for rich toffs, who roasted their geese and put up their Christmas trees and gave each other expensive gifts. Not for the likes of the Irregulars.

The words of the song that floated down the street to Flynn were something about a silent night. Which was just stupid. Nothing about London was ever silent—day or night.

But Flynn felt the sentiment within the song, and he decided against making Lonnie climb the ladder. He used his key to open the outside front vestibule door that led to the narrow downstairs hall and the steep flight of stairs that would take them to their room. "Everybody quiet now," he said.

When they got into the vestibule, they could hear the wails of babies. "Mrs. Rigsby's out of medicine," Bart said. The wailing was another reason why Flynn didn't like being indoors in this particular building. Though to be fair about it, the wails didn't happen too often. Mostly at this hour either Mrs. Rigsby didn't have customers, or the parent or nurse had picked up the baby, or there was enough medicine to keep the babies quiet.

At least with the babies going on like this, Flynn thought, they wouldn't have to worry about Shaw hearing them come in.

It was cold in the vestibule, and dark. At the top of the stairs, one small electric bulb was lit, enough to show the door to their room, which was the first on the left.

A steel padlock hung on their door.

"Around back, then," Flynn said. He turned to reopen the outer door.

But at that moment the wails of the babies got louder. Looking up, Flynn saw old Shaw, in his thick wool vest and shirtsleeves, leaning on his walking stick and pivoting away from the babies' room. Two strides later, Shaw looked down at them the top of the stairwell.

"You lot," he said. "You owe me three weeks back rent."

"We paid," Flynn said.

"For the first week."

"You said it was the month."

"The rest was a deposit. You owe me three weeks. The padlock stays on until you pay."

"We need to get our things," Flynn said. Though their things didn't amount to much. A few coins, a couple of medals, and their spare clothes. Nothing they couldn't do without for a few days.

Bart stepped forward. "I've got money," he said.

"Hand it over," said Shaw.

He put one hand on the stair railing and leaned his walking stick against it. Then he held out his other hand, rubbing his fingers together in a hurry-up gesture.

"Let me," said Flynn to Bart.

Flynn was the most experienced of the four, and the others respected him. Straw-haired and scrawny, he had been on the streets as long as he could remember or at least as long as he wanted to remember. He had never told anyone what happened to put him there or where he had been before. He had never told anyone his first name. His parents were both dead, for almost as many years as Flynn had been alive.

Bart handed him a handful of coins.

Flynn took it up the stairs. "I give you the money when you take off the lock," he said.

"You don't dictate terms with me, you young imp."

Flynn could see Mrs. Rigsby poke her head out the doorway behind Shaw, irritation on her face. She didn't want the door open because of the noise, Flynn thought, but she needed something. When Shaw ignored her, she pushed the door open hard and stepped out, but she seemed to trip over something. She grasped the wall. "Now, see what you made me do," she said. "Perfectly good skirt."

"Not now, woman," Shaw said.

"They need the medicine, or they'll be crying all night, and tomorrow people will notice."

"You heard me," Shaw said.

Mrs. Rigsby glared at him. Then she untangled her right boot from where she had stepped on her skirt hem, the cause of her stumbling. She gave an angry look at the tear in the fabric, then hoisted her skirts and stamped back into the room. The door closed. The crying kept on, but not as loudly, now that the babies were shut up inside.

"Now, let's have those coins," Shaw said.

"Give me the key to the padlock," Flynn said.

Shaw patted his vest pocket. "Money first." He held out his hand palm up.

Flynn heard Lonnie snuffling at the base of the stairs. He gave Shaw the money.

Shaw counted the coins and then stuffed them into his trousers pocket. "Only twenty here. You still owe five."

"That's not fair," said Flynn. "Open the door for us. We want to get our things. They don't belong to you."

"Whatever is in there belongs to me until you pay the rent in full," Shaw said.

Flynn was two steps below the top of the stairs, and old Shaw was taller, even if they had been on level ground. He stared contemptuously down at Flynn. "Now get out," he said.

Something in his tone gave Flynn hope. A note of urgency. Shaw wanted them to go. Maybe that was something to bargain with. "We're staying right here until you unlock our door," Flynn said. "We can stay all night."

"Oh, can you now," Shaw said, leaning forward, his face coming closer to Flynn's. Flynn could smell the man's stale tobacco breath, but he stood his ground and looked Shaw in the eye.

Which was a mistake.

Flynn was so intent on meeting Shaw's glittering blue stare that he didn't see Shaw's outside hand come off the rail, grip the cane, and with one quick move, swing it around, sideways, whip-like, lashing at Flynn's legs. The weighted head of the walking stick struck Flynn along the side of his knee.

A burst of pain.

Involuntarily Flynn's hand went to his knee.

Shaw pushed hard at Flynn's chest, sending him tumbling down the stairs.

Flynn got his body curled up, but the fall still knocked the wind out of him.

He was getting to his feet when he saw Shaw pull something from his trousers pocket.

It was a revolver.

"You come around here again, you will be trespassing, and

I can shoot you like the little dogs you are," Shaw said. "Now, get out."

Ashen-faced and trembling, the boys bundled Flynn out of the vestibule. Enough slush came through the cracks in Flynn's worn-out boots to make him feel the wet, along with the cold.

"You lost my twenty shillings," Bart said.

CHAPTER 2

They spent the night in a church, one of their usual places of refuge when they needed one. There were cushions on some of the pews, which made this place a favorite. But the throbbing in Flynn's knee kept him awake, as did the chimes from the church bell. In his mind he kept playing over the encounter with Shaw, running it over in his memory to see how he could have made it come out better. He hated to lose. And landing at the bottom of the stairs, hurt and looking up at a gun, that was losing, no question about it. When he lost, he always tried to see where his mistake had been, so he wouldn't make it twice. So, what had gone right, and what had gone wrong?

Well, he had stood up to Shaw, that was one thing right. You had to stand up to people like Shaw, or they'd kick you into the gutter. What he shouldn't have done, he thought, was to come up the stairs to meet Shaw. He should have stayed back, where Shaw couldn't hit him. Come to think of it, he shouldn't have been on the stairs at all. He shouldn't even have gone to the front door. That was his mistake. He had been soft about little Lonnie and his sore collar bone not wanting to go around back and climb the rope ladder. If they'd just gone up the ladder, quiet-like and not made noise, they could have spent the night

in the room and left the same way. But because he'd been soft
about Lonnie, they were out twenty shillings, and he had a sore
knee. Soft was the first mistake, he decided. Then the other
mistakes made it worse.

So, he better not be soft.

CHAPTER 3

The dark void above him turned to the outlines of church windows and then to shadows of people in robes in the stained glass. Flynn got up, gingerly favoring his knee, and hobbled the few paces to the pew behind his, where Bart and Lonnie were snoring softly. He put a hand on Bart's shoulder. The other boy, startled, sat up as though having a bad dream.

"We have to go," Flynn said, speaking quietly into Bart's ear.

Bart nodded and leaned over to wake his brother. Flynn did the same for Tom, in the next pew down.

On their way out, they saw Wiggins, another one of the Irregulars, running up the wide stone steps, a scarf around his hair and tied under his chin, a coat too large for him flapping around his legs. He stumbled on the frozen slush in boots that, Flynn thought, were too small.

"There's a job," Wiggins said. "Baker Street."

CHAPTER 4

Flynn led them up the stairs to Mr. Holmes's big room like he always did. He hadn't taken two steps inside before a blond-haired girl popped up from the sofa and narrowed her eyes at him.

"What happened to your leg?"

Becky Kelly was, in a manner of speaking, Mr. Holmes's grand-niece. At least, she was the younger sister of Mr. Holmes's daughter's husband—whatever that was called. She was eleven, same as him, and she also wasn't a bad sort, as girls went. But right now, Flynn wished she hadn't got such sharp eyes.

"Nothing," Flynn said, stepping aside so the others could flow in around him.

He might have known Becky wouldn't just let it go. "Dr. Watson? Flynn's hurt his leg."

Dr. Watson got up from where he'd been sitting by the fire. "What seems to be the matter, Flynn?"

Flynn blew out a breath. "I bumped it."

Lonnie said, "A man hit him with a cane. He took our twenty shillings, too. Bart's and mine."

"Where?" It was Mr. Holmes's voice, short and sharp, coming from behind. It made Flynn jump. Mr. Holmes had been standing at his desk, behind them as they walked in, so Flynn hadn't seen him.

"Now that it's winter, we needed a room," Flynn said. "The twenty shillings was for back rent."

Mr. Holmes made him explain what had happened. Flynn avoided looking at Becky while he told the story. Becky was also whip-smart, and he couldn't help thinking she would have thought of a way out of the whole mess. Or at least not been lack-witted enough to let old Shaw get away with the money.

When Flynn finished talking, Mr. Holmes took a long pull on his pipe. "The landlord's name?"

"Shaw."

Becky said, "Something's not right. Why would a man like Mr. Shaw have a gun?"

"We will look into it," Mr. Holmes said. "Dr. Watson, is Flynn fit for today's assignment?"

"Roll up your trouser leg," said Dr. Watson. Moments later he frowned and started tugging at the knot in the red scarf that Flynn had tied around his knee. "Where did this come from?"

"It's a brace."

"You can't run with it tied so tightly," Dr. Watson said, "and it will interfere with healing." The scarf came free. Flynn winced at the sudden surge of pain.

CHAPTER 5

They were in King's Cross Railway Station. Flynn and Bart stood by the main entrance, on the inside. Lonnie and Tom were posted across the station, on the other side of the ebb and flow of travelers who came and went with their luggage.

It was a spot-and-follow job, Mr. Holmes had said. The target would be wearing a black coat and top hat, like thousands of others, of course, but would have a red Christmas scarf. And he would be carrying a brown satchel, leather, with a two-strap handle. The leather would be tan. Not brown, not mahogany. Tan. He would arrive at eleven o'clock.

They were to spot the man and then follow the satchel.

The man would come in the entry gate that Flynn and Bart were watching. He would come in and wait for instructions. He should be easy to spot because he would be the only one standing about. All the others would be going this way or that, wanting to get to their trains or buy their tickets.

"He will hand the satchel to someone," Mr. Holmes said, "But not until someone gives him instructions. That may occur in front of you, in the station."

"What if someone stops him outside?"

"Others will be watching outside."

"Wiggins?"

"And others. There will be police. Plainclothesmen, and ordinary guards. But they will not interfere. Your job is to follow the satchel."

"What if the man with the satchel gets on a train?"

"Then you get on the train as well. Here is a crown for each of you to buy the necessary ticket. You will return it if not used. Or if you are successful, you will add it to your reward."

"What's in the satchel?"

"A great deal of money."

"What for?"

"Its purpose does not concern you. You are to concentrate on the satchel. Follow it until it no longer is moving. Then one of you stays with it while the other goes back. Flynn and Tom, you will be the ones to stay. Bart and Lonnie, you will be the ones to return here to report. Use your crown to pay for a telephone call if needed. Be sure to get proper change."

Flynn had been pleased to be designated to stay with the satchel. Who was to say that the satchel wouldn't go on the move again?

Now Bart's eyes were on the crowd, as were Flynn's. Neither boy looked at the other. Bart said, "A great deal of money."

Flynn said, "What about it?"

"Mr. Holmes wouldn't say what it was for. What do you think it's for?"

"I don't care."

"I think it ought to be for us," Bart said.

"Don't talk rubbish," Flynn said. "There's police about. They'll know about the satchel too."

"What if we found a way to get past them? We could get on the train and go somewhere."

"You're crazy," Flynn said. "We wouldn't get away. Not in front of the rozzers."

"I didn't say we would. I said that's what ought to happen."

CHAPTER 6

Flynn saw the man with the red scarf and the tan satchel about ten minutes later, just at eleven o'clock, just when Mr. Holmes said. The man looked worried. Flynn had expected him to look worried. Anyone carrying a satchel with a great deal of money into a situation where he didn't know what to expect would look worried.

"That must be him."

Flynn jumped when the voice spoke behind him. Bart had gone to make a circuit of the room a minute ago, just in case they'd somehow missed seeing their target. Which meant that whoever was talking to him now had to be—

Flynn turned around and saw Becky, dressed in boy's clothes, with her braids tucked up under a checkered cloth cap.

"What are you doing here?" Flynn demanded.

Becky shrugged. "The same thing you are. Waiting to see who that man"—she pointed to man with the satchel Flynn had already spotted—"gives all the money to."

Flynn gave her a narrow look. "Mr. Holmes said you could come?"

Becky had a way of looking completely innocent, like butter wouldn't melt in her mouth. It always meant that trouble was ahead. She looked just that way now.

"He didn't say that I couldn't. I might have given him the impression that I was going to go and bake scones with Mrs. Hudson in the kitchen. I didn't lie," she added. "I will go and make scones with her. Once this is all over."

Flynn knew from experience that arguing with Becky when she'd got her mind set on something was a waste of breath, but he still ground his teeth together.

"You can't be here!"

"Why not?"

Flynn stabbed a finger in their mark's direction. "Because whoever he's giving the money to is up to no good."

Becky rolled her eyes. "Obviously."

He should have known she'd have worked that one out. The police were outside, which meant this couldn't be a straight-up delivery job. The police or the Pinkertons or the bank men would be the ones to deliver straight money, and they would get their help from their nightsticks and guns, not from street kids. This money was being delivered to someone bad.

"Who do you think is going to come and meet him?" Becky asked.

Flynn didn't know. Maybe a spy. Or a blackmailer. "No one you should be tangling with, anyway."

Becky's eyes got slitty-looking. "Why is all right for you to be here but not me? Just because I'm a girl?"

Flynn wasn't thick enough to put a foot in that argument. Becky might look about as much a threat as a fluffy kitten, but he'd seen her fight. She was as good with her fists as any boy.

"Mr. Holmes wouldn't want you getting mixed up in whatever this is," he finally said.

"But he's *ordered* you to be mixed up in it. It's just as dangerous for you."

"That's different. I'm not a part of his family."

Becky looked like she was going to say something else—keep arguing, probably. But at that minute a fat man with a top hat and black beard came in from where the trains were, like he'd just arrived, walking fast, taking big bold strides.

The reason Flynn spotted him right away was that the fat man was carrying a tan satchel. The fat man went right up to the man with the red scarf and stopped. The man with the red scarf looked puzzled. The fat man set down his satchel, tipped his hat politely, and looked like he was asking directions. The other man still looked puzzled, but then he set down his own satchel and pointed back at the entry doors where he'd come in.

The fat man nodded, shook hands, picked up a satchel and strode off to the entry doors.

Becky sucked in a quick breath, and Flynn nodded. "We've got to round up the others and get them to follow the fat one. They just switched satchels."

CHAPTER 7

Flynn and the Irregulars had a good system for following targets for Mr. Holmes. As well they might, because they did it for a living, along with pickpocketing and a lot of other things that Mr. Holmes wouldn't approve of, though Flynn was sure that Mr. Holmes knew, because Mr. Holmes knew everything. The system was to fan out front and back and side to side. They had Tom, Bart, and Lonnie ahead of the target and Flynn in back.

Which meant letting Tom and Lonnie know right away there was a target to get out in front of.

Flynn did that with his own red scarf, the one he had tied to his knee that Dr. Watson had made him take off. He'd put the scarf back on as soon as they'd come out of Baker Street because it made the knee numb and easier to walk on, even if it still hurt and Flynn had to keep it stiff, like a peg leg.

He loosened the scarf, took it off, and gave it a wave in the direction of the other doors as soon as they had come out on the crowded street. That got Tom's attention, and then Flynn mimed a fat man by waving his arms wide and pulling them down around his sides, imagining himself as a snowman. Then he imitated carrying a satchel. All the while keeping his eye on the fat man, who stood at the curb as though waiting for a cab.

Becky was standing next to him. Flynn had quit arguing about her taking part in the job. For one thing, they didn't have time. And for another, the fact was that he and Becky had been in tight spots together before. This job was more likely to be a success with her here, even if he didn't want to admit it out loud.

The fat man ran out between two of the cabs, crossing the street. Which would have been a problem if Tom, Bart, and Lonnie hadn't spotted him already, thanks to Flynn. But they did, and Flynn saw with satisfaction that they were crossing the street, separating so Tom and Bart could get on either side, with Lonnie up ahead, as soon as they knew which way the fat man was going.

"Your knee's hurting," Becky said.

Flynn grunted. It was, but he didn't want to admit that, either.

The fat man kept on for about ten minutes, and then turned right, into a shopping arcade.

Becky and Flynn stopped short on the other side of the street arcade. The fat man was stopped at the window of one of the shops. "Brown's Haberdashery," Becky read.

Flynn couldn't read the sign over the shop door, but he could recognize the top hats and spats and braces in the window right enough to know what kind of a place it was. Although what the fat man wanted here was anyone's guess.

Lonnie and Tom sauntered past, one on one side of the arcade and Tom on the other. Bart was over on the far side of the arcade.

So far, the fat man hadn't even looked in their direction. Which was the reason Mr. Holmes used street boys for this work, Flynn knew. Because even if you looked at a street boy, you didn't see him. Because you didn't really want to see him.

"Flynn—the window!" Becky's whisper was urgent, although for a second, Flynn didn't know what she was getting at.

"It's like a mirror," Becky hissed. "If you thought you might be followed, but didn't want to be obvious about looking behind you—"

She didn't have to spell it out. The fat man could be staring into the haberdashery's window to get a look at the arcade behind him.

Another thought came hard on the heels of that one. He'd put the red scarf back on around his knee. That would make him stand out, and memorable, and maybe spook the fat man when he saw a boy with a red scarf tied around his knee a second time. Flynn knew the scarf had to go.

Best do it now, he thought, and tugged it off.

"Better," Becky murmured.

Flynn ignored the hot rush of pain and stuffed the scarf inside his coat, all the while keeping his eye on the fat man.

Who stepped away from the shop window and, without looking behind him, moved on to the next shop.

And went inside.

"We need to get closer." Becky didn't wait for an answer, just darted towards the shop. Flynn went after her.

The fat man had gone into a lady's dress shop. Flynn couldn't read the name of the shop any better than he had the one on the haberdashery, but this shop's sign had the silhouette of a woman's dress on it.

At least Becky knew enough not to just stare straight in through the window. When he caught up to her, they both waited a minute, and then came forward again, till they were just at the edge of the glass. Flynn kept walking, keeping his eyes front but looking in the window, and trying to spot the fat man while taking care not to limp. The man would remember a limp. Flynn could walk without limping for a few steps, and that was all it took.

But Flynn couldn't see the fat man inside the shop. Just a woman in a black wool cap. The woman was saying something to the clerk lady, getting her scarf and hat adjusted and plainly about to leave the shop.

"He's gone!" Becky gasped.

A hollow feeling bloomed in the pit of Flynn's stomach. He turned and made a quick signal to Tom, Bart, and Lonnie, pointing away down to the end of the arcade and making a sweeping, curving gesture with his arm and hand, to indicate they should go to the end of the arcade and to the rear entrance to look for the fat man.

The three of them nodded and set off.

Becky tugged him away from the door to the shop. "Do you think he went out the back?"

"Must have."

Flynn wanted to run in right then, but he thought he had better wait for the woman in the wool hat to leave. She was fiddling with a wrapped parcel, tucking it into her carpetbag. Flynn and Becky stood to one side of the entrance as she came out and walked away with her big carpetbag, head down, swishing her skirt.

"I'm going in to ask," Flynn said.

He'd expected Becky to argue about that one, too, but she just nodded.

Flynn pushed open the shop door and faced the clerk lady. She stared at him as though he were a rat scuttling across her floorboards.

Flynn asked, "Did a fat man with a tan satchel come through here?"

"Get out!" the clerk lady said. She picked up a flower pot containing a big red flower as if she was about to throw pot and all at Flynn. Again, louder this time, she said, "Get out!"

Flynn did.

Becky had seen, of course, and heard it too. "She's not very nice. Maybe she's hiding the fat man in one of the changing rooms?"

Flynn could have told her the clerk lady's treatment of him was about average for grown-ups around the city. "Why would she do that?"

"I don't know." Becky frowned at the shop's awning. "Maybe you were right the first time and he went out the back. Maybe Tom and Lonnie and Bart are after him now."

She also didn't have to spell it out that if the other lads weren't after the fat man, it meant that they'd lost him, and would have to report as much to Mr. Holmes.

Flynn felt sick, and his leg hurt. He remembered another time, a couple years earlier, when he had lost another important target and had to tell Mr. Holmes face to face. He had the same sick feeling now as back then.

He turned back to the shop window. Saw the clerk lady glaring at him and picking up a telephone. He waved at her and gave her a cheeky grin. Might as well darken someone else's day.

"Flynn!"

Becky had been standing stock-still next to him, looking like she was lost in thought. But now all of a sudden she startled, grabbing onto his arm.

"What?"

"The woman with the wool hat," Becky said.

"What about her?" Flynn didn't see her among the shoppers that crowded the arcade.

Becky's brows were knitted together, her face screwed up like she was trying to remember something. "I don't know, but there was something… something about the way she was walking that seemed familiar—"

Flynn drew in a sharp burst of air. Becky might have recognized the way the woman was walking. But he was recalling something else. Her skirt, swishing around when she walked. He concentrated, forcing the remembered image back into his mind.

Her head down, her face tucked into her scarf.

The swishing hem of her skirt.

The *torn* hem of her skirt.

Mrs. Rigsby.

Then he saw her, all the way at the end of the arcade. She was getting into a cab.

He caught hold of Becky's hand. No time even to explain. "After her! Run!"

CHAPTER 8

Becky was making better time than he was. Flynn hustled himself along after her as best he could with his sore knee, jostling through the shoppers and trying not to fall.

It was all clear to him. Mrs. Rigsby had picked up the satchel at the train station, dressed as a fat man. A fat man, because she had her skirt bunched up under her coat, along with her carpetbag. In front of the arcade shop, she had looked inside to see that there were no other shoppers and maybe that the lady clerk wasn't watching. Then she had gone inside, probably pulling off the black beard and flattening the top hat with a quick move, while letting her skirts down at the same time she pulled out the carpetbag. Beard, hat, and satchel had gone into the carpetbag. Then she had bought something from the lady clerk and had it wrapped in brown paper. The wool cap had been in her coat pocket, and she'd put it on before leaving the shop.

If they could get to the end of the arcade in time to see the cab number, he could let Mr. Holmes know. At least they would be able to ask the cabman where he'd taken his fare.

But by the time Flynn had reached the end of the arcade, the cab was no longer in sight.

Becky turned to him, breathing hard and clenching her hands

in frustration. She didn't like failing any more than he did. "We lost her!"

Flynn shook his head. "Maybe not."

At the end of the arcade, another cab was pulling up to let out a passenger. Flynn waved to get the driver's attention.

The man's dubious look faded when Flynn showed him the half-crown, the one Mr. Holmes had given each of them for train fare. The driver asked, "Where to?"

Flynn had a moment's hesitation. Then he told the driver the address of old Shaw's building in Whitechapel.

Becky got into the cab first, then barely waited for Flynn to sit down before she started in with questions.

"I don't understand. Who is that woman? How do you know the address where she might be heading?"

Flynn's stomach knotted up. He'd always avoided letting Becky—or anyone else for that matter—know how he lived when he wasn't on a job for Mr. Holmes. The thought of how she'd look—maybe disgusted, or even worse, pitying—when she saw old Shaw's building was like nails dragged on a chalkboard inside his mind. But the thought of disappointing Mr. Holmes was worse.

Flynn looked out the window as the cab started to roll, avoiding Becky's gaze. "Her name is Mrs. Rigsby. She rents a room in the same building as me and the lads. Makes a living minding other people's babies for them."

Becky's eyes widened. "And you're sure she's going back there now?"

"Pretty sure." It was true, of course, that Mrs. Rigsby might have been going anywhere with the money she had in the satchel. "Remember the padlock old Shaw put on the door to our room?"

Becky nodded, looking like she'd put the pieces together, too. "You're right. Why would Shaw care about twenty shillings back rent enough to padlock your door?"

"Exactly." The cab stopped to let a wagon loaded down with Christmas trees trundle into the stream of traffic. Flynn ground his teeth together, waiting for the cab to get rolling again. Christmas really was nothing but a nuisance. "Shaw wanted to keep us out of our room because he had something to hide in there."

"And now Mrs. Rigsby is taking the money in the satchel to Shaw?" Becky said. "That would mean that they're in whatever this is together."

She didn't say it, but Flynn would bet that she was thinking about old Shaw's gun, and the fact that this job had just gotten a lot more dangerous.

CHAPTER 9

The cab drew up at the house in Whitechapel. In the daylight, it looked even worse than it had last night—which was saying something.

Becky studied the sagging roof and boarded-up windows. "So this is where you live?"

To give her credit, she didn't sound like she was feeling sorry for him, but Flynn still growled, "It's not that bad!"

"I didn't say it was. You saw the neighborhood Jack and I used to live in, before he got promoted."

That was true. Flynn sometimes forgot that Becky hadn't always been a rich girl. She and her brother had been poor, back when Jack Kelly hadn't yet got promoted to Scotland Yard and had been just a lowly beat constable, trying to support them both on a few shillings a week.

Becky started to climb out of the cab, but Flynn stopped her.

"Listen," Flynn told Becky. "You need to go back to Baker Street and get Mr. Holmes. Tell him where I am."

Becky frowned. "What are you going to do while I'm gone?"

"Try to get a look inside at whatever secrets Old Shaw is hiding in there."

Becky's frown got even deeper. "I'm not the one with a hurt knee."

"No. But I know the layout of this place, and you don't. Besides. Shaw and Mrs. Rigsby both know me. If I'm spotted, they'll think I'm just trying to get back into the room to get our belongings. They might chase me off, but they're not going to try that hard to catch me."

Becky didn't look as though she liked it, but she couldn't argue with that. It was safer for Flynn to be the one to stay.

The cab driver also didn't look any too happy when Becky told him she wanted him to take her to Baker Street, but at least she'd thought to fill her pockets with some money before coming out. She handed over some coins, promised the driver more when he delivered her, and the cab rolled away.

Flynn watched them go. Should he act now? If he got into trouble, there would be no one to help him. But then, he might be wrong about everything. Mrs. Rigsby might have taken the money satchel somewhere else, and he would be dragging Mr. Holmes here for nothing.

Flynn went around the back and climbed up the ladder, slowly, because of his knee. The window was unlocked, the way the boys always left it. Before he slid it upward, Flynn peered through the dirty glass to be sure old Shaw wasn't waiting for him.

Shaw wasn't.

But someone was.

Someone was lying very still, on one of the four canvas cots that Flynn and his mates had been sleeping on. A woman. She wore a dark blue overcoat. Some kind of a uniform. Flynn wondered how long she had been there. Had she been behind the locked door when they'd come in just after midnight? Was she a prisoner?

Balancing on the swaying rope ladder, Flynn lifted the window up, just an inch or so, and listened.

He heard the sound of the woman breathing. That was all. No cries from babies in the room next door. So the babies were asleep or gone.

Gone made more sense. Now it was clear why Shaw had padlocked the room. Shaw and Mrs. Rigsby were hiding the woman. They couldn't put her into the other room, because the mothers or nurses would be coming in to pick up the babies.

CHAPTER 10

He slid the window open and clambered over the sill, leading with his good leg. His bad knee hurt more, but he pulled that leg through and stood, his boots soaked through with slush, listening hard. Had someone heard? He shut the window.

The woman on the cot must have felt the change in the air with the window opening and shutting, because she woke up. She moved on the cot and opened her eyes.

Flynn's heart started pounding. He held a finger to his lips.

"It's all right," he said.

"Who are you?"

"I live here. I mean I spend nights here. We pay rent. Those other three cots are for my mates. I came to get our things. Who are you?"

The woman thought this over and then she sat up straight, getting her feet on the floor, ready to stand up.

Then she yelled, "Shaw!"

At that moment, two things happened.

From the room next door, through the thin wall, came the sound of Shaw's voice, tight and low. "Will you shut up?"

And from down the stairway came the sound of the outside door, opening, and Mrs. Rigsby's voice. "I've got it!"

The uniform woman turned to the doorway at the two sounds, and like a flash Flynn was at the window, pushing it up, hard and fast. He had an idea, but it didn't include staying here and letting Shaw come in with that gun. With the sash now up, Flynn rolled out the window, grabbed the rope ladder, and swung himself all the way out. He slid down fast.

But he watched the open window as he went down.

Just as he was hitting the ground, Flynn saw the uniform woman's face, looking down at him. He took off running as best he could with the knee and the slush.

Then he came back, keeping close to the wall, to where the ladder hung beneath the window.

He spent a long minute thinking, trying to imagine himself being as smart as Mr. Holmes. He decided that the money was for Shaw and Mrs. Rigsby and that the lady in the uniform was in on it.

So, they were all bad guys.

So, taking their money wouldn't be wrong. If Flynn could take it, he and his mates would be set for life. He could even return it. There would be some kind of a reward, he was sure about that.

He backed away from the wall of the building, supporting himself by the ladder, and looked up to where he could see the window.

Still open.

That meant that the uniform lady and Shaw and Mrs. Rigsby weren't in there. And they hadn't come out of the building to chase after him. Why would they, after all? Like he'd told Becky, they would think he had just come back to his room to get his belongings and those of his mates, and that now he'd run away frightened. They wouldn't think he knew about the satchel or the money.

A minute later he was up the ladder and looking through the window into the room.

No one there. Flynn eased himself back in.

They had left the door to his room open. He could hear voices coming from the room next door.

CHAPTER 11

There were three voices. Shaw, the uniform woman, and Mrs. Rigsby. Walking as softly as he could, Flynn moved into the hallway and crouched down outside their door. It was halfway open.

They were standing over one of the cribs, at the far side of the room, near the window, next to a rocking chair. On the crib was the carpetbag Mrs. Rigsby had been carrying. It was open. A brown paper parcel was on the shabby little mattress beside it. Shaw had leaned his walking stick against the crib and was holding on to the crib rail, hovering over the open carpetbag. He pulled out a black beard, and then a top hat, still flattened. Then he pulled out the satchel.

"The moment of truth," Shaw said.

But at that moment, from a crib near the doorway, just to the right of where Flynn was standing, came a baby's cry.

Flynn involuntarily looked at the crib. He saw a dark blue blanket, wrapped around something very small. The dark blue color of the blanket was the same as the uniform lady's overcoat.

Flynn could see the baby's pink forehead.

Old Shaw wasn't looking at the baby. He was looking down into the satchel. Rummaging his hand around. "Looks like it's all here," he said.

The two women looked back at Shaw, as though seeking direction.

"We have to do it now," Shaw said.

"With the medicine," Mrs. Rigsby said. "He won't feel it."

The uniform lady was by the window, looking out, her back to them.

"I don't want to do it," she said.

"You said you would," said Mrs. Rigsby. She took a few steps to stand in front of the uniform lady. "He'll take it quicker, coming from you. He's used to you."

Shaw said, "You two just get it done."

And at that moment, Flynn changed his plan.

Flynn dove for the walking stick and grabbed it. Before Shaw even realized Flynn had come into the room, Flynn took the stick by the smaller end, came up into a crouch, and swung the heavy weighted handle in a good, hard arc that smacked into Shaw's kneecap with a loud crack. Shaw gave an outraged roar, but he bent down, involuntarily clutching at his injury. By this time, Flynn had the walking stick drawn back and ready for another swing, and he took it, good and hard, catching Shaw on the side of the head, just above the ear.

Shaw went down like a felled ox. The two women had turned at the sound and were staring at Flynn in disbelief. Flynn knew he had to do something about them too, but all he had was the walking stick. He threw the walking stick at them. It missed, of course, but it shattered the window glass, showering the rocking chair and the floor with shards and then clattering to the floor. By the time the two women recovered, Flynn had the baby in his arms and was through the doorway, heading for the stairs.

CHAPTER 12

The baby weighed less than a cat, Flynn thought. It wouldn't
slow him down, though he worried about his unsteady knee.
He didn't want to fall on the stairs. He hesitated at the top.
The stairs were steep, and it was a long way down. From the
room behind him came the sounds of the two women stumbling
through the glass and the rocking chair on the wood floor, and
then Shaw's bellow of rage.

"He's seen us! Get out of my way!"

Flynn sat on the top step and clutched the baby to his chest
and stuck out both feet and lay back and slid down the stairs,
feet first.

Flynn's plan was to stand up and keep moving forward as
soon as his feet reached the tile floor of the vestibule, but with
the knee and the baby and puddles tracked in from the slush
outside, the movement wasn't as smooth or quick as he had
hoped for. Finally, he was on his feet getting the door open.
Glancing back, he saw Shaw was at the top of the stairs, with
his gun in one hand and the other on the stair rail, staggering
forward, his face a deep scarlet.

Flynn spun out through the vestibule doorway and shut the
door behind him.

A shot rang out, and a bullet smacked through the heavy wood. It missed Flynn, but then he slipped on the slush on the front stoop and went down, clutching the baby against his chest. The baby let out a wail like a siren.

"Shhh." Flynn knew nothing about babies, nor did he especially want to, but he gave it an awkward pat, hoping it would quiet down and let him think, because he'd never needed to think harder or quicker in his life. Shaw would have made it down the inside steps by now and any moment would be opening the door, and taking aim, with a clear shot, point-blank, at Flynn and the baby. Shaw wouldn't hesitate. He had the money, and he needed Flynn dead. He was probably going to go back upstairs and shoot the two women, Flynn thought.

Then Flynn remembered. He still had his key to the front door. He could hear Shaw clumping across the tiles of the vestibule. Flynn jammed the key into the front door keyhole and turned it, hearing the lock click, leaving the key inside, twisting it hard and bending it for good measure.

Out on the street, a horse and cab pounded around the corner, the driver hauling on the reins. Right behind them came two more horses, pulling a police wagon.

Both drivers brought their horses to a halt, directly in front of the house.

Flynn glimpsed a face at the cab window.

Behind Flynn, the front door of the house was rattling. Flynn dragged himself off the stoop and down the steps and off to the side, hoping to get out of Shaw's sight in time. He heard a loud crash as the door behind him burst open.

But Flynn did not turn around to look. The cab door had opened. Flynn was staring in disbelief at Dr. Watson.

Crouched in the cab, Dr. Watson held a revolver in a dead-steady hand, aiming straight at the front door of the house.

From the police wagon, other guns appeared, pointing in the same direction.

From the cab came a familiar voice. *Two* familiar voices. Becky called out, "It's all right, we're here!"

And Sherlock Holmes said, "Drop your weapon, Shaw, and put up your hands."

In Flynn's arms, the baby stirred, fighting against the restraint of its blanket. Flushed and toothless, the baby stared into Flynn's eyes, the little face red and contorted with what looked to Flynn like pure outrage.

"I don't blame you, little guy," Flynn said, as the baby screamed. "I don't blame you one bit."

CHAPTER 13

They rode in the cab back to Scotland Yard, where Flynn handed the baby over to a policewoman. He didn't expect to see the baby ever again. Lestrade was there, and he shook Flynn's hand. Lestrade remembered when he and Flynn had found a warehouse of dynamite together. He said that he always thought Flynn would amount to something in the world. Flynn thought he had better not say he had come back to the Whitechapel building because he intended to take the satchel.

He rode in the cab with Mr. Holmes and Becky and Dr. Watson back to Baker Street, where he noticed Mrs. Hudson had put a holly wreath on the front door. Dr. Watson helped Flynn up the seventeen steps to the big room and made him sit on the couch across from the fireplace. Soon both Flynn's boots were off, and his bad leg was stretched out. With the warmth of the fire on his face, Flynn almost immediately fell asleep.

He came half-awake when the telephone rang—and even more awake when someone poked him on the shoulder.

"Are you awake?"

Becky was sitting on the sofa beside him.

Flynn rubbed his face. "I am now."

"That was very brave, rescuing the baby," Becky said. She frowned. "Not very smart, but very brave."

Coming from her, that was probably the best Flynn was going to get, so he said, "Thanks."

Mr. Holmes hung up the telephone and moved a chair from a table, positioning it across from Flynn.

"Now then," Mr. Holmes said. "Becky here and I have been having a talk about you and your future."

Flynn sat up. He didn't entirely like the sound of that. "We make out all right, me and the lads. I can look after myself."

Mr. Holmes steepled his long fingers together. "I do not doubt it for a moment. However, you and the other boys might do even better with a new room, since Mr. Shaw will be incarcerated for the foreseeable future, and thus unable to provide accommodation."

Flynn felt himself scowling, wondering how he was going to admit that they couldn't afford a better place than Shaw's, when Mr. Holmes said, "The rent will be paid for as long as you wish."

Flynn bristled. "I don't take no charity—"

Mr. Holmes raised a hand. "Nor do I dole charity out. Consider it an investment. You have done good work for me—valuable work. I would like you to continue to do so. However—" He nodded towards Flynn's knee. "You cannot continue to work for me at full capacity if you continue to live in sub-standard, unhealthful environments that carry a risk of injury. To protect my own interests, it is only logical that I should prioritize your safety and health."

That was a lot of big words, but Flynn supposed what Mr. Holmes was saying made sense. He gave a cautious nod.

"Also—" Mr. Holmes looked sideways at Becky. "It has further come to my attention that you might be an even greater asset to my investigative practice if you were to learn to read. Therefore, a tutor will be engaged to teach you."

That sounded like staying indoors. Flynn scowled again.

"Cheer up." Becky grinned at him and nudged his shoulder. "I'll sit in on the lessons with you. It won't be so bad." She looked at Mr. Holmes. "Tell him everything else that's happened! About Shaw and the others."

"Shaw and the two women are locked away in Newgate Prison," Mr. Holmes said. "All three will be tried for kidnapping and attempted murder. They were about to kill the baby, as you thought. Mrs. Rigsby said they had agreed not to do the murder unless they had the ransom money safely in hand. A curious scruple, but it worked to our advantage. The woman you saw in uniform is Mrs. Rigsby's sister. She was the child's nurse. The parents are a very wealthy couple who live nearby, in Regent's Park. They received a note saying both nurse and baby would be killed unless the ransom was paid. All the money was recovered from the satchel when the police stormed the building."

Dr. Watson came in, carrying a bowl of ice and some towels, and a brown tube made of heavy leather with brass hinges and buckles on one side. He looked down at Flynn. "Now about that knee of yours," he said. "Ice will reduce the swelling, and this is a proper brace that will not cut off circulation. If you take care of yourself, you will have a full recovery."

He was about to put the towels under Flynn's leg, but at that moment there was a ring at the doorbell. Flynn heard Mrs. Hudson's voice, and others, quieter, and footsteps coming up the stairs.

Flynn sat up and got his feet off the couch as a young man and woman entered the room. The man doffed his sleek top hat and reached out for a handshake with Mr. Holmes. Flynn saw particles of snow glittering on the woman's fur coat. She was holding the baby. Father and mother, Flynn thought.

"We just had to come and say thank you in person, Mr. Holmes," the father said.

The mother said, "And we had to bring this little fellow, because I'm not letting him out of my sight."

"I hope the arrangements will be satisfactory," the father said. "I have already done as you asked. I would also be quite happy to pay a fee—"

Mr. Holmes held up his hand to interrupt. "A fee is quite unnecessary," he said. "It was no more than my duty."

The father was looking at Flynn, who was standing up by now, awkward and embarrassed by the holes in his socks. "And you, young man. You are the one we have to thank for your quick action and bravery, are you not?"

The mother was looking at the baby, her dark eyes filled with emotion, and then at Flynn, He knew both parents were expecting a polite reply.

Still, for a long moment, Flynn was unable to speak.

In his memory, he saw another pair of dark eyes, and they were looking down into his own. The eyes were different, of course, but they were filled with the same emotion. He had seen them before, in a dream that sometimes came to him. The eyes always vanished before he could see whose they were. In the dream, the eyes were accompanied by a warm and comforting voice, and a feeling that bloomed inside his chest and spread throughout his body, a feeling for which he had no words.

Then the memory passed, and Flynn could speak again.

He said, "It was no more than my duty."

The young couple and their baby left soon afterward, and Dr. Watson wrapped up Flynn's knee with a towel packed with ice.

Becky dropped back onto the couch next to him. "I've got one more surprise for you!"

She had that innocent look again. Flynn looked at her warily. He still wasn't quite ready to forgive her for giving Mr. Holmes the idea of a tutor, even if it might come in handy to know how to read sometimes. "I think I've had about enough of your surprises for one day."

"You'll like this one," Becky said. "Mrs. Hudson has been busy in the kitchen since morning, and Lucy and Jack will be here soon. And Mr. Holmes has made sure that Bart and Lonnie and all the other boys are invited too."

Out in the street, Flynn could hear carolers singing. Something about joy to the world.

"And as soon as they get here," Becky said. "We're all going to have Christmas dinner."

THE
CLOWN
ON THE
HIGH WIRE

"I hope you can tell us how he got up there, MR. HOLMES."

WATSON

CHAPTER 1

My story begins just after nine o'clock on the morning of March 10, 1898, when we first entered the vast interior of the London Olympia Amphitheatre. The body of a circus clown hung nearly one hundred feet above us, looking very small within that great chamber. As we gazed upward, I heard a shrill whistle blast from a train departing the nearby Olympia railway station. The sound of the whistle took on a mocking note, or so it seemed to me. On that very train, I thought, whoever had done this deed might be making his escape.

I hoped this puzzling new case would bring Sherlock Holmes out of the dark mood that had followed our most recent adventure. That case, involving a gang of opium smugglers, had ended with the escape of one of the criminals, a murderous woman named Mrs. Torrance. To date Holmes had not captured her, and his growing frustration had been painful for me to observe.

* * *

"An odd murder, Mr. Holmes, and no mistake," Lestrade said. His ferret-like features twisted as he squinted upward at the body. Around us, all the thousands of amphitheatre seats were empty now, but they soon would be filled with clamouring crowds eager to watch the performers of the Great American Circus. "Worth an early-morning trip for you, I'd say."

The body drooped motionless in its white costume, dangling like a pendulum at the centre of a long circus high wire, suspended by a rope wrapped around its obviously broken neck. Daylight from a thousand glass panes streamed into the vast emptiness of the amphitheatre, illuminating floppy red clown shoes on the feet and chalk-white makeup on the face and nearly bald head. Around the head a bright fringe of false red hair created a grotesque halo. The eyes, made ominous by black greasepaint, seemed to stare directly down at us.

"I hope you can tell us how he got up there, Mr. Holmes," Lestrade said. "It may help us catch his killer."

Holmes made no reply. He was no longer looking upward. He seemed to be concentrating on the sturdy circus pole nearest us, one of two that supported the tightrope. A ladder ran up the pole to a small platform at the top, about a hundred feet high. Two trapezes hung from the platform, one short, one longer. Then Holmes was looking down at the sawdust that covered the ground within the circus ring.

I could tell that the sawdust had been recently raked.

"No footprints," Lestrade went on. "So how did he get up to the pole? And how did he get to the middle of that tightrope? He couldn't have walked out there on a high wire in those ridiculous big shoes."

Holmes said nothing.

"And why would he put a rope around his neck? Someone had to have done that."

Holmes nodded to Mr. Debary, the circus manager, who stood with us. "Mr. Debary, do you know the identity of the deceased?"

A ruddy-faced, clean-shaven man, powerfully built, Debary projected an air of confidence and energy that would make him, I thought, successful as an impresario. "Hard to tell from this distance," Debary said.

"How will you get him down?"

Debary did not hesitate. "I have the crew ready. We'll lower the tightrope poles, same way as we do every time we fold and move on," he said.

"How many in the crew?"

"Four roustabouts. Experienced men. I had them awakened as soon as I saw the body. They're in the commissary."

"I should like to observe."

"I'll bring the crew in now," Debary said. "We need to get this over with. The matinee starts in three hours. We need to begin setting up. Five thousand people will be here, and it's costing us an arm and a leg to rent the Olympia. We can't afford to lose that revenue!"

Lestrade put a hand onto Debary's chest. "No one else is allowed in until I give permission. This is a murder investigation. And we're dealing with a most clever murderer here, that much is certain."

Debary stared. "Murder?"

"The clown didn't get all the way up there to the centre of the tightrope by himself. That's plain enough. Somebody didn't want to leave footprints. But they wanted this fellow dead, and they wanted him not only dead but humiliated. Strung up for all to see, in the centre ring. Stopping the show. Literally. That's a cruel person, sir, and a clever one too, and we can't have people like that escaping justice and running at large to do more harm to an innocent and trusting public."

He paused, folded his arms, and fixed Debary with a determined stare. "Now, sir, do you have any idea of who might have perpetrated this crime?"

Debary shook his head. "I don't even know who this man is!" He gestured to the guard at the entrance to admit the four roustabouts. They brought with them a wheelbarrow and a large block-and-tackle apparatus. Soon they were at work lowering the pole, and with it the body.

"Who discovered the body?" asked Holmes.

"I came in early as I always do. I saw it," Debary said.

"Why do you always come in early?"

"To check up on the performance of the cleanup crew."

"And what did you see this morning?"

"I saw a shadow. Something made me look up, and there it was. I thought, some poor devil's gone and hanged himself."

"But you called the police."

"Had to. Can't take a chance."

"And you disturbed nothing here?"

"You mean did I sweep or rake the sawdust? Certainly not."

"Do you have a program of the circus? We need a list of all the acts and attractions."

"I can get you that."

By now the pole was lowered to within twenty feet of the ground, and the body was very nearly within reach. "Hold there," said Holmes. He strode to the centre, positioning himself directly beneath the body. "Dr. Watson, would you kindly assist? We want no impact as the body reaches the ground."

Though it was cold, the body did not display the stiffness of rigor mortis, and I felt somewhat awkward guiding it to flop onto its side and rest upon the sawdust.

Seen from closer range, the noose around the neck of the body was revealed to be a rope that had been clamped to the tightrope at one end and to some sort of harness affair behind his belt at the other.

"Safety line," said Debary.

"Must have got tangled in it when he fell," Lestrade said.

Holmes said nothing.

He looked at the clown's hands and then at the feet. He bent over the body. Kneeling, he pushed on the clown's chest.

After a moment he stood. "The body should be taken for mortuary examination," he said. "I detect the scent of bitter almonds. Dr. Watson, would you please confirm?"

I bent close to the inert white-painted features. The characteristic odour was indeed present. "Cyanide," I said.

"Can you see into his mouth?" Holmes asked.

"His jaws are clenched. I advise waiting until we have the proper instruments."

"At the police mortuary," said Lestrade. "Were you thinking that he must have taken the cyanide just before his death? That would be suicide rather than murder."

At that moment there came a woman's cry from the entrance, and then came the woman herself, running at full speed with a graceful stride. She was lovely, very trim, dressed in a leotard but with a short linen jacket over it against the chill.

"My husband's gone missing," she cried, "and I have to know—"

Debary gave her a sympathetic look. Stepping aside, he said, "If it will set your mind at rest. Go ahead, Linda, by all means."

To Holmes and Lestrade he said, "This is Mrs. Linda Sadler, one of the aerialists in our troupe. She and her husband, Sam, are known as the 'Soaring Sadlers.' " He paused. "Mrs. Sadler reported him missing a few hours ago."

Mrs. Sadler was kneeling over the prostrate figure, but only for a moment. Then she crumpled to the ground, her shoulders hunched, her body shaking with sobs.

She raised herself up onto hands and knees and turned to Debary, her eyes wide. "It's Sam," she said.

Still shaking, she placed her fingertip at the base of the clown's collar and pulled down at the elaborate silk ruffle. When she finally spoke again, her voice was thick and hoarse. "You can see the star," she said.

I bent down to observe. On the dirty bare skin below the collar, a small tattooed blue star was plainly visible.

Holmes knelt between Mrs. Sadler and me, glancing at the tattoo for only a moment. "Mrs. Sadler, we shall need to ask you a few questions, but only when you have recovered yourself."

"Did he fall?" she asked.

"We're trying to determine what happened," Lestrade said. "That's why we need to ask you the questions. But we can wait for that."

"I will be in my wagon," she said.

We watched her walk quickly away, arms folded and head down, as though hugging something precious.

Holmes had gone off to where the big circus pole was resting on the ground, with its supporting cables streaming from it like garlands from a maypole. The aerialists' platform, once a hundred feet above us at the top, was now at his eye level. Holmes ran his fingertips lightly over the surface. Then he returned to stand with us.

"Mr. Debary, could you please unclamp the rope from the

high wire and have your crew raise the pole and stabilize it once more? I should like to climb the ladder on the other pole to inspect the other platform."

While Debary was occupied, Holmes turned to Lestrade. "It is of particular importance that I accompany the body and attend the autopsy."

"I'll see to that."

"Dr. Watson, while I am inspecting the other platform, will you please remain with the body and see that no one touches it? Other than the police orderlies who prepare it for transportation, of course."

I did so, though I glanced somewhat nervously at Holmes as he climbed up the tall, narrow trapeze ladder to the platform and then made his way down again.

He returned to my side, giving no indication of whether he had seen anything of significance.

By now, Lestrade had returned.

"Police wagon is just coming," he said. "You and Dr. Watson are cleared to ride inside if you wish to do so."

Holmes nodded his thanks. "Lestrade, while Watson and I are away, might I ask if you and your men could establish the time that the theatre was unoccupied? All members of the troupe must be questioned, and very quickly, in an orderly and efficient manner. I say 'very quickly,' because it would not do to delay the performance. Can you get some help for that? I would suggest Jack Kelly and also, if you can arrange it, Lucy James."

CHAPTER 2

Jack frowned at his moustached reflection in the looking glass. "I look like a stage villain in a cheap melodrama. You *had* to pass us off as a family of magicians?"

I bit my lip, stifling a smile. Under ordinary circumstances, Jack's lean, darkly handsome good looks and muscular build gave him an air of watchful, focused intensity blended with an edge of danger—which was useful in his chosen profession as a sergeant with Scotland Yard. He rarely had to threaten; criminals took one look at him and decided to either cooperate or run.

At the moment, though, his high silk top-hat and red-satin-lined black cape—not to mention the false black moustache from Holmes's store of such items—did rather push him into stage-villain territory.

"It could be worse; I could have said you were a lion tamer. Besides, wouldn't you rather pass ourselves off as the Magical Kennedys than, say, a family of clowns?"

Jack turned away from the mirror. "I'd rather pass myself off as a policeman."

"Which would get us exactly nowhere. You know as well as I do that circus folk are an insular, secretive lot—distrustful of strangers and outsiders at even the best of times. How far do you think you'd get by striding in here as Detective Sergeant Jack Kelly and asking whether anyone knows who among the performers had a motive to murder Sam Sadler, and please be honest now?"

"And what happens tonight, when we're actually expected to perform some kind of a magic show?"

That was, of course, the flaw in the scheme. Since literally no one within the circus could be ruled out from the list of suspects at this stage in the investigation, even the circus's manager, Mr. Debary, didn't know our real identities. The loss of Sam Sadler and his wife's acrobatics routine had left the circus one act short, and we had applied as being willing to fill the gap on an immediate and temporary basis—and here we were.

"We ask for volunteers from the audience?"

Jack gave me a look. "Careful. I may just start twirling the ends of this idiot moustache and threatening to tie you up on the tracks of some oncoming train."

Becky giggled. "Well, I think you look very dashing, Jack."

We were in the spare caravan that had been assigned to us as newly arrived members of the circus. A small wooden-built structure on wheels, the caravan had walls painted in a brilliant shade of blue, with a pattern of red flowers curling around the small windows and door. Twin built-in bunks covered in bright patchwork quilts lined the walls in the back, and at the moment, Becky was sitting perched at the small table and two chairs that were bolted to the floor at the front of the caravan, her eyes on the wooden box that had come from Holmes's nearby hideaway on Russel Road.

The box had been the source of Jack's hat, cape, and moustache, and I knew Becky was itching to see what else it contained.

The circus hadn't officially been cleared to open for performance tonight, but from outside I could hear the bouncing strains of calliope music and the shouts of a troupe of tumbling acrobats who were rehearsing their routine nearby.

Jack moved his eyebrows—likewise enhanced by some of Holmes's techniques in the art of disguise—in an expression of exaggerated menace at his sister. "And maybe my first trick will be to make you disappear—all the way back to Baker Street."

I could tell from the shadow that crossed his gaze that he wasn't entirely joking about sending Becky back to the safety of Baker Street. As per usual, the potential danger of letting his ten-year-old sister be involved in an investigation was giving him—giving both of us, if I was honest—serious cause for worry.

The trouble with Becky, though, was that the danger she could get into if left to her own devices was exponentially worse than anything she might encounter with us here. At least this way we would both be able to keep an eye on her.

"Holmes suspects that Linda Sadler, the dead man's wife, is hiding something," I said. "So Becky's and my first order of business will be to try to speak with her—see whether we can induce any confidences. And you—"

"I'll ask around among the roustabouts and the other performers," Jack said. "Try to find out anything I can about Sam."

I nodded. "On the bright side, this gives us motivation to solve the case quickly. The Magical Kennedys don't have to perform in the afternoon show. We aren't scheduled to perform until the evening show at seven o'clock tonight—which gives us just under eight hours to find out the truth about Sam Sadler's death."

"That makes me feel a whole lot better." Jack was smiling, but he caught hold of my hand as I started towards the caravan door, and he pulled me close for a second. "Just be careful out there."

I sobered as well. "I will be." This murder investigation wasn't just clowns and acrobats and play-acting. A man was dead, and someone in the small, isolated world of the circus had very likely killed him. "You be careful too."

Jack nodded. "Always am."

* * *

"Where shall we start?" Becky asked.

I frowned, gazing up at the big Olympia hippodrome, where the circus performances would be held, and then taking in the expanse of the circus grounds all around us. The circus really was like its own small town. Strings of laundry were hung up to dry between the wagons that had been brought in by train. Children were running between tents, shouting and kicking a ball—although I noticed that a baby elephant made up one member of the team.

"It's nearly midday," I told Becky. "People will probably be starting to gather in the cookhouse tent for luncheon. We can try asking around there first to see whether anyone knows where to find Linda."

The cookhouse tent proved easy enough to find from the wafting smell of fried meat and potatoes that filtered through the tent flaps. Becky and I entered and found ourselves in a big open space lined with wooden tables and benches. A blond-haired man whose huge frame and bulging muscles made him almost certainly the circus strongman was sitting alone at one table, hunched over a plate of food and shovelling fried pork into his mouth as fast as he could. Three girls wearing bright rouge on their cheeks and sequined leotards were sitting together at another table, laughing and talking.

And a man who couldn't be more than three and a half feet tall was shaking a fist and bellowing into the face of a harried-looking woman with untidy wisps of gray hair framing her face and half-moon spectacles perched on the end of her nose.

"What is the meaning of this?" the small man demanded. He had brown hair slicked down over his skull, and despite his stature he was possessed of a surprisingly deep and powerful voice with a trace of a Russian accent. "I went to put on my jacket for the show tonight and found *this* atrocity!"

He held up the offending garment, shaking it at the gray-haired woman. "The gold braid on the left sleeve has started to come loose! When I expressly directed that you fix it last week!"

The gray-haired woman examined the sleeve and sighed. "Now, now, Mr. Dubrovnik. There's only a tiny spot where the thread has started to pull. But leave the jacket with me, and I'll see that it gets fixed."

Mr. Dubrovnik pulled himself up to his full height—which still only reached to the level of the woman's waist. "It had better be!" After turning on his heel, he marched from the tent.

I gave Becky's hand a squeeze and moved to approach the gray-haired woman with a sympathetic smile. "Goodness. He doesn't seem very pleasant."

The woman turned to look at me, her pale-blue eyes blinking behind the polished lenses of the spectacles. "Oh, Mr. Dubrovnik doesn't mean any harm, really. It's only that he gets tired of people patting him on the head and saying how adorable he is—it's enough to give anyone a chip on the shoulder. Besides, we're all on edge this morning." She folded the black velvet jacket that the small man had given her across her arm, then studied me and Becky more closely. "You must be the new act of magicians I heard had joined us. American, are you?"

"That's right. I'm Lucy Kennedy, and this is my sister-in-law, Becky."

The gray-haired woman returned the introduction with a vague smile and an attempt to poke her loosened wisps of hair into order. "And I'm Mrs. Mitchel, the costumes mistress. Be sure to let me know whether you need any sewing done— although I'm that rushed off my feet at the moment, I don't know when I might get to it."

"Thank you." I squeezed Becky's hand again, which she correctly interpreted as a signal to move off. It was a constant source of indignation to Becky, but most people were freer with their tongues when a child wasn't present.

Becky skipped over to the food table, where a man in a cook's hat and apron was ladling food into huge trays of warming dishes.

Mrs. Mitchel looked as though she was about to move away, too, so I hurried on, "We've just finished a run at the Dome Theatre in Brighton." That was the cover story that we had given Mr. Debary during our interview. "We didn't have another job booked, though, so it was lucky that Mr. Debary had space to take on another act. Although I suppose maybe I shouldn't say that." I lowered my voice. "We heard about how that poor man died last night. What a terrible upset it must have been for you all."

I had never met Mrs. Mitchel, but I did know the word of the theatre. Mrs. Budge, our costumes mistress at the Savoy, invariably knew everything there was to know about any gossip flying around the company—and she could never resist the opportunity to share that gossip with a sympathetic listener.

Mrs. Mitchel's long nose twitched as she lowered her voice to match mine. "It was indeed! We even"—she shot a glance around the tent—"had the police called in, asking questions and poking into everything. One of their constables turned over an entire basket of my spools of thread and never bothered to pick it up again." She snorted indignantly. "As though the murderer was likely to be hiding in there!"

"How inconsiderate. So they do think it was murder, then, and not some accident or a suicide?"

"Well." Mrs. Mitchel drew herself up virtuously. "Of course, I'm not one to gossip, but that's what I do hear."

I arranged my expression to look suitably shocked. "How awful for everyone—and for his poor wife, especially."

Mrs. Mitchel sniffed. "Well, that's as may be, but it's my belief that Mrs. Hoity-Toity-Thinks-She's-A-Cut-Above-All-The-Rest-Of-Us Sadler won't be shedding too many tears over poor Sam."

Nosy, gossipy, and inclined to both hold grudges and believe the worst of people. Definitely Mrs. Mitchel was proving to be a witness worth cultivating.

"Really?" I let my eyes widen. "Was their marriage not a happy one, then?"

"Well, I don't know about that. They always seemed happy enough with each other before this. *But*—" Mrs. Mitchel paused dramatically. "They were overheard quarrelling before the performance—just hours before poor Sam must have died."

"Really? Who by?"

If Mrs. Mitchel stopped to consider, I would have to come up with some sort of convincing explanation for why a complete stranger might want to know those details. But fortunately, she was far too carried away with the excitement of her story and her own sense of self-importance.

"I heard it from Ruby, she's one of the bareback riders—" She glanced around the cookhouse tent. "Oh, there she is now."

Mrs. Mitchel raised her voice. "Ruby? Ruby, come over here a minute."

One of the girls in sequins who had been talking and laughing with the rest of the group rose and came over to us. Thin and sharp-featured under the rouge and makeup, she had blue eyes and a fringe of frizzed red hair over her forehead. "Yes, Mrs. Mitchel? What is it?"

"I was just telling this young lady—she's part of the new magician's act, Lucy—" Mrs. Mitchel broke off. "I'm sorry, dear, what was your name again?"

"Lucy Kennedy."

"That's right. I was just telling her how you overhead Sam and Linda arguing before the performance last night."

Fortunately for my purpose, Ruby seemed just as happy to impart gossip as Mrs. Mitchel. "That's right, I did! I happened to be passing their wagon, and I heard them, clear as anything. At it hammer and tongs, they were."

"What were they arguing about, do you know?"

Ruby gave a regretful shake of her head. "I didn't hear enough to find out, even when I—" She broke off and for the first time looked slightly uncomfortable. "What I mean to say is, that the … the lace on my slipper had happened to come untied just then, just as I was passing Sam and Linda's wagon." She gestured to the pink ballet-style slippers she wore, with crisscrossed ribbons tied around her ankles. "So I had to stop and retie it, didn't I? Didn't want it to get torn or dirty."

"Of course," I agreed.

"So I stopped and retied it, just as I say. But I still couldn't make out what Sam and Linda were fighting over. Just Sam saying over and over again something about, 'No, I won't do it.' And Linda saying back, 'You've got to!'" Ruby stopped and glanced at Mrs. Mitchel. "But I reckon they must have made up with each other later, because their act last night was spot-on. So maybe the quarrel wasn't about anything important after all."

Mrs. Mitchel sniffed again. "Well, that's as may be. But just this very morning, I went to Linda and Sam's wagon to see …" Like Ruby, she looked slightly discomfited. "I mean to say, naturally I wanted to stop by to offer my condolences and make sure that Linda had everything she needed."

Murderess or no, I was beginning to feel sympathy for Linda Sadler, who couldn't seem to get five minutes of privacy, even in her own caravan wagon.

"Naturally," I agreed. "I'm sure it was very kind of you."

Mrs. Mitchel looked pleased by my reassurance. "Exactly! Well, I knocked and knocked, but there was no answer. It's my belief she was going to pretend not to be there and not come to the door at all, but then I heard her knock something over inside the wagon—so that it was plain to anyone that she was inside—and she finally opened the door."

Mrs. Mitchel paused for a much-needed breath, then went on. "She wouldn't let me inside—just stayed in the doorway. She had a handkerchief up to her face as if she'd been crying, and her voice sounded all shaky when she spoke to me. But before I left, she happened to let the handkerchief slip a little, and her eyes were bone dry—not a bit wet or even red. Mark my words, she'd not been shedding anything but crocodile's tears for her poor husband. Why, she cried more when those flowers came for her last month, remember, Ruby?"

My pulse quickened, but I kept my voice casual. "She cried over receiving flowers? How odd."

Ruby broke in eagerly. "Yes, wasn't it just! A big bunch of beautiful red roses they were, too—ever so pretty, and they must have cost whoever sent them a fortune. But Linda, she took one look at the message on the card and turned white as a ghost. Then a bit later, I saw her crying on her own—sitting on a barrel back behind the elephant trainer's tent. Sobbing her heart out, she was, like the whole world was ending."

Mrs. Mitchel nodded; she'd plainly heard that part of the story before. "It's my belief that the flowers were from an old sweetheart of hers—someone she knew before she married Sam. Or maybe it was someone she'd met recent-like, someone she would have married, if only she weren't already tied down with Sam. Well." Mrs. Mitchel paused, her long nose twitching. "She's free and clear to take up with whomever she likes now, isn't she? I suppose we shall just see what we shall see."

* * *

"Did you find out anything interesting?" Becky asked.

We were outside of the cookhouse tent, making our way past a row of cages where three enormous brown bears were sleeping in the pools of sunlight slanting through the bars. One of the bears snorted in its sleep, and Becky startled, gripping my hand a little tighter.

"I found out that circuses are certainly hotbeds of gossip. Linda and Sam Sadler had a quarrel in their wagon just before the performance last night—and this morning, Linda was apparently only pretending to cry over Sam."

"Do you think she had anything to do with her husband's death?" Becky asked.

I frowned, considering. "Without actually talking to her, I don't know. I will say it's difficult to see how one woman could have gotten Sam Sadler up into the position where his body was found. That would have taken a fair bit of strength. It's possible she could have had help, though."

I stopped. Something was nagging at me about this case—something to do with what Uncle John had told me about the discovery of the body? Or about Linda Sadler's reaction?

I hadn't been present, true, but Watson was a keen observer and had described the scene to me in his briefing before we arrived at the circus grounds. Holmes had already given his opinion that Sam Sadler's widow was being less than fully truthful—but I couldn't shake the feeling that Uncle John had mentioned some other detail that was important.

"At any rate, we'll know more after we speak to her."

Becky's brows were knitted together. "It's odd that Mr. Sadler was dressed up as a circus clown—when he was supposed to be a high-wire acrobat."

"Yes, it is odd."

I looked around the circus grounds. A lady wearing a red satin evening dress and elbow-length black satin gloves—and with a spectacularly bushy beard tracing the line of her jaw—was lounging on a chair in front of a tent, idly flipping through a magazine.

Through the flaps of another tent, I could see a girl wearing a clown's costume rehearsing with a troupe of fluffy white dogs, making them jump through hoops and walk on their hind legs. Across from the caravan wagon that had been assigned to the Magical Kennedys, I saw another pair of clowns, dressed in white and with comically large orange gloves, carefully tossing what looked like an orange croquet ball back and forth, as if they were planning to use it in a juggling act.

I didn't see any sign of Jack, but then he could be anywhere amidst all this hive of activity.

"Do you see any likely candidates to ask about which wagon belonged to the Sadlers?" I asked Becky. I hadn't wanted to ask Mrs. Mitchel and Ruby; that might have pushed them over the edge of beginning to wonder why I was so inquisitive about Sam and Linda.

Becky eyed the dogs regretfully but shook her head. "Oh, we don't have to ask anyone. I found that out from the cook in the food tent. I said that I'd heard someone had died last night, and wouldn't it be terribly spooky if his ghost were to come back and haunt the circus. The cook laughed and said he didn't think there'd be any hauntings, but if I was worried about ghosts, I should stay away from the Sadler's wagon. And then he told me where it was."

"Perfect." I tilted my head. "Do you hear that?"

Becky looked puzzled. "Hear what?"

I put my arm around her shoulders and squeezed. "The sound of your investigative-genius points being added to your already full account."

* * *

Sam and Linda Sadler's caravan proved to be the third in a row of similar wagons parked not too far from the one where Becky, Jack, and I had begun here. Bright red, the Sadlers' travelling residence had a flock of painted bluebirds on one side and a wreath of daisies painted over the front door. Blue drapes hung in the small window, preventing us from seeing inside.

Becky stopped as we approached. "How are we going to explain why we've come to see her?"

Becky made a good point. If Linda Sadler was innocent, intruding on her grief would be rude, bordering on cruel. And even if she proved to be guilty, we could hardly march in and ask outright whether she'd had anything to do with her husband's murder.

"We can say that although we never met her and her husband, we've seen them perform several times and were great admirers of their work—so much so that we had to come and pay our condolences when we heard what had happened to Sam."

Becky still looked slightly dubious, but she nodded. "All right."

I was prepared for Linda to pretend that she wasn't at home, just as she had with Mrs. Mitchel. But the door to the caravan flew open almost the instant my knuckles connected with the wood.

"Oh." Linda's face fell with disappointment at the sight of Becky and me. "I thought you were the movers."

Her appearance matched the description that Uncle John had given me: slim, somewhere close to thirty, and very pretty, with golden-blonde hair and wide, thickly lashed blue eyes.

She also matched up to Mrs. Mitchel's assessment, in that I very much doubted that those eyes had shed a single tear yet today.

"Movers?" I looked past Linda into the wagon, which seemed to be in a state of half-packed chaos: clothing and books and other personal items flung all about, some tumbled into cartons and bags, others lying in heaps on the narrow wedge of the caravan floor. "Are you leaving, then?"

"Yes!" Her thin shoulders hunched forward. "I'm packing up everything and having it shipped to my sister's in Bristol—and I'll be off there myself just as soon as the police tell me that I may. Sam is dead, and I don't intend to stay here another moment beyond what I absolutely must."

I studied her. Linda Sadler might not appear grief-stricken to me, but she was certainly in the grip of some powerful emotion. Agitation, at the very least—or even fear? Her whole body was rigid with it, her muscles almost quivering with keyed-up tension.

So much so that it didn't even appear to have occurred to her to wonder who Becky and I were.

"I'm so sorry to hear about your husband, Mrs. Sadler. He was one of the circus's clowns?"

I watched Linda closely. Something about her was oddly familiar to me. Not her name—I couldn't remember ever having heard that before—but her face. I'd seen her somewhere, I was nearly certain of it, but when and where?

"Not really." Linda spoke almost absently, rubbing her hands up and down her arms as though she was cold. "That is, he was afraid he was getting too old to perform on the high wire. It's an act only for the very young and agile. So he had the idea to train as a clown. He thought it would be safer."

Her voice broke slightly on the final word.

"I'm so sorry," I murmured again. "Have the police made any progress in finding out what happened?"

"Not that they would consent to inform me! They seemed to treat me as a suspect—as though I could have done anything to harm Sam!" Her eyes were bright with outrage.

Behind us, the red-satin-clad bearded lady minced by on teeteringly high-heeled evening slippers, presumably on the way to her own caravan. I waited for her to pass, then asked, "Have you any idea who could have wanted to hurt Sam?"

"I—" Linda seemed on the verge of saying more, but then clamped her lips shut. "I don't know. I don't have any idea!"

Her blue eyes were wide and unwavering in their gaze as they met mine. In the back of my mind, Holmes's sardonic voice commented: *Classic liar's stare.*

Most people grew up with the notion that liars were unable to look someone directly in the eye while they lied to them. Which frequently led to the belief that the converse must be true, as well—if someone met and held your gaze directly, they must be honest.

I might not have quite as much experience as Holmes in being lied to, but I'd seen enough to recognize the signs in Linda: the stare that was too unblinking, too unwavering, as though willing me to believe she was speaking the truth.

"But what if they should come after me next?" Linda went on, her voice climbing. "That's why I'm leaving—going somewhere I'll be safe!"

As she spoke, a light breeze sprang up along the circus causeway, stirring her hair—and sending a scrap of paper that she must have dislodged in her frenzy of packing spinning down the caravan wagon's set of wooden steps.

I picked it up automatically, about to hand it back to her. It was a newspaper clipping, although I had only time to read the partial headline: *Murwald Sen*—

Then Linda snatched the scrap out of my hand so fast that the edge of the paper tore a little. "Give me that!" She drew a ragged breath, seeming to recollect herself, and shut her eyes a brief half second. "That is, I beg your pardon. It's just that I've so much to do. Packing and … you'll excuse me. Please."

Stepping back into the wagon, she swung the painted door shut behind her, and a moment later I heard a key scrape in the lock.

"She's afraid of something," Becky said in an undertone as we turned away.

I nodded. Linda was an acrobat, not an actress. If she hadn't been able to feign crying well enough to fool Mrs. Mitchel, I doubted she could pretend to feel fear convincingly either. Sam Sadler's widow was genuinely terrified of someone or some-thing. Although whether she actually feared Sam's killer—or simply feared that the police would identify her as Sam's killer—I hadn't yet made up my mind.

"What's next?" Becky asked.

"Let's go back to our caravan. We can see whether Jack's there and whether he's learned anything of value."

* * *

Even though I knew Jack could take care of himself better than anyone else I knew, I still felt a quick rush of relief at the sight of him sitting on the caravan steps, with the black top-hat beside him and the magician's cape slightly askew.

"Jack!" Becky raced forward to greet him. "Did you find out anything about—"

"About how to saw you in half?" Jack spoke over her, picking her up and swinging her high into the air.

He was grinning, but his eyes met mine over the top of Becky's head, and he nodded once. "I did find out a couple of things," he said in an undertone. He glanced across to where the two clowns were still practicing with their juggling act, now with red hoops instead of the orange balls. "But not here. Let's get inside."

Becky kept silent until the caravan wagon's door was closed and locked behind us, but then burst out, bouncing up and down a little in her chair, "What did you find out, Jack?"

Jack gave a quick check of the area just outside the caravan's single window, then let the curtain drop back into place. "Well, for one thing, I found out that Sam Sadler was last seen going into the arena late at night after the cleanup."

"Who saw him? Were they certain that it was really Sam?"

"Pretty certain. The witness was one of the roustabouts whose job it was to sweep up all the popcorn and peanuts scattered on the ground after a show. He was just finishing up and putting his brooms away when Sam passed by him, wearing his clown costume and carrying his red shoes."

"Still, with all that makeup on his face, it would have been difficult to recognize him for certain. Uncle John told me that even Mr. Debary didn't know the dead clown was Sam."

Jack shook his head. "Tom—that's the roustabout's name— said he didn't just see Sam, he actually spoke to him. Sam asked him to help adjust his collar and clown's ruff. He mentioned the star tattoo at the base of Sam's neck particularly, said he'd told Sam he'd never noticed it before. Sam said it was a relic of a misspent youth and that he usually kept it covered. Then Sam said he was looking to get in some extra practice for a new act he'd been working on."

"So, unless this Tom is lying for some reason, we can take it that Sam went to the tent willingly, under his own power," I said. "And that his killer found him there and surprised him."

"Anything else?" Becky asked.

I could already tell from Jack's expression that there was.

"Sam had apparently just taken out a life-insurance policy on himself—to the tune of a thousand pounds."

I drew in a quick breath. "A thousand pounds! There are a lot of wives who would consider that an amount well worth becoming widows for."

Jack raised an eyebrow at me. "Should I be worried?"

I rolled my eyes at him. "You know what I mean. I assume Linda is the beneficiary of the policy?"

Jack shrugged. "Well, I don't know for certain—I couldn't ask too many questions without raising suspicions. But it seems likely. The person I talked to was Father Benjamin, the circus's priest."

"The circus has its own priest?"

"Seems so. Father Benjamin was a lawyer before taking the cloth. He said that Sam came to him and asked for his advice on how to go about taking out life insurance, so that Linda would be provided for if something happened to him. Father Benjamin took it to mean Sam was worried about having an accident up on the high wire, but—"

"But it's also possible that Sam knew of some other outside

danger and was in fear for his life." I bit my lip. "How long ago was this?"

"About a month ago, or so Father Benjamin said."

Becky had been silent until now, but she piped up, "It doesn't sound as though Sam didn't trust Linda. Not if he was worried about making sure she was taken care of if he were to die."

"You're right," I said. "Then again, Sam Sadler wouldn't be the first man who failed to perceive a threat from the person closest to him. It's always possible that Linda was the one who put the idea of life insurance into Sam's head in the first place, pushing him to apply for a policy. We should ask Father Benjamin whether Sam mentioned anything about that."

Becky sighed. "I suppose you're right."

I looked at her. Holmes might dismiss instinct and personal likes or dislikes as unreliable in an investigation. But even Holmes would admit that Becky was almost always a good judge of character.

"You don't want Linda to be guilty?" I asked gently.

Becky shook her head. "No. I liked her. But she did have a quarrel with Sam on the night he died."

Jack's head lifted alertly. "She and Sam fought?"

"Yes. That's part of what we discovered today. They were overheard quarrelling in their caravan wagon just before last night's performance. Although actually … " I stopped.

Jack's eyes met mine, and he nodded. "Yeah, you're right."

"Right about what?" Becky complained. "It's not fair when the two of you start finishing each other's sentences and no one else can understand what you're talking about!"

Jack smiled and tugged one of her blonde braids. "Sorry, Beck. Lucy was just going to say that actually the fight with Sam could count as a point in Linda's favour. If she were planning to kill him, she'd make sure not to quarrel with him so that she'd be less likely to be suspected."

"Exactly," I agreed. "The life-insurance policy—if that was Linda's motivation for killing Sam—points towards premeditation. And the cause of death may point that way, too. We won't know for certain until after the autopsy, but Uncle John said that he smelled bitter almonds—cyanide—in Sam Sadler's mouth. No one keeps cyanide capsules lying around just on the off chance that they may decide to murder someone one day. Especially—"

I broke off.

Jack looked at me sharply. "What is it?"

"Murwald!"

Jack frowned. "What?"

My breath went out from the force of realization that had just slammed into me. "Do you remember a case ... it must have been two or three years ago ... where a man called James Murwald was convicted of murder?"

Jack's brow furrowed, but he nodded almost at once; his memory for such things was easily the equal to Holmes's or mine. "James Murwald. Nasty piece of goods. He was convicted of having lured an old woman—a flower vendor—into a back alleyway and then killing her for nothing but the sake of the few shillings she'd made in sales that night. He had a criminal record, too, if I remember. Burglary. Assault. But what really sealed the case against him was the account of a witness, a woman who actually saw him commit the murder and was willing to testify—"

Jack broke off. "Hold up. Are you saying that that witness—"

"Was Linda Sadler. Exactly. Although she wasn't calling herself Linda Sadler then. She was going by another name. But I'm certain—or nearly certain—that it was her. I thought when we spoke to her that her face looked familiar to me. I must have seen her photograph in the papers; it was splashed all over the news at the time of Murwald's trial. And she had saved a clipping of a newspaper article from that time—it had fallen out from somewhere while she was packing, and she snatched it back from me too fast for me to read most of it. I caught the name Murwald. And you should have seen her face, she was absolutely terrified!"

Jack was already on his feet. "Becky, stay here. Lock the door up after us, and don't let anyone inside unless it's me or Lucy, you understand?"

Becky nodded, wide-eyed. Even she didn't argue when Jack spoke in that particular tone.

"Where are you going?"

"To find Linda Sadler." I spoke over my shoulder as I followed Jack to the door. "If we're right, then she's in grave danger."

* * *

Jack and I sped through the circus fairgrounds, weaving through the stalls where games of chance like Ring the Bottle were being set up and passing by coloured lantern shows and candy floss and popcorn machines.

"There's one thing about this theory that doesn't make any sense. Why wouldn't Linda have told the police about Mur-wald?" I asked Jack.

Jack's expression was grim. His gaze, like mine, was moving rapidly across the circus grounds, cataloguing details and identifying any potential points of threat.

The gates hadn't yet been opened to the public, but the hour for the afternoon performance was approaching, and there were far more people out and about than before.

The back of my neck prickled.

A single outsider could far too easily slip in and pass unnoticed amongst the crowds of performers and roustabouts.

"Maybe she was scared," Jack said. "If she's changed her name and identity and gone unrecognized all this time, it's possible she was too afraid to let anyone know the truth about who she really was."

"It's possible. But she must have suspected James Murwald killed her husband. If I'm right about this, Murwald has been stalking her for weeks now. According to the circus's costumes mistress, Linda was sent a big bouquet of roses and was seen crying over them. And that was around the same time that Sam took out his life-insurance policy."

The evidence we had was all circumstantial, but it hung together.

"I was going through police training when James Murwald was arrested and charged," Jack said. "I remember sitting in for one day of his trial. He sat in the dock and never showed a flicker of remorse. Just swore revenge on everyone who'd put him there."

We walked faster.

"Why isn't he still locked up, though—or dead? He surely can't have been released."

Jack shook his head. "Don't know. It's something we'll need to find out—after we find Linda Sadler."

We were within sight now of the Sadler's red caravan wagon.

The door with its bright wreath of painted flowers hung on its hinges, slightly ajar.

Dread pooled in the pit of my stomach.

Jack took the short flight of wooden steps two at a time and pushed the door fully open. I held my breath, my imagination painting images of Linda Sadler lying dead in her own blood.

"Empty," Jack said.

I released a breath, climbing up the steps and looking past him into the caravan's interior. The same chaos of crates and shipping containers I'd seen before reigned, but Linda Sadler was nowhere to be seen.

"Did she run away, do you think?" I asked.

Jack was scanning the inside of the wagon. "There's nothing to say one way or the other. No blood or any sign of a struggle, anyway."

"You're right." The caravan was a mess, but there was nothing smashed or broken as one would expect if there'd been a fight.

"I need to report this," Jack said. "Let the Yard know that we suspect James Murwald might have had a hand in Sam's death—not to mention find out whether Murwald's escaped from prison."

I nodded. I'd been expecting that. "I know you do. I have an idea, though."

Jack looked at me. "A good idea?"

"Well, I'm going to say yes, and you're most likely going to say no."

Jack's brows edged together, but I kept going before he could speak. "If he really has escaped from prison, James Murwald could be anywhere. But the one thing we do know is that he's certain to be coming after Linda. And isn't it most likely that he'll come back sometime during the circus performance—at a time when it's easy for a stranger to just walk right onto the fairgrounds, but everyone is occupied inside the amphitheatre, watching the show?"

"Yeah, but—"

"He has to know that Linda herself won't be performing today. So he's likely to come here—to the Sadlers' wagon—to try and catch her. What if we stay here—light the lamps, make it look as though the caravan is definitely occupied? We'll be able to catch him when he does come back."

Jack's expression got even grimmer. "And by we, you actually mean—"

"Well, me. But only for the next half hour or so."

"You're forgetting the part where that nice, neat plan turns to rubbish," Jack said.

"You go and call Scotland Yard and then come back here. I'll be fine on my own for at least that long."

The tight line of Jack's mouth told me he wasn't convinced by my attempt at confident assurances. Neither, if I was being entirely honest with myself, was I. My heart was beating too fast and too hard. But James Murwald was a dangerous man— a killer twice over, if we were right. We couldn't let him slip away to kill again.

"I've got my pistol." I showed Jack the small revolver I carried in my inner pocket. "And if he does come here, Murwald is going to be expecting Linda—alone, unarmed, and terrified. I'll catch him completely by surprise."

Jack expression lightened just a fraction. "That I believe. All right, Trouble." He leaned over and kissed my forehead. "I'll be back as quick as I can."

CHAPTER 3

Returning from the mortuary to my medical office in Padding-ton, I hastily organized my notes from what Holmes and I had observed at the autopsy earlier that afternoon.

I reproduce those notes here.

1. The hands of the victim are calloused and stained dark, and the fingertips and nails ingrained with dirt.

2. The callouses at the base of the victim's fingers and the palms are consistent with an acrobat's grasp of the trapeze or an aerialist's grasp of the balance bar.

3. The well-developed muscular structure of the chest, shoulders, and upper arms are similarly consistent with an aerialist's activity.

4. However, Holmes notes that the callouses and dirt around the fingertips are, to use his exact word, "inconsistent."

5. The tattoo on the victim's neck was obscured slightly by grime, but following application of a wet washcloth it is revealed to be an old one, the ink around the edges of the design somewhat dispersed.

6. While removing the white makeup, also with a wet washcloth, I observe a peculiar instability in the right temporal
   area of the skull. This last observation is puzzling.

7. The red clown shoes appear to have been specially made
   to fit over other shoes. There is a gap at the centre where
   they do not come in contact with the ground. The actual
   shoes worn beneath are those of an aerialist, supple thin
   leather enabling the wearer to sense his contact with the
   tightrope.

8. Rigor mortis has still not set in. Possibly because the body
   was hung downwards in that odd position and then disturbed while being lowered.

9. The time of death is uncertain.

10. The jaws open readily. Inside I observed a broken capsule.
    From the odour, I believe that analysis will confirm that
    the capsule contained potassium cyanide.

11. There are newly formed abrasions on the right ankle of
    the body.

12. I return my attention to the right temporal area of the
    skull, palpating the skin gingerly with my fingertips. The
    bones, fragile in their normal state, are definitely broken,
    as is the skin at what would likely have been the point of
    impact. I invite Holmes to look at the fracture, which, in
    my experience, would be fatal. It could easily be the cause
    of death, just as the broken neck might have been. There is
    no additional bruising visible beyond the discolouration
    of the skin over the entire skull and neck, and that was

caused, I believe, by the downward positioning of the head as the body hung from the rope.

13. I posit a theory to Holmes, namely that the clown, climbing the ladder, slipped while attempting to mount the aerialists' platform, struck his head, and, rapidly losing consciousness, in his doomed attempts to regain his footing, entangled himself in his safety rope, with his motion and inertia carrying him to the centre of the tightrope, where he was found. I acknowledge that this theory does not account for the cyanide capsule.

14. Holmes leaves me in haste, promising to reconvene at 221B Baker Street that evening. "Your theory covers most of the facts, Watson," he says. "I congratulate you. But now I must gather more data."

Completing my notes, I waited for my regularly scheduled patient to appear, all the while preoccupied with thoughts of Holmes. I wondered where Holmes had gone to gather the additional data of which he had spoken. In my imagination, I pictured him at the circus, climbing the ladder once again to inspect the edge of the aerialists' platform for traces of an impact with the skull of the clown.

Then my telephone rang. I heard Jack Kelly's voice on the line, telling me to meet him at the circus grounds as soon as I could manage to get there.

LUCY
CHAPTER 4

With Jack gone, I shut the front door of the Sadlers' wagon, then sat down on one of the slightly rickety-looking chairs. Beside the door, a row of white wooden juggling clubs was arranged neatly on a rack. Next to the clubs was a standing coat hanger, over which was hung a white-silk clown suit, and at the base was a pair of large, floppy red clown shoes. Alongside the coat rack, what looked to be a window was covered with dark-blue satin drapes.

Investigation frequently resembled a potter's art: shaping a container, building it up from the lumpy, misshapen clay of assorted clues. Smoothing, refining—firing it in the kiln of logic and then holding it up to see if it actually held water.

The trouble with this current case was that I wasn't certain that our theory was entirely solid enough to hold water. Just sitting here, I could easily identify half a dozen leaks—spots where the actions of Linda Sadler and even her dead husband didn't appear to make any sense. For one thing—

I sat up sharply, the thought snapped off by the sound of footsteps directly outside the wagon, followed by a creak as someone mounted the wooden steps.

I was already on my feet, the revolver in my hand, when the caravan door swung open, revealing a broad-shouldered man with dark hair and a rugged, square-jawed face.

His eyes flared wide at the sight of me, gaze flashing from me to the pistol in my hand.

"Who in blazes are you? Where's Linda?"

In my head, I silently acknowledged to Jack that this was indeed the moment when all carefully laid plans flew out of the proverbial window.

I kept my gun hand steady, trained on the man's midsection.

"I'm someone who wants to ask you some questions. As for Linda—"

Before I could get further, the man's hand darted into a side pocket of his coat, coming out with a Webley .455 revolver.

My heart skipped. Guns weren't readily accessible to London's criminal classes—particularly not to an escaped felon like James Murwald. This was a particularly nasty trick on the part of Fate that he happened to be not only armed, but with a higher-calibre gun than mine.

He shook the weapon at me, advancing another foot or so into the caravan.

"I'm not going to ask again! Who are you, and where's Linda?"

I drew in a slow breath. This wasn't the first time I'd been held at gunpoint, but the hollowed-out, icy feeling of fear never entirely faded.

That didn't, however, mean that I had to let Murwald see that I was afraid.

"Didn't you just assure me that you *weren't* going to ask those two particular questions again?"

A fierce snarl twisted his mouth, and for a second I thought that I'd pushed him too far and that he would simply shoot me where I stood. But instead he ground out, "Talk, curse you! And put down that gun!"

His hand shook slightly on the revolver.

Good.

An angry man was, generally speaking, a careless man—and right now, I had two options. One: keep Murwald talking until Jack returned. Or two: ensure that he was angry and off-balance enough that I eventually got an opening for attack.

"Only if you put down your weapon first."

"Not bloody likely!" Murwald made a harsh, scornful sound between an exhale and a humourless laugh. "I don't want to shoot you—"

"I am delighted to hear it."

The voice came from directly behind Murwald, and a figure appeared in the caravan's doorway. I gasped as I recognized the bearded lady—now wearing trousers and an overcoat.

Only, it wasn't.

In a single swift movement, the new arrival stepped into the wagon, pressed the barrel of Uncle John's service revolver into Murwald's back … and continued to speak in Sherlock Holmes's voice.

"I would strongly advise you to drop that weapon, unless you wish this to be your last moment of enjoying the privilege of breathing."

Murwald's face had gone pale, but he had better nerves than I would have given him credit for. He kept his grip on the Webley, maintaining its aim at me. "You can shoot me—but I could still get off a shot at her first! And I will, unless you tell me right now what you've done with Linda!"

I was still staring at Holmes. "You … you were …"

Holmes permitted himself a glance and a small smile in my direction. "It is gratifying to know that I can still surprise you. Now." He shifted to address Murwald. "Perhaps I might suggest that we *all* lower our weapons, our present circumstances being melodramatic to the point of verging on the ludicrous."

"What's going on here?" Linda Sadler, her face blanched with shock, appeared in the doorway behind Holmes.

"Linda!" Murwald instinctively tried to spin in Holmes's grip, his attention diverted—which allowed Holmes to knock the gun neatly out of his hand.

The Webley clattered to the wooden floorboards, and I released a breath.

Several missing pieces of the puzzle had just slotted together in my mind with what felt like an almost palpable snap.

"It's all right, Mr. Sadler," I added. "As you can see, your wife is quite unharmed."

Holmes still had the gun planted against Sam Sadler's ribs, but he gave me a quick glance and a nod of approval for having pieced that together. Although I was silently kicking myself for not having realized it sooner.

Mr. Debary hadn't recognized the dead man in clown's makeup as Sam—because it hadn't been Sam at all. Likewise, Linda Sadler didn't dare bring up the case of James Murwald with the police. Not when it was Murwald himself who was lying dead on the circus-ring floor.

"I pray you will sit down, Mr. Sadler," Holmes said. "And you also, Mrs. Sadler."

He guided Sam to the small built-in cushioned seat that ran

along one wall of the wagon, gesturing for Linda to join him.

The Sadlers both sat down, casting nervous glances at the weapons in both Holmes's and my hands. Although Sam Sadler's jaw was still hard with determined anger.

"I don't even know yet who you are or what you're doing here!"

"My name is Sherlock Holmes." With a single quick jerk, Holmes peeled the false beard away from his jaw and faced the Sadlers. "You may perhaps have heard of me."

I could tell by the fear that etched the Sadlers' faces that they had. Linda reached reflexively for her husband's hand.

"Now," Holmes went on. "I propose to ask you some questions, and what happens afterwards depends entirely on how satisfied I am with your answers. I would therefore caution you to speak honestly. I shall know if you prevaricate or tell an untruth."

Sam Sadler swallowed visibly, the muscles in his throat contracting. The anger had gone out of him, and, seen up close in the harsh afternoon light filtering in through the window, he looked exhausted, his face stamped with the marks of what had probably been a completely sleepless night.

"What do you want to know?"

"Why don't you begin with James Murwald?" I said. "Mrs. Sadler, your testimony was crucial in seeing him convicted at his trial, isn't that right?"

Linda squeezed her eyes shut a moment. Although when her husband opened his mouth to speak, she pressed his hand lightly and shook her head. "No, it's all right, Sam. I'll tell it. After I saw Murwald kill that poor old woman, I went straight to the police with what I had witnessed. I told them I was willing—happy—to testify for the prosecution. I wasn't even afraid … then. My favourite uncle was a policeman. A constable in Liverpool. All I thought about was doing the right thing."

She swallowed. "Then, at the trial, James Murwald would sit in the dock every day, simply staring at me. It may sound fanciful, but I swear to you, it was as though the devil himself had me in his sights. No pity, no mercy, or even fear—just pure, deadly evil."

Her shoulders hunched forwards with remembered fear, and a shudder went through her slender frame.

"But I told my story. And then afterwards, when they read out the verdict of guilty and the sentencing, Murwald swore he'd get revenge on all those who'd helped put him away. I was even more terrified. I went to the police and begged them for protection. But they said that Murwald would be locked up tight in Dartmoor prison. So I had nothing to fear."

Her mouth twisted a little on the final words. "At the time, I was performing at the Alhambra Theatre. I had a musical act—singing and dancing, with a bit of acrobatics. But then soon after James Murwald was sent away, I met Sam." She glanced at her husband. "That wasn't why I married him. But I was glad of the chance for a fresh start—a new name, a new life on the road with the circus. Somehow, I had the feeling that Murwald would manage to find me and make good on his threats. I would dream of him at night—of his face when he swore vengeance. But I thought that surely even he would have trouble finding me as a member of a circus act, without even so much as a permanent address."

"But he did find you?" I said.

"Yes. About a month ago. We were camped in Leeds for

a week of performances. I was walking back to our wagon in the dark after the evening show, and suddenly … suddenly Murwald was there. As though he had just appeared out of the night air." Linda's voice shook. "I thought that I was hallucinating at first. But then he spoke. He told me that he was going to kill me for having put him away in jail. But not right away. That wouldn't be punishment enough. He intended to make me suffer first."

Linda laced her hands together, her grip so tight that the knuckles stood out white. "He said that from that moment on, he would always be watching me. I wouldn't see him, but he would always be there, somewhere, hiding in the shadows. Waiting for the right moment to strike. He told me that when I least expected it, he would kill Sam first and make me watch— and then he would kill me. And after that … after that, every stop we made, every town the circus camped in from that day on, there would be some message sent to me. A note. A postcard. Even a bouquet of flowers." Her voice broke. "Always something to let me know that he was out there, watching and biding his time."

Holmes and I exchanged a look. I didn't have to wonder whether Linda was telling the truth. No one could put on that convincing an act of being terrified; right now, even the memory was enough to make her look almost ill with fear.

"Did Mr. Murwald reveal how he came to have escaped from prison?" Holmes asked.

Linda gave a shaky nod. "Yes. He said that he had contrived to bribe the prison's doctor to help him fake his own death. I don't know all the details. But he said that as far as the police and the prison wardens were concerned, he was dead and buried in an unmarked grave. That he had nothing to fear because no one was looking for him."

Holmes shifted his attention to Sam. "I take it that is when you purchased a revolver and took steps to ensure your own life?"

"It was." Sam's big, powerful hands flexed on his knees. "Didn't seem like enough, but it was all I could think to do. We knew Murwald was coming. All we could do was try to be prepared and make sure that if Murwald got me, Linda and—" he stopped. "Linda would be provided for."

Linda's arms were folded protectively across her middle. I saw Holmes's brows go up slightly, and knew he hadn't missed the significance of that gesture, either.

"You will pardon me for the question, Mrs. Sadler, but you are … with child?"

Linda's eyes filled with tears as she nodded. "Yes. Two months. We haven't told anyone. Not a soul." She hugged her middle more tightly, her gaze haunted. "I was terrified above anything of Murwald finding out. God alone knows what he might have done."

"You didn't think to go to the police?" I asked.

Sam and Linda looked at one another, and then Linda answered. "I didn't think the police would believe me. According to all official records, Murwald was dead and buried. They'd think I was just a hysterical female, afraid of my own shadow. Besides, Murwald said—"

She swallowed hard. "He swore to me that he would know if I ever tried to contact the police to let them know that he was alive. And that if I did, he … he wouldn't kill me right away after all. He would take me and keep me locked up somewhere— somewhere no one but him would ever find me. So that he could spend some time … amusing himself with me, before he finally ended my life."

The police might have believed Linda, or they might not have done. But I could easily see why Linda would be too much afraid to take the risk.

The muscles of Sam's shoulder's bunched, and his face turned ruddy. "He was a demon, Mr. Holmes, I swear it. A veritable demon."

Holmes's face was characteristically impassive; I couldn't tell what effect the Sadlers' story was having on him. "We come now to the events of last night," he said. "Can you give me an account of what happened?"

Sam and Linda looked at one another, and then Sam cleared his throat.

"It was about an hour or so before the performance. Linda and I were here, in our wagon, when Murwald burst in." His gaze travelled to the caravan's painted door, as though he were seeing it happen all over again. "We'd been living in terror for weeks now, starting at every noise and shadow. I swear to you, mad as it sounds, it was almost a relief to see Murwald there, in the flesh. At least we didn't have to wonder when he was coming."

Holmes inclined his head. "Such a sentiment is understandable. Pray, go on."

"Linda screamed." Sam's eyes were still unfocused, lost in the memory. "I shoved her behind me, trying to get her out of the way. Murwald had a knife—a big butcher's blade. He swore he was going to carve me up and make Linda watch. I went for the gun I'd bought just in case—I kept it in the table drawer, just there." He gestured to the small table at the front of the caravan.

"But before I could get there, Murwald lunged for me, swinging the knife. He caught me on the arm—here."

Sam rolled up the sleeve of his shirt, revealing a gash on his inner wrist. "I swear to you, Mr. Holmes, I don't know exactly what happened next."

Holmes was looking at the doorway. "You picked up one of your juggling clubs," he said.

"How do you know that?"

"There are only five clubs in the rack. It holds enough space for six."

Sam's shoulders slumped. "You are too much for me, Mr. Holmes. Yes, I grabbed one of my juggling clubs and lashed out at Murwald, more by instinct than anything else. Trying to keep him away. But I hit him, just a glancing blow I thought, and he somehow lost his balance and went crashing down. Just there. By the stove."

Sam gestured again towards the tiny kitchen area, with its pot-bellied metal stove. "It shouldn't have hurt him or done more than made him even madder with rage than before. But he went down and didn't get up again. And when I went to look, he was dead."

Sam passed a hand across his face.

Holmes turned to make a swift examination of the stove and kitchen area. I heard his breath go out in a slight hiss of satisfaction.

"You dropped the juggling club," he said, "and it rolled beneath the stove."

Holmes held up the club, white, bottle-shaped, painted with a red stripe, matching the five others in the rack. "You struck Murwald with the bottom edge of the club. On the white paint I can see traces of blood and a hair that matches his in colour. It is a peculiar quirk of human anatomy that the skull is particularly fragile just there. It takes a comparatively slight blow to cause death."

Holmes spun again, fixing the Sadlers with one of his penetrating stares.

"Very well. Continue. Murwald was dead, if accidentally so. What did you do then?"

Linda had been silent until now, her face very pale, but she answered in a voice little above a whisper. "We argued. Sam wanted to call the police in. But I said—" She stole a quick glance at her husband. "I was frightened that they might not believe Murwald's death had really been an accident, given how much reason we'd had for wanting him to die. I was afraid Sam might be charged and brought to trial—even hanged for having killed him."

I still couldn't be certain what Holmes was thinking, but I could understand Linda's not having a particular confidence in the criminal-justice system that had dragged her into this nightmare in the first place.

"I'd been practicing a clown act," Sam said. "Something for the future, because I'm not getting any younger and the trapeze won't forgive an older man's mistakes. And Murwald and I were similar in face and build."

"So you hit on the idea of passing Murwald off as Sam, and claiming that it was Sam who had been killed," Holmes said. "Not to mention being able to collect on the life-insurance policy that Sam had the foresight to take out."

Linda swallowed and nodded. "Yes. We thought it would be a help in letting us travel somewhere new, somewhere we could start over."

Holmes's gaze was still keenly penetrating, but he inclined his head. "Very well. So you decided on your plan. I take it you dressed Murwald in a clown's garb and made up his face with white paint, then concealed the body somewhere—perhaps even in the clown's props cart, beneath the props—while the rest of the circus personnel were occupied with the show that was taking place?"

Sam's eyes widened. "Yes, but how did you—"

"It requires very little in the way of deduction. I myself saw and examined the body. The hands were calloused, but where I would have expected to see ingrained white rosin powder, I saw darker stains, consistent with the discolouration acquired by prisoners when put to the forced labour of picking oakum. That argued against your story, Mrs. Sadler. I did see the star tattoo, which appeared quite genuine, according to Dr. Watson. I suppose that you, Mrs. Sadler, drew a new star tattoo on the base of your husband's neck, so that it might be seen by a witness as a mark of positive identification. And you also broke open a cyanide capsule inside Murwald's mouth, hoping to distract from the genuine cause of death. I observed you when you were with us and bending over the body. Were you checking to see if the capsule was still present?"

"Yes." Linda's voice was still a low whisper. "The cyanide was my … my last resort, you could say. If Sam was dead and Murwald came for me—I knew I would rather take my own life than allow Murwald to end it at his leisure."

Holmes turned to address Sam. "After the performance—and after you took care to be observed and recognized going into the tent—you took out Murwald's body, hooked up the safety rope, and then hoisted the body to the acrobat's platform using the same rope-and-pulley system that the roustabouts used to raise and lower the pole. You then climbed the pole yourself, hooked the safety-rope clamp to the high wire, and passed it around the neck of the dead Murwald. The long rope you had used to haul the body up, you now loosely looped around Murwald's ankle, which caused the slight post-mortem abrasions I myself observed. Then, after climbing down, you manoeuvred the body to the centre of the wire. You swept the sawdust free from any footmarks and made your escape."

Sam's head hung low, his hands dangling between his knees and his expression bordering on despair. But he gave a miserable gesture of confirmation.

"You're right, Mr. Holmes, about everything. It's as though you were standing there, watching it all." He drew a breath, straightening and seeming to force himself to meet Holmes's gaze. "I killed James Murwald. I didn't mean to do it, but he's dead. And I can't pretend I'm anything but glad of it. If I'd had the chance, I *would* have killed him—so if that makes me guilty in the eyes of the law, then guilty I stand."

Holmes's gray eyes rested on Sam for a long moment. Then he turned. "You will excuse us. Miss James and I would like a private word."

He drew me several feet away, to the rear of the caravan. "Well? What say you?"

I felt my eyebrows go up. "You're asking for my opinion?"

Holmes had reached a point where he might value my thoughts on a case, but I couldn't recall his ever having asked my advice before.

Holmes's lips twitched without quite becoming a smile at my surprise. "In the absence of Watson, I must ask that you serve as the voice of my conscience." He glanced towards the Sadlers. "What are we to do?"

Sam and Linda were sitting with their hands clasped together and their heads bowed—like prisoners in the dock waiting to hear a verdict. Linda's free hand rested protectively against her stomach, as though she could somehow shield the child inside.

I made up my mind. "In this case, bringing them to trial would be an injustice."

Holmes frowned, then gave a quick, decisive nod.

He spun back to Sam and Linda. "As far as the authorities are concerned, James Murwald is dead—and now, so is Sam Sadler. I see no reason to trouble that assurance."

Sam's head came up, and he stared at Holmes as though he could scarcely take in what Holmes was saying. "You mean—" he said hoarsely.

"I mean that you and your wife are free to depart. Free to start your lives anew in a new location, untroubled by the past."

Sam stared at us a moment longer, then sprang to his feet, seizing hold of Holmes's hands. "God bless you, Mr. Holmes. God bless you, sir."

"Yes, well." Holmes might have become slightly softened at the edges from the thinking machine that Watson had first encountered at St. Bart's hospital all those years ago. But he still looked approximately as comfortable as a cat in a roomful of bathtubs at being the object of Sam Sadler's gratitude.

He detached his hands. "You had best make yourself scarce, Mr. Sadler, before you are spotted by anyone of your acquaintance. You will need a new identity, which will require some funds."

"I don't have any funds," Mr. Sadler said.

"I'll use the insurance money," Mrs. Sadler said.

Holmes shook his head and, after taking out his wallet, handed over several bank-notes. "I would advise you to be most careful in how you make any claim against your life-insurance policy, since it has been so recently issued. And please do consider that while your unintended killing of Mr. Murwald may not be a crime, your collection of insurance proceeds certainly will be. You and your wife will be subjecting yourselves to criminal prosecution for insurance fraud. And for that there will be no defence."

"I will think that over," Sam said. Then he recollected himself. "Yes, indeed, Linda and I will think that over."

"I advise you to depart immediately," Holmes said. "When you have found a safe place, you can send word to the circus regarding your belongings. I wish you good day and"—another of those brief touches of a smile just flickered at the edge of his mouth—"and a more peaceful existence than has been yours up until this point."

Holmes led the way down the caravan's steps, and I followed, shutting the wooden door behind us. Walking quickly with him down the sawdust-strewn causeway, I was surprised to see him duck behind another caravan, one close enough to see where we had just left the Sadlers. He held a finger to his lips.

We watched in silence for only a short while, until we saw the Sadlers depart together. Each was cloaked and hooded in the dark-blue fabric that I had noticed on the drapes inside their caravan window. They carried no luggage. Plainly they were following Holmes's instructions to leave at once and avoid being identified. The moment that they passed us, Holmes gave me a look that indicated he was about to follow and that I should come with him.

We walked together for a few paces. Up ahead, a crowd had formed up and looked ready to march into the great Olympia Amphitheatre for the matinee performance. I saw a brass band in red and gold uniforms, clowns in white silks, three big elephants–two forming a chain by holding its predecessor's tail in its trunk–other animals in colourfully painted cages, and a crowd of cowboy-costumed performers on horses. All were coming our way.

The two Sadlers had been walking quickly in the opposite direction but now they hung back, shrinking beneath their blue cloaks, not wanting to be more conspicuous to those who would recognize them.

"They are heading for the Olympia train station," Holmes said.

The procession continued. I could see more clowns–some dressed in red-and-black-striped leotards and frilly red tutus. I saw a gaggle of white geese and perhaps a dozen pigs, all roped together with collars, and wondered momentarily what kind of act those animals could possibly perform. I saw a man in a soldier's khaki outfit, wearing a pith helmet and doffing it and waving to the others in the crowd.

And I saw Becky.

She was walking behind the man in khaki, a red satin cape over her shoulders and a reticule of matching red fabric dangling from her hand. Her tightly pressed lips showed her anxiety as she searched the perimeter of the crowd, glancing from time to time back at where the caravans were parked.

A surge of guilt went through me for getting so caught up in the investigation with Holmes that I had forgotten her. Left alone in the caravan wagon that had been assigned to the Magical Kennedys, she must have grown impatient. Or someone had come into the wagon and told her the Kennedys needed to perform at the matinee after all. Otherwise, why would she be wearing the costume cape?

At the same time, I realized that the Sadlers were in danger.

Someone had invested the money required for Murwald's escape and surely would have known that Murwald wanted to kill the Sadlers. That someone might be harbouring the same lust for vengeance that Murwald had shown so flagrantly.

My heart pounded in my chest. I nudged Holmes and inclined my head in Becky's direction.

Holmes nodded. "Quickly, then," he said.

* * *

About twenty paces separated me from Becky, and I ran them all, holding my finger to my lips the moment I saw that she'd recognized me. I had expected to take her hand and run back to Holmes in silence, but Becky as always was full of surprises.

"Mrs. Torrance!" she said, as soon as I came close enough that she didn't have to shout.

The name sent a cold chill through my body. A few months ago, we had taken on the investigation of a ring of opium smugglers operating from a seaside town on the northern coast. Most of the criminals responsible for the smuggling were either dead or in jail, but the woman we suspected of having been the mastermind behind the whole operation– Mrs. Torrance, otherwise known as The Duchess–was still at large.

I knew that our failure to capture her was, to Holmes, roughly the equivalent of a nail in the sole of one's shoe that jabbed painfully with every step.

"I saw her!" Becky went on. "I know Jack said to stay in the wagon, but I saw her!"

Becky grabbed my hand and turned me so that I could see past the far side of the crowd of circus performers, where the matinee ticket holders were lining up.

Yes, full of surprises indeed.

For there was Mrs. Torrance, the murderer, wearing a gray coat and a cranberry-coloured wool hat and waiting in the line just as if she were a perfectly ordinary person, eager to see the circus.

It flashed through my mind that there must be some connection between the opium ring and the circus—or possibly even with Murwald.

"Did she see you?" I asked.

"I don't think so. She was walking along the causeway between the caravans. I was in my cape, practicing for our magic act, and I just happened to look out the window. Well, I was looking for Jack, really. Or you. I didn't know when you'd be coming back."

"Just now?"

"Yes."

"She went straight to the line where she is now?"

"That's right. She's been there maybe not long, maybe three minutes. I'd just gotten myself into position when you arrived."

I could see Holmes looking impatiently at me. Ought I to go back to him and explain, or should I stay here and watch Mrs. Torrance? I had my revolver in my pocket.

I shifted my weight and cut my eyes in Mrs. Torrance's direction, hoping Holmes would understand.

The Sadlers were moving now. Holmes would follow them.

Then the line of ticket holders shuffled forward a few steps. As the motion thinned them out briefly, I noticed that Mrs. Torrance had a companion. A tall, rough-looking man with an evil furrow to his brow, dark haired, no hat, gray coat and scarf. Tall enough to see over her head. Tall enough to notice me. And Becky in her cape.

The rough-looking man bent down and whispered something to Mrs. Torrance.

Instantly her dark, sharp eyes flicked up. Looked in our direction. Of course she knew me and Becky. She'd seen us both in Shellingford, at the hotel where she and her late husband had stored and distributed illegal opium.

Her dark eyes met mine.

At the same time, two shrill whistle blasts came from the train station behind me, signalling that a train was about to leave.

It took all my willpower not to look away, to hold Mrs. Torrance's gaze rather than turning around to see whether the Sadlers were close enough to the station entrance to catch that train. If indeed Mrs. Torrance had come to the circus to watch over Murwald, the last thing I wanted was for her to notice the Sadlers as they tried to make their escape.

But I knew what I had to do.

"Stay right here, Becky," I said, and I took off at a run, heading straight for Mrs. Torrance, who was in the ticket line about thirty yards away. I might not catch her, but at least for the moment she would be watching me and not the Sadlers.

I hadn't taken more than a few steps before I saw her duck behind the tall, rough-looking man. Now she was behind the others in the line and out of my sight, and he had detached himself from the line and was running straight at me, his hand inside his jacket pocket. I tried to see where Mrs. Torrance had gone, but my view was blocked by the people in the ticket line, staring at the two of us running at each other. I turned my body to the left, intending to dodge past him and keep going. Two steps more and I would have been past him. But he tackled me.

I saw a gun. He was pulling it from his coat.

Then I heard a smacking sound, as if someone had been slapped, and the gun, the man's coat, and his face—everything I could see at that moment—turned to orange.

Orange dust, inexplicably, was everywhere. I blinked and shook my head, trying to see more clearly.

"Come on, Lucy!" It was Becky's voice. "Hurry!"

I got to one knee, fumbling for my revolver. The rough-looking man was getting to his feet, teeth bared in an ugly snarl as he rubbed orange powder from his eyes with the back of one hand.

His gun was in the other.

And then something big and bulky hurtled past me and smashed into the rough-looking man, hitting him with a pow-erful impact that took him off his feet and sent him sprawling onto the ground. Above the orange-coloured cloud I saw a black topcoat and black shoes and a tangle of legs. I heard Uncle John's voice, an angry grunt, intense with effort. "You'll stay down this time. By God you will!"

And from above me, another voice.

Jack's voice.

Relief washed over me as I heard him say, "Sir, do not move. You are under arrest."

CHAPTER 5

I reproduce here the seven notes that remain from my files on the Olympia circus case:

1. Holmes thanked me for intervening to prevent an attack on Lucy. He had been close by, he said, but otherwise engaged, and he was grateful that he had not been required to turn his attentions from watching Mrs. Sadler safely board the first train that left the Olympia station, and confirming that she had not been followed.

2. The tall man I tackled outside the circus ticket line was taken into custody. He complained bitterly about having his face and clothes discoloured by the orange smoke powder, which little Becky had thrown at him before he could harm Lucy. He refused to give his name. He denied any knowledge of knowing Mrs. Torrance, claiming to have merely been assisting a woman in distress, who believed she was about to be attacked by a strange young woman. He was charged with assault with a deadly weapon, brought to trial, and convicted. Lestrade has him under observation at the Newgate prison in hopes that

there may be a clue as to his name and his associates, and thus to the location of Mrs. Torrance.

3. That evening Becky, Flynn, and many of the Baker Street Irregulars attended the Great American Circus with free tickets, courtesy of Mr. Debary, the circus manager, who was so relieved not to have any further distractions to the show or interruptions to his ticket sales that he gladly forgave Lucy and Jack for masquerading as magicians—and Becky, for her theft of the orange smoke bomb from the clowns' wagon. Lucy and I went with the group. None of them had seen a circus before. It was an enormous pleasure to see their young faces as they watched the spectacle.

4. Lestrade took credit for solving the case of the death of Sam Sadler. At Holmes's suggestion, he had the aerialists' platform examined. Traces of white clown's makeup were found on the edge, supporting my thesis that the death had been caused by a blow to the temple of the victim, resulting from an accidental fall. The coroner held an inquest, and a verdict of death by mischance was the result.

5. Holmes put Mycroft onto the task of investigating Mrs. Torrance's financial records—those she kept under the name of her false identity as proprietress of the Grand Hotel. For the most part, everything was perfectly ordinary and above-board. Save for one transaction: six months ago, she withdrew a substantial sum of money and deposited it with another bank, in an account not bearing her name. The bank in question was in Dartmoor. Holmes soon determined that the account was in the name of the prison

doctor who had given the death certificate for Murwald. The doctor had since vanished from the area. Holmes is working on more leads to connect him with Mrs. Torrance. I am delighted to add that Holmes is pursuing these leads with his usual energy.

6. Holmes helped little Becky reproduce the orange smoke grenade she had taken from the clowns. The two of them did so one afternoon, using chemicals Holmes had at hand in his laboratory, some orange fabric dye powder, and some milk sugar and sodium bicarbonate from Mrs. Hudson's kitchen.

7. The body of the man the authorities had identified as Sam Sadler was never claimed. A letter was received at the police mortuary from his wife, asking that the remains be cremated. After public notice was duly posted for three days, the prescribed period of time in such matters, Mrs. Sadler's request was granted.

THE
COBRA
IN THE
MONKEY
CAGE

"A long, coiled, thick gray snake,
very much alive and gazing directly at me."

CHAPTER 1

The events associated with this adventure began on a cold, rainy morning in the spring of 1898. I had just completed my breakfast and was standing at our bow window at 221B Baker Street, grateful to be out of the weather. Then our esteemed landlady, Mrs. Hudson, knocked on the door of our sitting room. Behind her stood a pitiable figure in a dripping-wet black cape and homburg hat.

"I told this gentleman that Mr. Holmes was away," Mrs. Hudson said, "but he wants to speak with you. He claims the two of you were at university together."

I recognized Paul Archer immediately. His misshapen features were unforgettable. His eyes were abnormally large, and his nose looked to have been broken and badly set, although it had been that way, he had told me, from birth. His thick straw-coloured hair was perpetually unruly, like a haystack, and in school he had shaved twice daily to prevent his thick beard from covering his face like a monkey's. And as if his facial defects were not a sufficient difficulty for him to bear, a childhood bout with the ailment of rickets had rendered him bow-legged, so that he walked with a crouching, monkey-like stride, notwithstanding his efforts to straighten up and present himself as other men.

Now his brown eyes were wide with a desperate appeal.

Determined to help him if I could, I put on a smile of welcome. "Hello, Paul," I said.

"I need your help, Watson."

I had always got on well with him, and we had more than once assisted one another in our studies. He was a brilliant student. Moreover, he was very driven to achieve and succeed, the more so, I thought, to compensate for the undeserved handicaps with which nature had burdened him.

I had heard that he had been accepted into the army and shipped off to Afghanistan just before I had gone there. At the time, I felt gratified to know that his appearance had not stopped the queen's army from taking him on as a medical officer, since I was sure that his knowledge and drive would make him more than well qualified to serve.

Looking at Archer now, I was concerned by his obvious fear, but I took comfort from seeing him dressed in an expensive suit that compensated for his skeletal malformation. Somehow, I thought, he must have prospered after returning from the Afghan campaign.

He went on, his tone urgent. "One of my research cobras got loose yesterday and killed a monkey. I have no idea what happened. The snake has been recovered, but if another incident occurs, I will be utterly ruined."

I blinked. "Research cobras? Monkey? My dear fellow, perhaps it would be best if you were to begin at the beginning of your tale."

Archer passed a trembling hand across his eyes. "Yes. Yes, of course. I beg your pardon, Watson. My nerves are in such a state that I can scarce order my thoughts, but I will try. For the past several years, I have been conducting research into the effects of snake venom on human—" He broke off, shaking his head. "But this will not do. Will you come with me? There's no time to lose, I'm afraid, but perhaps I might offer you a further and more complete explanation on the way."

My sympathy was of course aroused by both my past memories and his present state of distress. And plainly I would get nothing more coherent out of him when he was in such an advanced state of agitation. "Where are we going?"

"Not far. Just across Regent's Park. I have a cab waiting. The London Zoo. The monkey house, to be specific."

My puzzlement must have been apparent in my expression. "Where the monkey was killed, Watson!" he said. "Now, please will you come?"

* * *

Archer gave instructions to the cabman and bade me get in first, so that I sat on the right of the cab. Then he spoke, earnestly and rapidly. "I want you to understand why I need your help. Have you heard of Calmette's serum? It is an antidote for the toxic effects of snakebite, just announced recently by the Pasteur Institute. I have a technique to make Calmette's far more effective. Mass-produce it. Every snakebite could be immediately cured. An enormous benefit for mankind. And for our soldiers, who must march through snake-infested frontiers and battlegrounds."

Then he sat back, as though marshalling up his words had cost him too much effort and he needed rest. After we had travelled for a few hundred yards, he said, "Please look out your window now."

Beyond the wide green expanse of parkland perhaps a hundred yards away, a magnificent curved white limestone facade of townhouses, tall and resplendent, rose up out of the spring mist.

"The Park Crescent," I said. I had long admired the architecture from afar. The monthly expense to rent even the smallest flat would have exceeded my annual income.

"Would it surprise you to learn that I live in one of the townhouses?"

"You certainly have done well, Archer," I said.

"Indeed, I have been the most fortunate of men. Before he died last month, my father was a wealthy sheep farmer with five thousand acres of good Buckinghamshire pastureland, and he took out a mortgage loan to set me up in Harley Street. There I have earned enough to pursue my research. I utilize the family flocks of sheep to create my serum samples, and I test the efficacy of the serum on smaller animals or barnyard fowl."

Then he shuddered. "Sometimes a test does not prove successful, and then I am pained to observe the suffering of the poor rabbit or chicken who must die in agony brought on by the poison I have given it. I feel responsible, though I know that it is for a greater good and that I ought to take a scientific attitude. Yet lately I am keenly aware that the poor animal is consumed by its own desperate and painful struggles. Sometimes at night I awaken with indigestion or the sharp pains of a migraine headache, and I pace the floor, knowing my sharp discomfort is nothing compared to the misery I have brought upon my fellow creature."

"Yet as you say, it is for a greater good. It may alleviate human suffering and save human lives."

"That is what drives me forward, of course. I have every hope that one day I shall succeed. I have arranged financial matters so that the funds from Father's estate will enable me at a minimum to carry on my development of antivenom while living on the farm in Buckinghamshire. For a time, my wife and I will also be able to maintain our London home, possibly even indefinitely, if I am successful in exploiting the commercial potential of my research. In fact, I have just taken the final financial steps to securing my dream by selling the railway shares that were the principal asset in Father's estate. Tomorrow the proceeds will pay off the burdensome mortgage loan that still encumbers the family farm."

"I congratulate you."

"Thank you, my friend. Yet the sweet taste of my victory may turn to ashes at any moment, because my sleeplessness and worry have caused me to genuinely become careless. I shall be pilloried in the press and the scientific community for my shortcomings."

I understood his meaning, though I believed that due to his emotional state he was exaggerating the consequences. "The incident with the cobra," I said.

He gave a grim smile. "You do understand. I am glad I thought to call upon you for help. Unless you can help me clear my reputation and prevent a recurrence of what happened, all of my life's work will be undone. Worse, the reputation of the zoo will be blackened and the whole of London may suffer accordingly."

Whereupon he shuddered and seemed to withdraw into himself, sitting hunched, his chin on his chest, until we reached the monkey house.

* * *

The sign on the doorway proclaimed the open hours to be from 11 a.m. to 5 p.m. Inside the spacious, high-windowed enclosure, a tall man in a well-tailored gray frock coat was waiting for us. He looked pointedly at his watch and then replaced it in his waistcoat pocket. "You are on time, Paul. Even a trifle early. We have forty-five minutes until feeding time."

"Hoping to get our little problem sorted," said Archer. "This is my friend and colleague Dr. John Watson. He also served in Afghanistan."

The tall man nodded and held out his hand. "Colonel Rupert Bryce. I am deputy keeper here at the zoo. Also an army man, but ten years ahead of you two lads." He spoke in a rather hoarse voice, as though his vocal cords had been somehow damaged. "I served in Magdala."

"The Abyssinian Campaign," I said, to demonstrate that I knew whereof he spoke.

"As a military man, I feel we ought to stick together. That is why I have kept silent up until now about Paul's king cobra. Somehow it escaped, came in here, and killed a rhesus monkey over there in that cage."

The colonel gestured to one of a long row of cages, the only one not occupied by an ape of one size or another. The animals appeared despondent, and the smell was a trifle overpowering, In the corner was a larger ape, of the gorilla species, I believed.

"Rhesus monkeys are common and easily replaced," the colonel went on. "That's why I was able to turn a blind eye, so to speak. Had it been one of the larger species, such as young Gordon, that gorilla you see over there, I would have been compelled to report the incident. Which I must still do, according to my duty as deputy keeper here, unless you gentlemen can demonstrate to me how the snake escaped and what measures you are taking to prevent a reoccurrence. I shudder to think what the public would say if they knew that a ten-foot-long king cobra might be lying in wait for them as they were innocently touring the grounds with their wee ones."

I winced. Archer was looking positively ill with worry. "I've asked Dr. Watson to help," Archer said, looking more miserable still. "He is an army man and a doctor and also a detective, and—"

"I've read some of your reports of Mr. Holmes, Doctor," the colonel replied. "I will be glad to help."

"Thank you," I said. "Now can you tell me what you observed?"

"Well, I came in early yesterday morning, due to the fine weather, and was on my way to look in on the eagles. One of them we thought might be breeding. Then I heard horrible screams from the monkey house. I unlocked the door, entered, and saw Archer's king cobra inside the cage of a dead rhesus. The cage is the one that is empty now, for I disposed of the poor creature."

"No one else heard the screams?"

"No one that I know of."

"And are you certain that the cobra was the cause of death?"

"Well, I know cobra venom is excruciatingly painful. And there was the snake. And a mark on the monkey's shoulder. And the monkey had been screaming in agony."

"What did you do?"

"We have netting for the monkeys, as you see, and the grappling hooks we need to use to handle them worked well enough in this instance. I was able to get the net over the cobra, and then I wrapped it up in a canvas bag. After disposing of the monkey, I took the snake to the reptile house, just across the drive from here. No one was there at that hour, but I have a passkey to all the exhibit buildings. I entered Dr. Archer's laboratory area, which adjoins the part of the exhibit open to the public. Lo and behold, one of the reptile tanks was empty, and the glass door was ajar. I returned the snake to its tank."

Archer nodded. "I keep a dozen of the cobras for my research. My laboratory is partitioned off on the north side of the reptile house."

"And no one was on duty in your laboratory at the time the snake escaped?"

"We locked everything up, my assistant and I."

"When was that?"

"Before tea. We generally do not stop work until suppertime, but that evening there was a social gathering that my wife wished me to attend, and my assistant was invited as well. She also is a scientist, of course."

I formulated my thoughts, striving to utilize my experience gained from observing Holmes. *Footprints*, I thought.

"The track of the snake," I said. "That will be our paramount objective. That and determining the points of potential exit from the reptile house and the points of potential entry to this building."

The colonel nodded thoughtfully. "There is ventilation for both buildings, of course. And we can examine the openings. The doors were locked. We can assume that they remained so. It is possible that even after the rain there may be some traces."

"Why would the snake choose to travel in this direction?"

"This is the nearest installation with living animals. There is a tunnel coming from the site of the reptile house as well, so the snake need not have crossed the road. It would have scented prey. Fortunately for our inquiry, the rain would not have washed away a trail within the tunnel."

"But why would the snake want prey?" I asked, turning to Archer. "Had you not fed it recently?"

"On the contrary. I feed all the snakes on a regular basis. I see to it that they do not lack for anything. It is important that they be able to produce their venom in as great a quantity as possible."

"For your research?"

"Such as it may be," Archer said, suddenly despondent. "If I can go on with it."

"Come on, Paul," said the colonel. "You've been in bad spots before." He turned to me. "Did he tell you how he got his medal in Afghanistan?"

Archer looked downward, modestly. "That was not scientific."

"But brave," said the colonel. "Don't sell yourself short, man. It won't do you any good, and it's not like you. You're not usually this diffident."

He turned to me. "It was in the mountain country. A sawtooth viper. Deadliest reptile in that part of the world. Archer here was with the soldier when the accident occurred. He killed the snake, lanced the bite on the spot, and personally sucked out the venom, even though there were more snakes about. Well, that soldier was my brother. Paul saved his life —got a medal for his action. And when he came back, he wanted to save more soldiers from the same fate. I did what I could to help him. Introduced him to my friend Dr. George Norman, and some good came of that as well. So, Dr. Watson, don't let this fellow get down in the dumps. I don't want his bravery and dedication to go for naught."

"Then I suggest we get on with our investigation," I said, "while we have privacy. Has the floor of the monkey house been swept?"

"Yes, by custodial routine. It wouldn't have done to change. The last thing I wanted to do was have Paul come into the lime-light for the wrong reason. Though I must repeat, we cannot have this happen again."

"We can examine the tunnel for snake tracks, as you suggested," I said. "And we can examine the snake itself. Surely it would have picked up some evidence of where it had been."

"It may have," said the colonel. "But remember that I put the creature into a canvas sack and brought it back to its cage, so whatever clues to its travels may very likely have been sloughed off."

The colonel picked up his walking stick. "Now I must bid you farewell. My schedule has other commitments, and I do not want to break with routine, for reasons I have already mentioned."

During the next twenty minutes, Archer accompanied me as I carefully examined the passageways and possible points of entry. I found no tracks in the tunnel other than those of ordinary shoes and boots. When we reached the reptile house, I found no markings either at the ventilation portals or on the floor inside the airy, greenhouse-like structure. The snake itself lay coiled behind the tall glass window of its tank-like chamber, beneath a short tree that it could climb for exercise and partially obscured by fresh sawdust. I could see no distinctive marks either on or between its pebble-like scales.

"My assistant will be here soon," said Archer. "It is important that she not know. I do not want her to be distressed."

Then to our surprise came a female voice from behind us. "You do not want *who* to be distressed about *what*?"

Both Archer and I spun round at the interruption. A young woman of perhaps twenty-two or twenty-three stood in the entrance to the laboratory.

Archer's face reddened, his jaw dropping open as he gaped at her. "I—" He cleared his throat. "Watson, may I present to you Miss April Norman, my research assistant. Miss Norman, this is Dr. John Watson, an old friend of mine from medical school."

April Norman was slight, dark haired, and remarkably pretty; it passed through my mind that I would sooner have expected to see her on the stage in the role of ingenue than in a laboratory full of venomous cobras.

She smiled in response to Archer's introductions. "A pleasure to meet you, Dr. Watson, I'm sure." She refocused on Archer, a slight frown marring the smoothness of her brow. "But what were you saying just now, Dr. Archer? Has something happened?"

Archer's shoulders slumped, but he evidently determined that attempting to conceal the cobra's escape was a vain endeavour. Indeed, I should have strongly objected if he had tried to do so.

"I'm afraid you must brace yourself for some bad news this morning, Miss Norman. It appears that Number Seven here"—he gestured toward the enormous cobra's tank—"escaped sometime during the night and killed a rhesus monkey."

"No!" April clamped a hand over her mouth, her eyes rounding in horror. "But how could such a thing have happened?"

"That is what we are endeavouring to discover," I said. "Miss Norman, is there any chance that you might have accidentally neglected to lock the cobra's tank?"

April started to shake her head, but it was Archer who answered. "That is not possible. It was I who locked up, and we left together, and we went to the event together, where we met with my wife. The event was in Hanover Square, where we heard an informal presentation of a scientific paper at the society. Afterward, Miss Norman and I went our separate ways. My wife and I returned home, had our supper, and went to bed."

"I see." I frowned. "Can you tell me more about the production of the antivenom? You mentioned using the sheep on your family estates?"

"Yes, quite so." Archer's face kindled with enthusiasm at speaking of what was plainly his pet subject. "You are no doubt aware, Watson, of the work of the German scientist Van Behring in Berlin, injecting small amounts of diseased tissue into rats and letting the immune systems of the little creatures produce substances that combat diphtheria and tetanus. As I mentioned earlier, the Frenchman Calmette reasoned that the venom of a snake might produce a similar immune response when a small amount is injected into a large animal, such as a cow or a horse."

"Or a sheep."

"Yes, my own work builds upon those two researchers, following the same principles but using sheep to fulfil the function of the host animal. Sheep are docile and easier to work with in large numbers, and they are readily accessible to me."

He rubbed his hands together, warming to his subject. "I am

also quite hopeful for success with a machine I have developed to extract the immunizing serum from the blood of the sheep. My innovation is based on a device created by a German named Prandtl to separate butterfat from cow's milk using centrifugal force—"

He stopped. "But you look sceptical. Or else I am boring you."

April interjected. "Oh, that would be quite impossible, Dr. Archer. I'm sure Dr. Watson finds your explanation fascinating and most instructive!"

I opened my mouth, then closed it again without speaking. A suspicion had just dawned—one that I would have been glad to dismiss as impossible. But the thought clung on, stubborn. Would not monkeys, as being closer in physiognomy to humans, make for better host animals for the production of antivenom? And if so, might Paul Archer himself have introduced the snake into the monkey house, in some sort of botched attempt to create simian hosts?

True, Archer's distress this morning had struck me as absolutely genuine. But he would of course not have intended for the monkey to die—and now that disaster had occurred, he might have sought to cover what he had done by pretending complete ignorance.

In any case, I could not think of a way to phrase the question without alienating Archer and most probably giving him reason to terminate his request for my help.

Instead I asked, "Has anyone besides yourselves been inside the laboratory in the last day or two?"

"No. That is—" Archer's brow furrowed. "I think perhaps Bryce may have stopped by. But not for long."

"There was your wife," Miss Norman said. "She was here to see you yesterday, remember?"

"Ah, yes, of course. Sarah came yesterday afternoon and stayed a few minutes."

"Is your wife interested in your research, then?"

A quick twist, as of pain or regret, passed across Archer's features. "No. I'm afraid that Sarah's interests lie in … quite different directions from mine. I had hoped that in time she might develop a greater appreciation for the work we are doing here but …" He trailed off, looking awkward, and spread his hands.

"Then you can think of no one else who might have—either accidentally or with malicious intent—left the lock on the cobra's tank ajar?"

"Malicious—" Archer's face blanched. For all his brilliance as an academic, apparently that most obvious of solutions had not occurred to him. "You think, Watson, that someone deliberately let the specimen out of its cage?"

"I don't know." For the moment, I could see no motive for anyone's having done so. Colonel Bryce would be the obvious suspect in terms of opportunity; by his own admission he possessed keys to both the laboratory and the cobra tanks. But I could see no reason for him to have wished to sabotage Archer's reputation—particularly since it was Bryce who had made the decision to keep silent about the monkey's death. "But I shall do my utmost to find out."

* * *

I returned home to Baker Street that afternoon, and was distressed to find Holmes positioned cross-legged on our settee in his dressing gown, smoking and deeply immersed in thought. I eyed him with some trepidation. Holmes had of late been showing signs of returning to his old paths of self-destructive habits: eating little, sleeping less. Thus far, to my great relief, there had been no reappearance of the red morocco case with its syringes filled with a seven-per-cent solution of cocaine. But I knew that his frustrating failure to capture the woman known as Mrs. Torrance continued to eat at him.

Holmes remained immobile as I stepped closer, picking up a sheet of paper from the floor. I saw that it was a message from Mycroft, which I assumed was the cause of Holmes's current reverie. I scanned the page, which was written in Mycroft Holmes's small, cramped hand.

According to the records I have been able to uncover, a woman matching the description of Mrs. Torrance was last seen entering the Savoy Hotel March 10, where she checked in under the name of Miss Edna Wallace, spinster, of the parish of St. George the Martyr, Southwark, in the City of London. There is no record of her checking out of the hotel, although her room was never occupied.

I have looked further into the parish records of births, as well as the census records from 1851. There was indeed an Edna Wallace born in said parish. Although if she was the lady at the Savoy I should be greatly surprised, as her age in 1851 was given as thirty-five years of age, and thus three years ago, she would have been eighty-two years old.

I have looked but failed to find any death certificate on record for the lady. It might perhaps be worthwhile to dispatch a force of your irregulars to Southwark in order to ask whether anyone there knows or remembers Miss Edna Wallace—by which I mean the genuine Edna Wallace? I admit freely that such a mission is akin to the age-old saw about hunting a needle in a haystack, but it might nevertheless be a place to start.

I set down the missive and opened my mouth, prepared to ask Holmes for his thoughts on this latest scrap of information. But before I could utter a word he spoke, without opening his eyes. "Mrs. Hudson tells me you left with a friend on an urgent errand this morning."

"It is a small matter, seemingly nothing of a criminal nature. A matter of possible negligence and the prevention of a recurrence."

He opened his eyes. "At the zoo. Do not look so astonished. There is no deduction involved. You have picked up some quite distinctive scents, and you really ought to clean your boots. Now, please tell me what has occurred."

I recounted my morning's tale, concluding with "I have made no progress."

"The reptile house was more vile smelling than the monkey house, I would imagine. Being of closer quarters and less well ventilated due to concerns of temperature. Did you see Gordon the gorilla?"

"I saw a large ape. He did not look at all impressive."

"He is a new arrival. According to the papers, none of his predecessors during the past ten years has lasted more than six months. I understand the concern of your new acquaintance, the colonel. As deputy keeper, his position cannot be strengthened by another dead resident, and one that is conspicuous and expensive to replace as well."

"I must confess I am at a loss as to what to do next," I said.

Holmes nodded. "You wish to help your school friend and to maintain the possibility that his medical achievement will come to fruition. I have two points of advice for you, if you are inclined to listen."

"Of course."

"First, regarding the death of the rhesus monkey. When you have eliminated the impossible, whatever remains, however improbable, must be the truth."

"Holmes," I said, "this maxim is no doubt accurate, and I have heard it from you before, but I do not see how it benefits me at this time."

He gave one of his little smiles. "Then you will appreciate my second suggestion."

"Which is?"

"That more time be given to questioning Archer's young assistant, which should be done out of his presence. Also, Archer's wife should be interviewed. As these subjects are both female, I suggest you employ Lucy for both tasks."

"What can Lucy hope to learn from those two ladies?"

"I suggest you leave that to Lucy."

LUCY
CHAPTER 2

"Snakes." My voice sounded hollow even in my own ears. "Why couldn't Uncle John's friend have been doing research on kittens ... or puppies ... or parakeets?"

We were in the kitchen, doing the washing up after breakfast—and Jack's mouth was twitching. "Well, the easy answer is that kittens and puppies and parakeets don't make the kind of venom that doctors want to find an antidote for."

I made a face at him, reaching for another dirty plate to dunk into the washtub. "Be careful. I'm the one standing here with a tub full of soapy water."

I flicked my wet fingers at him, and Jack laughed. "Just thinking that I've seen you face down half a dozen armed men without batting an eye—but you're scared of a few reptiles?"

"I don't have to be actively afraid of snakes to think that I could have lived without a case involving ten-foot-long king cobras."

"I'm not scared of snakes either!" Becky piped up from the table behind us.

Between my performance schedule at the Savoy theatre and Jack's work at Scotland Yard, it wasn't very often that we were all three of us home together for supper in the evenings. So we had made breakfast our family meal of the day. Right now, Becky was theoretically supposed to be finishing her eggs— and in actuality was poring over a heavy medical textbook that I recognized as belonging to Uncle John. "I've been reading about all the different kinds of venomous species there are in the world. They're very interesting." Becky looked up, marking her page with one slightly sticky finger. "Did you know that the black mamba from Africa can kill a full-grown man within minutes of biting him?"

"Yes, well, luckily for us, Watson's friend Dr. Archer isn't working with black mambas." Although I wasn't sure that the king cobras sounded any better; according to Uncle John, their bites could prove fatal even to an elephant.

I glanced at Jack, who was drying the dishes as I washed them. "What time do you have to be at the Yard?"

"Nine o'clock. Unless you want someone to come along and protect you from the snakes?" He grinned as I raised my fingers threateningly at him again.

"I imagine I should be safe enough. My first task of the morning is to call on Dr. Archer's wife, Sarah. From what Uncle John told me, she has little to no interest in her husband's research."

"Can I come along with you?" Becky asked.

Regretfully, I shook my head. "I'm sorry, I don't think you'd better for this particular interview. Sarah Archer only just barely agreed to make time to speak with me at all—and she must have said at least five times that she only had a quarter of an hour to spare this morning, in between all of her direly important social engagements."

Ordinarily, I tried to abide by Holmes's strictures about pre-judging people before I had actually met them in person. But in this case, I was fairly sure I knew exactly what I thought about Sarah Sutton Archer after three minutes spent speaking to her on the telephone.

"But you can come along with me to the zoo this afternoon," I told Becky. "I promise."

* * *

Dr. and Mrs. Archer's address was in the Regent's Park neighbourhood of Park Crescent—which conveniently meant that I could drop Becky off with Mrs. Hudson on my way, since 221B Baker Street was just a short few minutes' walk.

The Archer residence stood within a curved row of many tall, narrow townhouses built in the Grecian style, with a white-stucco facade and slender white columns framing the front door. It should have been a handsome residence, but at some point in its recent history, someone had apparently decided to "improve" it by adding several elaborately decorated balconies to the windows on the upper stories and a pair of glassed-in bay windows to the lowest floor—all of which combined to look rather like warts stuck on an aristocratic lady's face.

A harried-looking parlourmaid in black dress and white apron answered my ring at the front door.

"Yes, ma'am. I know Mrs. Archer's expecting you. Come right this way."

She led the way towards a doorway near the back of the marble-floored front hallway. I could hear voices coming from inside, the first a woman's, which I recognized as belonging to Mrs. Archer, the tone strident and demanding.

"—and tell Cook that I wish her to serve the crème brûlée and the roast mutton for supper with Lord and Lady Wakefield tonight."

"But—" The second voice was also female, but lower-pitched and more than a little sullen sounding. "But I thought Dr. Archer said that he thought too much rich food wasn't agreeing with him, that it brought on—"

"Just do as I say!" Mrs. Archer snapped. "When I wish for your opinion, I will ask for it. Now go!"

I stepped back as the parlour door opened and another servant—this one a dark-haired girl wearing a kitchen maid's uniform—burst out, almost colliding with me.

She muttered a surly apology as she brushed past, disappearing through the green baize door at the back of the hall that in most houses like this one would lead to the kitchen and the servant's quarters.

"Go right in, ma'am." The parlourmaid who had showed me in sounded embarrassed.

"Thank you."

Inside the parlour, Mrs. Sarah Archer stood near the hearth, looking almost as though she were posing for a portrait: her head lifted, the skirts of her ruffled pink morning gown trailing across the carpet.

She held up her hand as I stepped forward to greet her, cutting in before I could open my mouth. "Before we begin, I wish to say that I consider this to be a waste of time and an unforgivable intrusion on myself and my husband's private affairs."

I felt my eyebrows climbing towards my hairline, but I clamped down on my automatic response—which was something along the lines of *Please don't hold back; tell me how you really feel.*

Instead, I manufactured a smile. Sarah Archer was far from the first uncooperative witness I had interviewed.

"Then let me begin by saying that I'm terribly sorry for the intrusion, Mrs. Archer, and very grateful for any time that you can spare me." When dealing with Mrs. Archer's type, I had no compunction whatsoever about lying through my teeth. I took out a notebook and pencil. "Do you mind if I take notes?"

I didn't usually need to write down the facts of an interview to remember them, but I'd found that people tended to be more comfortable—and thus speak more freely—when I had a ready excuse for not looking at them directly.

Sarah Archer frowned but waved a hand. "Do as you like."

"Thank you." I kept my pencil poised and my smile in place. "As I understand it, your husband asked for help from Dr. Watson as a more discreet alternative to the police?"

Mrs. Archer sniffed, her eyes narrowing. She was somewhere around thirty or thirty-five, with the look of a once-beautiful woman who spent a good deal of her time in front of the mirror, engaged in convincing herself that she was beautiful still.

Her fair hair was swept up behind and curled in the front into elaborate ringlets that framed her face. Her figure was plump, just beginning to turn matronly, and her features were pretty in a childish, slightly petulant way, with large blue eyes, a small chin, and a small bow mouth that when at rest seemed to lapse into a habitual expression of discontent. Her cosmetics were reasonably discrete—a light dusting of rice powder and a coat of rouge applied to her lips and cheeks. But it was still more than most women of her social standing wore to greet morning visitors in their own homes.

"The police." Her voice was scornful. "What would the police care about a missing snake and a dead monkey? I told Paul that the horrid thing probably just slithered out of its tank."

"Surely it cannot have unlocked the tank by itself, though."

Mrs. Archer shrugged dismissively. "Paul is absent-minded enough to forget anything—including locking up properly. And I have told him time and again that he ought to go into a more respectable line of research. Finding a cure for polio or cholera. Those are the types of discoveries that earn a man a knighthood." Her face lapsed into the habitually disappointed expression I had noticed before. "No one of any importance in society cares about a lot of beastly cobras."

And there went any need to ask Mrs. Archer's opinion about her husband's research.

"Dr. Archer's assistant—Miss Norman, is that her name? I believe she mentioned that you visited your husband's laboratory earlier this week?"

I bent my head over my notebook but at the same time watched Mrs. Archer closely out of the corner of my vision. I hadn't yet met Dr. Archer's laboratory assistant, April Norman, but according to Uncle John she was both young and very pretty. And I had already observed that both the kitchen maid I'd glimpsed briefly and the parlourmaid who had showed me in were decidedly plain—a fact which might have been pure chance but also might speak to Mrs. Archer's position on having any competition in the beauty department inside her own home.

She didn't at all seem the type of woman to tolerate a younger, prettier rival for her husband's affections—especially one who was a good deal more sympathetic to Dr. Archer's research. Unless she didn't actually care about her husband enough to be jealous?

Mrs. Archer looked momentarily surprised at my query, but she gave another dismissive gesture. "Yes, Paul forgot his medicine—the one he takes for indigestion—and I was forced to bring it to him at his work. He's dreadfully absent-minded that way, as I said. It makes him quite impossible to live with at times."

I opened my mouth, but before I could formulate my next question, the parlourmaid appeared in the doorway to address Mrs. Archer.

"Beg pardon, ma'am."

"Yes?" Mrs. Archer spun round, her voice snapping with barely concealed impatience. "What is it now, Helen?"

The maid gulped. "Beg pardon, ma'am, but the florist's shop is calling for you on the telephone again. Something about the bill for last week's garden party."

Mrs. Archer's lips compressed, but she swept off towards the hall without a backwards glance in my direction. A few moments later, I heard her voice—elevated now, and more shrill: "That is simply unacceptable! And unless I receive a formal apology from the management of your establishment, I shall be forced to take my business elsewhere!"

I gave the parlourmaid a friendly smile. "Your name is Helen, is that right?"

The Archers' maid was an overweight, nervous-looking girl with rounded shoulders, straggling dirty-blonde hair, and a weak chin. Her eyes widened in seeming astonishment at being spoken to directly, then she swallowed again. "Well … no. That is, not exactly. My name's actually Jane." She gave me a quick, apprehensive glance, as though she was unused to being able to talk freely to anyone. But when I didn't interrupt, she went on, "The mistress's last maid was called Helen. But when I took the job, she couldn't get over the habit of using the other girl's name. So she just calls me Helen."

"I see. Have you worked here long?"

"About three months."

Helen—or rather, Jane—startled and gave a worried look in the direction of the hall as Mrs. Archer's shrill voice rose again.

"I have not paid for the rhododendron you sent because it was a most inferior quality! I have yet to see a single blossom, and the leaves are already turning brown!"

"Is Mrs. Archer fond of flowers, then?" I asked.

At the back of the parlour, I could see the entrance to a glassed-in conservatory, crammed with plants of all varieties, from calla lilies and oleanders to ferns and hot-house orchids. Near the doorway, what I assumed was the offending rhododendron sat in a plain brown pot—and in Mrs. Archer's defence, it looked as unhealthy as she had claimed, its branches drooping and its leaves brown and curling up at the edges.

Jane looked dubious. "She hosts a great many parties for the Garden Society ladies—she's in some sort of club that takes it in turns to meet at each other's houses and give fancy teas. And she's always messing about with snipping off flowers and trying to boil them or some such. Says she intends to take their scents and make her own perfumes. Makes for a dreadful lot of mess to clear up afterwards, I can tell you."

"I see. What about Dr. Archer? Does he ever bring his research home with him?"

"You mean his snakes?" Jane looked at me, wide-eyed. "Oh, no, the mistress wouldn't hear of it. She'd never let any of those nasty creatures in the house, not that I blame her. But Dr. Archer himself is a nice enough gentleman. Deserves a sight better in my opinion than—"

She broke off with a slight gasp as Mrs. Archer swept back into the room, although her mistress ignored Jane completely, focusing on me.

"Will that be all?" Mrs. Archer asked. "I'm afraid that I have a great deal to do this morning, and that really is all the time I can spare."

"Yes, that will be everything." I stood up. "Thank you so much for speaking with me, Mrs. Archer. You've been very helpful."

* * *

"Dr. Archer would never have been so careless as to let one of our specimens escape." April Norman's brown eyes were alight with indignation. "Never!"

In person, Dr. Archer's research assistant was every bit as pretty as Uncle John had described: slender, with delicate features and a cloud of softly curling dark hair framing her heart-shaped face.

Becky and I had arrived at the reptile house at the same time that afternoon as April, and now we were all three of us inside of Dr. Archer's private laboratory, which was located in a back room. The air throughout the building was several degrees warmer than comfortable, I supposed to accommodate the cold-blooded zoo specimens on display. The laboratory itself was furnished with long metal tables, Bunsen burners, and an array of test tubes and glass vials that put me in mind of Holmes's chemistry equipment.

A row of glass tanks for Dr. Archer's test subjects took up one whole wall of the room from floor to ceiling. Becky had immediately upon our entrance gone straight to peer into the tanks, looking closely at the snakes that lay coiled inside like huge lengths of thick, scaly rope.

I had to fight the urge to pull her further away. I'd been telling the truth this morning to Jack; I wasn't really afraid of snakes. Maybe it was just that I'd encountered too many dangerous predators—albeit of the human variety—in my work with Holmes. Another of my father's rather pessimistic dictums was that if anything could work to your disadvantage during the course of an investigation, it generally did. And right now, the cobras in Dr. Archer's laboratory raised something like the same feeling I got when in the presence of a loaded firearm: the skin-prickling awareness of something dangerous, to be underestimated at your own peril.

April was busy removing the pins from her hat and hanging up her coat on a rack near one of the laboratory tables. I studied her, mentally running through what I already knew about her background.

At the moment, I had no reason to think she might wish to sabotage her employer's research here, but on Holmes's general principle of distrusting everyone in equal measure until they gave you a reason to do otherwise, I had dug as much as I could into April's history.

Not that there was very much to uncover. She was twenty-two years old and had thus far lived a quiet, fairly unremarkable life. A telephone call to Mycroft had put me in touch with a Dr. Penderwick of the Royal London College of Medicine, who had known April's father as a professional colleague.

"A good man, Michael Norman," Dr. Penderwick had told me on the phone. I had never seen him in person, but his voice on the line was slightly wheezing with age, making me picture him as stoop shouldered and white-haired. "Did some good work on the study of malaria while he was at college. A bit too fond of the bottle and had a weakness for gambling, as I recall. But most men have their vices, and so far as I saw, it never interfered with his work."

All of which told me very little about April herself—although it did lead me to place a mental query mark against Dr. Archer's name. It might be helpful to find out whether he had ever shared his friend's fondness for drink and gambling.

Now I perched on the edge of one of the hard metal stools in the laboratory and took out my notebook. "How did you come to work for Dr. Archer?" I asked April.

April finished hanging up her coat and turned to face me. "My father was his mentor when Paul—that is, Dr. Archer—was studying to become a physician. I had hoped to become a physician myself, but unfortunately when my father died a year ago, there were … I discovered that unfortunately there were no funds for me to attend medical school after all."

Her cheeks had flushed slightly in a way that had me silently deciding that the rumours about her father's gambling addiction were probably true.

"But it's all worked out for the best." April's expression brightened as she went on. "Dr. Archer agreed to take me on as his assistant here so that I could save up the money for tuition fees."

"So you want to become a doctor?" Becky looked away from the snakes' tanks.

"Yes indeed. I believe the time has come for women to take their rightful places in the world—when we cannot be held back from entering those professions traditionally thought to be an exclusively male domain."

I smiled. "Becky and I certainly wouldn't argue with you there."

Becky nodded. "I might want to be a doctor when I'm grown up." She so far had been much more interested in the snakes than in April Norman but now looked at her more closely. "Your ring is pretty, by the way. Was it a present from an admirer?"

I had observed before that the advantage to being Becky's age was that you could ask questions that would be considered far past the point of impertinence coming from an adult.

"Thank you." April's cheeks were slightly flushed, but she smiled at Becky's interest, turning the ring around on her finger. "And yes, it was a gift, but not from an admirer. My grandmother gave it to me. It was a family heirloom."

The ring was pretty—and no doubt valuable as well: a big central cabochon ruby surrounded by seed pearls. My first, slightly uncharitable thought was that it might have been a gift from Dr. Archer. He was old enough to be her father, true, but he would hardly be the first aging gentleman to fall in love with a pretty young girl.

But the ring, though clearly worth a good deal, was of a decidedly old-fashioned design. Besides which, the setting was slightly dirty and scratched at the edges as well. Surely if Dr. Archer had grown infatuated with his assistant, he would have gifted her with a new ring—or at least taken the trouble to have an old one polished and cleaned.

"So you've worked here in Dr. Archer's lab for the past year?" I asked.

"Yes." April nodded. "And the experience has been wonderful. I've learned so much. It's a privilege to work with a truly great mind like Paul's. And I've no idea how the cobra could have come to be in the monkey's cage," she added. "As I said, Dr. Archer would never have been so careless. I know that you may have heard rumours that he's been under pressure to produce results more quickly and that it's made him grow sloppy—or that he has been driving himself into a nervous breakdown, working such long hours at the cost of his health, and that as a result he is not able to give his full or best attention to his work here."

"No," I said slowly. "If such rumours exist, I hadn't heard them."

"Oh. Well." April looked rather as though she would have preferred to have me argue so that she could keep defending Dr. Archer's reputation. "Good. Because none of that is true in the slightest, I assure you!" She straightened, her hands tightening at her sides. "I work with Paul here every day, and I know better than anyone the care he takes to ensure proper safety measures!"

"I see. I'm sorry, but I do have to ask," I began. "Is there any chance that the cobra might have been placed in the monkey's cage deliberately? I understand Dr. Archer is in need of test subjects to study the effects of cobra venom—and the efficacy of his antivenom."

I didn't know Dr. Archer personally, but from what Uncle John had told me, even he was worried about the possibility that his friend might himself be responsible for the cobra's appearance in the monkey house. It certainly made for a more believable theory than that the snake had found its way into the monkey's cage purely by accident.

The other possibility, of course, was that April Norman was

responsible. She had equal access to the cobras, after all, and perhaps as much reason as Dr. Archer to wish for their research to succeed and therefore to try a different, more humanlike host animal. But her eyes widened with what looked to me like genuine shock at my question, as though that thought hadn't even occurred to her.

"He wouldn't—that is, I'm sure he would never—" She shook her head. "Paul is dedicated to his research, but I'm certain that he wouldn't …" She stopped, and for the first time since our arrival at the laboratory, she looked neither righteous nor indignant, just thoroughly confused.

"Look here," she said at last. "I'll show you how carefully our test subjects are kept and cared for."

Standing up, she crossed over to the wall of glass tanks, unhooking a key that hung on a chain from around her neck. "All the tanks are kept locked, and there are only two copies of the key. I have one, and Dr. Archer has the other. At the end of the day, he checks to make sure that each and every tank is locked for the night."

I watched April, wondering whether she realized that her testimony was only making it more and more likely that Paul Archer was responsible.

"And where is Dr. Archer this afternoon?" I asked.

"I'm not sure; I haven't yet seen him." April bit her lip. "I was here earlier, but then I had some personal errands to run, and so I didn't get back until after lunch—well, you saw me then as we came in together. It's odd, because he's usually in first thing every morning. I thought perhaps he was too upset to work and had decided to stay at home for today."

Uneasiness prickled across my skin. Wherever Dr. Archer

currently was, I already knew from my visit to the Archer residence that he had not elected to stay at home.

Becky suddenly spoke up. "This tank is empty." She pointed
towards a sawdust-lined tank in the lower right-hand corner of
the room, near to the floor.

"That's impossible!" April Norman drew in a sharp breath.
"All of the specimens were here last night and this morning,
I know they were."

Becky moved aside. "See for yourself."

She was right. The cobras weren't exactly easy to miss; it only
took a glance to see that the tank she had pointed out had no
massive scaled body inside.

Alarm dashed through me as I made a quick survey of the
laboratory floor. No sign of any loose snakes, and it wasn't easy
to see anywhere a snake that big might be able to hide. But the
fine hairs on the back of my neck rose all the same. "Has anyone
else been here in the laboratory, either today or yesterday?"

April was still staring in seeming shock at the empty tank.
"No. Just Paul and me. There's been no one besides us here all
week. Oh, except for Dr. Watson yesterday. And Mrs. Archer, of
course. She dropped by one afternoon. The first time that she's
ever come here, that I can recall."

"Yes, she told me. She said she had to bring Dr. Archer his
medicine."

April blinked, finally looking away from the glass tanks. "Was
that the reason? She never said. But of course, she wouldn't
have taken the trouble to explain herself to me."

"Was she ever alone in the laboratory?" I asked. "Even for
a short while?"

"No, never. She came through here, then went in to speak

with Paul in his private office. It's just through there." April nodded towards a doorway at the back of the room. "Oh." Her mouth rounded in sudden realization, and her expression cleared of the worry that had stamped it. "Oh, how silly of me! Paul may just be in his office right now. He could have come in while I was doing my errands and shut himself up in there. I'm surprised he hasn't heard us and come out."

Swiftly, April crossed over to the office door and knocked on the panel. "Paul? Dr. Archer, are you there?"

There was no answer, and she knocked again. "Dr. Archer?"

I moved to join her. Maybe there was no overt reason to be uneasy, but the cold, crawling sensation had spread to the pit of my stomach. "Do you have a key to this door?"

April looked up at me, startled. "Well, yes. It's this one here." She held up the second key on the chain around her neck. "But I don't see why we'd need it. Dr. Archer almost never bothers to lock up." She set her hand on the knob, which turned easily in her grasp. "There, you see? It's open. I suppose I must have been wrong, and Dr. Archer never did come in today after—"

She broke off with a sharp gasp. The door had swung open at her touch, revealing a small windowless office with a big mahogany desk pushed into one corner—and behind it, on the floor, the protruding legs of a man sprawled face down.

"Paul!" April's voice rose to a scream. "Oh, no, no, no!"

She took a tentative step towards the dead man, but I caught hold of her arm. "Don't!" I looked over my shoulder. "Becky, stay back!"

I'd already seen what was under the desk.

A long, coiled, thick gray snake, very much alive and gazing directly at me.

The missing cobra had just been found—along with its victim.

"But it's Paul!" April was crying now, the words coming between choking sobs. "He might … not be dead. We have to try injecting the antivenom! I know there's some in the cabinet—"

I couldn't risk taking my eyes off the cobra for long, but I let my glance flick just briefly to the body on the floor. I'd seen dead men before, far too often, and right now, all of my instincts were screaming at me that the man lying on the floor was far beyond help. But if there was even a slight chance that I was wrong and Dr. Archer might be saved …

I eyed the snake, trying to remember whether I'd ever heard or read anything about how fast a king cobra could move. Although I was fairly certain that *far too fast* was the answer.

"All right." The cobra looked even larger out here, in the open, than the specimens had in their tanks. It hadn't yet moved or raised its head, but I was fairly certain I remembered reading once that snakes responded to ground vibrations rather than noise. "I'll go in first as a distraction and make sure that the snake doesn't attack you. You drag Dr. Archer out of there as fast as you can."

April's face had turned pale. "But I can't … I don't think I'll be able to …" she stammered.

"If there's any chance of our saving Dr. Archer, you'll do as I say!"

I glanced towards Becky and found that she had already anticipated me by climbing up onto one of the metal laboratory tables. She would be safe there if the snake escaped into the outer room. Her face was even whiter than April's, though, her eyes huge and frightened.

"Lucy, be careful!"

"I promise." I forced myself to sound calm. "Getting bitten by a king cobra was more or less the very last thing I wanted to have happen to me today."

Beside me, April swallowed hard. "Try not to hurt it," she whispered. "It's a very valuable specimen."

"That's also low on my priority list, but I'll do what I can."

I edged back out of the room enough to pick up one of the swivelling metal stools. Then, my heart drumming in my ears, I held it out in front of me like a shield and advanced forwards into the small office.

The cobra's head lifted before I had taken three steps, its body swaying back and forth and its scaled hood standing out from its head. Slit-pupiled reptilian eyes tracked me. At least I now knew that the half-remembered fact about their responding to floor vibrations was true.

"April, now!" I shouted.

April had been standing as though paralyzed in the doorway, but she finally darted forwards, seizing hold of the prostrate man's shoes and tugging him towards the doorway ... and then through. In the same moment, the snake struck, launching itself towards me in a movement so fast it was almost a blur.

The cobra's head clanged against one of the stool's metal legs, and it fell back, momentarily stunned. I dropped the stool, spun, and raced for the door, expecting at every second to feel a stabbing bite, but I crossed the threshold and slammed the door shut behind me.

Safe. It took me a moment to register. I'd made it out of the office. I hadn't been bitten.

April was crouched over the prostrate body on the floor, still sobbing. "Paul ... Paul ..."

She put a hand on the dead man's shoulder, rolling him onto his back, then drew in a sharp gasp. "Why … it's not Paul." The blank shock in her voice cut right through the tears. "This is Rupert Bryce."

* * *

"Never thought you'd actually need protection from a snake today," Jack said. Despite his tone, his dark eyes were serious.

"I'm fine." Ordinarily when we met like this at a crime scene, I tried for the sake of Jack's career to stay strictly professional. But in this case, I let myself lean against him for just a moment. We were alone together in the hallway outside the laboratory. Uncle John was escorting Becky back to Baker Street to stay with Mrs. Hudson. April Norman had finished having hysterics and been taken off by a police constable to find a cup of tea in the zoo's canteen. Holmes and Inspector Lestrade were inside the laboratory, examining Rupert Bryce's body. And despite the reptile house's over-warm heating system, the chilled feeling inside me was so far refusing to be dispelled.

"Although if I never see another king cobra again, I won't exactly be sorry," I said.

I drew away from Jack as the laboratory door opened and Holmes emerged, with Lestrade following close on his heels.

"Cobras." Lestrade's narrow features were pinched with distaste, and he seemed to be repressing a shudder as he glanced over his shoulder, back at the glassed-in tanks. "How anyone spends day in and day out studying the beasts is beyond me."

This was one of the rare occasions when Inspector Lestrade and I were in perfect agreement, if only I'd had enough attention to properly mark the occasion. "What will happen to the snake that bit Rupert Bryce?" I asked. "At least, I assume that that's how he died?"

"A reptile handler in the zoo's employ is being summoned to capture and contain the animal," Holmes said. "At which time we shall be able to compare the span of the creature's fangs to the wound on the deceased man's leg and verify that it is indeed responsible for the unfortunate Mr. Bryce's death. However, a preliminary examination makes it appear virtually certain that he did indeed die of the respiratory paralysis brought on by a cobra's bite."

Holmes—typically—sounded as calm as though he measured a king cobra's fang span every day of the week. But I thought his gray eyes were more grim than usual as he rounded on Lestrade.

"Since Colonel Bryce is dead, it may well be too late. But it is imperative that we attempt to discover how exactly the rhesus monkey died. Tell your men to make inquiries among the rest of the zoo staff. Find out where a dead animal would have been disposed of."

Lestrade looked taken aback. "But surely we know how the animal died. Snake bite, just like the dead man in there …" He faltered to a stop as Holmes continued to fix him with a steely gaze. "Yes, Mr. Holmes, I'll see that it's done."

"Good." Holmes turned to me. "Am I correct that Rupert Bryce was the one to discover the dead monkey—and that he told no one of his discovery?"

I was quite sure Holmes didn't need my confirmation, but I nodded. "That's right. According to Uncle John, Colonel Bryce disposed of the dead monkey, returned the cobra to its tank, and offered to keep the matter entirely silent for the sake of not ruining Dr. Archer's reputation."

"Then our next task is to find Dr. Archer." Holmes glanced through the reptile house's front windows to where the sky was growing dark with approaching twilight. "Since it is no exaggeration to say that he might be anywhere in London, I propose that our most fruitful and efficient course will be to remain here."

Lestrade swallowed, casting an uneasy glance at the display cases nearby. There were no cobras here, but his gaze lingered on the tank of a bearded dragon and another with a plaque that proclaimed it to be a boa constrictor from Peru.

"But why—" Lestrade began.

I answered for Holmes. It was often difficult to keep up with my father's deductive leaps, but in this case I was fairly certain that our thoughts were running along the same lines.

"Because someone deliberately placed that snake in Dr. Archer's office. They must have done, unless the snake grew opposable thumbs and succeeded in opening its tank, turning the knob on the office door, and letting itself inside. That means that someone wants Dr. Archer not just discredited, but dead. Or else the intended victim really was Rupert Bryce all along. In which case, Dr. Archer has to be considered our prime suspect."

CHAPTER 3

I left little Becky with Mrs. Hudson at Baker Street. Thankfully, the child seemed none the worse for her experience. When I returned to Archer's laboratory, I found Holmes seated at Archer's desk, immersed in documents. Lestrade was at his side.

"Ah, Watson," Holmes said. "Lucy and Jack have gone to the zoo canteen, at my request. I hope you can accompany us there as well in a few minutes time. Meanwhile, you can help us. Please take a look at this."

He handed me a ledger. "It appears to be scientific records of Archer's experiments with the cobras."

I saw the neatly ruled columns and lines that formed a chart on each page, wherein words and numbers had been precisely, lovingly entered. Archer's handwriting was just as clear and crisp as it had been when we had exchanged lecture notes during our school days. On one group of pages in the ledger, columns indicated which snakes had been milked, the quantities of each milking, what batch of venom those quantities had gone into. Another group of pages listed which type of process had been used to chemically affect the venom prior to injecting it into a sheep, which sheep had been injected, and how much time had elapsed from the injection of the venom until the extraction of the antivenom serum. Another showed how the serum had been processed on Archer's centrifugal-force machine. Another listed particular chickens, their breed and weight, and the quantities of venom and serum injected. In two final columns were indicated the lethal dose per pound and the required dose of antivenom. All entries had been marked and coded for cross-checking so that the results on the last page—indicating whether a particular chicken had lived or died —could be monitored and traced.

"Lestrade, What conclusions do you draw from these entries—about the man Archer?" Holmes asked.

"From the abundance of detail and the orderly nature of the records, I would say that he is a patient, orderly man who has great organizational skills and enjoys his research immensely. Even glories in it, I might add."

"Thank you, Lestrade. Watson, would you describe your friend's recent state of mind as matching Lestrade's account?"

I shook my head. "Archer was nervous and unhappy. He was even having second thoughts about his research and the suffering it caused his animal subjects."

"When was the most recent entry in this record book?"

"About two weeks ago."

"When did Archer's father die?"

"About two weeks ago."

"He may have been distressed about his father's death," said Lestrade. "That may account for his unhappy state of mind."

"Are these entries all in Archer's handwriting?"

"Yes, I can attest to that," I said.

"Here is a letter written by the same hand, Watson. What do you make of it?"

"It appears to be the beginnings of a speech," I said, and then I read aloud, "Mr. Secretary, Madame Chairman, ladies of the auxiliary, honoured gentlemen. Herewith are my results. When you have heard me out, if you are so inclined, I should be grateful for your support. As will many a British soldier."

"Has he given the speech yet, I wonder," said Lestrade.

Holmes was rummaging in the back of a desk drawer. Now he produced a metal deedbox enamelled in black.

"Lestrade," Holmes said, "it may be that the murderer was after what was in this box and that Bryce surprised him. We ought to examine the contents at once."

Lestrade made no objection. In a few moments Holmes picked the lock.

Inside the deedbox I could see two black leather-bound journal books and perhaps a dozen ordinary white envelopes.

"A cheque-book and a ledger," Holmes said, "both in the name of 'British Scientific Research, Ltd.' The account appears to have been opened two weeks ago. The ledger indicates two deposits on the credit side. A small deposit to open the account, written in ink, and beneath it a large deposit, written in pencil. The debit side indicates a number of other cheques, apparently drawn against the larger deposited amount. Those entries are in ink."

"The cheques themselves are here in envelopes," said Lestrade.

"How many cheques are listed on the register?"

"Thirteen."

"How many envelopes?"

Lestrade handed the envelopes to me, and I counted. "Twelve."

"Please open the envelopes. We must determine which cheque is missing."

I did so. The cheques were all signed by Paul, but the entries were made in a different handwriting.

"The cheque that is missing is number four. According to the ledger, it is the one large debited amount. Twelve thousand pounds. The note says it is for payment of the mortgage loan on the Buckinghamshire Farm."

"That accords with what Archer told me yesterday morning." I recalled our conversation in the cab. "He said that tomorrow— which would be today—his financial structure would finally be stable once again. Perhaps he took cheque number four with him to Buckinghamshire, to make the payment in person."

Lestrade nodded. "If he was paying off the mortgage loan, the farm would no longer have that interest expense to bear."

"The other cheques in the ledger are for far smaller amounts," Holmes said. "Together I believe they add up to only about two thousand. The ledger indicates a balance remaining of four hundred fifty pounds."

"That accords with what Paul told me.," I said, but Holmes was not listening. He was riffling through the pages of the book containing the remaining cheques. Then he put the ledger, cheque-book, and envelopes into the deedbox and locked it again, then replaced the box into the desk drawer.

He closed the drawer and stood, consulting his pocket watch.

"This has been most instructive," he said. "We are fortunate that the hour is now past four. However, we have one remaining question that must be answered."

"Only one?" Lestrade's tone was ironic, but Holmes did not appear to notice.

"For the answer, I believe we might ask Miss April, who I trust is still in the company of Lucy and Jack at the zoo canteen. Do you fancy a cup of tea?"

* * *

"Why did Bryce go into Dr. Archer's office?" Holmes asked April Norman.

The young woman hung her head, as though sorrowful and recalling the distressing scene, and Holmes's question hung awkwardly in the air for a short interval. Around us was the continued bustle of visitors to the canteen impatient for their afternoon tea, queuing up to place their order at a central counter and then returning to bring their treasures back to their tables.

Finally, Miss Norman sat up. "It may have been because he hoped to converse with the doctor. To find out from him what preventive measures he was going to take, so that the escape of the snake would not have to be reported. He wanted to be discreet, I expect, so he went into the office. Possibly he wanted to be very discreet, in case I came in first, and so he shut the door behind him."

"And then he encountered the cobra."

"Yes. That must have been it."

"And how did the cobra get out of its locked tank and into the room?"

"I really have no idea. As I said before, all the tanks were locked when I left this morning to run my errands and then go to lunch. Now, I am very tired and shaken. I wish to go home. May I?"

"Of course," said Holmes. "But there is just one more question. Or rather, two questions."

She waited, silent and wide-eyed.

"First, where is Dr. Archer now?"

"I really don't know." Miss Norman pressed her lips together as though in puzzlement. "He may have gone to his country farm. He said yesterday that he had some business to attend to there. Something to do with his inheritance, I believe. It is a pity that the farm has no telephone, for I am certain he would wish to be informed as to what has happened. I know he will be very distressed to learn what has happened to poor Mr. Bryce."

"Indeed. Which brings me to my final question. Please do not distress yourself at the suggestion, but might the cobra have been placed in Dr. Archer's office by someone with the intention of its encountering *you*?"

"Me?" She gave a short laugh. "I am only an unimportant research assistant. Why should anyone wish to harm me?"

"Therein lies my question. Do you know of anyone who might bear you ill will? Someone jealous, perhaps? Or someone who feels slighted or wronged by you for some reason?"

"Oh no. Certainly there may be people who dislike me, though I am not aware of any. But since my father's death I really have not had many encounters with anyone outside my very limited capacity as Dr. Archer's assistant. Mrs. Archer even remarked once that I ought to be out and doing more socially, and I am sure she is correct, but no, I can think of no one who would wish to harm me. Very few people even know I exist, I fear."

"Most reassuring," Holmes said. "Though it is growing dark and, given the circumstances, I should nevertheless recommend that Inspector Lestrade here provide one of his constables to see you safely home."

"That's very kind, but there's no need to bother. I live only a short walk from here, on Chalcot Road. The street lighting is quite effective. I have walked home on many late evenings."

"Nevertheless, I should like to be certain that there is no danger lying in wait for you when you arrive."

* * *

We watched Miss Norman depart in the company of a young constable. Then Holmes took Lucy and Jack aside for a brief word, which I did not overhear. Lucy and Jack departed.

Holmes and I then left the zoo canteen with Lestrade. In the darkening shadows of the park lawn, we walked swiftly until we reached another of the zoo buildings.

"The office that the late Mr. Bryce had once occupied," Holmes said. We reached the office doorway, and Holmes bent to pick the lock.

"I'm sure you have your reasons, Mr. Holmes," said Lestrade, "but before we enter, I should like to know. Why are we here?"

"Because I hope to understand why Colonel Bryce took it upon himself to enter Dr. Archer's office this morning."

Switching on the light, we saw a spacious room, neatly furnished with a bare desk and a side chair and a few wooden file cabinets. A poster photograph of the queen and a framed army certificate were the only decorations on the wall. On the floor at the entrance two letters had been slipped under the door. Holmes opened them and passed them over to Lestrade. "A reunion of his old regiment," Holmes said. "The other is an overdue bill."

"For his monthly rent," Lestrade said. "That gives us the address of his residence, which may be useful if we do not find here what you hope to find. Whatever that may be …"

He let his voice trail off in an obvious attempt to provoke a reply.

Holmes said nothing. He opened one desk drawer, then another. He bent and extracted a stack of envelopes bound by a thin red ribbon. "More overdue bills," he said.

Then he went over to the file cabinet and rummaged inside each drawer.

"You have not found what you were looking for?" Lestrade said.

Holmes was at the chair, lifting the seat cushion. Then he gave a murmur of satisfaction. He held up a schoolboy's journal, marked *1898*.

"The others are likely in his rooms," Holmes said. "He kept the current year in his office, where he made the entries for each day."

"What is the most recent entry?"

"It is dated three days ago. Somewhat cryptic. It is suggestive, but not conclusive." He handed over the journal, where I read:

A difficult choice to be made.

Then on the next page, the final entry:

I have made my decision. Let us hope it proves to be correct.

"What now?" Lestrade asked.

"We must return to the reptile house."

"For what purpose?"

"We need to find Dr. Archer. He may return to his office."

"Why would he not return to his home?"

"He very well may. But Lucy and Jack are watching that location."

* * *

I come now to the most haunting incidents of my narrative. After slogging through a rain-soaked park beneath a black night sky, Lestrade, Holmes, and I walked into the silent, alien atmosphere of the darkened reptile house. Lestrade moved to turn on the light switch, but Holmes stayed his hand. "No one must be aware of our presence," he said. "Otherwise our efforts will be in vain."

There was sufficient light from the electric bulb at the building entrance to see that the door to Dr. Archer's office remained open, apparently undisturbed from when we had searched his desk earlier in the day. At Holmes's instruction, the three of us stationed ourselves to wait uncomfortably on laboratory stools at the far corner of the space, away from the public entrance and Archer's office.

The darkness at that part of the room enveloped us. The night wind and the hiss of the rain put my nerves on edge. I could feel the presence of the many snakes, at least seven of which I knew to be deadly. I comforted myself that the snakes were dormant in the colder night air and that they were safely locked inside their glass tanks.

"Who are we waiting for?" I asked Holmes in a low whisper.

"For the murderer of Rupert Bryce."

"And who, then, is responsible for his death? Do you know?"

"You know my methods, Watson. Apply them. Indeed, you have yourself assembled the majority of the evidence in this case. As far as I can see, you failed only to make one crucial inquiry."

"And that would be?"

"Whether Dr. and Mrs. Archer occupy separate bedchambers."

My jaw dropped, but before I could speak, Holmes cut me off. "Now we must wait in silence, Watson, lest by some noise we inadvertently frighten our killer away."

I resettled myself into a more comfortable position and tried to focus my thoughts on Paul Archer. If Miss Norman's conjecture and our examination of the ledgers were any indication, he had gone to Buckinghamshire to pay off his mortgage debt so that he would own his family farm free and clear. Having accomplished that, why should he return here, to his office, on a cold and rainy night?

To get the other cheques? But the envelopes had all been addressed. Archer would need only to place them in the mail, which would not be picked up until the morning, at the very soonest. Quite useless to come in now for that purpose.

We waited. Beside me I could hear Lestrade breathing: sharp, shallow intakes and exhalations. Holmes was completely silent. I estimated the distance to the nearest snake tank. Possibly seven feet. The reptile inside made no movement.

I thought of the events of that morning. Someone had removed a cobra from one of the tanks and placed it in Paul Archer's office. Later, the snake had fatally bitten Rupert Bryce. We had not yet received confirmation from the snake handler and the medical examiner to that effect, but I could think of no other explanation.

Then with a chill, I realized that if someone had come here to release a snake earlier today, someone could be returning even now, about to perform the same deadly task.

Would that someone be armed? I wished fervently that I had brought my Webley revolver.

Outside, rain spattered and hissed on the roof tiles and the glass window just above where we were crouched. I thought I saw a shadow, cast by the entry light bulb and flitting across the arched window above the public entrance.

Then I heard a noise coming from that same direction. I held my breath. The sound was that of a key turning in the door lock.

I heard soft footsteps. The door to a cabinet opened and then closed. Another cabinet door opened and then closed.

I heard the soft gurgle and splash of liquid on concrete. A few moments later the gurgle and splashing noises came again, this time from the doorway to Archer's office. Amid the vile ammonia-ridden air of the enclosed space I now caught the scents of ethanol and ether.

The steps retreated, back to the public entry door. I heard it close. Then I heard the key turning in the lock.

Holmes's low voice came the next moment. "Quickly."

We walked toward the public entrance. I realized that beneath our shoes we were treading on something wet—from the fumes, I knew it was the ethanol and ether I had noticed a few moments earlier. I held my breath, not wishing to be overcome. We were soon at the door, which Holmes unlocked from the inside, opening it to allow the welcome rush of cold air to sweep in.

Outside the wind had picked up and a fierce rain lashed our faces. There came a flash of lightning. Illuminated in the harsh momentary glow, perhaps ten yards away, was a silhouetted figure. The sight made me gasp with horror.

It was a moving man, cloaked in a cape and homburg hat, shuffling forward, bandy-legged.

Paul Archer, I thought.

Then, almost instantly, came a clap of thunder.

The figure vanished. I heard Holmes's voice, low and urgent. "Heading for the tunnel. We must follow."

"Is that Archer?" Lestrade asked.

"We shall see," Holmes replied. "We are on the trail of a most dangerous and devious murderer. Do not let your sight waver, not even for an instant."

We entered the tunnel.

I kept the silhouetted figure within my gaze every step of the way. It reached the end of the tunnel, and another bolt of lightning flashed over it once again. It was hunched over and shuffling. It wore a cape and a homburg hat. Just as Archer had worn.

It moved rapidly, with its rolling gait, toward the entrance of the monkey house. But it stopped short of the doorway, waiting in the shadows, out of sight of the pathway that led down the hill towards the southern edge of Regent's Park. As it crouched there, I had the absurd thought that this was one of the apes from the zoo collection, escaped from its cage. But I knew that could not be. I realized that this was only my imagination, wanting to believe that my friend Paul Archer was not the figure in the cape. That my friend Paul Archer had not just poured explosive fluids onto the floor of the reptile house, where the single application of a flame would cause the helpless inhabitants and all Paul's work to go up in a terrible outburst of fire.

But why would Archer do such a thing?

He had seemed distressed yesterday but hardly mad enough to destroy his life's research, for which he had expressed such passionate hopes.

Then I blinked, shaking my head, convinced that in my musings I had lost sight of the figure in the shadows. But in another flare of lightning I saw it once again. The same silhouette. The same hat. The same hunched, shuffling gait.

Only now it was coming in our direction, up the pathway from the southern edge of the park.

It reached the entrance to the monkey house and used a key to open the door. Then electric lights went on inside, and immediately there was a cacophony of screeches from the inmates, rattling and protesting inside their cages.

Then, from the shadows outside the building entrance, the first hunched figure emerged.

It moved behind the other, which stood illuminated in the doorway.

Which one was Dr. Archer?

The first figure had something in its hand. Beside me, Holmes was edging forwards, closing in on the silhouetted pair.

I heard a woman's voice, shrill with fear. "It's down there, Doctor!"

Then like a tiger, Sherlock Holmes sprang forward.

CHAPTER 4

"It was clear to me," Holmes said, "that there were two explanations for the death of Colonel Rupert Bryce."

We were back at Dr. and Mrs. Archer's home in Park Crescent, all assembled in the conservatory, getting dry.

Archer, his hair still wet from the rain outside, sat between his wife and an equally wet and bedraggled April Norman.

Uncle John and I were sitting opposite them, while Jack—at Holmes' request—stood by the door. As my father had said, too often exposed murderers were seized with the futile urge to run at the moment their crime was revealed.

All eyes were fixed on my father as he went on. "If Colonel Bryce was the intended murder victim, then one individual clearly stood the most to gain from his death."

Holmes rounded on Dr. Archer. "Dr. Archer, can you please tell us what prompted you to come to the monkey house tonight?"

Dr. Archer swallowed, looking nervous, then dug in his pocket. "I ... I received this note."

Holmes took it from him and read aloud.

Paul,

I'm afraid Number Seven is loose again. I will try to stop him from doing any harm at the monkey house. Please come if you can, and alone so that we can stop any word of this from getting out.

"And the signature is yours, Miss Norman," Holmes said.

April's mouth dropped open. "That can't be! I never sent any such note!" She peered more closely at the missive in Holmes' hand. "Why, that's not even my writing! It looks like mine—it's a good imitation. But it must have been written by someone trying to make it look as though the note had been written in my hand."

"Can you think of anyone familiar enough with your writing to have created such a forgery?"

"Well—" April's brows creased. "Well, apart from my own circle of acquaintances, there is only Dr. Archer, of course. But he wouldn't … I mean, he would have had no reason—"

Holmes interrupted her. "We shall come to that in due time." His voice and expression were entirely calm, but I recognized the hidden energy that seemed to run through his tall frame like an electric current. If my father had been willing to admit to anything as human as having a favourite part of an investigation, I was nearly sure that moments such as these would be his choice.

"As I say, one individual stood the most to gain from Colonel Bryce's death. I refer, of course, to you, Dr. Archer."

Dr. Archer's eyes rounded, and his cheeks paled above the edge of his beard. "But I—"

Holmes held up his hand. "Rupert Bryce alone among the zoo staff knew of the death of the monkey due to a bite from one of your cobras. He had agreed at first to keep the matter quiet in order to protect your research. However, we found a journal of his, stating that he had a difficult decision to make. If he had altered his intention and determined to reveal the cobra's escape after all, then you, Dr. Archer, had good reason to wish for his silence. I have known men to kill for far slighter motives than a burning wish to save their own reputations and livelihoods."

Dr. Archer's cheeks had turned from pale to an unhealthy yellowish gray. "But I never … I swear that I had nothing to do with Bryce's death!"

His wife said nothing, although she was staring at her husband with her face gone slack with shock. Beside me, I heard Uncle John give a slight, near-inaudible murmur of distress.

Dr. Archer's hands shook. "You must believe me, I do not know who killed Bryce, and I swear it was not I!"

Holmes allowed the silence to rest for a beat. Then he gave a single decisive nod. "Fortunately for you, Dr. Archer, I do believe you. You are not responsible for either the death of the rhesus monkey or the murder of Rupert Bryce."

Dr. Archer sank back in his chair, his breath escaping in a whistling hiss.

Uncle John sat up straighter. "Really, Holmes. Then who—"

Holmes once more held up a hand for silence. "We shall make more progress if we proceed in an orderly fashion. Miss Norman, will you kindly tell us what brought you out to the zoo tonight?"

"Why—" April's brow was crinkled in bewilderment. "Why, I received a note, just as Dr. Archer did, saying that a snake had escaped and asking me to come at once. Although mine said that it had come from Paul. It *looked* like his writing too."

"And I do not suppose that you have the note with you?" Holmes asked.

"Why, no. I'm so sorry, but I'm afraid that I left it at home …"

"No matter." Holmes gave her one of his fleeting smiles, then turned to me. "Lucy, when we arrived, I asked you to bring Miss Norman's cape, which she removed out in the hallway, into this room. Will you show us what is in the inner pockets of the garment now?"

I picked up the cloak, which I had concealed behind my chair.

April faced Holmes, lifting her chin. "Going through a lady's private possessions is hardly the act of a gentleman, Mr. Holmes!"

Holmes regarded her. "Alas, Miss Norman, I care very little. Lucy."

I had already searched the pockets concealed in the cape's inner lining outside in the hall. Now I dipped my fingers into the folds of the fabric and drew out two objects. "A bottle and a hypodermic syringe," I told Holmes.

"Is the bottle marked?"

"Cobra venom. Specimens Seven, Eight, and Nine, collected March 21-31."

"That's not possible!" April said. "That bottle contains antivenom. I—I brought it in case there was trouble with Specimen Number Seven!" She turned an appealing gaze on Dr. Archer. "Please, Paul, tell them—"

Holmes interrupted before she could finish her plea.

"Dr. Archer, can you kindly account for your movements since we saw you yesterday?"

Dr. Archer had been staring at April, his expression hovering somewhere between disbelief and distress. But at Holmes' question he squared his shoulders, turning his attention to Holmes. "I could not sleep last night. I went to the lab. I felt obsessed by the need to pay off the mortgage on my family farm as soon as possible. I retrieved the cheque from my desk and went directly to the railway station. I took the next train to Buckinghamshire and to the bank, where I paid off the loan just before noon. Gave me great satisfaction. The farm can now sustain itself without the heavy burden of interest to be paid on the debt. A symbolic journey for me."

At that, Sarah Archer yawned, covering her mouth with one hand. She was dressed in a frilled pink-silk dressing gown, with her hair done up in curlpapers. And so far, she had shown absolutely no curiosity as to why she had been rousted out of bed. "Mr. Holmes, is it really necessary that I be here? All this is nothing to do with me, and I'm quite tired. Couldn't I—"

"I pray your indulgence for just a few moments more." Holmes turned to her, one hand lifted in a gesture of pacification. "I assure you, Mrs. Archer, all will soon become clear."

Sarah Archer still looked sulky and far from satisfied, but she subsided back into her chair.

Holmes turned back to April. "Miss Norman. You realized that Dr. Archer had come in early and that he had gone to Buckinghamshire."

"Yes. When we were in the canteen, I told you that."

"What you did not say, however, was at which moment you realized that Dr. Archer had gone. That moment occurred when you realized that the dead man you had dragged from behind Dr. Archer's desk was not Dr. Archer after all, but Colonel Bryce."

"I'm not sure that I understand—" April began.

Holmes interrupted. "Shall I tell you what *your* movements were this morning, Miss Norman?"

She swallowed. "Of course, if you like. But I really don't see how it's relevant to poor Mr. Bryce's death."

"Ah yes, Colonel Bryce's death," Holmes said. "As I mentioned before, there were two possibilities. The first was that he was killed with malice aforethought, in which case the most likely culprit was Dr. Archer. The second possibility—" Holmes paused, letting the silence thicken a moment more. "The second possibility was that his death was an accident and that the intended victim was Dr. Archer all along."

Dr. Archer made a brief, jolting movement, half rising. "You mean to say that I was the one who was supposed to die of the cobra's venom?"

Holmes regarded him a moment but turned away without answering, back to April Norman.

"To return to your movements this morning. You left your home and went to a bank, where you deposited a cheque."

"You cannot possibly know that—"

Holmes interrupted. "I shall prove it soon enough. But to return to your movements of this morning, you went from the bank to Dr. Archer's office, arriving at your usual time, which was before Dr. Archer normally appeared. Upon arrival, you took one of the cobras from its tank and placed it in Dr. Archer's office, taking good care to close the door. Then you left the room and waited outside for Archer to appear, but he did not. Not wishing to appear conspicuous, you left the area. What you did not know at the time, of course, was that Rupert Bryce was having second thoughts about your arrangement. We found evidence of that in his journal, which he kept in his office."

I had to credit April Norman. Her pretty face was arranged in an almost-convincing expression of confusion. You had to look very closely to see something hard and brittle lurking at the back of her gaze. "I don't know what you mean. What arrangement are you talking about?"

"You induced him to invent a story about a cobra escaping from its tank and killing a rhesus monkey two days ago."

Dr. Archer startled at that, and even Mrs. Archer sat up straighter.

"I don't understand," Dr. Archer said. "We know that the monkey was killed by snake venom—"

Holmes held up a hand. "We know no such thing. Whose word have we that the cobra escaped from its cage and entered the monkey house? Colonel Bryce's alone. Who saw the dead monkey? Again, Colonel Bryce and only Colonel Bryce. In fact, there was no such event. Cobra Number Seven never even left its tank. You may ask your assistant there, Dr. Archer, if you do not believe me."

Shock etched Dr. Archer's face.

April folded her arms across her chest. She would no doubt hate the comparison, but in that moment, her petulant expression was not unlike Sarah Archer's. "Rupert Bryce said there was," she replied. "It is your word against his. And he is dead."

Holmes shrugged. "In any event, you wished to adhere to routine. It was lunchtime. So you had lunch at the canteen as usual and then returned. Still no one came. Then Lucy appeared, and you could not risk having her enter alone. So you had to accompany her inside. You directed her attention to the office, where you expected to find the cobra alive and Dr. Archer dead. You opened the door and waited for Lucy to enter ahead of you, knowing the cobra was inside." Holmes' voice hardened slightly as he spoke the final words. "But then you discovered that the dead man was Colonel Bryce. He was no loss to you, and you may even have planned to kill him some other way, in order to silence him. But his death at that moment was an inconvenience, because it isolated the crime scene, which contained the cheques and cheque-book that would upon close examination prove you had committed the crime of embezzlement."

April's cheeks flushed, and I could almost see the rapid series of calculations flashing across her face as she tried to settle on the correct response. Evidently she decided on *outraged*, because she leapt to her feet. "How dare you? I must say, Mr. Holmes, that I take the greatest offense—"

Holmes cut in. "Again, Miss Norman, I must declare my absolute indifference to whether you are offended or not. To return to the facts of the situation. For your purposes, Dr. Archer still had to be killed. So you waited until this evening. You knew he would be returning home from Buckinghamshire, so you composed a note to lure him, knowing that he was mortally fearful of another death at the monkey house."

April's mouth opened and closed without any sound emerging. "You cannot prove any of this," she finally managed.

"I hear that so frequently from people in your position," said Holmes. "When you had left the note, you came to the reptile house, where you entered the office and picked up the venom and the hypodermic syringe with which you planned to kill Dr. Archer. We saw you. The syringe and venom are in your possession."

"It is not venom. It is antivenom. I was concerned that one of the snakes had escaped. So I went to the office for the antivenom. But the office was dark, and I may have mistakenly picked up the wrong bottle."

"You were followed from your home, Miss Norman," Lestrade said. "Constable Collingsworth, who escorted you there, waited and followed you when you came out. You did not go anywhere near Dr. Archer's office until after you had come here, to his home, and delivered your note one hour ago."

The colour was slowly draining from April's face, and instead of sullen hardness, her gaze now held something trapped and desperate. If she hadn't knowingly allowed me to walk into a room containing a giant, live king cobra earlier today, I might— almost—have felt slightly sorry for her.

As it was, I straightened and faced her. "You're in debt. That ring you're wearing—I thought yesterday that it was odd you wouldn't take better care of a ring that you said was a family heirloom. But I also found these in the pocket of your cloak." I drew out several pink slips of folded paper. "A pawnshop ticket. You've been pawning that ring when you need ready cash and then redeeming it. I don't know the source of your debts, but my guess would be that your father wasn't the only gambling enthusiast in the family."

April turned a look on me that could have frozen lava, but she said nothing.

Holmes cleared his throat. "Returning to your activities of this evening, Miss Norman. It was clever of you to don a homburg hat and cape and assume a shuffling gait similar to your employer's," Holmes said. "If someone saw you going into the office, they would assume it was Dr. Archer, working late at night. But Constable Collingsworth was not taken in by your deception. He followed you from your room to Park Crescent and then to the grounds of the zoo, where Inspector Lestrade, Dr. Watson, and I saw you enter Dr. Archer's office. You spilled flammable chemicals on the floor, which you intended to ignite to destroy your financial records after you had murdered Dr. Archer at the monkey house. We watched you walk through

the tunnel to the monkey house, where you attempted to strike
Dr. Archer with his own walking stick. You intended to render him unconscious so that you could inject him with cobra
venom."

"I told you! I thought I saw a snake! I was trying to hit the
snake!"

"Really, Miss Norman, you do disappoint me," Holmes said.
"I would have thought you would be able to come up with a more
credible lie than that. Based on the more likely interpretation of
your behaviour, Inspector Lestrade and I telephoned Scotland
Yard from here a few minutes ago. The police have obtained
a warrant to search your rooms."

April sucked in a sharp breath.

"I believe that the search of your room will find that your
suitcases are packed and ready for a quick departure. We will
also find some evidence of a bank account under your control,
and when we examine that account, we will find that you have
this morning deposited a cheque in the amount of fourteen thousand four hundred fifty pounds from British Scientific Research,
Ltd."

"But I did not sign any such cheque!" Dr. Archer exclaimed.
"That would wipe out every last shilling from in the account!"

"Of course you would not do that, Dr. Archer. But there
was one cheque missing from those at the back of the cheque
register in your office. You were careless enough to sign a stack
of cheques and allow Miss Norman to fill in the names of the
respective payees."

Archer stared at Miss Norman, who averted her gaze.

Holmes went on, his tone inexorable. "Miss Norman, we saw
your handwriting on the other cheques. No doubt it will be on

the larger cheque that went into your account as well. That will be sufficient to have you convicted of the crime of embezzlement, and I have every confidence that enough additional evidence will come to light to convict you of the murder of Colonel Bryce."

At this, Miss Norman covered her face and slumped forward.

Archer's face turned ashen. "Good God! If the cheque she deposited has cleared—"

"We will explain to both banks, Dr. Archer," said Lestrade. "The fraudulent cheque will be returned to you."

Jack was still standing beside the door, but as Holmes continued speaking, his gaze left April Norman and met mine.

I shook my head briefly. Unless I was very, very much mistaken, this wasn't over—not quite yet.

Mrs. Archer came over to sit beside her husband. "Well, there's a relief," she said. "Paul, you have had an incredibly lucky escape, but it's no wonder you have been so careless. You have been overworking yourself. You need a good night's rest. And you must take your medicine. I have it waiting for you—"

But Holmes interrupted. "I would not recommend you do that, Dr. Archer."

Mrs. Archer's posture stiffened, her head rearing back. "What do you—"

"You have indeed had a fortunate escape, Dr. Archer," Holmes went on. "It is not every man who can say that he has survived two separate attempts at murder in a single week."

I was beginning to feel more than slightly sorry for Dr. Archer, for whom this night seemed to be one unpleasant shock after another. He looked at Holmes, blinking rapidly.

"Two attempts? What do you mean?"

"The first attempt was April Norman's. The second and

more prolonged attempt on your life has come from far closer to home," Holmes said. "Your wife has been attempting to either kill or discredit you for most likely these past two months or more."

Mrs. Archer's hand went to her mouth for a moment, although I had to judge her performance as far less convincing than April Norman's.

"How dare you suggest such a thing?"

"You are a city woman of wealthy background."

"What of it?"

"You were not pleased with the risk your husband was taking. If he failed, you faced the prospect of spending the rest of your life on his country sheep farm."

"She has her own money," said Dr. Archer.

"*Had* would be the correct term. It is all gone. I am confident an examination of her bank accounts will confirm as much."

"It was my money to spend," Mrs. Archer said.

"Yet now it is gone," I said.

Unlike Holmes, this wasn't my favourite part of an investigation. Forcing miserable people to admit to the ways in which they had wasted and ruined their own lives always left me feeling slightly soiled and slimy by association. But I straightened and faced Mrs. Archer. "I heard you speaking on the telephone, unable even to pay your florist's bill."

Mrs. Archer's cheeks were mottled red, but she seemed unable to speak.

Holmes gave me a nod of acknowledgement and went on. "Two weeks ago, when your husband told you his plans for his inheritance, you decided to stop him. Your first thought was to make him out to be mentally incompetent and have him committed. You tried to do that with herbs from this conservatory. I notice you have calla lilies and oleander, either of which would have produced the confusion, discomfort, and distress which you, Dr. Archer, have experienced in increasing intensity during the two weeks following your father's death. Also, you have rhododendron, which releases a poisonous gas when burned and can cause severe headaches."

Uncle John had been silent, but at that he sat up with a sharp inhalation of breath. "That was why you asked me whether or not Dr. and Mrs. Archer occupied separate bedchambers!"

"Indeed." Holmes turned back to Dr. Archer. "I imagine your wife has been adding snippets of the plant to your bedroom fire. You have been away for nearly twenty-four hours, however, and I expect you are feeling better now, is that not correct?"

Dr. Archer's nod gave his answer.

"And then you, Mrs. Archer, decided that snake venom would be a faster and more efficient alternative," Holmes said.

"She made up the story about him forgetting his medicine as an excuse to go the lab," I said. "Mrs. Archer, you really should have come up with a better story. Anyone with even a slight degree of intelligence would find it odd that you did not care enough about your husband's health to alter your dinner menu to accommodate his indigestion, but yet you were supposedly willing to travel to the zoo just to deliver his medicine."

"One of the bottles of venom was missing when we examined the laboratory stock," said Lestrade.

"I did not take it," said Mrs. Archer.

"I believe a search of these premises will prove differently," said Holmes. "I also believe that an analysis of the medicine dose you have laid out for your husband will show, in addition to the toxic herbs, the presence of cobra venom."

Dr. Archer's incredulous stare at his wife indicated that he had grasped Holmes's meaning.

Holmes went on, calmly. "Not that the dose would have proved fatal, of course. Cobra venom must be injected into the circulation, either by a snake's fangs or by a syringe, in order for the toxins to do their work. Judging from your present expression of surprise and chagrin, Mrs. Archer, you did not know that. However, the charge of attempted murder does not require proof that the attempt would have been successful."

Mrs. Archer had finally regained her ability to speak. "I will not listen to such wicked insolence! You are to leave my house this instant!"

Dr. Archer stood up. He was breathing quickly, but he straightened his shoulders. "It is my house," he said, "and whatever searches are necessary shall be performed."

"I am going to my room," said Mrs. Archer.

"I think not," said Lestrade. "Mrs. Archer, you are under arrest for the attempted murder of your husband. Miss Norman, you are under arrest for the murder of Colonel Rupert Bryce. Neither of you ladies is obliged to say anything at this time, but anything you do say may be taken down in evidence and used against you in a court of law."

CHAPTER 5

A short while later, the two women were in the police carriage, under the guard of Constable Collingsworth, soon to be driven away to Scotland Yard. Lestrade was gathering evidence upstairs in Mrs. Archer's room. Archer–after vigorously shaking my hand and effusively expressing eternal gratitude to Holmes–was now hunched over his telephone receiver, trying to persuade someone on the zoo security staff to meet him at the reptile house and help clean the flammable chemicals from the floor of his office.

I was looking at Holmes.

"How did you know?" I asked.

"I told you yesterday, Watson. By eliminating the impossible."

I had experience with Holmes' ways, but this had been a remarkably long night. Evidently my expression was put-upon enough that Lucy felt compelled to explain.

"You had gone over the grounds and both buildings, Uncle John," she said, "and you determined that the king cobra could not have travelled to the monkey house on its own. So that was impossible. What improbable alternatives were left?"

"That someone else had moved the cobra," I said.

"That was one alternative, but another was the simplest: the colonel was lying. That was improbable, for he was an honourable military man who considered himself a friend to Paul Archer. But he may have noticed Archer's strange behaviour, and no doubt Miss Norman spun him a tale exaggerating the doctor's carelessness and her fears that something harmful to the zoo could come from that. Likely she convinced him that a simple fabrication would be the shock necessary to bring Dr. Archer around and cause him to focus on essential, practical matters. No one other than the three of them needed to know about the supposed presence of the cobra in the monkey cage, and no one did, until Dr. Archer decided to call on you for help."

Jack had returned from escorting the women outside. "Are we ready to go?"

Lucy smiled. "More than ready."

I smiled to see Lucy take Jack's arm, resting her head against his shoulder. On a night like this, confronted with the basest and most reprehensible parts of human nature, it did one's heart good to remember that qualities such as love and loyalty still existed in the world.

I thought that even Holmes' expression softened slightly.

As we reached the outside pavement I turned to Holmes. "So all the colonel needed to do was kill a rhesus monkey and dispose of it—or, simpler still, all he really needed to do was add the monkey to his story. After all, no one saw him with either a snake or a dead monkey."

Holmes tossed the ends of his scarf over his shoulder. "And when you ask yourself why the colonel would do that, the most profitable path of inquiry gradually opens before you." He regarded me, one eyebrow slightly raised. "Really, Watson, your grasp of investigative methods is really coming along quite … adequately."

"Adequately," I repeated.

I had thought Lucy was too far away to hear our exchange, but at that she looked over her shoulder, still resting one hand on her husband's arm, and smiled. "I would count that as a win, Uncle John," she said.

EPILOGUE

Two days later, I entered the door of 221B with some trepidation. Although I had not intended it that way, the case of Paul Archer and the monkey house had proven a welcome distraction from the frustrations that were besetting Holmes' mind. Now that the matter of Colonel Bryce's death was resolved, I feared lest my friend should fall into his former state of relentless drive to uncover the whereabouts of Mrs. Torrance.

I fully expected to find the sitting room awash in a fog of shag-tobacco smoke, with Holmes, unshaven and seated in a nest of cushions, on the floor. Instead, though, I discovered him at the breakfast table, poring over a selection of papers that had evidently been delivered this morning. An opened envelope lay beside him on the table, with a seal I recognized as having come from Scotland Yard.

"Ah, Watson."

Holmes's breakfast plate lay beside his place, untouched, but his eyes were bright and there was a contained energy about him that I had not seen in weeks.

"Is there news on the Mrs. Torrance case?" I asked.

"You may see for yourself." Holmes spread the papers out before him. "These were found in the lodgings of Miss April Norman, our erstwhile murderer. She had indeed packed her suitcases, indicating she was about to flee with her embezzled funds."

I examined the papers with some astonishment. They were:

- a birth certificate for a Miss Violet Gerrard;

- a certificate of marriage, registering a union between that same Miss Gerrard and a Sergeant Edward Small, of the First Infantry Brigade in Her Majesty's army;

- a death notice for Sergeant Small, dated 31 August 1880, recording that he had died of wounds received at the Battle of Kandahar; and finally

- a sheaf of clerical papers with the heading of Barclays Bank, London, recording the monthly payment of a small pension that Mrs. Small—formerly Violet Gerrard—had drawn as Sergeant Small's widow.

I looked up. "I don't understand, Holmes. Do these documents have a connection with Mrs. Torrance?"

"Indeed, that is the central question." Holmes was leaning back in his chair, his fingertips steepled, his eyes vacant with the look that meant the majority of his attention was engaged elsewhere. "You will recall that Mrs. Torrance, when last we heard of her, was using an assumed identity of a real individual. It may be that Miss Norman planned to assume the identity of the real Widow Small, using these documents. The identity of whomever Miss Norman paid to procure them would be very valuable information indeed."

"To lead us to Mrs. Torrance?"

Instead of answering, Holmes rested the tips of his joined fingers against his upper lip. "Do you recall my saying once,

Watson, that I was conscious of some power behind the male-factors I encountered in the course of my investigations, some deep organizing force which forever stands in the way of the law and throws its shield over the wrongdoer?"

A chill ran through me. "I should say that I do. You were speaking of Professor Moriarty and his criminal organization."

"Indeed. I have that identical sense now, of a greater power that lurks below the surface of the London underworld." Holmes' expression as his gaze rested on the papers spread before him was as grim as ever I had seen it. "I shall one day come face to face with the evil individual who controls that power, and I shall not back away from the confrontation." He paused and looked up at me. Then he gave a deprecatory shrug. "The outcome, of course, remains to be seen."

A
FANCY DRESS
DEATH

"Then light flared up between them,
and she saw Flynn scowling at her."

Chapter 1

Flynn had broken their rule.

Becky tugged on Prince's leash, quickening the pace. Drury Lane wasn't the worst street she'd ever been on at night. She and Jack had lived in St. Giles before he married Lucy, and neighborhoods around there made Drury Lane look like Buckingham Palace. But on the other hand, Mrs. Hudson would probably be horrified if she knew where Becky and Flynn were right now.

Becky felt a quick twinge of guilt at the thought of Mrs. Hudson. With Lucy and Mr. Holmes off in Dartmoor on a case and Jack on duty at the yard, she and Flynn were supposed to be staying under Mrs. Hudson's care in Baker Street tonight. Well, Becky was. Flynn never slept inside a house if he could help it, not unless the weather was truly bitter cold. Tonight, even with the wet March wind, Flynn would probably have found a doorway to bed down in or taken shelter under a railway bridge.

Except that he wasn't doing anything of the sort.

Becky tugged on Prince's leash again, trying to keep the back of Flynn's ragged cloth coat and flat-topped cap in sight. There was a heavy, yellow-tinged fog tonight that crawled along the narrow alleyways and seemed to swallow up the rickety buildings on either side. Becky was lucky that nearly every other shop on Drury Lane was a gin palace, with burning red-colored lanterns hung outside, otherwise it would have been next to impossible to keep her eyes on Flynn.

She banished the guilty thought of what Mrs. Hudson would say if she happened to go into Becky's room to check on her tonight and found it empty. With any luck, Mrs. Hudson wouldn't find out—and if she did, this was all Flynn's fault anyway.

After Christmas, Mr. Holmes had engaged a tutor for Flynn and Becky to teach them how to read and write and do arithmetic. Well, the tutor was mostly for Flynn, since Becky could already read and write and study her multiplication tables. Dr. Watson had told her that she could sit in on the lessons to keep Flynn company—which she suspected was grown-up talk for, "Make sure that Flynn doesn't try to duck out after five minutes."

Which Flynn hadn't, so far. They'd been studying together every Monday, Wednesday, and Friday afternoon, and Flynn had gotten so that he could write and spell his own name, and he was good at sums. Their tutor, Mr. Everett, wasn't a bad sort. Sober and serious, but Flynn had got used to him, and no longer drummed his feet and fidgeted every time Mr. Everett read to them from Shakespeare or their history reader of the Kings and Queens of England.

Becky was fairly sure that Mr. Holmes hadn't chosen that part of their lessons. Mr. Holmes would have picked chemistry or studying footprints or blood stains. Becky liked the stories— especially the ones about queens like Elizabeth, which was the chapter that Mr. Everett had been reading from tonight.

But the second Mr. Everett had declared their lessons finished,

Flynn had shot out of his chair as if someone had stuck him with a pin. When Becky had asked where he was going, he'd just shrugged and said, "Nowhere in particular."

Because apparently, he thought Becky had been born yesterday.

Becky watched Flynn pass by a butcher's shop and a cigar vendor's cart, then duck around a shabby barrel organ that was grinding out a creaky, bouncing tune that would have made Lucy wince the pitches were so far off-key. He *was* heading somewhere in particular, that was absolutely certain. Which was the reason she was also sure—or almost sure—that he was breaking their first and most important rule.

There were two little girls huddled on the muddy pavement outside the next gin palace up ahead. Both of them looked younger than Becky, with bare feet and draggling wet hair matted down across their foreheads. Probably they were waiting for their father or mother to finish drinking and come out to collect them. Flynn paused and Becky saw him grimace as he looked at them and toss the older of the girls something as he passed by. The girl caught it, and peering through the fog, Becky saw that it was the orange Mrs. Hudson had given him earlier that day.

Then Flynn plunged into the narrow alley just past the gin shop.

Becky pulled on Prince's leash so that he'd stay close to her as she followed. She was dressed like a boy, and her clothes were as shabby as Flynn's—which generally meant that barely anyone gave her a second glance on a street like this one. But just in case anyone thought she had anything worth stealing, having a huge dog walking along with her mostly kept any trouble makers at arms' distance. Lucy had been teaching her how to fight, too, but as Lucy always told her, fighting was your last resort, what you turned to when you had no other choice.

The alley Flynn had gone into was so dark that Becky couldn't even see shapes in the gloom. And she couldn't see any sign of Flynn, either.

Her stomach dropped. She couldn't have lost him, not when she'd come all this way.

She turned back to the little girls outside the gin shop. "Do you know where this leads to?"

Be safe. That's what Lucy and Jack always told her. London's a dangerous place, but you can stay out of trouble if you keep your eyes open and don't take risks that you don't have to.

Well, Becky was trying to be sensible and not take any chances tonight. That was how she was stopping herself from feeling too guilty at the thought of what Lucy and Jack would say if they knew she was out here at all.

She'd brought Prince along, and she was keeping her head down and avoiding any grown-ups who even looked as though they might possibly be trouble. And now before she walked straight into a blind alley, she was going to find out what might be waiting for her on the other side.

The younger girl looked at her, wide-eyed, and put her thumb in her mouth. The bigger one gave her a suspicious look. "What'll you give us if we tell you?"

Becky dug into the pocket of her trousers and took out a single coin. "A penny."

She had a lot more than that in the inner pocket of her coat, but she also knew better than to go flashing money around, even with a pair of kids younger than her.

Another way she was being safe and sensible tonight.

The bigger girl's lip curled up. "One rotten penny?"

"It's better than none, which is what you had a second ago," Becky said. She shrugged. "Take it or leave it."

If it hadn't been for Jack—and Lucy—Becky could have been one of those girls. She could have ended up right where they were, after her mother took sick and died.

But even while feeling sorry for them, Becky also knew the two girls would turn on her in a second if they thought they could get something more valuable out of her.

"Fine." The older girl snatched the penny out of Becky's hand so fast it was clear she thought Becky was going to change her mind about the offer. "Don't know why you'd want t' know, but go through that way and you come out in the courtyard behind a public 'ouse on the next street over."

"Thank you."

Becky gripped Prince's leash tightly and edged into the alley. After a dozen or so paces, her eyes adjusted to the darkness, sort of, at least enough that she could see a long square of grayish light up ahead that she took to be the end of the passageway. But she still had to keep her hand stretched out in front of her to make sure she didn't crash into anything, and she could have kicked herself for not thinking to bring some kind of a light— a lantern, or even just a couple of matches—along.

Although on second thought, maybe she didn't actually want to know what she was stepping in. The ground was squashy with rotten garbage, and the smell felt strong enough to crawl down her throat.

Prince whined. He didn't like it any better than she did.

Becky put a hand on his neck. "Shh, it's all right."

At least they were almost at the end of the alley. Becky stepped around a pile of broken packing crates, heading for that patch of pale light up ahead—and crashed straight into a solid body. Hands grabbed hold of her upper arms.

She stamped down hard, aiming for the other person's instep, just the way that Lucy had showed her. She heard a grunt of pain and followed up with a sharp jab of her elbow into her captor's ribs before she realized that she recognized the voice that was using words that would probably make Mrs. Hudson wash his mouth out with soap.

She jerked back. "Flynn?"

"Becky?" Flynn sounded just as shocked as she did.

She heard a rustle and then the scratch of a safety match. Then light flared up between them, and she saw Flynn scowling at her.

"What do you think you're doing here?"

"What am *I* doing here? Have you forgotten our bargain?"

Two months ago, after the opium smuggling case, they'd promised each other not to go off on any mission for Mr. Holmes— or any other case involving danger—without at the very least telling the other one where they'd be and what they were doing.

Becky had proposed the rule, and Flynn had agreed to it. Given that before he'd started working for Mr. Holmes, Flynn had been a first-class pickpocket and thief, maybe Becky shouldn't have been surprised to find he wouldn't keep his word. But she'd thought after all the danger they'd run into up in Shellingford that Flynn had at least seen the sense of having someone know where you were at all times so that they could summon help if you got into trouble.

Flynn scowled even harder, which for him meant that he knew he was in the wrong but was going to try to convince both of them that he wasn't. "You still don't have any business following me! How did you get here, anyhow?"

"I walked. The same as you." Coming all the way from Baker Street, it had taken forever, too. "And you're going to burn your fingers if you keep holding onto that match," Becky pointed out.

Flynn looked down, sucked in a breath, and then dropped the match on the ground just before the flame burned down to touch his first finger and thumb. Without the light she couldn't see his face, but from his voice, she could tell he was still scowling. Probably because she'd managed to follow him without him spotting her.

"Well, you can just walk back to Baker Street again."

"No."

"What?"

"No." Becky drew herself up straighter. "That's one of the nice things about being me—I actually don't have to do what you tell me to. Now, tell me what you're doing here."

She didn't know whether Flynn would have answered her or not. She was leaning towards not, but before he could get a word out, a voice spoke from out of the darkness behind them. "Flynn? Flynn? Are you there?"

"Yeah, here." Flynn turned, striking another match. This time, he held it up so that Becky could get a quick glance around the small courtyard they'd entered. It was tiny, paved with cracked flagstones, and crammed with overflowing trash bins, she supposed from the public house that the girls back in Drury Lane had told her about. Underneath the reek of the garbage, Becky could smell the thick, yeasty smell of spilled ale and hear shouts and the occasional snatch of someone singing from inside.

She also caught just a glimpse of the boy who'd joined them:

tall and skinny and older than she and Flynn were by three or four years, which would make him thirteen or fourteen. He wasn't wearing a hat, which left his mop of curly red hair bare, and his face was long and thin with freckles scattered across his cheeks and nose.

He took a few steps towards them, then stopped short at the sight of Becky and Prince.

"Who's this?" He sounded about as happy to see her as Flynn had.

Flynn dropped the second match, too. But a wind had sprung up, clearing away enough of the fog that the moonlight from overhead could shine through. And now that they were out of the alley and Becky's eyes were adjusting, there were also a few chinks of light coming from gaps in the public house shutters.

"I told you to come alone," the older boy snapped at Flynn, without waiting for him to answer.

"She's just leaving," Flynn said.

"She?" The red-haired boy peered at her more closely— which made Prince growl, low in his throat, the fur on the back of his neck bristling. The boy gave a startled yelp and jumped back, his hands flying up into the air.

"I'm Becky. A friend of Flynn's." She shot a look at Flynn. "And I'm not just leaving."

She tried to speak calmly, but the truth was, a sick feeling was pulling at the pit of her stomach, and not because she was afraid of the red-haired boy or even because of the filth and smell all around.

Flynn wasn't supposed to steal things anymore. Mr. Holmes paid him and the other Irregulars good wages for the work they did for him with the understanding that they wouldn't break the law, at least while they were in his employ. But this secret meeting in a dirty back courtyard had all the signs of being the start of something illegal—the kind of something that could get Flynn arrested and sent to prison.

The red-haired boy was still eyeing Prince nervously. "Fine, fine, she can stay. Maybe it's better that way, anyway."

There was just light enough for Becky to see that Flynn looked like someone had made him take a drink of sour milk. But he started at that. "Better? How d'you mean?"

"She's the girl you told me about, yeah? The one who stays with Mr. 'Olmes sometimes? Well, she might be able to 'elp with this trouble I 'ave."

Second to being lied to, the other thing Becky hated most was being talked about as if she wasn't even there.

Still, she took what felt like her first full breath since she'd left Baker street. Whatever Flynn was doing here, it sounded like they couldn't be up to anything criminal. Not if the boy knew that she knew Mr. Holmes and still wanted her here.

"What trouble? Is it something to do with the public house?" She nodded towards the building. "You obviously work there."

"What?" the red-haired boy looked shocked all over again. "You d'you know that?"

"You're not wearing a hat or a coat," Becky said. "Which on a night as cold as tonight usually either means you're stupid or desperate. But you've also got shoes on and decent clothes, too, so desperate's probably out. And you don't seem stupid. That means you didn't have far to walk to meet us—and you knew this place would be empty at this time of night. Besides, your clothes all smell like spilled ale and gin. So, my guess is you work in the public house."

She winced a little as she heard herself accidentally use the word guess. She knew how Mr. Holmes would feel about that. But the red-haired boy didn't seem to notice. He was staring at her.

"The name's Boyan," he finally said. "Frank Boyan." The more he kept talking, Becky heard a hint of an Irish accent underneath the East End in his voice. "And yer right, I work at the Yellow Dog. In a manner of speakin', anyway." He smiled briefly, but it wasn't a happy kind of smile, and there was something hard-edged that Becky didn't quite understand in his voice. "But that's not why I called Flynn out 'ere."

"You said it 'ad to do with Mr. 'Olmes," Flynn said. "So what is it, then? We don't 'ave all night."

Flynn sounded surly—which Becky put down to him still not being happy that she had not only succeeded in following him but now was here, listening to everything he and Frank said.

"Awright, awright, keep yer trousers on, I'm getting to it, ain't I?" Frank said. Becky thought his heart wasn't really in the grumble, though. He looked nervous, his shoulders hunched and his hands shaking a bit as he pushed them through his hair. "The fact is, it's about me brother. Me older brother, Tom."

Flynn frowned. "Tom? What about 'im? I thought last I 'eard tell, 'e was in Coldbath Jug."

"Yeah, 'e was." Frank bobbed his head. "Got 'imself nabbed for fakin' a blowen's flag. But 'e got 'is discharge two months ago."

Becky had spent the first seven years of her life in Liverpool, but she'd lived in London long enough that she could mostly understand what Frank and Flynn were saying. Frank's brother had been in prison for stealing a lady's handbag, but had gotten out two months ago.

"Trouble is—" Frank swallowed, his thin shoulders hunching

all over again. "Trouble is, 'e's like to get 'imself lagged for life if 'e goes through with what 'e's planning now."

Flynn tugged the brim of his hat down lower and folded his arms. "'Ow d'you mean? What's 'e got planned?"

"You know Tom," Frank said. The words seemed to tumble out of him faster now. "'E's not a bad sort. None too bright, maybe. And 'e'd rather dream about strikin' it rich than ever work a day in 'is life, but—"

"Yeah, I know." Flynn's voice sounded short. "So what's 'e got 'imself into now?"

"That's just the trouble," Frank said. "Tom, 'e's got 'imself in with a rough lot of customers 'e met in the jug. Not just dippers an' bug 'unters, but 'igh tobers an' even snuff men."

Becky thought that Frank had just said his brother had gotten mixed up with highway robbers and even murderers—as opposed to petty criminals like pickpockets and robbers who preyed on the very drunk. But she'd apparently just hit the limit of her knowledge of thieves' cant. Becky felt a flare of annoyance with herself. She should have spent more time sneaking out to the ale halls in St. Giles and listening in on the conversations there while she had the chance.

"An' now they've got Tom dreamin' about a big score," Frank went on. "Got 'im convinced 'e'll be set up for life if only 'e does what they want 'im to."

"What's the job?" Flynn asked. "Smash an' grab at a jewelry shop?"

"I wish." Frank shook his head glumly. "No, they're planning to 'it some kind of charity ball that one of the nobs up in Mayfair is having tomorrow night. They got Tom thinkin' all they've got to do is dress up like waiters and nick the sparks right off the blowers' necks. He's going to get nabbed for sure."

Becky had got that one. Tom and his fellows were planning to dress in waiters' uniforms at a fancy ball in Mayfair, and steal the diamonds right off the rich ladies' necks. And Frank was sure they'd be arrested for it.

Flynn grimaced. His hands were thrust deep into the pockets of his jacket. "And what d'you want me to do about it? And what's that got to do with Mr. 'Olmes?"

Frank shuffled his feet, looking uncomfortable. To judge from his expression, Becky would guess that he didn't have to ask other people for help very often. "Well, I just thought … bein' that you work for Mr. 'Olmes and all, there might be some way you could think of t'get Tom to call the whole job off."

"Me?" Flynn snorted. "Pull the other one, why don't you? If Tom's not listening to you, 'e's not going to give a toss what I tell him 'e should and shouldn't do."

Frank blew out a long sigh. "I suppose yer right. But maybe—" He dropped his head, looking up at Flynn sideways from under his messy thatch of hair. "Maybe there's another way? If you went to the ball yourself, maybe?" He sounded hopeful.

Flynn snorted again. "Oh yeah. All the nobs up in Mayfair are just trippin' over themselves to ask me to their swank parties. Got to beat the invitations off with sticks sometimes."

Frank's shoulders dropped and he looked so discouraged that Becky's heart cramped.

She'd kept quiet up to now, but she spoke up. "Flynn. We probably could think of a way to get in."

Sneaking into a charity ball in a posh neighborhood would hardly be the hardest or the most dangerous thing she and Flynn had ever done. In fact, just last summer they'd both squeezed into the Jubilee ball at the Duchess of Devonshire's, which had been loaded with security forces there to protect the Prince.

But Becky made a habit of trying very, very hard not to remember details about that night– especially at moments like this one.

Flynn rounded on her, his mouth pulling down. "Yeah, and what d'you think we're going to do once we're inside? Ask Tom and 'is friends to put the jewels and silver they've stolen back, please?" He snorted again. "They'd laugh us right out the door—and then cut our throats to make sure we kept quiet."

Becky's skin prickled with goose bumps, but before she could open her mouth to argue again, Flynn asked Frank, "Where an' when's this party?"

"It's tomorrow night, like I said. Nine o'clock. I don't know the address, but it's Lady Dulwich that's giving the ball." Frank's gaze fixed on Flynn. "Awright, now I'll come straight out with it. Couldn't you talk to Mr. 'Olmes an' get him to do something? 'E knows all those posh birds. I reckon 'e could get 'imself an invitation right enough, couldn't 'e?"

Becky opened her mouth, about to say that Mr. Holmes was away until the end of the week at the earliest, but Flynn stamped down hard on her foot.

Frank scratched his chin. With the light from the public house right behind him, his face was in shadow so that she couldn't really see whether his expression had changed. But his voice sounded different when he kept going. Not threatening, exactly, Becky thought. But harder, with an edge of something calculating underneath.

"I wasn't going to bring it up, but—"

Flynn cut him off before he could say anything else.

"Aw'right!" he told Frank. "I got it. Fine."

"You'll talk to Mr. 'Olmes, then? See if he can be there tomorrow night? You could say 'e owes you a favor, doesn't 'e? All the work you've done for 'im? So 'e should be willin' to 'elp you out."

Flynn glanced at Becky as if he was worried she was going to try to say again that Mr. Holmes wasn't in London now. She glowered at him, letting him know that she could take a hint.

"Mr. 'Olmes doesn't owe favors to nobody," Flynn finally said. "An' no promises, but I'll see what I can do."

Frank's head jerked in a quick nod. "That's all I'm askin.'"

Flynn looked like he was about to turn away, but at the last moment he seemed to change his mind. "You know, you could talk to Mr. 'Olmes yourself. About coming t' work for 'im, I mean. It's not too late."

Becky wasn't used to hearing Flynn sound awkward, but that was how he sounded now.

Frank's head turned so that the light from the public house windows fell on his profile. His mouth was twisted up at the edges, but his eyes didn't look like he was smiling. "Yeah, that's exactly what it is for me, chum. Too late. But maybe not for Tom. You'll talk to Mr. 'Olmes and try and get 'im to come?"

"Said I would, didn't I?"

"Then that's it, then." Frank jerked his head once in another nod, and without saying anything else, he turned around and headed back towards the public house. A moment later, Becky heard a door open and then close somewhere in the shadows behind them.

"What was all of that about?" she asked. "You wanting Frank to come and work as an Irregular for Mr. Holmes?"

"Doesn't matter, 'e won't do it." Flynn kicked at a stray lump of coal on the flagstones, his voice sounding gruff, almost angry, now. "Frank's job with the Yellow Dog Tavern's to keep an eye on the customers and follow the roaring drunk ones out the door so's he can rob 'em blind in the nearest alley. Makes a good living at it, too. Even if 'e's got to split the profits with the landlord."

Flynn started back through the alley the way that Becky had come, striding along as if he could see in the dark like a cat. Becky followed with Prince trotting along at her heels—although at her first step, the foot that Flynn had stamped on throbbed.

"Ow," she said. "You didn't have to break my toes, you know."

Flynn grunted something under his breath that might have been an apology—or it might have been him muttering that Becky was the one who'd followed him here in the first place. She couldn't tell for sure, but she suspected it was the second one.

"I just didn't see any call to go blabbin' that Mr. 'Olmes wasn't in town. You know 'e likes to keep 'is movements dark."

Becky did know, but that didn't stop the lump of anger inside her from turning into a hard block of ice. "No, what you're planning to do is try to handle this all on your own."

She would also be willing to bet a gold sovereign that if they were talking about owing people favors, then Flynn owed one to the boy who'd just left them. But she'd bet even more money that asking him about it would get her nothing but a lot of silence and maybe a bad word or two.

Instead she finished with, "You're going to try to sneak into Lady Dulwich's party tomorrow night without telling anyone else—not Mr. Holmes, not even me. Even though it means you'll be breaking our rule again!"

Flynn muttered something else under his breath, but at least he didn't try to deny that she was right.

Then they heard a commotion coming from the Yellow Dog. Becky felt a strong pull on the leash as Prince lunged forward, but she dug in her heels and held the big dog steady.

Turning, they saw a small crowd had gathered outside the now-open door. The yellow gas light showed at least four shadowy men, huddled and hunched, clustered around something.

A woman's voice screamed, "Murder!"

FLYNN
CHAPTER 2

Flynn recognized the red curls right away, and the white shirt-sleeves, now stained and torn. Even from where Flynn stood, he could identify the motionless figure lying face down between the four men, a glistening pool of liquid spreading over the courtyard flagstones.

Frank.

Flynn's breath came faster, and his heart raced. For a moment he saw darkness all around him and had to put out a hand to steady himself. He shut his eyes, but he couldn't shut out the memory of another horrible sight, one he had always kept to himself. But the words still echoed in his mind.

Just a sack o' bleedin' rubbish, ain't yer!

He waited until the words went away.

Then he felt the heat of anger surge through him and opened his eyes. He wanted to hurt someone. That was a good sign, but he didn't know who to hurt. Becky had come up beside him. Her eyes were wide as saucers.

"'Op it," Flynn said.

She nodded bravely and turned, giving a yank on Prince's leash.

"Meet up at Baker Street," Flynn said.

He kept watch over her on the way back, staying close to the buildings alongside the narrow streets, where Becky and her dog were making their way through the theatre crowds. From time to time he stopped, melting into the shadows, and tried to determine whether anyone was following them. His mind was racing with what to do next, but he knew he couldn't afford to be careless or hasty either. That was why he had told Becky to meet up at Baker Street. One: they had already been there many times, so he wouldn't be giving anything away if someone was watching. And two, Dr. Watson was there. And Dr. Watson was a good person to talk things over with.

But Flynn wasn't going to let Frank's death go unavenged, no matter what Dr. Watson said.

Somehow, Flynn would make someone pay. Because this was not only a crime, it was an insult.

* * *

"An insult?" Dr. Watson asked. He had drawn up his chair closer to where Flynn sat, next to Becky, on the sofa in front of the coal fire.

"Yeah," Flynn said. "They want Mr. Holmes to come to that fancy-do costume party, so they spin me a tale—or Frank spins the tale—they make him do it—you could see he was reluctant, hesitatin,' not as if he'd thought it up himself. And that business of doin' Tom a good deed, rescuin' the poor dumb bloke from his path to sin—I didn't believe that for a minute."

"Why?"

"If Tom's in on a job, he can't back out. Won't make no dif-ference whether I tell him to, or Mr. Holmes tells him to, or the Queen tells him to. If he's in, he's in. Only way out is—feet first."

"Like his brother," Becky said.

"Do you think the owner of the Yellow Dog ordered the murder?"

"I dunno. Maybe. Frank—the way he acted, he was sure to have been followin' orders. Like he didn't think I'd believe him, that rubbish tale of his, but he couldn't do no better and had to say what he said. So, who bosses Frank around like that, makin' him say rubbish stuff? The owner, I guess. Frank wouldn't have a choice but to obey. The owner could throw Frank out in the street if he weren't happy with his performance."

"Or have him killed," Becky added.

Flynn hadn't thought if that. "Maybe he did. But that's a pretty stiff punishment, for makin' a mistake."

Dr. Watson said, "In a time like this, I always try to imagine what Mr. Holmes would do. I think he would start by having us tell him the facts. So what are those, if you please?"

"Frank puts out the word he wants to see me. Wiggins tells me. I go to the Yellow Dog. Becky follows me."

"In disguise," Becky put in. "As a boy."

"Yes. Then what happened."

"Why, what I said. Frank spins us this tale, we tell him we'll think about it, and he goes back inside. Not more than a minute later, Frank's outside again, only this time he's down on the ground bleedin' and dead."

"With people around him."

"It's got to be connected. Can't be just bad luck that Frank walks back into the bar and goes outside again and gets topped."

Dr. Watson said, "It would be odd indeed, for the two events not be connected, when they were almost simultaneous."

Becky said, "Was it because he talked to me and not just

to you? Because if Prince and I hadn't followed you—" She stopped, looking so miserable that Flynn felt sorry for her.

"Whatever killed Frank wasn't your fault. Besides, I didn't see no one watching us from the Yellow Dog. Nobody in there knew you and Prince were with me."

"Frank did look around a couple times," Becky said.

"And he didn't see nothing. And they didn't kill him because he told about the robbery job. Like I said, it happened too quick. Frank wouldn't have gone into the tavern and said, 'Well lads, I just spilled the beans about that fancy dress ball—' "

"And if anyone who knew had to die …" Dr. Watson's voice trailed off.

"Then we wouldn't have made it back here," Becky finished.

"So, it's like I said all along." Flynn folded his arms across his chest. "They were usin' me from the start, orderin' Frank to bring me in and spin me a tale, and then killin' him, all to get at Mr. Holmes."

"Who is presently investigating something at Dartmoor Prison," Dr. Watson said. "So the likelihood of him returning to attend a ball tomorrow night in order to avert a jewel robbery is, at best, remote."

"I'm goin' back to the Yellow Dog," Flynn said.

"No, you're not," Becky said.

"In disguise," Flynn said.

"I have a better idea," said Dr. Watson. "When does Jack get off duty?"

* * *

They changed clothes and went in a cab. Becky dressed as a girl, and Flynn took one of Mr. Holmes's flat caps and a bright scarf that took attention from his ragged coat. Just for safety, he and Becky watched from the bow window as Dr. Watson hailed the cab, and then ran out to scramble inside the open door. Prince stayed behind with Mrs. Hudson.

* * *

Jack listened as Flynn went over what had happened earlier the evening. Then he called New Scotland Yard.

A minute later Jack hung up the phone and turned to them.

"No murder reported at the Yellow Dog. Not unusual, for that neighborhood. But the Yard knows about the costume ball at Lady Dulwich's. Special protection. Lots of jewelry and such. A dozen men will be watching."

"If the police know all about it, then why would Frank make up a story to bring in Sherlock Holmes?" Flynn asked.

"Yes, it's not like a crook to want extra attention from the police. And he could hardly think that bringing in Mr. Holmes would improve the robbers' chances of success. But you're sure that Frank wasn't sincere in wanting his brother to call off the plan?"

Flynn shook his head. "That's one thing I know. In the first place, like I told Dr. Watson, there's no calling it off. Tom's anything but a master criminal. He's following orders, I'm sure of that. And second, maybe they are brothers, but Frank never liked Tom."

"You're sure?"

"He never batted an eye when Tom went to jail. I know that much. Never even mentioned him getting out till today. Least, not to me."

"We'll leave that question for now, then," said Jack. "Let's see what evidence we can find about Frank's murder at the Yellow Dog. I'll go in and talk to whoever's in charge."

Flynn said, "I'll watch the courtyard from outside. I'll be down the alley."

"I'm coming too," said Becky.

"And I," said Dr. Watson. "I brought along my Webley. It may prove useful."

* * *

The dark pool of blood was gone. But there was a stain. And Flynn caught the odor of something chemical when he crouched down over the courtyard flagstones. Something burned. As if they had poured out oil or kerosene and then lit it, in order to destroy Frank's blood.

Becky stood nearby, with an armful of flowers they had bought from one of the nearby stalls. "What's that smell?" she asked.

Flynn shook his head and motioned for her to go away. It still bothered him that they'd tried to use him to get at Mr. Holmes. That they'd even think about baiting him with such a rubbish story as saving poor Tom from a life in prison due to trying something as hare-brained as stealing diamonds right off the necks of rich ladies in the middle of a crowded party. And that was the worst thing. If you were gullible, you wouldn't last long. The word would get around. Flynn knew that. But he couldn't very well let on that he was wise to whatever game they were playing him for. It was a hard spot to be in, like having someone see you lifting a watch and chasing you for it, and then running into a cop. Someday he would be out of spots like that. He didn't know how, or where, because he didn't dare hope that far ahead. But Mr. Holmes had said that the way for Flynn to better himself was to improve his own skills and knowledge. Mr. Holmes had warned Flynn that he would have to fight to do that—fight others who would ridicule him out of jealousy, and fight his own weaknesses, when he got tired or lost hope.

Flynn thought of Frank, whose body had probably been dumped into the river with a load of garbage.

Then Flynn saw Jack come out of the Yellow Dog, banging the door shut behind him.

Jack walked past Flynn and Becky without showing any signs of recognition. He walked past where Dr. Watson sat on one of the barrels outside another tavern, draped in the shabby cloak that Holmes used sometimes for camouflage in these parts of town.

Flynn could barely see Jack as he turned the corner and vanished. Then, sensing something, Flynn turned quickly.

A shadowy figure detached itself from the darkened sidewall of the Yellow Dog and moved to the doorway. Flynn tried to get a good look as the figure slipped inside, but the tavern lights were coming from the wrong direction for Flynn to see more than a brief silhouette. A flat cap and a seaman's coat.

He stifled the urge to follow the figure inside. Someone had been watching Jack and had gone inside to report. That was good information and enough for now. Besides, someone in the Yellow Dog might recognize Flynn from his earlier visit.

He gave the signal to Becky and Dr. Watson. One by one, the three of them made their separate ways, walking the short distance to Charing Cross Station.

There they found Jack, standing at the tobacconist's stall where they had agreed to meet, his uniform now covered by the shabby cape Dr. Watson had worn.

Jack's eyes shone with grim satisfaction.

"No one at the Yellow Dog remembers anyone named Frank Boyan," Jack said.

"They're all lying," Flynn said. He told of the shadowy figure.

"A watchman," Jack said. "No surprise there, if they've just covered up a murder."

* * *

Lady Dulwich's Ball was the next place to investigate, and if the robbery plan really was to involve false waiters, the catering company had to be looked at. So, the next morning Flynn and Dr. Watson arrived at the Carlton, a huge hotel with brick decorations and turrets like castles that reminded Flynn of new Scotland Yard. The hotel was not yet open, since the lobby and upstairs rooms were still being finished. Escoffier, the famous chef formerly of the Savoy, had been hired by the Carlton to be the new hotel chef. The papers had reported that Escoffier had also been hired by Lady Dulwich to cater her grand event this evening. To gain entry, Dr. Watson would claim to be interested in catering arrangements of his own and ask to inspect the kitchen.

But the construction and the impending event had brought in many new workers, and Flynn and Dr. Watson slipped into the crowded hotel entrance without being challenged. They found the kitchen area crammed with people, some washing dishes and polishing silver and crystal, others hurrying to load metal trays and wooden boxes onto a large cart. Two white-hatted chefs labored over huge pans of meat and vegetables on a large countertop. Nothing seemed to be cooking yet.

And at the back of the kitchen, bent over a slop sink, elbow deep in a large baker's kettle, was Tom Boyan.

Flynn recognized him immediately. A bit taller than his brother, and heavier. Same ginger-red curls. Same close-set eyes. Clean-shaven and dressed in kitchen whites of heavy canvas-like fabric. Flynn's heart skipped for a moment. He wondered if Tom knew what had happened to his brother. Flynn didn't want to be the one to break the news.

Tom looked up as they approached. "Flynn?" His eyes showed curiosity, but not suspicion. "What are you doing here? And who's this?"

"This is Dr. Watson," Flynn said.

Dr. Watson held out his hand, with a half crown visible in his palm. A moment later the coin was in Tom's pocket and Tom's face wore a cooperative half-smile.

Flynn said, "I saw your brother yesterday."

"What's Frank on about, then?"

"It was about you, Tom."

A blank look was Tom's only reply.

"He said you had something planned for Lady Dulwich's ball," Dr. Watson said.

Tom's voice dripped sarcasm. "Oh, yeah, big plans, sure. If that's what you call packin' up the dirty pots and plates till dawn and then comin' back here to get 'em cleaned up. Real big plans. But I need the work."

His gaze narrowed. "But how did Frank know that? I 'aven't told him. Haven't seen 'im in two weeks. And what's Frank care about my job, hey? And what's it 'ave to do with you?"

Flynn hesitated. He really didn't want to get into what Frank had told him, if that had been a complete lie, which it certainly looked to have been. Much less did he want to tell Tom Boyan that the last time he had seen Frank, he was bleeding to death on the courtyard pavement.

At that moment a yell from the chef demanded that Tom quit chattering and get back to work. And a look from Dr. Watson convinced Flynn that there was no need to continue the conversation.

"We must have misunderstood, then," Dr. Watson said.

"No 'arm done," said Tom, turning away, hands in his pockets, giving no indication that he even thought of returning Dr. Watson's half-crown.

* * *

"Either Tom's lying, or Frank was," said Flynn, once they were outside.

"How did Tom seem to you?"

"Not lying," Flynn said after a moment's thought. "Just puzzled. And glad to get the money and not wantin' to give it back."

"My impression as well," said Dr. Watson. "Which rather leaves us with nowhere else to turn, for the moment anyway. I will report our results to Jack. Do you want to come with me?"

"No thanks," said Flynn.

He had another idea. But he didn't want to talk about it.

* * *

Lady Dulwich's place was a big brick affair in the middle of an enclosed park, not far from the Carlton, which was probably why whoever was in charge of the ball had picked that particular chef and kitchen to supply the food and drink. Flynn could see the high wrought iron fence wouldn't present a problem if he wanted to get in. There were trees around it with limbs low enough for him to clamber up and over. As he waited, though, the cart from the caterer's arrived, and that was too good a chance to let pass. He timed his jump well and got enough of a foothold so that he could reach the latch on the back and hang on. They sailed through the gate with Flynn unnoticed. Just as the cart was slowing to make its delivery at the rear entrance of the Dulwich mansion, Flynn dropped lightly to the gravel drive and slipped into the shadows of the tall perimeter hedge.

He was watching the kitchen entrance, calculating his next move, when he heard a twig snap behind him. He froze.

He was about to turn to face the new arrival when something hard slammed into the back of his skull.

He saw a flash of white light, and then it vanished, swept away by a wave of darkness. Flynn crumpled, completely unaware of the branches and undergrowth that scraped his face before he hit the ground.

* * *

He had no idea how long he had been unconscious. He opened his eyes and couldn't see anything. Not even shadows. Well, maybe shadows. Some kind of gray darkness. His head hurt. *Means I'm alive*, he thought.

Then it *really* hurt. Like a hot knife, stabbing through the top of his forehead right into his eyes. He pulled himself up and tried to stand, but he was bundled into something, some kind of cloth fabric.

Well, that explained the gray darkness. He was inside a bag. Rough, like canvas. And in here with him was something that smelled like towels or sheets or maybe both. He was getting ready to reach out with his hands and try to feel it, but a wave of nausea came up from his stomach and shook him. *Like a dog shakes a rabbit,* he thought. *But it'll pass off. Got to pass off.*

He decided to wait till it did. Meanwhile, he would try to figure out what had happened to him. All right, he had been trespassing and taken from behind, hit over the head. Who would do that? Not the police or real straight up grounds people or servants. They might give him a swat or a kick and send him on his way, but they wouldn't rap him on the head and put him in a bag.

It had to be connected with whoever had ordered Frank Boyan to spin a tale and get Flynn to come here. Flynn had thought it was Mr. Holmes they were trying to trick and trap, but maybe it was Flynn they wanted.

Or maybe, Flynn thought, they wanted to trap Mr. Holmes by using Flynn as bait. If Mr. Holmes came to rescue him–

In yer dreams, a voice in his head taunted. *No one's going to think Mr. Holmes would go anywhere to rescue the likes of you. He's got dozens more, all eager to run his errands and take his shillin's after you drop down and die.*

"But I'm different," Flynn whispered, in his mind. "Mr. Holmes is *making* me different. Got me a tutor, he has, and proper lessons—"

He might have kept arguing back and forth with himself, but at that moment Flynn felt a jolt and a bump, as whatever he was in was picked up, and then dropped down, and then picked up again. He nearly had to bite his tongue to keep from crying out, first in surprise at the sudden move, and then in pain, as the jolting shook his already-aching head.

* * *

It felt like they were stopping for a moment, and then going forward. His container tilted backwards. But it kept moving upward in bumps and jolts.

They were going up steps. Flynn counted them, because he knew Mr. Holmes would demand to know that. And he wasn't going to let Mr. Holmes down or let him think that he, Flynn, hadn't been– what was the word–observing, that was it, during this time. He had to catch the enemy unawares.

Fourteen steps up.

Then they were on level ground again, moving forward, and then stopping.

Dropped down with a bang. Another jolt that made Flynn's head throb.

A voice. One Flynn didn't recognize. Older. Educated. Authoritative. "Is he awake?"

Then a reply. "Not a peep from 'im. 'Asn't moved, neither."

This voice was younger, and a lot less educated. There was something familiar about it. Flynn tried to remember, but his head hurt too much to focus and his ears still rang, so he couldn't even hear very clearly.

He did know one thing, though. He couldn't let them know he was awake. Maybe he could surprise them.

The younger voice continued. "Want me to do 'im now?"

The older voice dripped contempt. "You *are* a stupid fellow, aren't you? Now why on earth would you want to do that?"

"Then we could 'ave a smoke. Wouldn't need to watch him."

"And he'd be nice and cold when they find him, too, you lazy, brainless oaf, and there would go the whole plan, literally up in smoke."

"I didn't—"

"Never mind. I've brought something. But someone'll still have to keep an eye on him till the time comes."

There was a period of silence. Flynn caught the scent of

something chemical. Then the older voice, "All right, let's have a look at your little prize."

Flynn heard the creak of a wicker lid being lifted on wicker hinges. He realized he was in a laundry basket. Then he felt the sack he'd been in jerked roughly and hauled upward. And dropped unceremoniously on the floor. Carpeted floor, though, Flynn thought, determined to remember that detail. *Fourteen steps up, and a carpeted floor.*

He let his head loll on his neck and kept his eyes shut. But he could see light through his eyelids, so he knew that they'd opened up the bag.

Flynn stayed limp. A hand touched his forehead and a rough fingertip pushed at his eyelid. He kept his eyes rolled up, trying not to look. The fingertip let go. Flynn let his eye go shut in what he hoped looked natural.

"Is he awake?" said the older voice.

Then a sharp kick in his ribs made Flynn's breath go out in a rush, and then back in as he gasped at the impact. But he still kept his eyes shut and his head lolled back.

"Guess he isn't," the younger voice said.

"Still."

Then the chemical smell got stronger. He knew that smell. It was chloroform.

And he felt something cold and wet, a cloth, clamped hard over his nose and mouth. He tried to hold his breath, but he was still gasping from the kick, and the mist came into his throat and down into his lungs.

CHAPTER 3

"Now, remember," Jack said. "You need to make sure that you're either with me or with Dr. Watson. The entire time we're here."

They were standing on the sweep of gravel drive outside of Lady Dulwich's house, which was a big towering brick place. The windows blazed with lights, and inside Becky could see party-goers in all sorts of fancy-dress costumes passing by. Even out here, it was noisy: people laughing and talking, and somewhere a group of violins playing music for them to dance to.

Becky nodded. "I will. I promise."

Jack was still frowning, as if he was thinking about what he'd just said and looking for possible loopholes. Becky couldn't entirely blame him. The last time she'd disobeyed his order to stay somewhere, she'd used the excuse that he hadn't specified how *long* she was supposed to stay.

"Really," she said again. "I promise, Jack."

Jack gave her another long look as though he still didn't completely believe her. But she really, honestly had every intention of doing exactly as he asked. Tonight, for once, she would almost have been happy to stay safe at Baker Street with Mrs. Hudson. Well, not *happy*. The lump of worry for Flynn was knotted up too tight in her chest for that—and even if Jack and Dr. Watson had tried to forbid her coming, she would have felt duty-bound to sneak in somehow, just in case she could pick up some clue as to what had happened to him.

But she would much, much rather not have been here.

Jack finally nodded. "All right. Let's go in."

He led the way, not in through the grand front entrance, but around the side of the house where the servants and people making deliveries would go in. Dr. Watson was already somewhere inside, among all the rest of the people in fancy costumes. But Jack was going to talk to the other police officers who'd been asked to keep an eye on things tonight, and rich people like Lady Dulwich didn't invite policemen to come in through the front door.

The rear entrance led them into a narrow passageway, with the sound of pots and pans clanking in the kitchen up ahead. Becky had to ignore the way her insides went cold and her heart jumped.

She'd fallen behind; Jack looked back over his shoulder at her. "All right, Beck?"

Becky took a breath and tried to stop her heart from thumping so hard. She definitely wasn't going to tell Jack that she was nervous about being here.

Jack and Dr. Watson had agreed to let her come because she knew Flynn the best, and stood the best chance of thinking like he would, trying to piece together what he might have done if he'd come here.

If he really *had* come here. They didn't even know that much. "Fine."

Jack might have kept asking her questions. That was the trouble with having a policeman for a brother: you were just wasting your breath if you thought you could ever get away with lying or even telling only half the truth.

But then Inspector Lestrade—easily recognizable by Becky since he wasn't wearing a costume—came up the passageway and started talking to Jack. Something about the watch they'd set around the perimeter of the house.

Jack turned away from her to listen, and Becky snuck a peek in through the doorway to the kitchen.

No sign of Flynn. Not that she'd really been expecting to see him safe and sound, sitting at the table with a biscuit and a cup of tea. Actually, if he *had* been here, unconcerned and safe, she'd have considered dotting him one on the nose for worrying them all like this. But her stomach dropped all the same as she scanned the whole room.

It was the biggest kitchen she'd ever seen in her entire life. A huge black oven range that was practically double size of Mrs. Hudson's back in Baker Street took up one whole wall. People—probably the catering staff from the hotel—were rushing around every which way, carrying big pots of soup, platters of meat and fish, and trays of grapes and strawberries and other fruit.

Becky edged her way in past a maid carrying a platter of toasts covered in what looked like black jelly, wrinkling her nose at the smell. Whatever the black stuff was, it had the same fishy odor as the Thames at low tide.

Everyone looked too busy to pay any attention to her coming in here—which was good, but it also meant everyone was too busy to stop and answer any questions.

Everyone except a plump, heavyset boy maybe a year or two older than her, who was standing at a table off in a corner and polishing silverware. He had blond hair and a snub-nosed face, and he was scowling as he went about his task, plainly either bored or in a bad temper.

Becky's heart sped up as she crossed the kitchen towards him. But Jack was still standing right near the kitchen doorway. She glanced back at him over her shoulder, and he gave her a nod. He'd seen her. Everything was all right. Nothing bad was going to happen while Jack was keeping an eye on her.

She reached the blond-haired boy and stopped.

"Hello."

The boy looked up from his polishing for a second, but he didn't answer. He just frowned at Becky for a second, then transferred the scowl back to the silverware—as if he suspected the forks and knives had been planning to jump off the table and try to escape while he wasn't looking. Then he went back to rubbing some kind of cleaning powder all over one of the knives.

"I'm looking for a friend of mine," Becky said.

This was the other reason that Jack and Dr. Watson had let her come along tonight; even Jack had admitted that servants, especially young ones like this boy, would be a lot more willing to talk to her than the police.

Although this boy seemed not to have gotten the notice about that, because he still didn't say anything at all.

"He's around eleven? Thin, with blond hair, and his clothes are usually dirty?"

It wasn't the best description of Flynn, but it was all she could think of. She'd have to get more practice at sketching people out in words, the way that Mr. Holmes did.

The boy still frowned down at his polishing, working the cloth—very, very slowly—into the corners of the swirling design on a knife handle. But he did at least answer. One word: "No."

"Have any strangers been here at all today?" Becky asked. Then she realized that was probably a stupid question, given what was going on in the house tonight. "Anyone besides the caterers and all the ball guests, I mean?"

If the boy thought she was an idiot, he at least didn't say so. Although on the other hand he didn't say anything helpful, either.

"No." He sounded every bit as bored with her as he was with polishing dinner knives.

Becky ground her teeth together. She was doing this all wrong. Being nervous and trying not to remember … things … was making it hard for her to think of the right questions to ask. What would Mr. Holmes—or Lucy—say right now?

Lucy would come up with some friendly way of making conversation, something that would make the boy *want* to talk to her.

"You're doing a good job with that," Becky tried. "They must really trust you to give you an important job like polishing all that silverware for the party."

"No." He didn't look at her again.

Probably Becky would be better off bashing her head against one of the house's brick walls. At least she wouldn't be accomplishing any *less* than she would in talking to this boy.

The door to the kitchen swung open, and a waiter carrying an empty tray swept through. They were too far away from the ballroom or wherever it was that the party was happening for Becky to actually see anything. But she heard the distant sounds of string music playing, which was all it took for her stomach to clench all over again. Clammy sweat prickled on her face and the back of her neck.

"You all right?" the blond-haired boy asked. He was looking at her in alarm. "You're not going to be sick or something, are you?"

Of course he would pick *now* to suddenly get interested in her.

"I'm fine," Becky said shortly.

She was, she told herself. She wasn't back at Landsdowne House, the way she sometimes was in her nightmares.

The boy gave her the same critical frown that he'd been giving the silverware. "You don't look fine."

"Well, I am." Becky didn't give him a chance to argue any more. "Has anything strange or out of the ordinary happened today?"

The boy finally stopped looking at her and went back to his polishing. Although Becky could practically hear him winding up to give her another one-word *no* of an answer.

The boy's forehead creased again. "Mr. Eldridge carried a laundry basket upstairs. That was strange."

For a second, Becky was so surprised to hear him give an actual answer that she couldn't think what to say. "Who's Mr. Eldridge, and why shouldn't he carry laundry?"

"Lord Dulwich's valet, of course." The boy sounded like *anyone* should have known that. "And it was strange that he'd take the laundry upstairs himself, because he always gets one of the housemaids to do it. Thinks he's a cut above the rest of us servants," the boy added, his voice sounding resentful. "Too good to be fetching and carrying and such."

Becky sighed. She really was wasting her time. She pictured having to tell Jack and Dr. Watson that the best she'd been able to do was hear about some stiff-necked valet and a basket of linens. She pictured Flynn. Something had to have happened to him. He might have broken their agreement before about going someplace without telling her where he'd be. But he wouldn't have been gone this long and not found a way to at least send a message unless something was really wrong.

She wasn't going to do him any good staying here—or being scared of going into the rest of the house.

"Thank you."

The boy grunted something and attacked his polishing again. Becky looked up and saw that Dr. Watson had come around and had joined Jack and Inspector Lestrade just outside the kitchen door. Judging by Dr. Watson's expression, he hadn't found anything useful out, either, but Becky still ducked quickly around the bustling kitchen and catering staff to ask.

"Has anyone seen Flynn?"

Dr. Watson shook his head, his face regretful. "I'm sorry, I haven't yet found anyone who recalls a boy answering his description." Looking down at her, he cleared his throat. "I'm sure that he's quite all right …"

Becky kept looking at him, though, and his voice trailed off. Dr. Watson wasn't as bad as some adults were for treating her like a baby who could be cheered up with a smile and a pat on the head. But he was also too kind-hearted to want her to worry, even when they both knew that there was a good reason to be scared.

"Jack, can I go with Dr. Watson into the ballroom?" Becky asked.

Jack gave her a considering look. He probably hadn't forgotten that she'd seemed nervous before. But another police constable was coming up to ask him something, and he finally nodded. "All right. We'll meet back here in an hour, all right?"

Becky nodded and Dr. Watson agreed, and they moved off together through the kitchen and into another long hallway that led towards the music and the other noise from the party.

* * *

The ballroom was crowded with people in all sorts of costumes: French queens in tall white wigs and Egyptian kings wearing crowns with snakes on them. Becky saw three women dressed as Queen Elizabeth—she recognized the costumes from the pictures in her history book—with their faces painted white and wearing ruffs around their necks.

It would have been entertaining to pick out what other costumes she could recognize, but mostly Becky was trying to keep from clutching onto Dr. Watson's hand—or turning around and running straight out the door.

"Are you all right, my dear?" Dr. Watson asked.

Becky was getting very sick of people asking her that, although Dr. Watson was too nice for her to say so.

Besides, Dr. Watson had been there, the night of the ball at the Duchess of Devonshire's. If she gave him a reason to think about it for too long, he might remember that the last time she'd been to a grand ball in a big house like this one, a criminal they'd been after had caught her.

He'd held her out an upper-story window, threatening to drop her, until Lucy and Mr. Holmes had stopped him.

Becky still had nightmares about it. Sometimes she dreamed that he really *had* dropped her, and she only woke up right when she was about to hit the ground.

Jack hadn't been there. He knew about what had happened,

partly from her and partly from Lucy telling him. But he'd been shot, and no one had even been certain that he wasn't going to die. That was probably why it hadn't occurred to him that coming to Lady Dulwich's would remind her of that other night.

Becky gulped in a breath. Lucy said that had always helped her, when she was first performing on stage and used to get nervous.

"Flynn isn't here," she said. There weren't any other children, not that she could see—and if Flynn had been here, his ragged clothes would have stuck out like a sore thumb in the middle of all the silks and satins and velvets on display.

"Not at the moment, no," Dr. Watson agreed.

The musicians struck up a new tune, and more people started to move onto the dance floor in the middle of the room. Becky squeezed her eyes shut for a second, trying to imagine what Flynn would have done if he *had* come here.

Would he have tried to sneak in through an upper-story window? Climb up the ivy on the side of the house, maybe?

He'd steer clear of the ballroom, unless he had a good reason for wanting to be here. Flynn didn't like crowds.

All the same, Becky looked all around the ballroom one more time, hoping that a miracle would happen, and she'd spot some kind of clue that would tell them whether Flynn was anywhere nearby. All she saw, though, were more and more fancy costumes. Waiters carrying trays of food and drinks. Still more costumes—

Becky's breath went out as if she'd been punched in the stomach. Beside her, Dr. Watson said something, but she didn't even hear the words. She was staring across the ballroom at the other side of the dance floor, where someone was wearing a Bedouin sheik costume: a long white robe and a turban with a scarf that wrapped around the whole lower part of his face. The upper part, though—

That was what Becky was staring at. Because she would swear that she'd seen those eyes and that forehead before, and recently, too—on the figure of Frank Boyan.

Becky felt like her thoughts were trying to scramble up a slippery snowbank. Frank Boyan was dead. He couldn't be here tonight, alive. She must be imagining things or making a mistake, or maybe worrying about Flynn had addled her brain.

But the more she kept staring across the room, the more she was certain she wasn't imagining things or going crazy. The figure wearing the Bedouin costume really was Frank.

She turned to Dr. Watson, ready to tell him what she'd seen— and discovered that Dr. Watson wasn't there.

Becky's heart skipped. She couldn't see Dr. Watson anywhere; all she saw was a sea of grown-ups, taller than she was, penning her in on all sides. She craned her neck, but still couldn't see a single sign of him. What she did see, though, out of the corner of her eye, was Frank—the person she *thought* was Frank Boyan— turn away from the ballroom and start heading for a doorway.

Becky felt sick. This was like one of her nightmares. She couldn't find Dr. Watson, she didn't see Jack anywhere, either— and unless she followed after the Bedouin right now, he'd get away without her finding out whether it really was Frank, not dead but somehow very much alive.

Becky gulped in a breath. Lucy and Jack would tell her to be careful, not to take risks. But if Lucy were here herself, she wouldn't let something that had scared her in the past stop her from what had to be done *now*.

Becky took another breath, then darted across the ballroom. She bumped into a few people on the way, but she managed to get to the door just in time to see the boy in the white robe and turban start climbing up a flight of stairs.

Becky let him get up past the first landing and out of sight. Then she crept forward, slid off her shoes so that she wouldn't make any noise, and started to climb.

CHAPTER 4

The door lock clicked, and Flynn came awake.

His head hurt, only not so badly as the first time he had wakened, when he had been all done up in that laundry sack.

Now he was still done up, but with ropes, tied over some kind of padding around his wrists and ankles. And the throbbing in his head was coming from all around, not just the spot on the back where he'd been struck before. Flynn could hear faint music, violins maybe, and clarinets. And people talking.

Maybe he was at the fancy-dress ball.

He was lying on his side, bent over, his hands close to his ankles. *That was good*, he thought, because he could reach the bonds on his ankles and maybe undo the knots.

But the door was opening. So, whoever was coming in could see him fiddling with the knots. That was bad.

He turned his head. Now he could just see the edge of the opening door. He narrowed his eyes to slits. A shadowy figure was coming in. Tall, bulky, bullet-headed, strong, in a white tie and tails, and wearing white gloves. He didn't think he'd ever seen this man before. Quickly he shut his eyes.

"Hurry up," the man said. The voice was familiar. It was the voice of the older man he had heard in this room earlier, before they had put the chloroform rag onto his face and made him inhale the fumes.

"Yes, sir," came another voice. And that one was familiar too. The younger voice.

Flynn risked another opening flicker of his eyes and saw the older man closing the door and locking it.

The younger man was removing a white cloth hat and a long white robe, tossing them onto the large four-poster bed that dominated the room.

Then the younger man unwound a long white silk scarf that had hidden the bottom of his face. He tossed the silk scarf onto the bed beside the robe and hat. Then he turned so that Flynn could see his face.

Flynn had to swallow down a gasp of surprise. He realized why the younger voice had sounded familiar.

The face was Frank Boyan's.

Suddenly Flynn remembered the smell from the paving stones. The chemical smell. It hadn't been the sheen of blood that Flynn had seen in the courtyard, at the feet of the four men who had surrounded Frank. It had been the sheen of oil.

Tricked, Flynn thought. *They tricked me in all sorts of ways. But why would they do that?*

"Do him now?" Frank asked.

"First get him up on the window ledge, and then get the ropes off."

"He might wake up."

Flynn could hear a window opening behind him. The noise of music and people got louder.

"And so? A scrawny little nothing like him? That's got you worried?"

Flynn felt cold air blowing around him. He wondered if he ought to reveal that he was awake. He thought maybe they would expect the cold air to revive him.

But if they were going to remove the ropes—

A hard slap stung his cheek. He opened his eyes. Saw Frank.

"Thought you were dead," Flynn said.

"'Cause you're stupid," Frank said. "Now, where's Mr. 'Olmes?"

"'Ow should I know?"

Another hard sting, as Frank slapped his other cheek. "Where?"

"You're the stupid one," Flynn said. "I've been trussed up 'ere. 'Ow am I goin' to know anything?"

Frank drew back his hand, but he froze at the sound of the older man's voice.

"No bruises, you idiot!" The older man was holding a black crowbar in his white-gloved hands. Two steps forward and the hard metal slapped into Flynn's palm. "Now, get his fingers onto this."

Frank squeezed Flynn's hand.

"Now the other."

The crowbar was in Flynn's other hand, and Frank was squeezing Flynn's fingers.

"Good. Now get him onto the window ledge."

Flynn tried to think what to do. He decided to wait till his hands and ankles were untied. He let Frank move him and set him with his back against the ledge and his feet on the floor but far away, propping him up like a chair tilted under a doorknob.

Flynn realized that if he moved, with his legs tied together and stuck out so far from under him, he would just fall down.

So he stayed put.

The older man was using the crowbar to pry open the drawer of a cabinet, making a real mess of the wood. But the noise wasn't great enough to be heard from the outside.

Frank untied Flynn's wrists, letting the ropes and pads drop to the ground.

The older man jerked open the drawer and pulled out a leather-bound box that looked about the same size as a brief-case. He set the box on the top of the cabinet and tried to open it. It was locked, so he used the crowbar. The lid popped up. He tossed the crowbar onto the bed.

Then he shook the box over the bed. Packets of papers, some big and some small, dropped onto the white bedspread. The packets were tied with red ribbons.

The older man picked up the white silk scarf that Frank Boyan had taken off. Carrying the leather box and the scarf, he walked over to where Flynn was still propped up awkwardly against the window ledge.

"Grab this," he said to Flynn, and held out the box.

"You want my finger marks on the box," Flynn said. "Like the crowbar."

"Shut up," Frank said, and clamped one hand around Flynn's wrist, slamming Flynn's palm against the edge of the box and pressing down onto Flynn's fingers.

Flynn was trying to think what to do, but he was having trouble just staying upright, and if he struggled, he would fall and then the two would be on top of him. He felt a rush of frustration and helpless anger, and humiliation, but knew he had to keep those feelings bottled up and put away where no one could see them. It never did, to let anyone see you like that.

So he waited, knowing that to them he was just a dupe they had successfully lured into whatever game they were running, that they had no more feelings for him than they did for the white robe they'd discarded on the bed.

The older man and Frank Boyan made more finger marks on the box, with Flynn's other hand. When they were done, Flynn saw the older man set the empty box down on the window ledge.

Frank was pulling something out from his trousers pocket. Flynn knew what it was.

A cosh. Lead shot wrapped in a leather sack, with a short leather handle. What Frank had used to knock Flynn out in the garden, hitting him from behind. Frank was going to use it again, this time killing Flynn, and then they were going to throw Flynn and the leather box out the window.

Frank was standing up now, holding his cosh, tapping it against his palm, looking at the older man, as though waiting for permission.

"Not yet," said the older man.

He bent down beside Flynn, and wrapped the silk scarf around Flynn's lower legs, pulling it tightly so that it pinched Flynn's calf muscles. He held the other end of the scarf in his hand and stepped back.

"Now, untie his ankles."

Frank knelt down and tugged at the knots.

Flynn had his eyes on the older man, who was holding the scarf in one hand and taking something out of his coat pocket with the other, gloved hand.

A pistol.

The ropes fell away, but Flynn's legs were still tightly bound by the windings of the silk scarf.

Outside, the music was loud and the noise of the party-goers continued unabated. Flynn was about to call out for help anyway.

Then he realized what else was about to happen.

Flynn said, "He's going to shoot you, Frank."

Frank's brows knit up in puzzlement. "Don't make this any 'arder for yourself than it has to be," he said.

"He's got a pistol in his hand!" Flynn felt his voice rising as he tried to make Frank understand what he, Flynn, knew: that Frank and he had both been tricked by this older bullet-headed bloke.

"After you do for me, he's going to shoot you in the head, and then push me out the window, and then put your fingers onto the gun!"

Frank was just staring at Flynn, not even looking at the older man.

Flynn was yelling now, starting to panic. "Then he'll take those papers and scarper! People downstairs will hear the shot and find me dead in the bushes, and when they come up they'll find you dead right here. What everyone will think is that we fought for the gun and you lost, then I tried to get out by the window with the box and fell!"

Suddenly Flynn felt exhausted from his effort. All he could do was stare at Frank, silently willing Frank to change his mind.

"Rubbish," said the older man. "Get on with it, Boyan."

Frank hesitated.

"*Now*, Boyan!"

Frank raised the cosh.

No, not now, Flynn thought.

He twisted and tried to grab the cosh, but he couldn't reach it and, as he'd expected, fell hard to the floor, hitting his elbow, and then, barely noticing the pain, rolling his body, trying to roll out of the scarf windings, but he was going in the wrong direction for that, he was just making them tighter, and getting closer to the older man's legs, but that was a good place to be now that his hands were untied. He grabbed at the man's striped trousers and the black-silk clad ankles beneath them, and got a good hold and yanked hard, hauling himself up, trying to get at the white-gloved hand and the pistol that it held.

But they were out of his reach, and in one horrible moment it seemed that for as long as he could remember he had always been alone, struggling, clawing and scratching his way up to something he'd always wanted, and never reaching it. And no one gave a sod.

That was only for a moment, though, and he kept struggling, and the voice in his head was loud and clear.

If yer goin' out, go out fightin'.

Then came a loud crash, and the door to the room burst open, and Flynn heard Dr. Watson's voice.

"Eldridge. Put the gun down."

* * *

"Very sagacious of you, Flynn, to explain the situation in a loud voice the way you did."

It was Mr. Holmes talking, just back from Dartmoor with Lucy, the two of them standing with Jack by the fireplace. They were at 221B Baker Street. Flynn was on the couch, getting the bandage on his head looked at by Dr. Watson, in his official medical capacity, and by Becky, who wasn't any kind of an official, but was watching with interest.

"'Tweren't nothin,'" Flynn said.

He recalled how Dr. Watson had broken into the room, with Detective Lestrade and Jack and two uniformed constables right behind. Dr. Watson had grabbed Flynn and the others had tackled the older man—Eldridge, he guessed the name was—and also collared Frank, who looked to be getting up his nerve to dive out the open window.

"You are entirely too modest on that point," Mr. Holmes went on. "Had you not said what you did, Lestrade and Jack would not have had cause to break down the door to Lord Dulwich's bedroom, an act which I am sure you appreciate they could not do on a mere suspicion or a whim."

"We didn't even know which room you were in," said Jack. "Becky got us all up to the corridor, but we couldn't do more than just listen, and we couldn't hear much of anything what with all of the noise of the music and the party going on."

Becky said, "Then we heard you say, 'You want my finger marks on the box,' and of course I recognized your voice."

"Then the rest of what you said gave us everything we needed," Jack said. "And when we got Eldridge and Frank Boyan down to the station, the truth came out. It appears that on his evenings off from his job as valet to Lord Dulwich, Eldridge likes to pretend he's gone to one of the theatres near Drury Lane, when really he's drinking at the Yellow Dog."

Mr. Holmes said, "Lord Dulwich is in the Foreign Service. Those were diplomatic papers in his dispatch box. They would have fetched a very substantial sum from foreign spies, and caused our own government a great deal of trouble."

"What did they want with me?" Flynn asked.

"Eldridge had to pin the theft on someone," Jack said. "They were hoping to drag Mr. Holmes into it as well, because people know that he's paying for you to be educated."

"How did you know they were going to steal the papers?"

"We didn't, silly," Becky said. "We were just trying to find you."

"Me?"

They were all looking at him. Mr. Holmes, Dr. Watson, Jack, Lucy, and Becky, all around him. Flynn had to hold his breath and shut his eyes and kind of turn away, because of all the feelings that welled up inside him at that moment, and because it *really* didn't do for anyone to see you when you were like that.

"And don't you ever go off without telling us," Becky said. "Never, ever, *ever* again."

THE SONS OF HELIOS

"With a nod, the butler stepped back and allowed us to pass."

WATSON

CHAPTER 1

The first time Holmes and I entered the great hall, I could immediately see the problem that had brought us to Shepperton House.

The towering curtains that normally covered the thirty-foot-high glass-paned windows had been drawn back. The incoming daylight shone on an enormous wall, on our right, which was crowded nearly to the ceiling with a checkerboard hodge-podge of decrepit paintings, all displayed in dust-covered gilded and varnished frames of varying sizes. The paintings themselves had also been neglected. Grime-covered, their colors and shapes would remain barely recognizable until someone gave them a proper cleaning.

At the centre of this collection of old paintings was the problem that had prompted our visit: a large barren rectangle of dirty white plaster. The gap was about four or five feet in both width and height—as stark and obvious as a missing front tooth. A single nail remained near the top of this bare space. The plaster that a painting had once covered was lighter in shade than the surrounding border, where grime had been permitted to accumulate.

"We gave it pride of place," said Lord Shepperton. Taller than Holmes, excessively thin, and with a deeply tanned face that contrasted with luxuriously thick white hair and bushy white eyebrows, he looked down his long nose at the two of us. "Good to know you're going to get it back for us, Mr. Holmes."

Holmes said nothing. His gaze was directed at something glittering beneath the edge of the tall curtain.

"They broke the glass," said Lady Florence, Shepperton's tall and highly aristocratic wife. Perhaps sixty, clad in a long, purple, silken dressing gown and matching purple satin slippers, she resembled her husband in her overly-thin, handsome features and luxurious gray hair. Her complexion, like her husband's, was deeply tanned.

"You can see the shattered pane. Directly above the door handle," Lord Shepperton said.

"Was the curtain drawn when you came in?" Holmes asked.

"No," said Lady Florence. "I pulled it back. I wanted to see how the thieves had come and gone. Did I do wrong?"

"That is immaterial."

"What is material," said Mr. Lloyd Crutchley, manager of The Capital and Counties Bank, "is how long it will take to recover the painting." It was Mr. Crutchley's call that had brought us to this fashionable section of Wembley, where the grand but obviously now-decaying estate of the Sheppertons had stood for nearly three hundred years. Holmes also had his accounts at Capital and Counties, which was the reason why he had taken the call from Mr. Crutchley.

"You are under some time constraints?" Holmes asked.

Crutchley gave an embarrassed nod toward Lady Shepperton. "A somewhat delicate issue."

"He means foreclosure," said Lady Florence. "And don't think I don't know all about it, Mr. Crutchley. My husband and

I have no secrets from one another."

Crutchley gave a delicate cough. "Then I can tell you, Mr. Holmes. The painting is collateral for Lord Shepperton's debt to the bank."

"I owe the bank far more than this crumbling pile of bricks and mortar would fetch on the open market," said Lord Shepperton. "There are no buyers for it, even though it's in a posh neighborhood." He gave an airy gesture towards the park-like grounds outside. "And no one cares that it is the home of my ancestors."

"But the stolen painting has value," added Lady Florence. "In fact, it is more valuable than the house. Considerably more valuable."

"I might have erased my debt with it, had I chosen to sell," Lord Shepperton said. "Christie's gave me an estimate last year."

"Yet you did not sell," Holmes said.

"I have some other ships that may come in," he said. "Besides, I had a sentimental attachment to the subject matter of the painting."

"Which is?"

"Oh, I thought you knew. The painting is called 'The Burning of Parliament, as seen from Westminster Bridge.' Wonderful likeness of the building, and the images of flame—well, they are just quite splendid, really. Resembles a sunset. People admired it greatly."

"People saw it here?"

"Of course," said Lady Florence. "We have a sort of social club, you see, and entertain in this room. Well, actually, it's a group of like-minded individuals, of a spiritualist bent, if you follow me."

"I should like a list of names," said Holmes.

"Of course," said Lord Shepperton. "We call ourselves 'The Sons of Helios.' Though women are encouraged to participate."

"And who is the artist?" Holmes asked.

"I'm surprised you don't know, Mr. Holmes." said Lady Florence. "Several of his paintings are in the National Gallery. The name is Turner. He's famous, you see."

"And dead," added Crutchley. "Which adds to the value, of course."

"And his dying words," said Lady Florence, with a conspiratorial air, "were uncannily suited to our group. Many of the wealthier members offered to buy the painting. One man was ready to make out a cheque right here on this spot."

I thought Holmes would be interested, but he had gone to the broken window pane beside the tall curtain and was looking through the open space. The early summer weather was relatively clear, for London, revealing some of the park-like setting that surrounded the Sheppertons' family estate.

"What were the artist's dying words?" I asked.

Lady Florence replied in a worshipful, awe-inspired tone, "As he lay dying, he said, 'The sun is god.' You appreciate the significance, of course."

I understood. "Helios is the name of the ancient Greek god of the sun. And you, Lord Shepperton, described the artist's concept of the fire in Parliament as resembling a sunset."

"Very astute," said Lady Florence. "You must come to one of our meetings, Dr. Watson. It would open your eyes and your heart and your mind and your soul."

I was about to reply when I was interrupted by Holmes, speaking from the window and ignoring my exchange with

Lady Florence. "We had rain in Baker Street," he said. "Did you have rain here last night as well?"

"Oh, yes. Buckets," said Lady Florence.

"There are two distinct sets of footprints," Holmes said. "One set comes towards the house, stopping before the door here, where the window is broken. The other set moves away from the window, into the grounds."

"Well, that's wonderful!" Mr. Crutchley exclaimed. "We can follow the tracks."

"Some tramp in the park; I shouldn't wonder," said Lady Florence. "We've heard several complaints from our neighbors."

"Ought we be leaving now?" asked Lord Shepperton. "Catch the blighters in their lair?"

"Dr. Watson and I will perform those investigative functions," said Holmes. "You will please remain here."

"Well, I jolly well hope you find it," said Lord Shepperton. "Otherwise, Crutchley here will foreclose on his loan against our home, and the sheriff will evict Lady Florence and me. Chuck us right out on our noble ears."

"My husband cloaks our anxieties with his humour," added Lady Florence, "as do I. Although we also take more of a sanguine outlook upon the vicissitudes of the world and universe than one would expect, given our strained financial position."

"We are enlightened, in short," said Lord Shepperton.

"Due to the tutelage of the Sons of Helios," Lady Florence went on. "But I fear that my sister-in-law, my husband's sister, whom you have not yet had the pleasure of meeting, will not be as capable. She will be devastated, and I feel great dread for how she may react."

"She is emotional?" Holmes asked.

"Indeed," said Lord Shepperton. "She is a spinster, and inclined to be erratic in her behavior. It was for her sake, to avoid a public spectacle, that I have taken Mr. Crutchley's recommendation of you and not reported the theft of the painting to the police. But I do hope, Mr. Holmes, that you will give this matter every attention."

"I shall not be idle." Holmes gave one of his sharp, succinct nods. "I shall make appropriate inquiries within the art world. And later this afternoon, I shall send over an associate of mine to interview your servants."

Lord Shepperton grimaced. "An *associate*?"

"Quite competent, I assure you, and better suited to the purpose than I. Her name is Lucy James."

LUCY

CHAPTER 2

"Such heathenish goings on!" Mrs. Bourie snorted. "It's no wonder that the house has been robbed. People coming, willy-nilly, after midnight for their worship hours, or so they call them. What's wrong with going to church on Sunday mornings like respectable Christian people, that's what I'd like to know?"

Mrs. Bourie, the Sheppertons' cook, was a middle-aged woman who broke the usual stereotype of cooks being stout, rosy-cheeked, and comfortable looking. Tall, raw-boned, and angular, she had a square, almost masculine face, bushy gray eyebrows, and strong hands. So far, all I'd been able to get out of her was a voluble indictment of all and sundry connected with the Sons of Helios—which seemed to be a quasi-religious organization—delivered in stentorian tones that might have rattled the pots and pudding molds on the kitchen walls.

"Were any of the group here two nights ago?" I asked.

"Well, no," Mrs. Bourie admitted. "But they're here more often than I can stomach, waltzing in at ungodly hours so that they can all watch the sunrise together, or some such nonsense!"

I gave a sympathetic nod. "Waking you up, I shouldn't wonder?"

"Oh, it's not that," she said, "It's not my place to complain about such things. It's the goings-on I can't abide. I don't hold

with that sort of thing, and so I told the master. I'm Church of
England born and raised, I said to him, and I won't stay in any
house where there's such goings on as I've seen here. Dressing
up like a lot of monks and chanting their so-called prayers out
on the lawn! For tuppence I'd have handed in my notice, but the
master begged me to stay till they leave for their yearly fishing
trip up to Scotland, and I agreed. I will say for his lordship; he's
not mean or stingy. Lets us have butter at the servants' table at
every meal. But there's some things not even butter makes up
for, and that's a fact!"

I bit down on the urge to ask how she really felt about the
Sons of Helios.

Then I turned to the second member of the household staff
in the room: Leah, the Sheppertons' housemaid.

"You were the one who first noticed that the painting was
missing, is that right?" I asked.

Ordinarily, a house of this size would be staffed with far more
servants, but the financial troubles of Lord and Lady Shepperton
had winnowed the staff down to Drake the butler and these two,
plus a boy who ran errands and weeded the garden, and a char
woman who came in daily to do the rough cleaning.

Leah was a red-haired girl who made up in stoutness everything Mrs. Bourie lacked. At the moment, her round, freckled
face was flushed and her eyes were bright. Plainly, this robbery
was the most exciting thing ever to have happened to her. She'd
been pressing her lips together while Mrs. Bourie and I spoke,
as though trying to hold back the words, but now she burst out,
"I did! It's one of my morning duties to sweep up in the great
hall and see that the fires are laid and such. Well, yesterday
morning I'd just come in, and I looked up at the wall and saw

that one of the paintings was missing, as plain as plain. So, I called for Lady Florence, and she came and spotted the broken glass all 'round the curtain under the window, and she told me not to sweep it up, so I didn't!" Leah finished triumphantly.

"I see. Did you hear anything the previous night?"

"Well, now." Leah screwed up her face as though in an effort at remembrance. "Now that you come to mention it, it seems like I might have heard something. A sort of crash!" Her eyes rounded with renewed excitement. "Do you suppose that was the thieves breaking in?"

"Perhaps. Was there anything else you might have noticed? Any strangers who might have come to the house recently, for example?"

"Well." Leah frowned again. "Do you know, I do remember seeing a man hanging about the place! Rough-looking fellow. Didn't come to the door; just walked all around outside. I saw him while I was doing the dusting in the dining room, just looking up at the windows. Gave me the shivers, it did." She shivered dramatically.

Mrs. Bourie gave her a censorious look. "You never said anything to me about it."

"Well, I never thought it was important, but now that I think about it, he must have been the thief, plotting how he was going to get in here!" Leah shivered again, with obvious pleasure.

"Can you remember anything about the man's appearance?" I asked.

"Well, he was a suspicious character, that's certain. Nasty, sly sort of fellow, I thought so at the time! He had that look about him, the sort where you can just tell someone's up to no good."

"Did he happen to have a dog with him?"

"A dog?" Leah's expression registered surprise, then turned thoughtful. "Do you know, now that you mention it, it seems to me that he did have a dog with him. I remember now, a great, big black one, it was!"

I gave up. I'd encountered witnesses of Leah's type before. Without intentionally meaning to be dishonest, they were the sort who would obligingly remember anything you asked them to. Right now, if I suggested the dog had actually been an elephant with purple and pink spots, she would probably recall that as well.

What was I doing here? Not here, specifically, questioning the cook and maid. Holmes's imposing demeanor sometimes terrified female domestic staff without him even trying, so it made far more sense for me to do this particular job of questioning. But ever since walking in through Lord and Lady Shepperton's front doors, I'd been wondering why Holmes had chosen to accept their case.

True, Mr. Crutchley was associated with Holmes's bank—but that alone wouldn't have led Holmes to feel obliged to tell Mr. Crutchley the correct time of day, much less investigate what looked to be a reasonably mundane theft of a painting, however valuable it might have been.

A bell mounted on the kitchen wall rang, loud and insistent.

Mrs. Bourie sighed, heaving herself to her feet. "That'll be Miss Shepperton, up from her afternoon rest and wanting tea to be served to her." She gave the still-clanging bell a resentful look. "Wouldn't need an afternoon rest if she didn't stay up half the night to greet the sunrise with the rest of them."

"Miss Shepperton—that would be Lord Shepperton's sister?" I asked.

"That's right. Never married, had no place else to go but to live here with her brother," Mrs. Bourie said. "I'll tell you something, though," she added. "Lady Florence might be sweet as honey to Miss Shepperton's face, but she doesn't like her much. Leah overheard her talking to the master just the other day, didn't you, Leah?"

"That's right." Leah bounced up from her chair to start assembling a tea tray, speaking over her shoulder. "Plain as plain, I did. They were talking together in his lordship's study, and I heard Lady Florence say that they hadn't got money to spare for another mouth to feed and why couldn't his sister go and live with their aunt instead, on account of the aunt's rich as sneezes."

What Lady Florence had probably said was that the aunt was as rich as Croesus, the ancient Greek king, but I let it go.

"And Miss Shepperton is a devotee of the Sons of Helios as well?" I asked.

"That's right." Mrs. Bourie spooned tea leaves into a teapot, then poured in boiling water from the kettle on the stove. "Worst of the lot of them, she is. If you're hoping she can tell you something about the robbery, you'll be wasting your time. Never notices what's right in front of her face, that one. Always going on about her dreams or visions or some such rubbish. Tried to tell me about it, just the other day." The cook drew herself up to her full height. " 'Miss Shepperton,' I told her, 'I'm a respectable Christian woman, and while I may be paid to cook your meals, I am not paid to listen to a lot of heathen nonsense!' "

"Oh, I thought it was sort of interesting," Leah objected. A dreamy look came over her plump features. "All about princes and princesses and them ... what are they called? Pyramids out in Egypt?"

"Heathen nonsense!" Mrs. Bourie repeated firmly. She set the kettle back on the stove with a clatter and snorted again. "They ought to all go back where they came from, and stay there!"

I frowned. "Where do they come from?"

"I asked Lacy Florence once. She wouldn't say."

"Why would she keep it a secret?"

"Oh, she did say some nonsensical babble. But she said it strange, as though it meant something to her and she was getting a lot of satisfaction. I took her serious at first, and I've racked my brain trying to think if she really did mean anything by it."

"Can you remember her words?"

"Oh, I do. Puzzled over them long enough, because it made me angry, the more I thought of it. She said they came from the land where the grave shall be no more and where hope shall flow strong as a mighty river. Which sounded like outright blasphemy to me!"

"I can see why. It sounds like something from the prayer book."

"And I told her so. Then she gave me a funny look and said, 'Mrs. Bourie, this group is my one true path to new life.'"

"What happened then?"

"She gave me another funny look, and she left my kitchen. Hardly set foot in it since."

"I wonder why."

Mrs. Bourie dismissed the question with a sharp jerk of her shoulders.

Leah added a cup, saucer, and plate of biscuits to the tea tray.

I made up my mind. "When you bring her tea up, will you ask Miss Shepperton if this would be a convenient time for her to speak with me?" I asked.

Miss Shepperton might not be able to tell me anything of importance about last night's robbery, but I was becoming more and more certain that finding out about the theft of the Turner wasn't my sole reason for being here.

* * *

"I have no idea whether or not the painting was insured," Miss Shepperton said. She was a thin, washed-out looking woman somewhere about fifty, with a mild, slightly sheep-like face and very pale blue eyes surrounded by light blonde lashes.

"You would have to ask my brother and sister-in-law. Although I very much doubt that they have any insurance. We have all risen above such mundane matters, you see. Money, I do so strongly feel, is at the root of all evil." Miss Shepperton clasped her hands and brought out the cliché with all the solemnity of an entirely original idea. "We have no thought at all for the cares and troubles caused by monetary loss and gain."

It was tempting to say that her philosophy didn't appear to be working out especially well for any of them, given that their home was in danger of foreclosure. But I didn't. Instead, I asked, "Will you tell me about the Sons of Helios?"

We were in Miss Shepperton's bedroom, a small chamber with slanted ceilings. Leah and Mrs. Bourie were evidently right about Lady Florence begrudging her sister-in-law house room. I'd passed several empty guest chambers on the lower floors, but Miss Shepperton's room was located all the way at the top of the house, near the servants' quarters. It must be boiling hot in the summer and freezing cold in the winter. Now, in March, it was unpleasantly damp and chilly, but no fire was in the grate, nor even coal to make one. Although, an incense burner of Eastern design was on a small stand by the bed. A sweet, slightly spicy odor still lingered in the air.

Miss Shepperton brightened at my question—although her hands, I noticed, remained tightly clasped in her lap. "Of course! My enlightenment from The Sons of Helios has been wonderful—such a revelation! I used to feel so useless, you know. An unmarried woman, of my age…" She trailed off, her sallow cheeks turning slightly pink. "But thanks to the meetings and the meditations, I have become entirely enlightened. My soul and mind have been opened to the realization that this existence is but one of many lives I have lived. I have seen my past lives in dreams—marvelous dreams. I was once a priestess at the Temple of Horus in ancient Egypt! Horus was the sun god, you know. And now I worship the same eternal sun again, so it all comes full circle, do you not think so?"

What I actually thought was that the Sons of Helios sounded as though it had been specifically designed to prey on the insecurities and frustrations of lonely, middle-aged spinsters of Miss Shepperton's type. Ordinarily, I would have felt sorry for the woman in front of me. But at the moment, my attention was caught by the underlying nervousness in her manner. Her hands were still tightly locked together, the knuckles standing out white under the skin, and her voice, as she'd rattled off the usual platitudes about past lives and reincarnation, had been a shade too high and fast.

"You mentioned seeing these … past lives of yours in dreams?" I asked.

"Yes, wonderful dreams!" Despite the enthusiastic words, Miss Shepperton's look of worry deepened. She glanced at the bed behind her, which was still unmade from her afternoon's rest, the covers rumpled. She then licked her lips. "Well, usually my dreams are wonderful. Today … today's revelation was most unpleasant. Violent, even. But then, one cannot escape suffering in this world. It would be too much to hope that our past lives might be free from all troubles."

Her hands shook slightly. She was wearing a dressing gown of deep cherry-red silk. A darker patch stained the left cuff, as though she'd gotten the sleeve wet while washing. But the basin and pitcher of the washstand in the corner were both dry.

"Is there a telephone I might use?" I asked.

Miss Shepperton blinked at the abrupt change of subject but nodded. "Yes, my brother had one installed in the hallway downstairs."

"Thank you."

A bare few minutes later, I was ensconced in the small alcove of the hall, waiting for the operator to put through a call to Baker Street. Lord and Lady Shepperton didn't seem to be anywhere nearby. Miss Shepperton was still upstairs, and the servants were in the kitchen. But I still kept my voice lowered when Holmes at last came on the line.

"What do you know about the Sons of Helios?" I asked.

"The Sons of Helios?" I could picture my father's slightly elevated eyebrows.

"That is why I'm here, isn't it? To learn something about the organization? This isn't the sort of case that would interest you ordinarily, so you must already know something about either the people involved, or the organization that they belong to."

I could have added that Holmes might have explained that fact before my arrival, but I didn't bother. In Watson's famous words, Holmes did and always would prefer to play a lone hand.

As though he'd picked up the thought, Holmes cleared his throat and said, "I was loath to prejudice your mind in advance, but certain facts have come to my attention about the self-proclaimed Sons of Helios that are, shall we say, suggestive. I have been unable to ascertain who actually is in charge of the organization. If there is an individual at the top, his or her identity is a closely-guarded secret known only to the initiates. But Lord Shepperton provided me with a list of names, and it reads like an entry from the book of Burke's Peerage. All are drawn from the upper echelons of society. Lords, Dukes, Viscounts. It appears that anyone without a title or at least a titled relative need not apply. It has also drawn notice that several of the wealthiest members of the Sons have died in the past six months. None of the deaths in and of themselves might have been cause for suspicion: one riding accident; one case of acute gastritis; one was killed by a runaway carriage in the street. However, there was this one common link."

"The Sons of Helios."

"Precisely."

The uneasy prickle I'd felt in Miss Shepperton's room was growing. Briefly, I recounted my conversations with Leah and Mrs. Bourie, as well as Miss Shepperton.

When I finished, I could almost feel Holmes's frown of concentration coming through the line. "I believe a thorough search of the premises would be productive," he finally said. "If Lord or Lady Shepperton objects, you can tell them that I believe the thieves may have concealed the painting somewhere on the premises, with the intent of returning for it later. The idea appears absurd, but then individuals who belong to such a group as the Sons ought to have little difficulty believing statements which strain the bounds of credulity."

"What exactly am I looking for?" I asked.

"That I cannot say. Although I have every confidence that you shall know when you find it."

* * *

Holmes was perfectly correct; Lord Shepperton made no objections at all to the proposed search.

"Certainly," he said from behind the desk in his study, looking up and smoothing his rumpled white hair. The desk was piled high with papers. He didn't appear to be reading any of them, but he waved at the piles with a vague hand. "I'm a bit tied up with work at the moment, but do help yourself and search anywhere you'd like. You can ask my sister or my wife if you need anything. I believe they're somewhere about." He gestured vaguely again.

"Thank you."

Outside his lordship's study, I stood in the corridor a moment, taking stock of the immense size of the house and wishing Holmes had seen fit to give me more explicit instructions as to what I was after. There was a time before I'd met my father, when I assumed Watson had invented Holmes's perpetual reluctance to share his theories as a plot device, to avoid giving away the mystery's solution before the end of the story. But no. Sherlock Holmes could be every bit as exasperating in fact as he was in fiction.

I might as well begin somewhere.

Straight ahead of me was the great hall, where the missing painting had been hung, but I'd already seen that room, and the parlor as well. To my right was a smaller doorway I judged must be a cupboard or cloakroom.

"There's nothing in there!" Miss Shepperton's high, nervous voice came from behind me just as I was about to set my hand on the doorknob.

I turned to study her. "No?"

"No! It's just …that is the room where my brother stores the robes and such that we use for our meetings." Miss Shepperton's hands were shaking badly, and her face had gone chalky pale.

"Are you all right, Miss Shepperton?"

"I'm quite … quite well!" Despite her words, Miss Shepperton trembled harder. "That is, I … the revelations of my past lives have been too strong for me today." She braced her palm against her forehead. "The spirit is willing, but the flesh is weak. Is that not what the Bible says?"

It was, although her use of that particular quotation was probably enough to make an entire divinity college of theologians have a collective paroxysm. My own skin was creeping, as if insects were walking up and down my spine.

"I should like to see them." I pulled open the door.

The room inside was, just as Miss Shepperton said, a small cloakroom, the walls lined with hooks on which white hooded robes hung.

But lying on the floor, atop another white robe, were the dead bodies of two men: one with a bullet hole in the center of his forehead; one with the hilt of a knife still protruding from his chest.

Behind me, Miss Shepperton gave a choked-off cry. "No—no!"

I recovered my breath. "Do you recognize either of them?"

The man who'd been stabbed was a rough-looking figure, his clothes shabby and caked with dirt, his face stubbled with several weeks' worth of scraggly beard. The other man was clean-shaven and dressed in a light gray suit. He had a receding hairline and narrow face that in life had probably been the essence of well-bred discretion. I had a cold suspicion I knew his identity even before Miss Shepperton gave another choking sob and bobbed her head in a nod. "It's … it's Mr. Crutchley! It was true, then. It was all … all true!"

Her hands were white-knuckled, clasped and twisting, and she was crying so hard, I could scarcely make out the words.

"What was true, Miss Shepperton?"

"I … I killed them. I must have killed them both!" Miss Shepperton's voice was a choked whisper, her gaze fixed on the bodies. Her eyes then rolled up, and she crumpled to the floor in a faint.

CHAPTER 3

I paced in the hall outside Lord Shepperton's office, observing the conversation going on inside between his lordship and the divisional police inspector for Wembley. The study doorway was open, and I could see his lordship cover his gaunt face with his hands for a long moment, then look up, as though he'd come to a decision.

"I must make it clear that if my sister did do this dreadful thing," Lord Shepperton said, "it was while she was of entirely unsound mind. I have been for some time concerned about her mental state. I am certain she was not responsible for her actions."

The Wembley inspector was a man I'd never met before: Inspector Pargeter. If he chose to bring Scotland Yard into the case, there was a chance the investigation might fall to Inspector Lestrade. But for now, we were saddled with Pargeter, a man whose abilities quite frankly impressed me not at all.

A rotund, cheerful-looking man in his middle fifties who looked better suited to life as a baker than a police officer, the inspector had grudgingly accepted my presence and Holmes's on the strength of Holmes's reputation. But I had the distinct impression he was itching for an excuse to evict us from both the house and murder case.

"Her mental state will be for a judge and jury to decide," Pargeter said now. "The facts remain. We found the gun that must have been the murder weapon hidden away under the mattress in her bedroom, and her clothes were stained with the dead men's blood."

Lucy had already given Pargeter her account of finding the bodies, then telephoned to Holmes, who'd asked me to accompany him to Shepperton House. Now, she and Holmes were making an examination of Miss Shepperton's room upstairs.

Inspector Pargeter cleared his throat. "There is also the matter of her confession."

"I know, I know," Lord Shepperton groaned. He had the look of a man who'd glided through life largely able to avoid all unpleasantness—but had now run into a brick wall of harsh reality.

"But she hardly knew what she was saying. There must be some mistake," Lord Shepperton continued, staring at the inspector with haunted, imploring eyes. "I must retain a competent barrister to represent her. That is her right, and my duty. I need to speak with my solicitor immediately."

The inspector was quite correct about the probable murder weapon. A Webley revolver from which a single shot had been fired had been found pushed under the mattress of Miss Shepperton's bed.

Miss Shepperton herself had indeed confessed to the crime, but when questioned she had become so hysterical that Inspector Pargeter had called on me in my professional capacity to give her a sedative. She now slept in one of the spare bedrooms upstairs, with a police constable on guard outside the door.

"Where is your solicitor?" Pargeter asked.

"Farrington. St. John's Lane," Shepperton replied quickly. "Do you know the area? I can take my coach and be there and back by suppertime. But I need to arrive before his firm closes their offices." He gave an ingratiating smile. "These chaps mainly do financial work, and they seem to think they're entitled to keep banker's hours. So, I had better leave at once. I want to be able to let my sister know she'll have competent counsel as soon as she wakes up."

"I don't know ..." Pargeter said.

"Besides, Holmes and that young woman upstairs may unearth something you'll need to see," Shepperton went on. "And I'm no use to you, just standing around here."

Pargeter shrugged. "Very well. I suppose ... I'll expect you here by seven this evening."

"Fine. I'll tell Mrs. Bourie to have supper ready by seven-thirty as usual."

With that, Lord Shepperton turned and left the room. He gave me a perplexed nod as he walked past, heading for the kitchen.

* * *

Pargeter asked me to accompany him to see the great hall and site of the theft of the painting. We were standing before the bare spot on the wall when the telephone rang.

A few moments later, Drake appeared. "The call is for Inspector Pargeter," he said. "Constable Briggs is calling from the Capitol and Counties Bank."

Pargeter bustled forward, spoke hurriedly on the telephone, then returned, flushed and excited.

"A new theory of the case may be required," he said. As he

continued, he led me to where the two bodies had been found.

"I had asked my constable to learn what he could about the one victim, the banker Crutchley," Pargeter said. "Well, it seems Crutchley was about to be given his notice by the bank! Into gambling trouble, he was, and his superiors had got wind of it. Changes things fundamentally, yes indeed!"

"In what way?"

"Don't you see? Crutchley may have been in on the theft! Probably worked it with that tramp fellow in advance, getting the bloke to take the painting and hide it somewhere. Then he comes back last night or early morning, and the tramp won't deliver! They fall out over it, they fight, and they kill each other!"

He paused for breath and looked at me, his eyes bright. "What do you suppose your Mr. Holmes will think of that?"

"He will probably wonder why the two men chose this cloak-room as the venue to settle their dispute."

Pargeter considered, but only for a moment. "They heard someone, and then they ducked in here to hide."

"He will also ask why, while killing each other, they obligingly placed one of the robes on the floor beneath their bodies in order not to stain the varnish."

"No need to be satirical about it. The robe may already have been on the floor."

"Finally, he will ask how the pistol from the cloakroom managed to make its way up two flights of stairs to where it was found beneath Miss Shepperton's pillow."

From outside came the rattle of a coach and horses, driving away.

Pargeter took no notice. He was not to be dissuaded from pursuing his argument, not by me, nor by the coach or the sound of footsteps hurrying down the stairs above us. He continued. "The pistol may have been moved by one of the servants. In fact, one of the servants could have had it in for Miss Shepperton. Taken a dislike to her. Saw the opportunity to cause her a bit of—"

"Inspector!" Holmes interrupted, coming down the staircase, followed by Lucy. In his hands was an iron incense grate heavily flaked with black and gray ashes. "Who was on that coach?"

"What coach?" Pargeter looked puzzled.

"The one that just drove away from the carriage house."

"Why, yes, I think I heard it," Pargeter said. "Must have been Lord Shepperton, on his way to his solicitor's. In Farrington, he said. He'll be back by seven o'clock for supper. Anyway, let me give you my new information. I've just had a call—"

Holmes interrupted. "Why was luggage strapped onto the back of the coach?"

A wary look came into Pargeter's close-set eyes. "Family was preparing for their annual fishing trip to Scotland when this— those bodies were discovered. I suppose he didn't have time to unpack the coach. Had to get to his solicitor's before the offices close this afternoon."

"Did your men search the carriage house?"

"I didn't see a need. The murder was done in here, and the painting was stolen from in here. Why go to the carriage house?"

Holmes gave one of his tight-lipped head shakes, dismissing the question. He asked, "And where is Lady Florence Shepperton?"

"Oh, I know the answer to that one right enough. She's at the Savoy Hotel in the city until this business gets cleared up. Said she was far too upset to spend another night here in this house, where murder had been committed."

"And you let her go?"

"Didn't see a reason to hold her. After all, she's not a suspect. And she is a lady. Besides, we know where to find her. The Savoy."

"I suggest you test that hypothesis by telephoning—never mind. Lucy, can you please make the call? I need to explain something to the inspector here."

Lucy strode quickly toward the telephone.

Holmes asked, "Do you see this incense grate, Inspector?"

"I do."

"Can you detect any particular scent or identify any part of the residue?"

Pargeter shook his head. "I know you're the expert when it comes to tobacco ashes, Mr. Holmes. But you say these ashes are from an incense burner. What scent should I be looking for?"

"These are not ashes from incense. They are the remnants of hashish, and devil's claw, two tropical herbs that, when ingested, create what medical men like Doctor Watson here refer to as a 'fugue state.' "

I nodded. "A trance," I said. "Patients—or more properly termed, victims—become disoriented, and overly placid. Almost sheep-like."

"They would be extremely susceptible to the power of suggestion, is that correct?" Holmes said.

Pargeter watched me nod, then turned to Holmes. "And where did you find this grate?"

"We found it in Miss Shepperton's little room, on the upper-most floor," Lucy said.

Pargeter stared at the grate. "You're not suggesting she sniffed the fumes of this exotic—whatever they are—and it drove her to murder two men?" He paused, thoughtfully. "On the other hand, that may be true. Lord Shepperton maintains that his sister wasn't in her right mind. Probably a good thing for this barrister he's going to retain—"

"I am saying precisely the opposite," Holmes said. "She killed no one. While she was under the effects of the drug fumes she had inhaled, someone walked her downstairs to the room with the dead bodies, put the Webley revolver used to shoot one of the victims into her hand, and convinced her that she had murdered them both. As an added touch, they smeared some of the blood onto her dressing gown and placed the revolver under her pillow."

"Fanciful." Pargeter's plump features tightened. "But worth considering. And I may just be able to work it into my own theory about the case, based on new knowledge about the victim Crutchley. You see, the bank was about to fire him for running up gambling debts, and, needing money, he may have been in league with that tramp fellow to steal the painting—"

Lucy, returning, interrupted. "At noon today, the Savoy took the reservation from Lady Florence Shepperton for a suite. But she has not checked into the hotel. As yet."

"She never will," Holmes said. "Now we must bid you farewell, Inspector. It is nearly five o'clock, and we have much to do. I shall telephone from Baker Street when I have something to report."

CHAPTER 4

"Have you any idea what he has in mind?" Watson asked me in an undertone.

We were on our way to Baker Street, seated together in the four-wheeler cab Holmes had kept waiting for us outside of Shepperton House. Holmes was on the seat opposite ours, muttering to himself under his breath as he pored over the writing on a sheet of paper.

"I think so." Before leaving Lord and Lady Shepperton's estate, Holmes had liberated three hooded robes from the downstairs cloakroom. Now the carriage jounced over a deep rut, and I gestured to the paper in Holmes's hand. "That is the list of names that Lord Shepperton gave him—back when he wanted it to appear that he was cooperating fully with our investigation. Holmes is trying to determine which if any of those persons his lordship mentioned might now be helping him to escape with the stolen painting."

I hadn't thought Holmes was attending to us, but at that he raised his head.

"It is perhaps too much to hope that his lordship would have been foolhardy enough to include the most important name—"

He broke off, his attention apparently caught by something on the handwritten list.

"What is it?" Watson asked.

"Lord Sonnebourne." Holmes's gaze turned at once both keen and speculative. "He is a shipping magnate, who leases cargo vessels. He has an estate which is situated near Gravesend. Those facts coupled with his surname—Sonnebourne, which might be interpreted as one who is born of the sun; an appropriate moniker for one who styles himself the leader of a cult of sun-worshippers—are suggestive, but unfortunately not proof positive. And we cannot afford to go haring off on a wild goose chase. The deaths of Mr. Crutchley and the second man will most likely demand that charges of murder be brought if Lord and Lady Shepperton are apprehended—charges that they will be most anxious to avoid. Not to mention the associated charge of insurance fraud. Every hour that passes makes it less likely that we will succeed in capturing them."

"You believe that Lord and Lady Shepperton killed Crutchley and the tramp themselves?" Watson asked.

"Perhaps. Although if they did commit the murders, it was only at the bidding of those persons to whom they report."

Holmes was giving us only half his attention, still running his gaze over the list in hand. "There are forces at work behind the scenes. Lord and Lady Shepperton are mere puppets dancing on the strings of—"

"Wait a moment." I held up a hand. Mrs. Bourie's words were nudging at the back of my mind, together with a mental picture of the maps I'd studied of London and its surrounding environs. "Gravesend. That is near the River Hope, isn't it?"

Holmes looked up sharply. "It is. That tells you something?"

"Maybe. Mrs. Bourie, the Shepperton House cook, told me that according to Lady Shepperton, the Sons of Helios came from the land where the grave shall be no more and where hope shall flow strong as a mighty river."

Holmes leapt up and hammered on the roof of the cab to attract the driver's attention.

"Take us to the London Bridge pier." He consulted his pocket watch. "At this hour, our most viable option to reach Gravesend will be the hire of a private steamer."

Watson gave a brief smile. "It will be quite reminiscent of old times. You remember, Holmes, our pursuit of Jonathan Small."

"Indeed." Holmes's expression remained grave. "And I have every reason to believe that the danger we face on this occasion will be equally great as that posed by Tonga and his poisoned darts."

* * *

The sun was setting in a blaze of fiery reds and golds as we came within sight of Sonnebourne House. Holmes had directed the captain of our hired launch to set us ashore a little upriver so that we might not attract the notice of anyone inside the mansion.

Sonnebourne House itself proved to be a magnificent estate built in the Palladian style, with slender white columns and an unbroken view of the river. Holmes drew in a quick breath of satisfaction as we saw the carriage parked in the sweeping gravel drive.

"That is Shepperton's coach." He handed over two of the hooded robes. "I believe it would be as well if we were to don these, and if you both were to go inside and attempt to locate the Sheppertons. But do not approach."

Watson pulled the robe over his head, and I did the same. "Where will you be, Holmes?"

Holmes gestured to the luggage strapped to the waiting carriage. "I intend to make a search of the Sheppertons' bags. The stolen painting may no longer be our primary objective, but it would be helpful if we can recover it, nonetheless. Oh, and Watson—" Holmes paused in the act of turning towards the carriage, looking at both of us. "I'm sure it goes without saying that we must exercise the highest degree of caution." He glanced towards the house. The windows were open, and I could just glimpse hooded figures moving to and fro inside. "My theory is still in what might be termed its larval stage, but if I am correct, this organization is more dangerous than we were previously aware. At the least, they have already proven themselves willing to commit murder in order to achieve their aims."

He turned for the Sheppertons' carriage, leaving Watson and me to finish tying our robes and drawing the hoods up over our heads.

"This thing is utterly ridiculous," Watson muttered. He kicked irritably at the folds of the robe as we made our way up the steps and towards the front entrance. "I feel like some sort of monk."

"I know." My own robe was several inches too long, dragged on the ground, and would probably trip me and land me flat on my face if I had to run or fight.

Although if I did wind up in a physical altercation with any of the similarly-dressed people within the mansion, I made a mental note to come at them from the side. I could personally testify to the hood's ability to limit one's peripheral vision.

A heavy brass knocker, molded into a stylized image of a sun with a human face, hung in the center of the door. Watson and I exchanged a look, then Watson gave the knocker a sharp rap.

A stiffly correct butler answered the knock almost immediately and gave us an expectant stare, plainly waiting for us to speak.

Beside me, I could tell Watson had tensed. He cleared his throat.

I opened my mouth. "The sun is god."

With a nod, the butler stepped back and allowed us to pass.

"How did you know that was the pass code to get in?" Watson murmured under his breath as we entered the white marbled entrance hall.

"I didn't. I just couldn't think of a more likely way to bluff our way inside."

Although now that we were in the house, I wasn't sure whether to be relieved or terrified that my guess had been correct. Arched doorways to both our right and left sides opened out into the house's formal receiving rooms—and on both sides, the space was so crowded with robed and hooded figures that there was scarcely room for them all to stand or move around.

If we came to be suspected as impostors, this wouldn't just be an uneven fight; we were so outnumbered that we'd be tied up and held captive before most of the attendees even noticed.

As we made our way towards what seemed to be a grand dining hall, I became aware of something else about the gathering. Watson had evidently come to the same conclusion.

"This is more like a banquet club than a religious cult," he muttered.

He was quite right. Several tables laid out in the dining hall were spread with a sumptuous buffet of food: grapes, roast capon, cheese tarts, ices, and cakes piled high with whipped cream. A waiter passed by us, carrying a tray with flutes of champagne.

"I suppose an organization that encourages its followers to gorge themselves on earthly delights stands a much higher chance of attracting members than one that preaches asceticism and self-denial," I murmured back.

I caught a sickly-sweet odor in the air and realized something else. "That's opium. They must provide it to members who prefer earthly delights of another—"

I stopped short, ice trickling down the back of my neck.

"What is it?" Watson asked.

"I've just realized something—I think. But there isn't time to explain now."

The chances of finding Lord and Lady Shepperton amidst the crowds were close to nil. There were no lamps or candles; the only light came from the dying rays of the sunset slanting through the windows, which made the rooms dim in the extreme. The hoods of the robes cast shadows that served to conceal the entire upper half of the wearer's face.

Excellent for maintaining our own cover; not so much for improving our odds of recognizing anyone else.

"Should we separate?" Watson asked.

I considered, then shook my head. "No, we might cover more ground that way, but there's too much chance we won't be able to find one another again. Besides, if one of us got into trouble, the other might not even be aware."

I took two of the champagne flutes from the waiter's tray and handed one to Watson. "For camouflage," I told him. "Now, keep an ear out for people's conversations. That's probably our best chance of recognizing the Sheppertons—by voice."

But as I led the way through the dining room, it came home to me that it would be nearly as difficult to distinguish voices as

it would individual facial features among the crowd. I'd spoken
to Lord Shepperton only twice, and to his wife not at all—and
Holmes hadn't been in jest about the requirements of nobility for
joining this club. Every single hooded figure I passed seemed
to be conversing in the drawling tones of society's upper crust.

So I said to him, I'm sorry, old boy, but it's simply not on …

*My dear, you really must try one of these, they're simply too divine
for words …*

At another time, the contrast between the mysterious, semi-
druidic costumes and banal drawing-room chit-chat might have
struck me as slightly comical. Now, though, my heart was beating too fast and too hard as the theory Holmes had alluded to
outside came together in my own mind.

If Holmes and I were thinking along the same lines, then it
wasn't just that the Sons of Helios were dangerous. We'd also
encountered them—and spoiled their plans—before.

I could expect whoever stood at the top of the organization
to possess a significant degree of irritation with us by now.

We passed from the dining room into a drawing room that
was still more dimly lit. In several curtained-off alcoves, robed
figures lay on sumptuous piles of pillows and puffed away on the
opium pipes I'd smelled before—looking like bizarre versions
of the caterpillar in Alice in Wonderland.

I kept my breathing shallow, ordering myself to think. Lord
and Lady Shepperton wouldn't be lounging on couches, smoking. They were wanted for questioning about a double murder,
and if we were correct, they had stolen their own painting to
fund their escape.

What had Mrs. Bourie said about Lady Florence's words to
her? *This group is my one true path to new life.*

Another door at the back of the drawing room stood only partly open, but it looked to me to lead into a library; I could see shelves filled with leather-bound books lining the walls.

Gas jets were lighted over the library's mantle, their glow illumining two more hooded figures who stood near an ornate mahogany desk at the back of the room. The flowing robes served to obscure body type, as well as individual features, but I thought one of the figures was tall and thin, with what could be Lord Shepperton's narrow build.

The second figure was … gigantic.

There was no other word possible to describe him. He had to be male, standing at least six and a half feet tall, and so broadly built that in his robe he looked like a solid wall.

Very big men were strong, but also often slow-moving, and they tended to be overconfident in their strength. I could hope.

"We need to get closer, Uncle John," I murmured.

Inside the library, the big man was taking something out of a desk drawer.

I continued. "Follow my lead."

I set my glass of champagne down on a table and moved towards the half-open doorway, then tripped, falling into a drunken half-stumble that carried me nearly to the wall beside the library. Watson caught me, and I gave the high-pitched drunken giggle of one who's intoxicated with alcohol or opium or both.

"Steady on," Watson said. He staggered and slurred his own words.

"Oh dear, I feel quite strange!" I giggled again and slumped against the wall, straining to listen to whatever was going on inside.

"—not now." Those were the first words I caught, spoken in what I was certain were Lord Shepperton's nasal tones. "Only when I am on board and the boat is underway. You can shoot me if I don't deliver."

"I assure you that I will not hesitate to do so."

I'd never heard the voice before, but I assumed it belonged to the giant of a man. From appearances, he ought to have had a low-pitched growl of a voice to match his size, but instead the tone was flat, urbane, and slightly bored-sounding.

Footsteps approached.

"They're coming out!" I whispered to Watson.

We had just enough time to lurch drunkenly out of the way before the door opened fully and the figure I'd identified as Lord Shepperton emerged, clutching two packets tied up with red ribbon. The taller man followed, then paused in the doorway to watch as Lord Shepperton wove his way back through the crowd.

Beside me, Watson glanced up from beneath the hood of his robe, in plain and silent question as to whether he should follow. I gave an infinitesimal nod, and he stumbled off in Lord Shepperton's wake.

I remained where I was. One semi-drunken figure happening to walk in the same path as Lord Shepperton might be overlooked; two would attract notice. Besides, the proof of what Holmes suspected—and a great deal more evidence, besides— was likely to be found in the library room behind me.

If only I could find it.

The question was whether I'd get a chance to make the attempt, or whether I'd have to create that chance for myself.

"Lord Sonnebourne, it's nearly time. The sun is going down."

One of the other robed and hooded figures approached the giant man, clutching a brass Chinese-style gong.

"Yes, yes." The big man gestured dismissively, and the second man struck the gong with a mallet: once, twice, then a third time.

An instant hush fell across the crowd, and as the ringing echoes of the final gong faded away, people began to file out of the room. Even the opium smokers struggled up from their nests of pillows and shuffled towards the parlor and a set of large glass doors that led out onto a terrace.

The Sons of Helios were presumably about to begin their evening's worship by watching the sunset.

The library didn't contain any places where I could be completely concealed, but I drew back into one of the shadowy alcoves and forced myself to keep my head bowed, *not* staring at the giant of a man who must be our host for the evening, Lord Sonnebourne. Unlike the majority of the other guests, he was neither drunk, nor drugged, nor stuffed with rich food. He would notice if any one of his flock appeared to be deviating from the normal routine.

From the edges of my vision, I saw him stand in the library doorway a long moment. Then with what looked to be an irritable twitch of his shoulders, he followed the man with the gong out of the room, and from there out onto the terrace as well.

I released a long breath, waiting as the last of the robed figures stepped outside. The terrace doors were swung closed, and a few moments later I heard dozens of voices take up a low, droning chant. For however long it took the worshippers to watch the sun slip beneath the horizon, I would be alone.

Except for any servants and wait staff who might be about.

Or guards Lord Sonnebourne might have directed to keep an eye on things.

I would have to move quickly, then. I stepped out of the alcove, crossed to the library, and pulled the door shut behind me. The red-ribboned packets Lord Sonnebourne took out had come from the upper righthand drawer of the desk.

Which, when I tried it, proved to be securely locked.

I let go of the drawer pull, silently swearing at myself for not having brought a set of lock picks. I scanned the desk surface, which contained only an empty sheet of blotting paper and a heavy brass paperweight that matched the stylized sun on the front door knocker. But there ought somewhere to be a letter-opener or some other tool I could use to force the catch—

The door to the library swung open, and Lord Sonnebourne appeared.

He stood stock-still a moment, staring at me in what looked like blank astonishment. His hood was still drawn up over his head, but I had a brief glimpse of a square jaw and mouth gone slack with shock.

"What the devil do you think you're doing?" he demanded.

My mind hectically flipped through options. *Bluff…fight…run.*

Running wasn't an option. There was only one exit, and Lord Sonnebourne blocked it completely; he was so broad, he took up very nearly the entire doorframe.

I was still wearing my own hooded robe, which meant I might be able to pass for one of the sun worshippers. But before I could decide between trying to come up with a convincing excuse for my presence and fighting, Lord Sonnebourne's hand dipped into a fold of his own robe and came out holding a pistol.

Strike out bluffing as an option, as well.

This would have been an excellent time for Holmes to appear suddenly, dressed in the guise of another group member—or reveal himself to be one of the library armchairs in disguise. But no such help materialized.

I caught up the heavy brass paperweight.

One chance. Make it count.

I threw the weight as hard as I could at Lord Sonnebourne's gun hand. It struck, knocking the pistol to the ground, and I stepped forward, lifting aside the skirts of my robe one-handed.

Come at him from the side.

I stepped to his left, kicked hard at his knee, and while he was knocked off-balance, I delivered a strike to the back of his neck.

Like hitting a solid tree trunk.

He staggered but made a grab for me, catching hold of the flapping sleeve of my robe. I stamped on his instep, twisted, and struck his throat a brutal chopping blow with the side of my hand.

He collapsed to the ground, wheezing, temporarily incapacitated, but not unconscious.

I ran. Out of the library, and across the drawing room.

The Sons of Helios had far less attention span for worship than they did for drinking and gorging themselves. Already some of the hooded figures were beginning to trickle back inside from the terrace.

And if I was right, Lord Sonnebourne would be severely averse to the majority of his group of worshippers knowing the true activities and purpose behind the Sons of Helios, which meant he wouldn't create a commotion.

He would be looking for me, and he surely had a select handful of chosen underlings he could order to do the same. But he hadn't seen more than a quick glimpse of my face, just as I'd never fully seen his.

I forced myself to slow to a sedate pace and joined a group en route to return to the dining room.

A hand took hold of my arm. Heart hammering, I nearly struck out again before I recognized Holmes's murmured voice in my ear.

"Have you had any luck?" Holmes's figure was cloaked in a robe like mine, and he was walking stoop-shouldered, the better to blend in with the rest of the crowd.

I kept my voice low and my own head bent. "That depends on your definition of luck. I avoided being shot by our genial host, but I had to come away without any proof of what he's really up to."

"And Watson?" Holmes asked.

"He was following Lord Shepperton. If the Sheppertons are attempting to get away, I would assume they're still outside."

From beneath the hood, I caught the momentary tightening of Holmes's lips. "Come, then."

Not quite all the Sons of Helios had returned inside. A few of the particularly devout—or particularly inebriated—remained on the terrace, lurching to and fro with raised hands and chanting in slurred voices to the last fading gilded rays of the sunset.

"There!" At the side of the house, a robed figure wearing boots that could only belong to Watson was standing and watching something on the river side of the estate.

"Holmes—Lucy!" Watson turned at our approach. "Your instructions were not to approach, Holmes, but you can see—" He gestured to the river, where Lord and Lady Shepperton, the hoods of their robes now drawn back, were just boarding a fast steam launch.

"Quite right," Holmes said.

"But—are we intending to let them get away?" Watson asked. "They may be guilty of murder!"

I could see the frustration in the set of Holmes's shoulders, but he shook his head. "The Sheppertons are small fry, Watson. I am after a bigger fish—a very big fish indeed. One that cannot be trapped if we show our hand now."

The Sheppertons' launch was beginning to pull away from the shore. Lady Florence picked up a long leather case of the sort made to contain fishing poles and handed it over to a tall, broadly-built hooded figure who remained on the riverbank.

"Lord Sonnebourne," I murmured. He seemed to have recovered from our encounter in the library.

"Indeed."

"How long have you suspected that he was part of the same organization that aided Mrs. Torrence in her opium smuggling and her escape?" I asked.

Watson's head snapped around. "*What?*"

"It's true." I nodded. "The Sons of Helios may offer quasi-religious nonsense to draw in the credulous. They may even discreetly murder the wealthiest of their followers, if they can convince them to make wills in the Sons' favor. But they also offer another service to a select few: new identities when needed. That was what Lord and Lady Shepperton received here tonight. Identity papers that will allow them to begin a new life somewhere. At least, that is their hope."

"As you say." Holmes's gaze was on the steam launch, which was rapidly heading downriver with the current. "However, tonight's adventure has not been an entire loss. We have cleared Miss Shepperton of two murders she did not commit. And although we may lack proof positive, we have a strong link to the organization that most likely aided Mrs. Torrance in her escape. And though we must beat a judicious retreat now, we can tackle the Sons of Helios again when we are more fully armed with both evidence and police reinforcement."

The sun had finally gone down, turning the sky deep blue-black, and thick curls of gray fog were rolling in off the water. With a final chug of its engines, the boat vanished into the mist.

Then a sudden shout from the riverbank drew our attention once more to Lord Sonnebourne's figure on the bank.

He threw down the leather case—now unbuckled.

In a fury, he called to a pair of uniformed waiters who were just coming towards him across the lawn.

"After them!" He gestured to the Sheppertons' boat.

"The case is empty?" I could hear the surprise in Watson's voice. "Surely, that was an extraordinarily foolish move on the part of Lord Shepperton, to draw the ire of Lord Sonnebourne by not handing over the painting after all."

"Not quite," Holmes said. "Although Lord Shepperton does strike me as an extraordinarily foolish man."

"And now his escape plans are spoiled," I put in.

Watson looked startled once again. "How do you mean?"

"His source of funds is cut off." I nodded at Holmes.

It was growing too dark to see clearly, but I could sense the brief twitch of a smile flitting across Holmes's mouth as he drew a rolled canvas from beneath the folds of his own robe.

I continued. "The missing Turner painting, is it not?"

Holmes nodded. "Without money to support their new life,

the Sheppertons will be significantly easier to capture at some later date, even if we must let them go now."

"Sonnebourne may hunt them down for us," I said.

Holmes put away the canvas. "Sonnebourne will be searching for us as well. We must return to our own launch, and from there to Baker Street." He tapped the side of his robe. "We will need to keep to the shadows."

THE VANISHING MEDIUM

""I see a voyage across zee water," Madame Yolanda droned."

LUCY

CHAPTER 1

"I see a voyage across zee water," Madame Yolanda droned. "And … yes, I see it now." She peered more closely into the crystal ball in front of her. "Yes, definitely you will journey across zee water, and there you will meet a—"

I had to stop myself from finishing the sentence for her with, *A tall, dark, and handsome man.*

"Zee dark and handsome young stranger!" Madame Yolanda concluded triumphantly.

I'd been inside Madam Yolanda's parlor—a small set of rooms in Chelsea with a sign over the door proclaiming *Seance Parlor, Fortunes Told*—for the past quarter of an hour. So far, the most remarkable part of her predictions was that she could see anything whatsoever, whether in the crystal ball or otherwise. The room was so dark, I could scarcely make out the details of our surroundings.

Heavy tasseled curtains covered the room's single window, and silk shawls draped over every available surface, from the small bric-a-brac tables, to the backs of the chairs, to Madame Yolanda herself, who wore no fewer than three silk wraps about her shoulders.

Above the shawls, she looked to be somewhere in her middle forties, though with so much makeup on, it was difficult to determine her actual features: heavily kohl-rimmed eyes; blood-red rouge painted lips and cheeks; and a wig that looked as though a small shaggy animal had climbed onto her head and settled in for a long nap. A long mantilla of black lace was pinned to the wig in the Spanish style, although her accent had veered more towards Russian, with a sprinkling of French thrown in for good measure.

She broke off in the midst of predicting the extremely vague details of my upcoming journey over the water—which she seemed barely more interested in than I was—and asked, "You have something more you weeesh to ask Madame Yolanda?"

I kept my expression of eager curiosity fixed in place, for I'd come to see her in the guise of a young lady's maid, telling her that I'd saved up my pennies to consult her on my afternoon off.

"I'd heard some people can tell fortunes just by looking at the lines in your palm?"

I half-extended a hand towards the velvet covered table, but Madame Yolanda waved it away, setting off a cacophony of clinks from the array of jangling bracelets on her wrist. "Stuff and nonsense!" For a moment, she forgot to drone mysteriously and sounded brisk, mildly annoyed, and originally from no further a distance away than South London. But she recovered and cleared her throat. "How else can Madame Yolanda help you? What guidance may zee spirits offer you today?"

I put my hands together. "Well, my mother died. Just last year." I faltered. "It would be such a comfort if I could speak to her again …"

Half an hour later, I'd given Madame Yolanda my profuse and insincere thanks and left her establishment, my ears still ringing with my fictional mother's rapturous descriptions of the spirit realm.

My appointment had been in the late afternoon, and evening shadows were falling as I walked down the steps and away from the *Fortunes Told* sign. Laborers were hurrying home from their day's work, wagons and carriages rattled across the cobbled streets, and lamplighters were kindling the gas lights.

I was rounding the corner nearest Madame Yolanda's establishment when a figure detached itself from the wall he'd been leaning against and came to meet me.

"Hello there."

Tall and strongly built, with a hard edge of competence—or sometimes even danger—he was the kind of person I might have thought twice about confronting alone and in the gathering dark; that was, if I hadn't happened to know he was a police sergeant with Scotland Yard—and also my husband.

I smiled at Jack. "Madame Yolanda did tell me I would meet a tall, dark young man. Although she got the stranger part wrong. Did you think I might need a bodyguard?"

"Well, it's been a good three days since your last brush with death, so I figured you were due." Jack grinned at the look I gave him, then shook his head. "No, I just got off duty at the Yard early and thought we could go home together. Did you find out anything?"

"Well, my mother is apparently frolicking in a place where everything is love, happiness, peace, and general sweetness and delight."

"That's a comfort."

"It would be if my mother weren't actually in Milan right now." I shook my head. "I don't understand. I went to see this Madame Yolanda because Miss Shepperton asked me to investigate her. You remember Miss Shepperton, from the Sons of Helios affair?"

"Sure."

A faded, middle-aged spinster with fair hair and pale blue eyes, Miss Shepperton had gotten herself mixed up with a very nasty crowd of people, from whom Holmes and I had rescued her. Yesterday, Miss Shepperton had telephoned and asked if I'd meet her for tea at the Criterion Restaurant. A few hours later, over a pot of tea and plate of scones, and with a deeply imploring gaze, Miss Shepperton made her appeal for my help. "I'm so dreadfully worried," she quavered, fingering the string of cheap beads she wore around her neck. "And you were so kind during that terrible affair of my brother's stolen painting."

So, more out of pity than curiosity, I had agreed to meet Madame Yolanda.

Now I glanced back over my shoulder, automatically checking to make sure we weren't being followed or purposefully observed by any of the other pedestrians. Without having to look, I knew Jack was doing the same, scanning the street ahead of us.

"Apparently, since she's now effectively homeless, Miss Shepperton has taken refuge with her aunt, Mrs. Trent, who's an extremely wealthy widow with an estate in Hampstead called Mulberry Walk," I went on. "And according to Miss Shepperton, Mrs. Trent has recently fallen under the influence of Madame Yolanda—so much so that she's even talking of leaving her entire estate and all her money to Madame Yolanda when she dies."

"Which Miss Shepperton would prefer she didn't do, especially if she's hoping to inherit everything herself?"

"Well, she didn't outright say as much, but I'd imagine that's certainly part of it. Although in Miss Shepperton's defense,

I wouldn't want to see Madame Yolanda ensconced in my family home either. What she told me was that she's afraid of Madame Yolanda actually doing away with her aunt once a will is made in her favor. She's absolutely certain her aunt's life is in danger, or more in danger. Apparently, Mrs. Trent is already in poor health and entirely bedridden."

Jack's brows edged together. "Hardly seems worth the risk of committing murder, then, if she's not likely to live long in any case."

"Exactly."

When Miss Shepperton had first come to me for help, my initial response had been somewhat uncharitable surprise that she herself would have identified Madame Yolanda as a fraud. Miss Shepperton's chief characteristic was credulity, as witnessed by her having fallen for the Sons of Helios' extremely dubious charms.

Now, having met Madame Yolanda in person, I no longer wondered that Miss Shepperton could have seen through her fakery. A three-year-old child could have deduced that Madame Yolanda had about as much chance of contacting the spirit realm as the proverbial pig did of learning how to fly.

"What's more of a mystery is how this aunt could have fallen under the influence of Madame Yolanda—or whatever her name really is—to the degree she apparently has," I told Jack, "even if she's elderly and infirm. It's hard to picture anyone finding Madame Yolanda's spiritualist nonsense anything but absurd."

"Do you think Miss Shepperton's right and Mrs. Trent's life really is in danger?" Jack asked.

"I don't know."

I frowned, playing back my interview with Madame Yolanda

inside my mind. Obviously, the medium had no qualms about earning a living by lying through her teeth. But not all con men or women were willing to go to the extreme of killing; in fact, most weren't. They were happy to bilk the overly credulous of their money, but preferred not to dirty their hands by crossing the line into violence.

"Madame Yolanda is ridiculously theatrical—like someone playing the part of a medium on the stage, and doing it badly, too. While I was in there, the biggest danger was that I'd forget my own part and start rolling my eyes at her predictions. But all the same …" I shook my head. "Something's not right about all this, whether Madame Yolanda does in fact intend to commit murder or not."

The more I talked it over with Jack, the more I felt there was something wrong at the heart of this affair.

"I suppose our next step is to go to Mulberry Walk and speak with the aunt," I said. "We'll leave first thing in the morning."

CHAPTER 2

We left Baker Street for Mulberry Walk just after dawn, taking the train to the Hampstead Heath Railway Station and hailing a cab for the short ride from there. A mist laden with the scent of impending rain hung over the roadway as the cab took us along the edge of the great, sprawling park that gives the Hampstead Heath area its name.

Few people were out at this hour, likely due to the disagreeable weather. Peering through the carriage window, I caught glimpses of the huge expanse of grassland that lay beyond the haze. For some reason I recalled the fog, spreading out across the great, open expanses of the moors in Devon.

"Watson?"

I came back to the present moment with a start. Holmes was at my side, and Lucy across from us.

"You appeared lost in reflection. Does the heath remind you of the green fields of Sonnebourne and the Sons of Helios?"

"I was thinking of Dartmoor, actually. But yes, it is reminiscent of Sonnebourne, now that you mention it."

"Those people in their white robes and cowls would feel right at home," said Lucy.

"The notion is suggestive," said Holmes.

I waited for him to explain, but he remained silent.

* * *

We rang the bell at the imposing doorway of Mulberry Walk, a majestic, turreted, gabled mansion perhaps one hundred years old, and far more well-kept than Shepperton House. Judging from the neatly trimmed shrubbery and well-manicured lawn, no financial dark clouds would be blackening this beautiful dwelling when the time came for it to be transferred to the next generation.

Our ring was answered within a few seconds by a dignified butler, perhaps fifty years old, with a well-nourished, competent air about him. He looked at us inquiringly.

"We have come to see Mrs. Trent," said Holmes. "I am Sherlock Holmes, and these are my associates, Lucy James and Dr. Watson."

"Our business is urgent," Lucy added.

"Indeed. I am Drake, Mrs. Trent's butler and head servant. Do come in. I know Mrs. Trent is awake, for she has just bid farewell to another visitor."

He held the door for us to enter a spacious front hall, with a two-story ceiling and impressive set of carpeted steps leading up to the second floor. I had thought he might usher us up the stairs, but instead he turned to a pair of double doors on our right, where I would have expected to find the dining room.

"Mrs. Trent has not been as active in the recent months as she was in her youth," Drake said. "She has taken to using this room as her bedroom." He knocked at the doors. "Mrs. Trent? You have three visitors."

We waited. There was no answer.

"Mrs. Trent?" After another pause, Drake said, "Mrs. Trent, I am concerned. I am coming in."

He turned the large brass handle, but the door was locked. He looked at us, as if for guidance.

"I would lose no time," Holmes said. "Have you a key?"

"Of course."

Drake produced a key from the large brass ring that hung at his side. Moments later, the heavy door swung open.

At first glance, the room and bed appeared to be empty. A pair of heavy maroon drapes, drawn, darkened the room. The bed was a tall four-poster, with an old-fashioned fringed canopy and curtains on all four sides. Those at the foot of the bed were only partially drawn, and visible behind them was what appeared to be a jumbled pile of a maroon quilt and several white pillows.

In two quick strides, Holmes was at the bedside, pushing back the curtain and lifting the topmost pillow.

The body of an elderly woman lay motionless, her face tilted upward by her thick, wispy gray hair, which was held in place by a hair net. Her mouth gaped open. Holmes touched her cheek very lightly.

"Watson, she is still warm."

I moved to Holmes's side and pressed my fingertips to the inside of her wrist, then searched for the subclavian artery above her left collarbone, feeling for her pulse. There was none. Nor was she breathing. Small purplish spots around her throat and a trace of foam around her pallid lips confirmed my diagnosis.

"She has been smothered," I said.

Holmes was already looking at the pillow, and the moisture darkening the white cotton fabric.

"Mr. Drake. The name of the visitor, if you please."

Drake stood motionless and silent for a moment, shoulders hunched forward, clasping his hands, as though summoning his powers of self-control. "That spiritualist woman, Madame Yolanda, came here at eight o'clock. She has visited here nearly every day for the past several weeks. She left just before you arrived."

"We did not see her."

"Well, possibly five minutes had elapsed. I was in the pantry, polishing the silver."

"The other servants?"

"They are all below stairs in the servants' hall. Miss Bramwell slept very poorly of late and takes—took—her breakfast just before noon. She preferred that the maids not disturb her by beginning the work of the house until after she had risen."

Holmes was across from the bed by now, pulling back the drapes to reveal a tall pair of elegant French doors, and beyond, visible through the glass panes, the dark gray morning. Rain had begun to fall.

"The door is locked," Holmes said. "Have you a telephone?"

"Yes."

"Then please give a description of Madame Yolanda to the police."

"Tell me first," Lucy said.

"Dark hair, spectacles, heavily rouged and powdered, in the European style. I believe she wore a floppy dark hat. Wide-brimmed. And a black cape."

"That describes the Madame Yolanda I saw," Lucy said.

"Tell the police to be on the lookout for her," Holmes said. "Possibly between here and the train station. Or on the heath. Tell them that Miss Bramwell has been murdered and that Madame Yolanda was the last person seen with her. And of course, summon an inspector and the police mortuary carriage."

"I shall do so. The telephone is just outside in the hall," Drake said.

"One more question. Are you prepared to swear that no one came out or entered the bedroom other than Madame Yolanda?"

"I can swear that I saw no one."

Holmes nodded as Drake left the room. We heard him speaking with the telephone operator moments later.

Holmes was at the French doors, looking at the rain coming down onto the patio outside. "Did Madame Yolanda strike you as being physically capable of doing this?"

Lucy shrugged. "It hardly requires a man's strength to smother an invalid old woman. But she might have used a key to let in a confederate, who might have entered and left by the French window."

At that moment, we heard the sound of the front door opening, then the wet rush of wind-driven rain coming from outside. Knowing Drake was occupied with the telephone, I stepped into the hall.

Backing into the room while shaking the rain from a black umbrella was a small woman. She turned, pale in complexion and extremely thin, and stared at me in astonishment.

It was Lord Shepperton's sister.

"Dr. Watson! What are you doing here?"

Drake interrupted before I had time to answer, calling out from the other side of the hall, where he held the telephone receiver.

"Miss Shepperton!" he said. "Do pardon me. I am on the telephone with the police. Please prepare yourself for a very bad shock. There has been a terrible occurrence."

By now, Lucy and Holmes had also come into the hall.

Drake waited a moment, then continued. "Your aunt is dead."

"The poor dear," Miss Shepperton said, gripping the handle of her umbrella more tightly, then leaning on it for support, as if it were a cane. "But it may be a blessing, after all. We've all known this day would come. I hope the end was quite peaceful—" She broke off and stared at Drake, who was still holding the telephone receiver. "Did you say you were speaking with the *police*?"

LUCY

Chapter 3

"Empty."

Holmes surveyed the seance parlor, a deep furrow between his brows.

"The newspaper boy on the corner is unusually observant. He says he saw her leave her rooms early this morning when he first took up station at his place of work, and she hasn't been back since."

"That's hardly surprising."

We'd come directly from Mulberry Walk. By a telephone call to Mrs. Trent's solicitor, we'd confirmed her original will hadn't been altered. A check of the actual document, in a safe in the library, had confirmed the entire estate had been left to Miss Shepperton. We left her discussing the funeral arrangements with Drake as they waited for the police to arrive.

Now Holmes and I were both standing in the narrow office doorway, taking a brief survey of the place before we risked entering and disturbing any potential clues. But it was clear, even at a glance, that no one was here. Madame Yolanda's parlor consisted of one single room, with only one window and the door we'd come through to serve as an entrance or exit.

Robbed of the mystery of semi-darkness, the place looked even more ridiculous than it had during my visit yesterday.

The heavy velvet and silk draperies were revealed to be moth-eaten and threadbare in spots, and the archaic symbols that hung on the walls—an Egyptian Eye of Horus, a pentagram, and a crescent moon—were cheap, shabby affairs of wood that had been hastily slopped over with gold paint.

"She would hardly commit murder and then come straight back here, just waiting to be arrested for the crime."

Holmes's frown remained in place. "But we have confirmed that Mrs. Trent's will remains unchanged. Her niece inherits the entire estate. So what motive would Madame Yolanda have to kill Mrs. Trent?"

"Maybe Mrs. Trent had promised to make a new will that left the estate and money to her, and Madame Yolanda misunderstood and thought it had already been done?"

I could see from Holmes's expression: this explanation did not satisfy him. For that matter, it was also unsatisfactory to me. Even if she had misunderstood the state of the will, Madame Yolanda had committed the killing in such a way that she was bound to be the first person suspected of the crime.

"Well, let us see whether any more can be gleaned from a more thorough examination of her place of business," Holmes said. He stepped from the doorway into the room, his gaze making what I was certain was a thorough catalogue of the tawdry decor. "Although if she departed from here this morning with the intent never to return, it is unlikely in the extreme that she will have left anything—" He broke off sharply.

"What is it?"

Holmes had crossed to the black velvet-covered table where Madame Yolanda had looked into her crystal ball—which in the daylight was revealed to be nothing but a large sphere of plain glass. He picked up the ball, lifting a sheet of paper that had been pinned to the table beneath the ball's weight.

Wordlessly, Holmes handed the paper over to me. It was a single sheet of ordinary writing paper, on which a message had been written in a shaky hand:

Let this, my last written testament, be also my full confession. I killed Mrs. Alexandra Trent this morning. I believed that the spirits were compelling me to set her free of her Earthly suffering, but I see now that I was led astray by the wicked powers that lie in wait, seeking to entrap us all. The spirits have shown me the right way, the true way, and I now cannot live with the guilt of what I have done. After I finish writing this, I will go to Westminster Bridge, and from there follow Mrs. Trent to the infinite Great Beyond, where I will beg her forgiveness and pray that I may be allowed to atone for my crimes.

I felt my eyebrows climbing as I read the words. "Suicide?"

"Or so she would like us to believe. In the absence of an actual body, one must entertain the distinct possibility that she wrote this in an effort to throw any pursuers off the scent."

"What? You doubt everything she said about obeying the spirits' directions?"

Holmes gave me a look. "To be thorough, we will have to make inquiries as to whether any women's bodies resembling the description of Madame Yolanda have been pulled from the river today. But the fact remains that if the law believes her dead, they will cease to search for her to prosecute her for murder."

"It's a very clumsy effort." I looked again at the letter in my hand. Although I had to admit, it was entirely in keeping with what I'd seen of Madame Yolanda: just as theatrical, just as absurd. "Does she really believe that the police will give up on looking for her based on her written intention to hurl herself into the Great Beyond?"

The door opened before Holmes could answer, and Uncle John came in, slightly out of breath.

"I've spoken to the estate agent who handles the rental of rooms in this building," he said. "A woman calling herself Yolanda DeSantos paid him to rent this place for the month. She handed over the money in cash, and other than the name she gave him, he knows nothing about her. This isn't the sort of neighborhood where anyone looks too closely at their tenants, provided the rent is paid up in full."

"So that's a dead end," I said. "Unless Yolanda DeSantos happens to be her real name, which is probably as likely as the idea that she's now thrown herself off Westminster Bridge in a fit of remorse. She left a letter, Uncle John," I added, showing him the paper, "purporting to be both a murder confession and a suicide note."

Holmes had been frowning at the remains of a fire in the room's single fireplace. "We had best finish our search. There may be something of value to point us towards Madame Yolanda's current location."

As Holmes had predicted, the room contained very little apart from the tawdry decorations and trappings of the spiritualist trade, and even those were few and far between. Holmes turned over the table at which Madame Yolanda's seances had been conducted and found it entirely ordinary. His dissatisfied look grew more pronounced.

"Not even the usual mechanism by which dramatic rappings and knockings from the spirit realm may be produced. Our fraudulent medium is either lazy or extremely willing to trust in the credulity of her clientele."

Watson gave a wry smile. "Not willing to consider the possibility that she really is in contact with the spirits and has no need of such trickery, eh?" He then picked up a small rectangle of red lacquered wood from the mantle and held it in one hand. "I say, Holmes," he added in a different tone, "this looks like one of those Chinese puzzle boxes—the kind with a hidden compartment. You know the sort of thing, you have to press on just the right spot—"

"Careful!"

With a sharp cry, Holmes sprang towards Watson and succeeded in wresting the box away from him. But the net effect was that the sharp blade that sprang out of the side of the lacquered wood punctured Holmes's hand instead of Watson's.

"Holmes!"

For a heart-stopping moment, both Watson and I stood staring at Holmes and the blood dripping from the wound in his hand. Watson then moved quickly forward, shaking out his handkerchief.

"Be careful, Uncle John!" I said quickly. "Don't touch anything. The blade was probably poisoned."

Watson turned astonished eyes on me. "But how do you—"

Holmes interrupted. "Lucy is correctly assuming that anyone who went to the trouble to set such a trap would wish to inflict more damage than a simple cut on the fingers or palm. However, I believe I can confirm the assumption, based on the effects I appear to be experiencing."

His voice was as calm as usual, but there was a slightly breathless quality to the words. "My own theory would lean strongly in favor of curare, best known from its use as a paralyzing poison by the indigenous tribes of South America. The natives shoot prey using darts dipped in the substance, which kills by asphyxiation, due to the inability of the victim's respiratory muscles to contract."

On those final words, Holmes sat down heavily on one of the wooden chairs.

Watson's face had turned pale. "Will you stop lecturing and tell us what is to be done, Holmes! Is there an antidote?"

Holmes drew a labored breath. "An injection of the extract of the West African Calabar bean, also known as physostigmine—while toxic in and of itself—has shown some efficacy as an antidote to curare … if administered in … time." His voice had faded to barely a whisper by the time he finished.

I looked quickly at Watson. "This physto—whatever it is called. Do you know it?"

"I do." Watson made a visible effort to collect himself. "It's used in the treatment of some eye diseases, such as glaucoma. I don't myself keep any in stock at my surgery, but a chemist might."

"Go! Go and find the nearest chemist's shop," I told him. "There must be one in the neighborhood. I'll stay with Holmes."

Holmes raised his head and spoke again, the effort clearly painful. "If all else fails, I have myself succeeded in isolating the derivative of the Calabar bean in my laboratory. However—"

He didn't need to finish. Baker Street was clear across London. Even if Uncle John found a carriage that could drive him there at top speed, there was a strong chance he wouldn't get back to us in time.

"Try the chemists' shops first," I told him. "Find a cab; the driver will probably know where the nearest one is."

Watson left the room at a run, and a moment later I heard his raised voice hailing a cab in the street outside.

I sat down on the chair opposite Holmes. My pulse was beating too fast and hard, and dread sat in a cold lump on my chest.

"How long—" I both needed to ask the question and didn't want to hear the answer.

"The timeline varies, according to … the dosage and the potency of the curare extract." Holmes's voice was the same labored whisper. "I should estimate that we have roughly twenty-five minutes before the respiratory muscular paralysis fully takes hold."

Twenty-five minutes for Watson to procure and return with the anti-toxin, after which it would be too late.

"Though there … have been instances," Holmes added, "where life has been preserved through artificial respiration, carried on until the poison's effects have worn off."

"I'll keep that in mind."

Holmes and I had faced danger often in the course of investigations, and I'd feared for his life almost more times than I could count. But I couldn't recall ever having to experience this particular brand of slow horror: being forced to sit, helpless, counting the seconds as they dripped past and waiting to see whether Holmes would live or die.

"What made you think that the box might be dangerous?" I asked. The lacquered square of wood lay on the floor where Holmes had dropped it, the blade glinting in the lamplight.

I could tell the curare was beginning to affect Holmes's muscles as well. He sat stiffly, his features even more rigid than before.

"I have seen … similar mechanisms before this, although I admit I had no concrete reason to believe that this particular one was armed with poison." Holmes's lips compressed. "While I am gratified to have spared Watson the curare's effects, I shall be provoked … in the extreme if I lose my life owing to what was little more than a hunch."

I could think of nothing to say; Holmes would scoff at empty reassurances or platitudes even more than I would have done in his place.

"None of this makes sense," I said instead. "If the suicide note is genuine, why leave a trap designed to kill anyone who examined that box? It's hard to imagine, but if she honestly left these rooms planning to kill herself in a fit of remorse, Madame Yolanda would presumably have had greater concerns on her mind than committing manslaughter—and by an incredibly uncertain mechanism, too. There was no telling who would come to search these rooms, and whether they'd even trigger the poisoned blade. But on the other hand, if the suicide note is a blind designed to stop the police from looking for her, then that still doesn't explain why she should have killed Mrs. Trent— when in the first place she had nothing to gain from Mrs. Trent's death, and in the second place she was bound to be the first person suspected of the crime."

"Indeed."

I waited, but Holmes said nothing more. Perhaps he couldn't. The curare would eventually rob him of the ability to speak. Each second that passed by in the silent room seemed to have weight.

"It's almost as though Madame Yolanda had some sort of a vendetta against Mrs. Trent personally," I went on, "and didn't care whether she were ultimately arrested for the crime. We're reasonably certain that Madame Yolanda isn't who she claimed to be, although we don't know her real identity. I don't suppose that they could have known each other when they were younger and Mrs. Trent did her an injury of some kind? Maybe Madame Yolanda was madly in love with Mr. Trent, but he married Mrs. Trent instead of her."

I'd thought Holmes's features were too paralyzed to register expression, but at that his eyebrows twitched briefly upwards. "You wouldn't … be attempting to offer distraction by proposing ever-more-absurd theories, would you?"

"Maybe."

It didn't appear to be working—either for Holmes or myself.

How long since Watson had left? I wished the room contained some sort of a device for telling time, but there were no clocks, and I didn't want to consult Holmes's pocket watch, only to find that a bare five minutes had gone by.

Holmes drew a shallow, painfully rattling breath. "I will say … that your analysis of the illogical nature of the crime … strikes me as accurate. We must therefore assume that there is some thus far undiscovered factor which makes the apparent illogic—"

The door burst open to admit Watson, panting heavily for breath and clutching a paper parcel. Quick relief crossed his face at the sight of Holmes, rigid in his chair but still alive.

"I've got it," Watson said. "The chemist two streets over had a supply of physostigmine, and I purchased the whole, together with a syringe." As he spoke, he was already at Holmes's side, drawing a small glass bottle out of the parcel and readying the syringe for injection.

I held my breath as Watson deftly rolled up Holmes's sleeve

to expose Holmes's sinewy forearm. I had to bite down on my impulse to ask if he was sure the dosage was exactly right—or whether the substance that had poisoned Holmes was without question curare. There had to be other poisons that would have the same effect but wouldn't be counteracted by the physostigmine.

Watson gave the injection, and another brief eternity of seconds crawled by. Holmes then drew a still-labored but full breath, his muscles seeming to relax.

"Thank you, Watson."

Watson stared.

Holmes turned to me. "I believe that our next step ought to be to ascertain whether any bodies answering our medium's description have been pulled from the Thames. Perhaps you might ask Jack to make the enquiry?"

I exhaled a shaky half-laugh. "It's reassuring to know that you're entirely back to normal. All right. I'll telephone him as soon as we return to Baker Street."

But when I telephoned, I didn't have to ask my question. Jack already had the news. A woman had fallen from Westminster Bridge at about noon that day. A bargeman on his boat in the water below heard the splash. By the time he reached the woman, she was dead.

Her body was at the nearby Westminster Mortuary.

WATSON
CHAPTER 4

I reproduce here my few notes from the Westminster Mortuary, taken prior to the official autopsy by the medical examiner, which I did not observe.

Over my strenuous objections, Holmes has insisted on attending the examination, although he ought not to have undertaken the journey to Horseferry Road and should be resting in our rooms on Baker Street. In a grudging compromise, he has yielded to my own insistence that he remain seated throughout and leave the initial examination to me.

The body is of a middle-aged woman of average height and weight. She has dark, matted hair.

Lucy cannot positively identify her as Madame Yolanda—the medium wore so much makeup, and the lighting was so dim. But neither can she say definitely that the woman is *not* Madame Yolanda.

There is no note found on the body, no identification, and no outward indication as to whether the dead woman committed suicide or was murdered.

The woman's pupils are contracted, suggesting that she may have taken opium or laudanum before she died.

Calluses on her fingers suggest she was at one point a typist.

Lucy says she never touched Madame Yolanda's hands.

I discontinued my note-taking when the medical examiner arrived. Since I saw no reason to stay for the formal autopsy, I had hoped to use this moment to depart, taking Holmes with me back to Baker Street and putting him under the watchful eye of Mrs. Hudson.

But this planned course of events, like so many other of my plans when Holmes was involved, failed to materialize.

Entering the room somewhat breathlessly, just behind the medical examiner, came Detective Sergeant Jack Kelly.

"The Sheppertons," he said. "They have been arrested and are at Scotland Yard. Lestrade is about to question them."

Holmes drew himself erect in his chair, holding up one hand. "We must go at once," he said. "Will you please telephone Lestrade and ask him to wait for us?" He turned to me and added, "It is only a short walk."

* * *

Lucy, Jack, Holmes and I climbed the stairs to the interview room at New Scotland Yard, Holmes leaning on my arm. Each breath came to him with difficulty it seemed, after the walk of several blocks. The effects of the poison on his respiratory system had obviously not yet worn off, and I felt a heavy burden of anxiety.

He hung on to the brass handrail and my elbow. I felt his weight with each step. I knew this opportunity to question the Sheppertons might yield insights into those shadowy, powerful figures who had helped them escape. Holmes would not pass up this opportunity, no matter what the continued exertion would do to his health.

Yet I still worried as we entered the interview room.

Lord and Lady Shepperton sat at one end of a large dark walnut table. Inspector Lestrade and a uniformed constable sat at the other.

The two Sheppertons appeared undaunted by their new condition as prisoners. They were dressed for a day in the country, both in sporting tweeds. They might have been preparing for a grouse shoot, or for their annual fishing expedition in the Hebrides.

We entered the room and took seats at Lestrade's end of the table, with Lucy and I on either side of Holmes.

Lord Shepperton's brows lifted in recognition. "Ah, Mr. Holmes," he said. "Have you found my painting?"

Holmes showed no impatience with this highly presumptuous greeting, which Lord Shepperton's reedy, nasal tone made particularly irritating. Rather, he shrugged, as though the question had an obvious answer, and said, "Yes."

"Indeed?"

"I removed it from your leather case, where it had been stored with your fishing poles. I delivered it to the Capital and Counties Bank."

"So that was you, at Sonnebourne House."

"It was."

"Well, Mr. Holmes, you have caused me a bit of inconvenience. My associates were considerably annoyed. But are you sure the painting you removed was the genuine missing Turner?"

I blinked in surprise, yet Holmes showed no emotion. "You would be in a position to know," he said.

"Indeed I am. And I can tell you that the painting you removed was a duplicate of the one that once served as the centrepiece of my painting collection. A copy. A forgery, if you will."

"Intended to deceive … whom?"

"My associates, of course. They agreed to provide new identity papers in exchange for the painting. You probably know that. But they demanded the painting in advance."

"A change in the terms you had agreed upon?"

"Quite. Yielding up the genuine article before attaining my safe escape would have placed me in an untenable position. Once in possession of the painting, my associates would have no further use for me or for my wife."

"So you have hidden the genuine article," Lestrade said.

"It is quite safe, at some undisclosed location known to me alone. However, I am in a position to provide the bank with directions."

"The bank has initiated foreclosure proceedings against Shepperton house," said Lestrade. "The doors are padlocked."

"I have no need to return there."

"There are charges against you," Lestrade continued. "A murder has been committed."

"Yes, I understand. My sister killed our banker when he was attempting to inspect the house, even before he had foreclosed. Some misguided zealotry to protect our family estate—the only home she had, I suppose. I told that fat policeman she wasn't in her right mind."

"Poor Crutchley," said Lady Florence. "So eager to do business for his bank."

"The police believe you killed both Crutchley and the tramp," Holmes said.

"Why should they believe that?"

"Because you fled the scene. Both of you, using one pretext or another."

"I am innocent," said Lord Shepperton, "and in the eyes of the law, I remain innocent until proven guilty."

"And to prevent that from occurring," Lady Florence said, leaning forward, "Lord Shepperton and I would like to employ you, Mr. Holmes, to clear our names."

"Your names are not something I could undertake to clear," Holmes said.

"Oh, you are witty, Mr. Holmes," said Lady Florence. "But I am sure you understand what we wish you to do. This false and unfair charge of murder must be quashed."

"Provided, of course, that your health permits, Mr. Holmes," said Lord Shepperton. "I must say, you are looking a trifle more peaked than when we last met."

"My health … is not a concern," Holmes said. He took a long breath, as though attempting to clear his thoughts, then said, "I regret that I have a conflict of interest."

"But we were your clients only two weeks ago."

"No, the Capital and Counties Bank was my client. Your interest and the interest of the bank converged, with regard to a missing painting."

"The same interests may converge again. If you clear our names of the murder charge, we just might agree to provide the genuine painting to the bank."

"This is foolishness," said Lestrade. "The two of you are in no position to bargain. You are prisoners, arrested for murder."

"We shall be free on bail within a few hours."

"Oh, will you, now?" A flush of red appeared on Lestrade's ferret-like features. "Just as easy as that, you think? Well, let me—"

Lord Shepperton interrupted, as though speaking patiently to a child. "There will be a hearing, and the decision to set me free will be made by a magistrate in consultation with my solicitor. Given my standing, and that of my wife, I expect the bail amount to be reasonable. My solicitor holds sufficient funds in his trustee account to enable him to pay."

There was an awkward silence. Holmes produced a neatly-folded white handkerchief and mopped his brow.

"Anything else?" Lord Shepperton inquired.

Lucy spoke up, the first time she had done so during this meeting. "Lord Shepperton, do you know that your aunt, Mrs. Trent, has died?"

"She never liked me. Nor I her."

"Do you know that your sister inherits your aunt's entire estate? Including Mulberry Walk?"

He shrugged. "Proves my point. Still, it won't be much use to my sister if she's to be hanged for Crutchley's murder."

"A remote contingency," Holmes said.

"Wasn't the gun found under her pillow? I seem to recall that little tidbit of evidence."

Holmes dabbed at his brow with his handkerchief once again.

Lady Florence said, "Dear me, Mr. Holmes, you are looking positively unwell."

Lucy said, "Might we adjourn for a moment?"

Jack, Lucy, Holmes and I left the Sheppertons with Lestrade. In the hallway, I closed the door to the conference room.

"We are not getting anywhere with these two," Lucy said. "They will be bailed out soon."

"We will set the Irregulars to follow them," Holmes said. He pocketed his handkerchief.

"You did not appear well in there," Lucy said.

I thought I saw a brief smile cross his hawk-like features. "The effect was deliberate, I assure you."

"For the benefit of the Sheppertons?"

"Who did not appear at all surprised."

"So they may have known about the poison in the Chinese box."

Holmes nodded.

"They certainly dodged away from the subject of Lord Shepperton's aunt."

"See if you can learn anything more from them along those lines," Holmes said.

"You're not staying?"

"Watson wishes me to return to Baker Street."

"I will learn what I can."

"And then take such action as you may find appropriate for the circumstances."

The look Holmes gave Lucy as he spoke was filled with a significance I failed to understand. Lucy, though, gave a quick, decisive nod.

"I shall."

A moment later, she and Jack were re-entering the Scotland Yard conference room, and Holmes and I were heading for the staircase.

When we had returned to 221b Baker Street, Holmes brought in Flynn, one of the Irregulars, and gave him instructions. If the two Sheppertons were indeed set free on bail, the Irregulars would be watching and following and reporting.

Holmes was resting when I left him to return to my surgery.

LUCY
CHAPTER 5

"Poor Auntie." Miss Shepperton raised a handkerchief to scrub at her eyes.

"I'm so sorry for your loss," I murmured. I hadn't yet told Miss Shepperton of her brother and his wife's arrest—and I hadn't the least idea how she'd take the news when it came time to break it to her. On the one hand, they were the only family she had left. On the other, although it might not have been proved, it was as close to certain as it was possible to come that they'd been instrumental in framing her for a double murder.

What I was still uncertain of was whether Miss Shepperton herself fully realized that fact.

She tucked the handkerchief away and seemed to recollect herself. "Oh, but where are my manners? I ought to have asked whether you'd like to sit down. Or perhaps you'd like some tea? Cook has most likely gone to bed, but I could ring the bell—"

I shook my head. "No, it's all right, I don't want to trouble anyone."

I'd come here directly after Jack and I concluded the interview with Lord and Lady Shepperton—during which time his Lordship and Lady Florence had shown all the varied expression of a solid brick wall. Every question we put forth was answered with either silence or a declared intent to say nothing more than what they'd already told us when Holmes was in the room.

I had a second reason for being here: Miss Shepperton had also been a part of the Sons of Helios. The question was, how much of that organization's true aims and purposes did she understand?

Now it was long past the dinner hour, and I'd found Miss Shepperton in her aunt's sitting room at Mulberry Walk, beginning to sort out the jumble of Mrs. Trent's papers and memorabilia. Old newspaper clippings, receipts, packets of letters bound up in ribbons, and ladies' magazines covered nearly every available surface, including the settee and chairs.

I stayed where I was, standing just inside the doorway. "And I won't stay long," I added. "It looks as though you've a great deal of work to do."

Behind Miss Shepperton were the double French doors that, like those in Mrs. Trent's converted bedroom, opened out onto the terrace, beyond which I could see the Mulberry Walk that gave the house its name. The rain from the morning had continued, and now a slight rattle of droplets pelted against the door's glass panels.

Miss Shepperton nodded. "Yes, Auntie was a great letter writer, and she always kept all the correspondence she received so that she could re-read the ones from those she cared for the most. She had such a loving heart."

Miss Shepperton was seated at what had been Mrs. Trent's writing desk. She laid aside the letter she'd been holding and wiped her eyes again. "It's so sad to think it was the very sweetness of Auntie's nature that killed her in the end. But then the Bible does say that the wicked flourish like the green bay tree."

"Possibly," I said. "Although Madame Yolanda isn't doing very much flourishing at the moment, considering that she's lying dead in a city morgue."

Miss Shepperton flinched at the intrusion of harsh reality and gave me a reproachful look. "That wicked, wicked woman. It may be uncharitable of me, but I am glad that she is no longer alive to profit from her crime."

"Yes, I'm sure that Madame Yolanda will never be seen alive again. But I don't think it's strictly accurate to say that she won't profit from what she's done."

Miss Shepperton had taken up another of her aunt's papers, but at that she looked up with a puzzled frown. "Why, whatever do you mean? I thought you said that she had confessed to her crime and taken her own life?"

"That is how it appears. But do you know what the curious thing about this case is?"

Miss Shepperton still looked uncertain. "No, I can't say … that is, I don't quite understand …" She trailed off.

"When you strip away all the nonsense about Madame Yolanda and her seances, only one thing of real significance happened. Your aunt died."

"Yes, poor Auntie—"

I interrupted. "Your aunt died, and you, Miss Shepperton, were the only one who actually profited from her death. You inherit this house and all your aunt's money, besides."

"Yes, but—but that dreadful Yolanda woman was scheming to take it all. She was poisoning my aunt's mind against me. That's why I came to you in the first place!"

"Was it? Or did you want an outside witness to corroborate your account of Madame Yolanda being not only a charlatan as a medium, but also an extremely dubious character? Because there are a few odd things about Madame Yolanda."

"Odd?"

"First, she didn't even make more than a cursory attempt to be seen as anything except a somewhat absurd fraud. There are countless tricks that a medium can employ to produce false manifestations from the spirits, but Madame Yolanda didn't bother with any of them. It's almost as though she wanted to be identified as a charlatan. Another odd thing is that no one knows where she came from. She simply popped into existence a little less than a month ago, when she took the lease on a room in Chelsea. Paying cash, and offering no other identification."

Miss Shepperton gave a confused shake of her head, her pale blue eyes still wide. "I'm sure I still don't understand what you're saying. Of course, she must have used a false name—"

"A false name and a false everything else. Madame Yolanda never existed."

"What?"

"She was *you*, in fact, Miss Shepperton. Dressed up and playing a part. Wearing a wig and swathed in shawls, using a false accent."

Miss Shepperton sucked in a sharp breath. "You must be joking—or mad!"

"Neither of those things, I can assure you. You dressed up as Madame Yolanda and came to see your aunt here regularly. Being bedridden and infirm, she didn't object to those visits. They probably offered her some entertainment, if nothing else. But I doubt she was very much more taken in by Madame Yolanda's so-called otherworldly abilities than I was. No one besides you, Miss Shepperton, ever mentioned that she was falling under

Madame Yolanda's thrall. The servants certainly had no notion that she planned to make a will in Madame Yolanda's favor. Neither did her solicitor. You were the only one to suggest that."

"No!" Miss Shepperton had gone deadly pale. She gave a shake of her head, her lips shaping the words, but almost no sound emerged. "No, it's not true!"

"It's quite true. You came here this morning, dressed up in your medium's disguise. You came to her bedroom, and you smothered your aunt in cold blood. That's why Madame Yolanda seemed not to care that she would be the first person suspected of the murder. She *wanted* to be suspected. Or rather, you wanted her to be suspected. You cultivated Madame Yolanda's persona with the sole intent of making her the villain in your murder scheme. Then after you killed Mrs. Trent, you walked out of here and resumed your own identity. There was no need to return to the room in Chelsea; I'm sure you'd set the stage there in advance, complete with a faked suicide note— and a little trap that might gain you the added bonus of killing me, my father, or anyone else who was looking too closely into Madame Yolanda's real identity." My voice hardened. "I'm not sorry to tell you it didn't work. Sherlock Holmes will be fine."

Miss Shepperton shrank back, her eyes darting back and forth, as though searching for an escape. "I didn't—"

I kept going. "The only thing I'm not sure of is the identity of the woman you threw off Westminster Bridge. Maybe she was another devotee of the Sons of Helios? Some lonely middle-aged spinster without any family to miss her, and who was roughly the same age and body type as you? You drugged her, giving her just enough that she'd be confused and easy to control. Then you took her for a walk along the Embankment and onto the bridge and pushed her over the railings. It would have taken a good bit of strength. But then people probably underestimate you a great deal, don't they? They don't realize how strong and determined you really are."

"I didn't throw anyone off Westminster Bridge. At noon today, I was right here. Making funeral arrangements. Drake can bear witness to that."

"I'm sure he can," I said.

I could not resist a smile as I continued. "But how did you know the woman was thrown off the bridge at noon?"

"Why, because you said she was."

"I only told you the place, Miss Shepperton. Not the time."

She said nothing.

"Obviously, you had help killing the woman," I continued. "A powerful organization, I would imagine. The same people who helped arrange for the escape of your brother and his wife. Those same people would tell you when the woman would be killed, so that you could arrange to have an alibi."

I'd dealt with murderers before, enough to know overweening vanity was the common thread that ran through nearly all their characters. I could see it in Miss Shepperton's face now: terror at having been caught warring with the odd desire to be recognized for how clever she'd been, and to boast of her crime.

Instead of saying a word, though, she reached suddenly into one of the letter slots of the writing desk and in a flash came out with a revolver. She aimed the gun at me.

My heart froze, although I forced my voice to stay calm. "You can't possibly think that you can shoot me and get away with it. Drake, your butler, let me in. He will hear the shot and come running. It's not as though you can even pretend to have mistaken me for a burglar."

"Stop talking!"

Miss Shepperton's hand shook as she aimed the revolver. Her face was deadly white and twitching, her gaze fixed with terror, empty of anything but the panicked fear of a trapped animal. Her voice rose in a high, hysterical scream.

"Not another word! I did everything I was supposed to do, and it all went perfectly—all of it! You're not going to spoil everything now!"

Her finger squeezed the trigger, and the revolver spat thunder, almost deafening in the confined room. I threw myself out of the way, although a flash of pain still seared my upper arm. As I collided with the carpeted floor, I looked up.

I was just in time to see Jack burst through the French doors and seize Miss Shepperton from behind.

* * *

I was lucky. The gun was a small-calibre weapon, and the bullet only grazed my arm.

Nevertheless, the wound burned as we stood with Miss Shepperton in the sitting room of Mulberry Walk, waiting for the police coach that would take her to prison.

She stood between two uniformed constables as Jack and I faced her. He had already told her she wasn't obligated to say anything more, and that anything she might say could be written down and used as evidence against her.

He then continued. "You'll be interested to learn that your brother and his wife have been caught."

"They are innocent."

"They confessed to the theft of the Turner painting."

Miss Shepperton's lips set in a thin line.

I watched her carefully. "They did try to blame two murders on you. The banker and the tramp."

"By putting that pistol under my pillow?" She gave an airy laugh. "That was all stage dressing. They knew they would be suspected—after all, Crutchley was forcing them to hand over the painting, and the painting was all the wealth they had left in the world. And I depended on them. So of course I went along with their plan. Sniffed that horrible incense. Made me quite dizzy. But you fell for it."

The unpleasant truth was that I had. I'd honestly believed Miss Shepperton to be a more-than-slightly pathetic victim.

Her eyes crinkled in a smug smile. "But in the confusion, after I took to my bed in my very convincing hysterics, my brother and his wife were able to escape. And we were confident that Mr. Holmes would prove that I didn't do it. So eventually I'd be free as well. I fooled you!"

Miss Shepperton's entire demeanor had changed, her features sharpening, her pale blue eyes malicious and triumphant. She'd been playing a part the entire time I'd been intent on proving her innocent of murder. And all the while she'd come and begged for help in protecting her aunt from Madame Yolanda, she'd also been lying—wearing a false face that I, of all people, ought to have seen through.

There was a saying back in America about *fool me once*. But I didn't say it out loud. Instead, I gave Miss Shepperton a calm smile.

"You're welcome to take consolation in that little triumph. I expect you'll need all the consolation you can get."

"What is that supposed to mean? I'm supposed to be worried

because I'm under arrest for murdering my aunt?"

I kept my voice pleasant. "I have to credit you, Miss Shepperton. You are one of the most accomplished liars I've ever encountered, and that is saying a great deal. But most people in your circumstances *would* be worried."

Miss Shepperton bridled. "Well, not I. I shall be out on bail soon, and then I can vanish. I'll do a better job of hiding than my brother and his wife, so I won't be caught."

Overweening vanity. I'd already underestimated Miss Shepperton more than once, and now I had the gunshot wound to prove it. If she could be lulled into a false sense of her own triumph, however, there was still a chance she might say more than she intended.

Jack gave me a quick, questioning glance, and I responded with a barely perceptible nod.

"The bail's not going to come cheap," Jack said. "And you won't be able to draw on your aunt's estate to put up the money, whatever her will says. You're not allowed to profit from a crime."

Miss Shepperton tossed her head. "I won't need my aunt's money."

"Would that be because you think the same people who helped you become Madame Yolanda will put up the money for your bail?"

Sudden caution shuttered Miss Shepperton's narrow features. "I'm saying nothing."

"But you've said quite a lot about the Sons of Helios, haven't you?"

"What about them?"

"You killed your aunt at their direction, for one thing."

"I deny that. Categorically. They are a wonderful, pious, enlightened—"

I cut her off. "They are a sophisticated criminal organization specializing in helping wealthy criminals escape the consequences of their crimes by hiding under new identities. And to maintain the fiction of their purpose as sun-worshippers, it is helpful if they have access to estates like Mulberry Walk, where they can organize gatherings to attract more wealthy followers who will make donations to the cause or even write wills in their favor."

"I have no idea what you are talking about," she said.

"You know your brother's solicitor, though."

Miss Shepperton's gaze narrowed. "What about him?"

"He made the arrangements to rent Madame Yolanda's studio. He drew up a will for you to sign, deeding Mulberry Walk to the Sons of Helios. You signed it one week ago."

Jack added, "That document was obtained by the police this afternoon. It will be shown at your trial."

Miss Shepperton stood silent, as though calculating. Her next words came out slowly, with unnatural deliberation. "Where … is … my brother's solicitor … now?"

"He's vanished."

"He has a powerful organization behind him." There was pride in her voice, and confidence.

"As did your brother and his wife. I saw them both this afternoon, at Scotland Yard."

"I trust they are well."

"They told me they would be freed on bail this afternoon," Jack said.

"I should think so."

I leaned towards her, still smiling. "But they couldn't say the same for you. They said you weren't important enough."

She lunged for me. The constables restrained her.

A short time later, we watched her being put into the police carriage, on her way to The Old Bailey.

* * *

I leaned my head against Jack's shoulder, wincing at the rattle of the wheels of our cab across the cobblestones. We were together in a hansom, driving home. We'd just come from Uncle John's surgery, where he'd treated the bullet wound in my arm.

The rain had stopped. The London sky hadn't cleared much, but the glow from the lamplights was pleasant, and the air was cool.

Jack put his arm around me. "I just wish I'd been quicker coming through the window."

I shook my head. "It wasn't your fault. And we got what we needed."

Having Jack as a witness had been part of our plan: Miss Shepperton was most likely to confess to her crime if she thought herself alone with me. Jack had been stationed just outside the French doors, on the terrace.

My final insult to Miss Shepperton had also been part of our plan.

"Do you think she'll be enraged enough to give away any information about the Sons of Helios?" I asked Jack.

"We'll have to wait and see what Holmes and Lestrade manage to learn when they interview her. They'll probably leave her to stew in a holding cell for tonight and then bring her in for interrogation tomorrow."

I shivered. "I never thought she'd try to shoot me."

Both of us had risked our lives before this; both of us had been hurt in the course of investigations. But the cold, sharp truth was that it never got any easier.

"We're alive," Jack said. His arm around me tightened. "And Miss Shepperton won't be for long, after she's tried and convicted."

"I know." I shut my eyes for a moment, listening to the creak of the carriage springs. Then I remembered something. "Becky is at Baker Street. We should go there first. We can bring her home with us."

Jack gave instructions to the driver. I settled back once again, and we rode in silence for a while.

"Penny for 'em," Jack said.

"It's just ... do you ever feel as though it's too much? All the ugliness we see every day? Having to think about all the despicable people and the crimes they commit?"

"Sure."

"What do you do about it?"

"That's easy." Jack leaned down and kissed my forehead. "I think about you instead."

* * *

About fifteen minutes later, the cab reached Baker Street.

Becky saw us as soon as I opened the door to the sitting room. "There's news!"

Holmes, recumbent on the sofa in his dressing gown, sat up.

"Flynn reported a few minutes ago. And I have just had a call from Scotland Yard," my father said. "I was just about to telephone Watson. Perhaps you should sit down."

We did so, I in Holmes's chair by the dark fireplace, and Jack in the chair opposite.

"A coach was waiting for the Sheppertons when they were released, following the magistrate's hearing at the Old Bailey," Holmes said. "Two of the Irregulars followed that coach to Whitechapel. There it stopped, but only momentarily."

He paused a moment, then continued.

"Two bodies were thrown out, one on either side of the coach. The bodies were those of Lord and Lady Shepperton. They were both quite dead."

I shuddered involuntarily.

"They had seen too many faces, and they knew too much," Holmes said. "Moreover, they had broken their promise to deliver the Turner painting in exchange for their escape. In the view of someone like Sonnebourne, that kind of behavior warrants no second chance, no forgiveness, and no mercy."

"But didn't Sonnebourne's organization want the genuine Turner painting?" I asked.

"The painting I took from Sonnebourne House and turned over to the Capital and Counties bank *was* the genuine Turner."

I stared at Holmes.

"Experts retained by the bank confirmed authenticity last week. I wished to keep Shepperton talking, so I let his falsehood go unchallenged."

"Why would he lie about that?"

"His barrister used the tale of the false painting to influence the magistrate at the bail hearing. 'Set him free, your honour,' he argued, 'and there is a chance the genuine painting may be recovered.' Something along those lines. The magistrate had no evidence to the contrary, so he granted bail. Ironic, considering the swift and deadly outcome for the Sheppertons."

"Do you think Lord Shepperton might have bargained with the organization when he was in that carriage?"

"I doubt it," Holmes said. "Sonnebourne did not send bargainers to pick up the Sheppertons after the bail hearing. He sent murderers."

I pictured the Sheppertons, stepping up into their carriage and coming face-to-face with the hard men who awaited them. In that single moment, they would have known. There would be no escape. I wondered if they had been allowed to say goodbye to one another.

I shuddered again.

"Was that what the call from Scotland Yard was about?" Jack asked.

Holmes shook his head. "*That* call concerned *Miss* Shepperton. She was being held in the Old Bailey." He was silent for a long moment. From his expression, I knew he was giving me time to prepare myself for another shock.

"A few minutes ago, Miss Shepperton was found hanged in her cell."

"Not a suicide," I said. "She had too much hope."

"There was an unidentified female guard seen closing Miss Shepperton's cell door a few minutes before the body was discovered," my father went on. "The police are investigating."

"Sonnebourne's people," Jack said. "Miss Shepperton was used and discarded."

"She was proud to be part of such a powerful organization," I said. "She trusted them."

Holmes nodded. "Now, having told you the news, I shall telephone Watson."

He stood and walked over to the telephone.

But at that moment, it rang.

He lifted the receiver and said, "Holmes."

He listened in silence, and his face went pale.

He then hung up the receiver. As he spoke, my heart plummeted.

"That was Lestrade," he said. "Fifteen minutes ago, three men broke into Watson's surgery."

His face hardened. His grey eyes were blazing.

"Watson is missing," he said.

CHRISTMAS AT BASKERVILLE HALL

"Holmes had lit his pipe and sat smoking in one corner,
looking on with half-lidded eyes."

LUCY
Chapter 1

"But you *must* write it all down and turn it into a proper story, Doctor Watson!" Becky was fairly bouncing up and down on the red velvet train seat with excitement, her blue eyes saucer-wide. "You absolutely have to, it's the most thrilling mystery I've ever heard!"

Outside of the train window behind her, the low hills of the Devonshire landscape flashed by, blanketed by a dazzling white snowfall that, we'd been told, sometimes occurred at this time of year. We had been traveling since early that morning, when we had boarded our train at Paddington Station, and to help pass the time of the journey, Uncle John had just finished telling Becky of the mystery that had originally brought him and Holmes to this part of England.

"I don't know." Uncle John tugged at his mustache. "It was one of our more lurid adventures. Family curses, devilish pacts, ghastly spectral hounds … readers are liable to think I made the entire thing up as a piece of sensational fiction. That's the reason I've never written it down before this, although my publisher has been asking for a fresh adventure for some time." He glanced sideways to where my father sat in the far corner of our railway carriage. "What do you think, Holmes?"

Sherlock Holmes took the stem of his pipe from his mouth. "I think that soon you will take pity on your longtime readers and succumb to your publisher's appeal for more tales of the lurid and sensational."

His tone was milder than usual as he said it, though. Today was December the twenty-third, and for the first time I could remember, we were traveling not for a case, but for a simple holiday. Sir Henry Baskerville had recently gotten back in touch with Uncle John and invited us all to spend the Christmas holidays at Baskerville Hall.

Holmes had made acerbic comments about being even less of an admirer of Charles Dickens's literary efforts than he was of Watson's, and declaimed the effects of boredom and too much rich food on the intellect. But he had in the end agreed to come, and now we were all on the train that would carry us to the small wayside station serving the village of Coombe Tracey: Watson; Holmes and I; Becky; and Jack, who had been granted a week's vacation from Scotland Yard. Even Prince, Becky's huge, tawny-brown mastiff, was accompanying us; at the moment he was sprawled out on the carriage floor, sound asleep and snoring, apparently unimpressed by the story surrounding one of his canine cousins. And Holmes, if not precisely relaxed, had as close to an air of holiday about him as he was ever likely to reveal.

"I want to see *everything*!" Becky was still bouncing up and down on her seat, setting her blonde braids dancing. "Baskerville Hall and the prehistoric huts on the moor where Mr. Holmes was staying and Merripit House where the Stapletons lived and the prison and the Great Grimpen Mire—" She had to stop since she'd run out of breath.

Uncle John smiled at her, and even Holmes's lips twitched. "We will certainly endeavor to oblige, weather permitting," Watson said. "Time moves slowly in this part of the world, and I imagine much of it is largely unchanged, though it has been getting on for ten years now since Holmes and I were here. Although I'm afraid that you won't be able to see much of the Great Grimpen Mire. Sir Henry has had it drained so that they can re-open the ancient tin mine in the center of the land there. He and his wife are making an effort to continue Sir Charles Baskerville's efforts at charitable outreach by providing jobs for the local populace."

As he spoke, I saw a shadow cross Uncle John's gaze. To Becky, the idea of the Grimpen Mire was as thrilling as the rest of the story. But to Watson, who had actually lived through the events at Baskerville Hall, it was clearly a source of memories that were grim even to this day.

Becky pounced on the last part of what Uncle John had just said. "Sir Henry's wife? Who did he marry? Was it poor Mrs. Stapleton?"

Uncle John's expression softened again. "Indeed it was. It took time for them both to recover from the horrors they had each lived through, but as I understand it, they met again nearly two years later and found that they each still harbored the same feelings of tenderness which they had begun to experience during that dreadful affair. Although I was somewhat surprised to hear that Sir Henry was able to forgive the young lady for the lies she had told him—"

"Lies?!" Becky broke in indignantly. "What other choice did she have? She was married to that horrible Stapleton man, who would probably have killed her if she'd told Sir Henry the truth! *And* she was brave enough to try to warn him about what Stapleton was planning! As for forgiveness, *she* ought to be the one to forgive *him*. If he really loved her, he ought to have had the wits to deduce how things really were for her! *Or* he could have done the sensible thing and just asked her straight out what the trouble was, instead of tiptoeing around, trying to be so proper and polite, and asking her supposed *brother's* permission to court her!" She snorted.

"Well…"

Uncle John looked dubious. As a gentleman and a man of honor, he had the highest respect for women. But he was also a man with his feet firmly rooted in the earliest days of Queen Victoria's reign, and Becky's thoughts on appropriate roles for the male and female of our species occasionally shook his world view to its core.

He began, "That might have been asking a bit much of Sir Henry—"

"Jack would have found out the truth!" Becky interrupted. "Wouldn't you, Jack?" She looked at her brother, who was sitting beside me.

"Well, but I had it easy." Jack smiled. "Lucy wasn't already married to a notorious criminal when I first met her."

"But you *would* have if she had been," Becky said. "Still, if Sir Henry and Beryl Stapleton are married now, I expect it's all come out all right in the end." She nodded approval. Becky, like the majority of Uncle John's readers, appreciated a happy ending.

Watson's fingers tugged at his mustache again. "I—yes. The two of them certainly deserve a chance at happiness after the horrors they endured. No one of feeling could say otherwise."

I thought there was a moment's hesitation or doubt in his voice before he answered—and it seemed to me that Holmes might have observed it, too, because he turned away from his study of the moving landscape outside the window and gave Watson a swift, keen look. But Becky didn't seem to notice.

"What about the L.L. woman—Laura Lyons?" she demanded of Uncle John. "What became of her? And what about her old father, the one who was always suing people? And Dr. Mortimer, what about him?"

"One at a time, one at a time!" Laughing, Uncle John held up his hands. "I can tell you that Sir Henry and his lady have a son who must be about four years old, and I understand from his letter that Lady Baskerville is even now expecting to be shortly delivered of another child. But I have not myself kept in touch with the majority of Sir Henry's neighbors, so my answer as to what has become of them will have to be that I do not know. It's likely that you will meet them for yourself and can find out, though; the area where we are bound is a small, closely knit community."

"I hope Dr. Mortimer is still there and that I can get him to show me his collection of skulls!" Becky said.

Whatever worry I'd seen or thought I'd seen in Watson's expression appeared now to be gone. But before I could hear his answer, Jack's voice pulled my attention away. "What's this?" he asked.

We were sitting across from Uncle John and Becky, in the opposite corner of the railway compartment from Holmes. Jack was holding a sheet of paper he'd just picked up from the ground, which was scribbled all over with Becky's handwriting.

"Oh, that," I said. "Before she persuaded Uncle John to tell her the story of the Baskerville hound, Becky was working on composing her list to be posted to Father Christmas."

"Lock picks, rubber cosh, skeleton key, *Anatomy Descriptive and Surgical,* by Henry Gray…" Jack read aloud, his eyebrows edging upwards. "This is what she wants for Christmas?"

"This is Becky we're speaking of here. You could hardly expect her to ask for a jack-in-the-box or a doll's pram."

I looked across the carriage to where Becky had hopped up to stand on the seat and peer out at the snowy landscape, craning her neck for the first sight of Dartmoor. Jack kept reading in a tone too low for her to hear above the rattle of the train and the roar of its engines.

"Fingerprint kit? That'll be easy to find on Christmas Eve in a village like Coombe Tracey."

"I know."

I at least had the medical anatomy book for her already; I'd seen her eying Uncle John's with fascination and bought a copy weeks ago. And lock picks were easy enough; I could just give her mine.

"I did try to get her to make her list earlier," I told Jack. "Since we're traveling, I told her Father Christmas might need a little more advance notice to get what she wanted, so that it would be ready to deliver to Dartmoor. But she kept changing her mind about what to ask for, and she said it wouldn't make a difference because Father Christmas would find her wherever she happened to be, and the reindeer would be bound to have an easier time of it in Dartmoor than in London anyway."

It was one of the endearing quirks of Becky's character that even after having been involved in far more criminal investigations than any other ten-year-old girl would normally imagine, she still believed wholeheartedly in Father Christmas and his reindeer-drawn sleigh. If she ever asked me for the full truth, I wouldn't lie to her. But visits from Saint Nicholas were a tradition her mother had begun with her when she was small, and I hadn't had the heart to spoil the magic for her, especially with her mother now gone.

"Did you believe in Father Christmas when you were young?" I asked Jack.

"I'm not sure I ever even heard the name."

It would have surprised me if he had, actually. Jack had grown up alone on the London streets, taking care of himself. At Becky's age, he'd been more concerned with not freezing to death or starving than with presents under a Christmas tree.

"You?" he asked.

"No. When I was six, I sat up late on Christmas Eve, calculating exactly how fast Father Christmas would have to travel in order to deliver a gift to every single child in the world in just one night—not to mention the cubic capacity his sleigh would require to hold all of those gifts—and decided that it was impossible."

The calculations had at least been a distraction from the fact that I was stuck at boarding school for the holidays, while all the other girls had gone home to be with their families.

I took Jack's hand, lacing our fingers together. "Well, we'll make sure that Becky has a merry Christmas. Even if we have to explain that the elves at the North Pole don't have the right equipment to produce a fingerprinting kit."

Chapter 2

The little railway outpost looked brighter than when we had first seen it years ago. A green holiday wreath hung from the apex of the metal roof that sheltered the small platform. The wood frame sparkled with a fresh coat of green paint. But the station still appeared small and insignificant, dwarfed as it was by the great snow-covered moor that extended far beyond us, surrounding the outpost and the little village of Coombe Tracey as far as the eye could see. I felt a pang of lonely isolation. I recalled the premonitions that had troubled me the past few days. And the moment Holmes and I stepped down from our railway carriage and saw our host, Sir Henry Baskerville, coming to greet us, I realized something had indeed gone wrong.

Outwardly, the bluff, genial baronet and heir to the Baskerville estate seemed to have changed little during the nine years since we had last seen him, although his forceful, square-jawed face had filled out a bit and it was apparent he had added a few pounds to his compact, muscular frame. Despite the cold weather, he wore his thick black wool coat open, only partially covering his gray tweed jacket and waistcoat. But his heavy dark brows were drawn together in a frown, and his lips were set in a tight line, not parted in the glad smile of welcome I would have expected on such an occasion.

He made no reference to his obvious discomfort until Holmes and I had shaken hands with him and said our hellos. Sir Henry then lowered his voice.

"Might I have a word before introductions are made? With just the two of you? I have separate carriages waiting, and you shall soon know the reason."

Turning, we could see Lucy, Jack, and Becky were out of earshot, just maneuvering Prince down the steps of the railway carriage. Holmes made a small gesture to indicate that they were to wait. We then turned to face Sir Henry.

"Mr. Holmes, I am at sixes and sevens," he said, "for I had expected this to be a merry and festive moment, as by rights it ought to be. I swear I had no inkling of this when I invited you to come to spend Christmas holiday. I must confess, I did have another matter I hoped to get your guidance on, but that is entirely different from this, this horror—" He broke off.

"Please tell us what has happened," Holmes said.

"I set out this morning to meet you at the station here. Without an inkling of what I would find. You must believe that."

Holmes nodded. "Please continue."

"I set out along the circular drive that connects with the roadway to town. Snow had fallen, so I was proceeding slowly."

"You were in your carriage?"

"I was driving my carriage. Yes. And then on the side of our drive, I saw a body. Covered in snow, it was. But unmistakably a body. I pulled up the horse and got down immediately. I bent to inspect the body."

"How was it positioned?"

"On its side. Curled up into a ball. Then I realized who it was. From the clothing, you understand. I had not yet uncovered the face. But from the clothing I realized it was Sir Vincent Percival, a prominent local citizen who had called on me just last evening. I was in shock at this, because after bidding him farewell, I swear I saw his carriage drive away down the hill and out of sight."

"Driven by Sir Vincent?"

"No, by his carriage driver. The man had waited outside throughout our interview, all muffled up against the cold in his bright red scarf and woolen cap."

"Why did he not come in?"

"Sir Vincent said the fellow had spoken of seeing something suspicious on the moor. Apparently, he wanted to keep watch to guard the horse."

"That may be significant," Holmes said. "Where were you when the carriage departed?"

"Standing on our front stoop. I waved as they first set out, and Sir Vincent waved back from inside the carriage. And then I went inside for our dinner and thought no more of the matter. So it was quite a shock this morning to find him there, on the ground, only a few yards from where I had seen him at his carriage window."

"What did you do when you found Sir Vincent's body?"

"I felt that I ought not to disturb anything. So, I ran back to our house and telephoned the police here in town. My wife overheard the conversation. I did not mention Sir Vincent by name during the call—I only said that a man appeared to have died outside my home and was lying in the driveway, and would the police please send someone to attend to it. I did not want to alarm Beryl, you see, and I am glad I did not. She is in what her midwife calls a 'delicate condition', and to upset her would not be good for her or the baby, whose time is so very nearly at hand that the midwife has taken up residence in one of our upstairs rooms."

He stopped, and I realized he was looking at Lucy and Becky, still out of earshot, standing expectantly beside several neatly-positioned suitcases, and at Prince, the Kellys' large mastiff, waiting patiently with Jack.

He shook his head. "I am sorry, Mr. Holmes. What kind of a host must you think me, keeping your friends waiting while I rattle on? Let us have the introductions now, and then we can go to the local hospital, where the police will have taken the bodies."

"More than one?"

"I found a second man's body later, on my way into town. It was along the road, about half a mile from the hall. Sir Vincent's carriage driver."

Forcing a smile, he gestured at the others in our party to come over. Lucy nodded. Jack bent to put the lead onto Prince's collar. As they approached, Sir Henry went on.

"Now I must quickly tell you, Mr. Holmes, why I arranged for two carriages. The first is for the three of us, and only the three of us, to go to the hospital. The second is for the others in your party, to take them directly to Baskerville Hall." Seeing Lucy and the others were nearly upon us, Sir Henry continued more rapidly. "The wounds on the two bodies are not a fit sight for a woman or a young girl, Mr. Holmes," he said.

"Indeed?"

Sir Henry went on, dropping his voice to a low, hoarse whisper. "The throats of both men have been torn apart."

I shuddered involuntarily as the words sprang immediately to my mind:

As if by a gigantic hound.

* * *

My mind whirled, and I barely listened as Holmes told Lucy, Jack, and Becky what had happened. My earlier premonitions—which I had felt from the time we had received Sir Henry's invitation in London—had returned in full force, and now they took on a ghastly shape, that of the spectral, phosphorescent, vicious hound that had terrified all three of us years ago. Despite all Sir Henry's best intentions to change the fate of the Baskervilles and bring fresh hope to the local citizens, the powers of evil, it seemed, were not to be denied. We had returned for a joyous celebration, only to place Lucy and Becky directly into harm's way. Their own family dog Prince, sitting at Becky's side, slack-jowled and wrinkle-faced, gazing up at Jack with adoring brown eyes, seemed naïve and wholly inadequate against the savage fury of the beast we had encountered when we were alone upon the cold and heartless moor that dreadful, fog-ridden night.

But that night had ended in victory, I told myself. Holmes and I had killed the beast. I drew inspiration from Holmes, who even now, in his crisp, factual manner, was explaining the need for Lucy and Jack to gently break the news to Lady Baskerville, and to reassure her so as to prevent unnecessary worry. I resolved that, come what may, Holmes and I would face down whatever evil awaited us now.

Soon afterwards, Lucy and Jack were off to Baskerville Hall, riding in the second carriage with Becky and Prince. I knew that all three were reluctant to miss the beginning of an investigation, but I was grateful all the same that little Becky would not have to witness the dreadful aspects of the two bodies that awaited at the local hospital.

The Coombe Tracey hospital was a small, freshly white-washed and landscaped affair that had once been a local inn. A worried-looking nurse greeted us in what was now the reception area.

"I understand that our old friend Dr. Mortimer is on duty," said Sir Henry.

"'E's with a family member," the nurse said, "'im and Chief Constable Penn. Just gone in to identify one of the dead ones." From the adjoining room came the keening wail that evidences a woman's grief. "It's the poor man's wife, and she's right broken up, poor thing."

"Lady Percival?" asked Sir Henry.

"No, that crying woman is Maud Hornsby. John Hornsby was Sir Vincent's driver."

Moments later, a small dark-haired man emerged from the room, assisting a sobbing country woman in shawl and head scarf. She was bent over in her anguish and clutching a red wool cap and red woolen scarf to her bosom. The two shuffled into the reception area and were nearly past us when the man glanced in our direction and saw Sir Henry.

"Sad times, Sir Henry," he said.

"Sad indeed, Chief Constable," Sir Henry replied.

The woman's eyes widened, and she spun around to face Sir Henry. "You!" she shrieked. "This is your doing. Your wretched family—"

"Now, now, Maud," said Chief Constable Penn. "There's no call for—"

"You keep away!" the woman shrieked. She held the cap and scarf up before her, brandishing it as if it were a weapon. "And now my man is gone and what is to become of me, God only knows!"

But at that moment, the expression on Sir Henry's face—horrified, pale, and utterly sympathetic to her plight—seemed to register with the poor woman. She then broke down in sobs and leaned against the chief constable, nearly crumpling to the floor.

"Let's go have a nice cup of hot tea at the inn across the way," Chief Constable Penn said. He firmly moved her to the doorway, assisted by the nurse.

After bidding farewell to the chief constable and the newly-widowed woman, the nurse then returned to her desk. "The old trouble," she said. "I'm sorry for you, Sir Henry, for I don't hold with folktales and superstitions. But tongues will be wagging all around the village by nightfall, and throughout the county by tomorrow."

"The truth will silence the tongues soon enough," said Sherlock Holmes. His grey eyes glittered with a fierce determination. "And we shall uncover the truth, Sir Henry. This I promise you."

At that moment, Dr. James Mortimer, our friend from our initial adventure with Sir Henry, emerged from the adjacent room, adjusting his gold spectacles. The smile of greeting on his narrow, long-nosed features was only brief and hesitant, almost embarrassed, and tinged with his obvious distress. We shook hands.

"Mr. Holmes, Dr. Watson, Sir Henry," said Dr. Mortimer. "Good to see you again, but I wish it were under happier circumstances. I'm sorry you had to undergo that ordeal with Mrs. Hornsby. The poor woman is quite beside herself, lashing out at whatever target she can find to blame—the hound and your family, in this instance. It is most instructive how, when under a great emotional strain, the human mind is prone to revert to superstition and wild beliefs."

"That was her husband's hat and scarf?" Holmes asked.

"She had knitted them herself."

"We have come to look at the bodies of the two victims," Holmes said.

"Of course. And you will not want to waste a moment, I am sure. Forgive me for prattling. My mind, you are well aware, runs on theoretical channels by nature, and this is a time of stress for me as well. Sir Vincent was a benefactor of the hospital and numerous other charities in our little village, and so he will be missed, not only by friends and family, but also—"

He stopped, mindful of Holmes's upraised palm, then continued. "Of course. The bodies. I have just returned Mr. Hornsby's to the surgery room, which was formerly the kitchen when this was the local tavern and inn. We shall pass through the patients' ward, but it is not occupied this afternoon. It once served as the dining room. Please follow me."

So saying, he led us, taking long, careful strides and hunching his rail-thin frame, lifting his knees high and placing each foot as though hiking over rocky ground. We passed through the ward, where a row of several beds stood empty, one of them very carelessly made up, and a forlorn rubber tree plant drooped lifelessly in the corner between a radiator and a large window. Holmes lingered beside the plant for a few moments.

"As you can see, we are quite understaffed," Mortimer said. "But we have no patients at the moment, so there is no harm done."

He then opened the door to the darker surgery room and switched on an electric light. We saw two metal surgical tables. On each table lay a man's body, facing upwards.

"This is Mr. Hornsby," said Mortimer, indicating the body closest to the entrance. "The other is, or was, Sir Vincent Percival. I knew him, as I mentioned."

"And I was with him at the hall just yesterday evening," said Sir Henry. "At first I thought the driver was to blame. But of course, it could not be the driver, since he is dead. I've worked it out in my mind as to what happened, though."

"Indeed?" Holmes asked, as he bent over the body of Mr. Hornsby.

"Yes, I think the first attack came far along the path beyond the hall, at the spot where Hornsby's body lay. The beast that did this horrid thing attacked Hornsby first, bringing him down from his seat on the carriage. Sir Vincent got out when the carriage stopped. He saw that he could not save Hornsby by himself, and then ran back to the hall to get help. But the animal overtook him."

Holmes did not appear to be paying attention. "What kind of a man was Sir Vincent?" he asked, moving away from Hornsby's body.

"A lonely fellow, I thought," said Mortimer. "Charitable in a public way. Very enthusiastic about the causes he supported. But I sometimes felt that was a way of atonement for his principal activity. He was a solicitor by trade, you see, and his firm, Percival and Merwyn, does the legal work for several of the mining companies with operations in the area."

"Why should that work require atonement?" Holmes asked.

"Working conditions in the mines are notoriously difficult and dangerous. Sir Vincent saw to it that the mines could keep operating, economically, notwithstanding numerous complaints about safety. Although I am somewhat incorrect in attributing that outcome to Sir Vincent. He laid off most of the work onto his junior partner, young Ferdinand Merwyn—overloaded him, you might say, to the breaking point and then some. I saw that for myself, just yesterday. Poor fellow wobbled over here from his office on his bicycle, he did, about an hour before teatime, and was in the ward all night, in one of those empty beds we just passed."

"What was the diagnosis?" I asked.

"Migraine. But the cause was—is—overwork, of that I am quite certain. We've seen him in here before, several times."

"With the same complaint?"

"Indeed, and we treated him here at no charge, since Sir Vincent was such a generous benefactor of the hospital. But I expect after this tragedy, that, too, will have to change…"

He trailed off as he realized Holmes was not listening. Bent over Sir Vincent's throat, Holmes was studying the wound, a great, ragged, gaping injury. He pointed to the jagged left edge of the wound, above the blood-stained white collar.

"Dr. Watson, will you please observe," he said.

I did so.

"Now, would you please observe the wound on the unfortunate Mr. Hornsby, also paying close attention to the left edge."

I did so. And drew in my breath. "The marks are identical," I said.

"Assuming it was the same animal, that is to be expected, surely?" said Sir Henry.

"It was not an animal at all," Holmes said. "The murderer was quite human."

"How can you be so certain?"

"Two additional points of observation are each indicative, and when taken together with the identical edges of each wound, they are quite conclusive."

I bent over the body once more and saw what Holmes had observed. "Dr. Mortimer," I said, "would you kindly raise the head of the body of Mr. Hornsby and tell me what you observe at the base of the skull."

He did so. "Why, the skull has been fractured," he said. "There is a small indentation, curved—no, in a circular pattern, but one side deeper than the other. There is also discoloration around the back of the neck, indicating that a bruise had begun to develop."

"I believe you will find—or the medical examiner will find, when the formal examination is made—that the fracture to the skull is the cause of death," I said. "The tearing at the throat came afterward."

Dr. Mortimer paused, reflected a moment, then said, "Because the blood stains are almost exclusively around the collar."

"Indeed. The heart had ceased to function when the wound at the neck was made," I said. "Had the throat laceration been the original wound, a great deal of blood would have poured out from the severed carotid artery and jugular vein."

"Thank you, Dr. Watson," said Holmes. "Now, Dr. Mortimer, if you will make the same inspection of the head and neck of Sir Vincent, I believe you will observe the same phenomena."

"Quite right," Dr. Mortimer said a few moments later, when he had completed his inspection.

Sir Henry stepped forward, examined the wounds on the necks of the two victims, then stepped back, emitting a sigh of relief. "A hand rake could have done this," he said. "A gardener's four-pronged iron hand rake. Whoever did this—"

Holmes cut in, "Whoever did this was strong enough to wield the hand rake in a powerful blow, doing a great deal of damage with one stroke. A cruel trick, intended to cause great emotional distress to you and your family, Sir Henry, as well as to the more credulous and fearful members of the populace."

"And it's certainly done that," Sir Henry said. "I'm sure fearful tongues are wagging, even as we speak. And when I go outside, I'll expect—"

"We must nip that in the bud," Holmes said. "Dr. Mortimer, would you kindly cross over to the inn and fetch Chief Constable Penn. Tell the nurse to stay with Mrs. Hornsby if necessary. And tell all three of them that your examination has determined that we are dealing with a clever human killer, not a spectral one. We have a straight-on murder investigation now."

"I shall tell them at once."

"And say nothing of my involvement, if you please. As an outsider and friend of Sir Henry's, my motives are suspect. Also, I would prefer that our murderer not become aware of my presence in the area until we are on firmer ground."

"But what did happen, Mr. Holmes?" asked Sir Henry after Dr. Mortimer had gone. "Do you think more than one murderer was involved? It might have required two or more men, to chase down the carriage and driver and Sir Vincent—"

"We must wait," said Holmes, "until we have more facts."

"Then let us get to it." Sir Henry consulted his pocket watch. "I expect you'll want to see where the two bodies were found. If we start now, we can get to the first location before sunset."

"Not quite yet," said Holmes.

Whereupon he took paper and pen from the laboratory desk and wrote out a few lines, then folded the paper. On our way out, he handed the folded paper to the nurse.

"When Chief Constable Penn returns, would you kindly give him this note," he said.

"Playing that lone hand of yours again, I see," said Sir Henry.

Holmes only gave one of his small smiles and laid a finger to his lips.

When we were outside, Sir Henry said, "I hope you don't intend to return to London or go hide in the hills, Mr. Holmes."

"Patience, Sir Henry," Holmes said. "I merely require data regarding the background and associates of the victims. As you know, one cannot make proper bricks without sufficient quantities of clay and straw."

* * *

Holmes, Sir Henry, and I were in an open dog-cart, driven by Bradley, one of the constables who had brought the body of Mr. Hornsby to the hospital. The cold wind stung my eyes. The bleak snow-covered moor ahead of us seemed to merge with the harsh gray sky. We had passed through the little village of Coombe Tracey, its shops gaily decorated for Christmas but largely bereft of customers. Around us, the few remaining houses cast their long shadows in the wan afternoon sun. The window curtains of most of the houses were closed. I wondered if they had been fearfully drawn shut against a spectral hound. I wondered if they would stay drawn when it became known that a clever and devious human murderer had been at work. I wondered if families would fear to venture out for evening vespers, or for Christmas Eve candlelight service, knowing that stealthy evil lurked nearby. Even Constable Bradley had been reluctant to ride with us, at first. But when Sir Henry explained that the impression of a killer hound had been deliberately created by the murderer, and that man-made implements, probably a hammer and a garden rake, had been used, the constable's jaw clenched with resolution.

"A fair wicked piece of work, then," Bradley said. "Like to get my hands on the one who done it. No call to kill poor Hornsby."

He shook his head, and we drove on in silence for several minutes. Holmes then asked, "Constable, who do you think would want to kill Sir Vincent?"

"Well, I don't know anyone in particular. But I can tell you he's not at all liked by the workmen at Grimpen Mine."

"Do you know why?"

The constable turned around to address Holmes, but Sir Henry stopped him.

"No need, Constable," said Sir Henry. "You can keep your eyes on your horse and on the road, there's a good chap." He turned to address Holmes. "Mr. Holmes, you may remember a tin mine on my land, where ancient deposits of tin ore were extracted from prehistoric times until a few decades ago. The entrance to the mine was on an island at the center of the Great Grimpen Mire."

"Watson and I saw it," said Holmes, "the day after we killed Stapleton's hound. And we have read of its recent transformation, brought about by your very substantial drainage project."

"I take satisfaction in that, Mr. Holmes. It is good to know that the lair of the villain who had threatened my life and done such harm to the woman I love no longer exists, and that the mine is now a source of employment for the village. Better still, my little boy can roam free on that part of the moor, which is now a grassy expanse of pastureland where sheep may safely graze."

"You commissioned the drainage work?"

"Oh, not with my own resources. Far from it. Fortunately, some businessmen from the area—old Andrew Throckmorton and his son—recognized the commercial potential of the mine, and they are now the owners. They own the mineral rights, and I own the land. New pumps now divert the ground water so that men can get at the valuable ore that lies beneath the surface. I am happy to say the project is on the brink of success."

"But not yet successful?"

"Nearly all the surface ore had been extracted before the mine was closed. But with judicious application of dynamite, the company has now created a great new chamber a hundred feet below the surface, exposing a rich lode of tin clearly visible in the granite wall. It only remains to haul up and cart away the rubble created by the explosion, so that the men can attack the walls with their picks and hammers."

"Can the work continue through the winter?"

"As long as the road is passable. Most days, the snow does not accumulate more than an inch or two, if at all. We can bring the men in on dog-carts, just like this one. And their work takes place underground, of course, out of the weather. We have a diesel-fuel generator, the very latest thing, that makes electricity to run the pumps."

"And you share in the success?" I asked.

"As owner of the land, there is a small percentage increase in the rent due me out of the profit of the enterprise. The lion's share of the gain rightfully goes to Throckmorton & Son. After all, they invested the lion's share of the capital."

"If we may return to the subject of Sir Vincent," said Holmes. "Why are the miners not fond of him? Is it because he enables the mine to operate even in unsafe conditions?"

"Oh, not just that, Mr. Holmes. They thought Sir Vincent would take their jobs away altogether."

"Can you explain?"

"The night he died, Sir Vincent was at Baskerville Hall, pressing me to support The Second Chance Society for prisoners. They are a charitable group who groom selected convicts in the Dartmoor prison for a 'second chance.' The chosen ones are sent to labor on a local project of some sort. Sir Vincent is the president of the organization. He thought the mining company, as a local business, ought to cooperate and allow prisoners to work there."

"I can think of few ideas less likely to appeal to a businessman than bringing in prison labor," said Holmes.

"Yes. The Throckmortons oppose it. And the workers, as I said, fear for their jobs. Yet Sir Vincent is—was—a prominent citizen and quite influential in charitable circles. And my wife, Beryl, is very much involved in local charities."

"So, you had a dilemma."

"Quite right, Mr. Holmes, and I confess that this dilemma was my ulterior motive in bringing you here," Sir Henry said. "Of course, I wanted to express my gratitude and perhaps show off the accomplishments that I have contributed to the region. But I also thought your counsel on how to solve my problem would be most valuable."

"But now there is a more pressing problem," Holmes said. "We must catch a murderer before he can kill again."

An idea came to me. "Might someone have killed Sir Vincent to keep the prisoners away from the mine?"

Holmes turned to Sir Henry. "What response did you give

Sir Vincent last night?"

"I agreed to support what you might call a compromise. A temporary arrangement. Let those Second Chance fellows into the mine for just part of one day. A trial run, so to speak. We agreed to do it tomorrow, December 24th."

"Who knows about that?" Holmes asked.

"Sir Vincent called his office with the news just before he left last evening. And I told the Throckmortons. We were to meet this evening at the hall to discuss the matter."

"Are the father and son both able-bodied men?"

"Oh, yes. Either one would be quite physically capable of the two murders."

"What about their characters?"

"Well, they are two domineering fellows. I don't take kindly to their pushing ways. But likely they will be at the hall when we arrive for our supper, and you can judge for yourself."

"I shall ask them where they were yesterday evening," Holmes said.

A moment or two later, the horse began to cut up rough, lurching the cart to and fro and jostling us. The constable snapped his whip against the animal's flank to settle it.

"We're coming to where I found poor Hornsby," Sir Henry said. "Perhaps the animal smells something."

Less than a minute later, our dog-cart stopped at the edge of a small copse, alongside a switchback bend in the lane. The path forked into two branches soon afterward. Wheel tracks and hoofprints could be seen in the snow, going in both directions.

Sir Henry pointed to the road on our right. "That one leads to Baskerville Hall."

"And the other?"

"The other leads to the Grimpen Mine."

Holmes was standing up in the dog-cart, surveying the snow-covered ground around us. "Sir Henry, where was the body when it was discovered?"

"Over there." Sir Henry pointed to a clump of brambles surrounding a tree.

"Inside the brambles?"

"No, against them."

"Was there snow on the body?"

"Enough to cover him, hat and all. But his muffler had been torn away, and the area of the wound showed through."

"Was the ground frozen before the snowfall?"

"Why, yes."

"And the carriage was not here when you found the body?"

"It was not."

"Constable, does this description tally with what you observed when you came to retrieve the body?"

"Oh, yes, sir," the man replied. "It was right where Sir Henry said he found it. We thought it was some sort of an animal what had done for poor Hornsby, but we didn't see any tracks."

"Because of the snow. And you did not search the surrounding area for a weapon?"

"No, sir. Like I said, we thought it was an animal."

"Where did you find the carriage?"

"Oh, we didn't, sir. The horse had pulled it into town. Someone in town found it and called us. Then we had the report from Sir Henry, so we came out and got the body."

Holmes shook his head. "We can learn nothing further here. Let us press on to the hall."

At the hall, two carriages were waiting in the circular driveway.

"That one will be the Throckmortons," Sir Henry said. "Not sure who came in the other."

"With all the snow and this carriage traffic, I doubt there is much to learn from this trampled ground," said Holmes. "Let us go speak to your callers, Sir Henry. Constable, thank you for your help. You are free to go."

Bradley thanked us, gave a long look at the darkening sky, then whipped up his horse, clattering away down the path and out of sight.

* * *

At the front portico of the hall, the door opened before Sir Henry could knock, and Lady Baskerville—Beryl Stapleton, as I had first known her—clutched at her husband's hands.

"Henry! I have heard the news that Sir Percival and his driver have both been killed!"

She looked scarcely a day older than when I had first encountered her, the day she had mistaken me for Sir Henry and warned me away from the moor. Dark brown hair curled about her proud, finely cut face, and her deep brown eyes were as beautiful as I recalled.

But she was clearly now, as she had been ten years ago, in great distress of mind.

"I don't understand at all. Who can have done such a terrible, terrible thing?!" she exclaimed.

"We don't know yet." Sir Henry's worry was apparent on his face, but he squeezed his wife's hands and endeavored to speak with reassurance. "But Mr. Holmes has determined that it was a human murderer, not an animal one. And I have every confidence that he and Dr. Watson will find the man responsible."

Lady Baskerville made a clear effort to recover herself, straightening and offering us a wan smile. "I beg your pardon, Dr. Watson and Mr. Holmes. I am glad to see you again, after all these years. And although I wish that the circumstances were happier, I can think of no better or more capable friends to assist us at this time."

Holmes bowed, and Sir Henry touched his wife's cheek. "Now I pray you don't upset yourself, my dear. It's bad for both you and the baby. As I'm sure Dr. Watson will agree."

I nodded. "Yes, indeed. Perhaps Lucy—"

Lucy had emerged from a door on the right that I assumed led into the drawing room. "Of course. I can help you upstairs."

She offered a hand to Lady Baskerville, who allowed herself to be led away. But I saw her shake her head as they started up the long stairwell.

"I don't understand." Her voice was little above a whisper. "I was so sure—"

She stopped as a gray-haired, matronly figure appeared on the landing above them, clucking her tongue. "Well, now, my lady, what's this? You ought not to be out of bed, much less running up and down the stairs. Come now, back to bed with you. You'll need your rest to deliver this babe into the world."

* * *

Mr. Jarvis—for that was the name of the butler—came into the hall and took our coats as Lady Baskerville and the midwife vanished upstairs. He was sturdy and middle-aged, and appeared a bit embarrassed that Lady Baskerville had rushed ahead to greet us before he could perform his duty.

I glanced around the great hall, pleased to see that the wide entryway, once dark and gloomy, had been freshened and decorated. A cheerful blaze crackled in the great stone fireplace. The firelight caught the shiny green holly and ivy leaves that hung on the great wooden beams overhead. The walls had been cleaned of their sooty haze and painted white, as if to proclaim that a new and livelier spirit now prevailed within the old mansion. I wondered whether the rows of foreboding family portraits still hung in the banqueting hall, daunting visitors with their ancestral presence.

Jarvis was speaking, his tone dignified and formal. "Supper will be served in one half-hour unless you wish to delay, in which event I shall notify the cook. Your business guests, Mr. Throckmorton and his son, and their solicitor, Mr. Merwyn, arrived a short while ago. They await you in the parlor."

"Thank you, Jarvis."

"I did not like to place them in the banqueting hall," the butler went on, "since the table there is laid for supper and I did not think you would wish to suggest that they were invited. I have, however, provided each of the three men with a sustaining beverage." He nodded towards me and Holmes. "May I presume these gentlemen are Mr. Holmes and Dr. Watson?"

"We are," said Holmes.

"Very good, gentlemen. Your suitcases arrived with the others in your party, and I have placed them in your respective rooms upstairs. I will be happy to escort—"

"No need for that now, Jarvis," said Sir Henry. "We'll see to our business guests first."

"There are sufficient refreshments in the parlor for all of you, sir."

This news was welcome to me after the long day. Sir Henry led us to the parlor door and flung it open to reveal the three visitors.

Two portly red-faced and red-haired fellows were perched side by side on the sofa, sitting bolt upright, faces tight with impatience, as though counting up the moments they had been waiting. A third man, bespectacled in a gold pince-nez, stood by the small fireplace. He was tall, thinner, darker, more handsome, and somewhat frail in appearance, dressed in a very well-tailored suit and elegant calfskin boots. He looked uncomfortable as he saw us enter.

"Ah, Throckmortons, father and son, and Mr. Merwyn," said Sir Henry. "Welcome, and my apologies for the late arrival. The unfortunate business—"

"I thought our meeting was to be private," interrupted the older and heavier of the two Throckmortons.

"You may rely on the discretion of these two gentlemen," said Sir Henry. "I have known and trusted them for nearly a decade, ever since I came to England."

"Well, we'll be brief enough," said the younger Throckmorton, after introductions had been made. "Merwyn here agrees with us that there's to be no work done at the mine by any jail-birds."

"But I had promised Sir Vincent—"

"—that there could be a trial session tomorrow," said Merwyn. "I know, for I had his message to that effect when I came into the office this morning. But I agree with my clients."

"That the murderer has won?" said Holmes.

"What do you mean by that, Mr. Holmes?" asked Throckmorton Senior. "How has the murderer won?"

"If his objective was to bar the Second Chance program from the mine, that objective has been achieved."

"What if that was not his objective? Sir Vincent may have had a thousand other enemies."

"He may indeed. And yet people will talk. Have you gentlemen considered the effect such talk will have on your own reputations?"

"I don't follow you."

"The chief constable will ask where you were last night, and if you have a strong alibi, then tongues will be stilled for the moment. But only for the moment, for people will say that your wealth would enable you to pay to have someone else remove the champion of prison labor at the mine."

"See here, Mr. Holmes—" said the junior Throckmorton.

"We have nothing to hide," said his father.

"Then where were you last night?"

"We were at home. You can ask my wife."

"Might we ask your servants?"

"Well, they had the night off. We went to bed. They didn't see us until this morning."

"So, to account for your whereabouts, you must depend on the woman who is wife to one of you and maternal parent to the other. In London, we would not call that a particularly strong alibi."

"London can go hang," said the father. "And so can you, Mr. Holmes."

"I was in the Coombe Tracey hospital all last night," said Merwyn.

"Why was that?" Holmes asked.

"I suffer from migraine headaches. Quite debilitating when one of them is upon me. I have recovered now, though."

Holmes nodded, as though he was hearing this information for the first time. This puzzled me, for I did not think it possible that Holmes's prodigious memory could have failed to recall the information Dr. Mortimer had conveyed to us only that afternoon. But I have learned to keep silent about such things.

Holmes continued, mildly. "And what brought on this migraine, if you don't mind my asking?"

"Oh, you will find that out soon enough," Merwyn said. "I had a quarrel with Sir Vincent yesterday morning. I fancy someone on the staff will tell the police when they come to investigate."

"What brought on the quarrel?"

"A business matter. We differed concerning an investment. But Sir Vincent was inclined to get emotional about his own views, and in this case, his emotion upset me. I found I could no longer get on with my work at the office. So, I was forced to go to the hospital. That was early yesterday afternoon."

"What was the treatment the hospital administered?"

"A large draught of laudanum. Then the nurse put me to bed, and I did not wake until this morning."

Holmes turned to me. "Is laudanum a standard treatment for migraine, Dr. Watson?"

"Assuming the condition is severe, yes, it is."

He turned back to Merwyn. "Then you, Mr. Merwyn, have a strong alibi. But of course, the same reasoning that applies to your two clients here applies to you. Those of your fellow citizens who are inclined to gossip might say that, upon quarreling with Sir Vincent and before you went to the hospital, you made arrangements with someone else to kill him. Are you a beneficiary in his will, by the way?"

Merwyn reddened. "Certainly not!"

"What becomes of his ownership interest in your legal partnership?"

"The partnership is dissolved with his death. The proceeds from assets available to sell would go to his estate."

"In which you have no testamentary interest."

"Quite right."

"Yet the effect of his death is that you, the former junior partner, now have control of the firm. A firm with a goodly number of prosperous clients. Some might call that a motive."

A slight smile appeared on the young man's bespectacled, handsome features. "I do believe you are testing me, Mr. Holmes."

Holmes shrugged. "I merely point out that public opinion, which always seeks out someone to blame when there is a murder, may fasten itself upon any of the three of you, whether you are innocent or not. For that matter, some might even gossip about Sir Henry here. Some might say that he did the murders and then returned to the hall, leaving the snow to cover the evidence of his footmarks."

"Now see here—" said Sir Henry.

But Holmes held up his hand. "My apologies, Sir Henry. I only point out the irrational nature of rumour, that many-headed serpent."

Throckmorton Senior got to his feet. "Holmes, you are a most annoying fellow," he said, "but I won't be baited. And I take your point. You think that having the prisoners in for a trial visit would stave off some gossip, is that it?"

"I do. And at the very least, it will delay gossip. And with luck, we will have caught the killer soon thereafter."

"Then bring in the jail-birds, and be damned," he said. "Merwyn, can you make the arrangements?"

"They have already been made," said Merwyn. "The office

called the society this morning, upon receipt of Sir Vincent's telephoned message. The society, in turn, called the prison. Unless we change the arrangements, the prisoners will arrive at the mine at noon tomorrow, accompanied by guards and the prison chaplain. The company foreman will meet them. The society will pay his wages for the day."

"My son and I will see you there, Merwyn," said the senior Throckmorton.

Merwyn's face clouded. "I hope you aren't intending to go down into the mine," he said. "Or at least that you won't expect me to accompany you. I tried going down there in the lift a few days ago, and my migraine—"

"We expect you to go wherever it's necessary to protect our interests," said Throckmorton Junior. "And you'll do just that if you want to retain our business."

The Throckmortons and Merwyn departed soon afterwards.

* * *

"I should like to use the telephone in your office, Sir Henry," Holmes said after we had seen them off. "And then I would deeply appreciate it if you would make one of your horses available for me to ride into Coombe Tracey."

"You won't be joining us for supper?"

"Regrettably, no. I should also appreciate the use of a latch-key to the hall, in the event that I am late in my return."

He gave no further explanation. I had no idea what he intended to do.

That night after supper I stood looking out from my cold upstairs bedroom at the sparse, wind-driven snowflakes that swirled between window and the cold, endless moor. Holmes was out there, alone. So also was the murderer, or murderers. Why, I wondered, had Holmes insisted on going by himself? What dangers would he be facing and what drove him, as Sir Henry had put it, to play a lone hand on so many occasions when I might be of help to him? Why did he insist on keeping his own counsel?

I went to bed but did not sleep. At two-thirty that morning I heard the latch of his bedroom door, next to mine, quietly open and then click shut.

I put on my robe and went into the hall. "Holmes," I said, "is that you?"

He opened the door and peered out, smiling, his tweed ulster still dusted with snowflakes. "Quite safe, old friend," he said. "Now let us both rest while we can. Tomorrow we will have a dangerous time ahead of us."

LUCY
CHAPTER 3

It was late afternoon at Baskerville Hall, the day before Christmas. Holmes, Watson, and Jack had left for the Grimpen Mine just after eleven that morning. Holmes was certain the murder of Sir Vincent Percival was somehow connected to the visit of the Second Chance prisoners planned for noon. The only way to uncover the mystery, he said, was to be present at the scene to observe as events unfolded.

Little Hugo had been clamouring to be allowed to go out and play in the snow, and when his mother finally consented, after the men had left, Becky didn't even have to be persuaded to join him. If this case seemed likely to overshadow our Christmas, we had at least ample distractions here to keep Becky away from the ugliest aspects of it all. She could barely wait for me to fasten up her coat and tug on her mittens before she was flying out to join Hugo on the small terrace just outside the drawing room.

Prince, who had been asleep with his head on his paws, whined to go out and join them as soon as he heard Becky outside—which was all to the good. With the fire burning cheerfully, and a Christmas tree already set up at the far end of the room, sparkling with colorful glass balls—and the dazzling purity of the snow stretching across the landscape outside—it seemed impossible to believe in violence or evil. But something or someone had killed Sir Vincent Percival. If there was danger, I had no doubt Prince would raise an alarm.

"Hugo could stay out there for hours if I let him," Beryl said. Her finely cut face still looked pale and drawn, but she smiled a little as she sat down on a chair that faced the window. "He loves being out of doors."

I sat down beside her. Becky and Hugo were making a game of tossing snowballs to Prince, who would lunge at them and snap them out of the air with his jaws, making the snowballs explode in a small shower of white flakes. Prince would then turn around and around in confusion, nosing at the ground and puzzling over where the ball could have gone.

Becky and Hugo were shrieking with laughter.

"Becky's never seen snow like this before, I don't think," I said. "It doesn't pile up this way in London." Most of the snow that fell in the city soon turned to dirty slush.

I waited a moment, then said, "Don't you think it would be as well if you were to tell me everything?"

Beryl gasped. "What do you mean?"

"There's something you're keeping back."

I tried to speak gently, mindful of both her condition and the fact that she'd endured more of the world's ugliness and cruelty than anyone should be reasonably expected to face in one lifetime. Unfortunately, though, life was practically never reasonable or fair. And that was the reason I'd stayed behind at Baskerville Hall this afternoon; there seemed a better chance Beryl might be willing to speak to me alone.

"Something that you haven't told anyone, not even your husband," I went on. "But it relates somehow to Sir Vincent's death. When you were speaking of his murder, you said, '*I was so sure...*'

What were you going to say?"

Lady Baskerville was silent a long moment, her eyes on her little boy and Becky. When she finally spoke, it was almost to herself rather than in answer to my question.

"I know the choice of Hugo might seem like an odd name, given the Baskerville history; the old story of how it was the wicked Sir Hugo who first brought the curse on the family. But that was the point—we intended our son to be a new beginning, for both the Baskerville line and for ourselves. A banishing of the old, unhappy, and wicked times in favor of better, purer, happier ones. And it's been *true*."

Her lips trembled briefly as she looked through the glass at the snow-covered scene outside. Becky and Hugo had abandoned their game with Prince and were now at work together building a snowman, rolling great lumps of snow about the terrace. The setting sun's rays fell on their two heads, gilding Becky's wheat-blonde braids and Hugo's golden curls.

"We *have* been happy," Beryl said. "Henry and Hugo and I. Happier than I could ever have dreamed possible." Her hand curved protectively around the curve of her unborn baby, then clenched into a fist as she finally turned her gaze to mine. "You asked what I was about to say when you first told me of Sir Vincent's death." She let out a shuddering breath. "I was going to say, *I was sure that it would be me.*"

For a moment, Beryl's words seemed to hang in the air between us. The only other sounds were the crackle of the fire in the drawing room grate and the voices of the children outside. Then with a sudden movement, as though she'd reached a decision, she struggled up from her chair and started to pace the room.

"I don't know you, Lucy. But I did know your father and Dr. Watson, once. I came to trust both of them. I will trust you now." She glanced at me, then pressed the heels of her hands against her temples. "I must speak of it to someone, I think. It's been driving me to distraction. And besides, Sir Vincent's death changes things. Though I don't see … I don't understand why it should have been he who was killed or what purpose his death could possibly serve, unless it was some terrible mistake …"

She trailed off, her gaze turning away as though her thoughts were following some complicated and unpleasant path. She shuddered once but didn't go on.

"Do you know who killed Sir Vincent?" I finally asked.

Beryl looked down at her clasped hands a long moment. "I can scarcely believe it, but I'm dreadfully afraid that I do. Though before I tell you, you must understand that not everyone in our part of the world was entirely … happy about my marriage to Henry."

"I suppose you've received a fair number of anonymous letters?"

Beryl's eyes flashed to mine in surprise. "How did you—"

"It stands to reason. If you'd been reduced to wandering the countryside in sack cloth and ashes after your first husband's death, everyone would have felt terribly sorry for you. But instead you committed the unforgiveable sin of moving on, building a new life, and being happy—and with the new lord of the manor. Spiteful people will always want to poke holes in someone else's success."

Beryl nodded. "It's just as you say. Almost from the time of my marriage to Henry, I've had letters—just nasty, spiteful things, all generally running along the same lines: that I'm an immoral temptress who snared Henry with my wiles, and he deserves much better. That sort of thing."

"Were they all from the same person, do you think, or was there more than one writer?"

"I'm not sure. Some were handwritten, although never in writing that I recognized. Others were typed."

"Typed?" One of the details Watson had told Becky in the train had just come back to me.

Beryl looked up. "Yes. Is that important?"

"It could be." Or it could mean nothing at all. "Go on?"

"Well, I didn't pay too much attention to the letters. As you say, it was just spite, and when you've lived with …" She seemed to have difficulty saying the name. "With a man like my first husband, anything other than outright cruelty and abuse scarcely seems worth bothering about. I burned them when they came and thought very little more about them. And gradually over the years, they've nearly stopped coming. I suppose even ill-natured, jealous people find it difficult to hold a grudge forever. In the past year or two, I don't think I've even had a single one." She swallowed. "Until two months ago."

"Did anything happen two months ago, anything that might have provoked a fresh attack?"

"No—nothing. That is, I suppose it was somewhere around that time that Henry became involved with the Second Chance Society." Beryl frowned briefly. "But I don't think there can be a connection, because these letters were … entirely different."

"Different how?"

Beryl drew in a shaking breath, pressing her eyes shut and seeming to brace herself for something. "Different in that they purported to come from the man your father and Dr. Watson knew as Stapleton. My first husband."

* * *

"Here." Beryl crossed to the small writing desk that stood in one corner of the room and unlocked one of the bottom drawers. "You had better see for yourself." She reached into the drawer and extracted a packet of letters, thrusting them into my hands. "I've kept them. They're all there."

I took up the topmost letter and read.

You filthy unfaithful wench, do you really believe that you can betray me in this way? I shall kill you before I allow you to belong to any other man.

Rodger.

I looked up. "Rodger?"

Beryl had started to pace the room again but stopped at the question. "That was his real name. He was named after his father, Rodger Baskerville, the younger brother of Sir Charles."

"And is this his handwriting?" A quick glance through the rest of the letters—she'd given me eight in all—showed messages very much along the same lines as the first, although the epithets used to describe Beryl became increasingly profane.

She raised her hand in a helpless gesture. "I … I cannot be entirely sure. It is ten years since last I saw a sample of anything he had written, and I've tried my best to expunge everything about him from my mind. I've tried not to recall even the way he looked and spoke, much less how he formed his letters. But it is … it is very like his. If the letters were not written by my former husband, then it was someone who has done a very good job of imitating his handwriting."

"I see."

"I thought he was dead." Beryl's hands fisted themselves at her sides. "*Everyone* was certain that he was dead, drowned in the mud of the Great Grimpen Mire. But no body was ever found. He *could* have escaped on that terrible day and fled somewhere he would not be recognized." She had gone very pale.

"But why wait the better part of ten years before resurrecting himself in this way?" I asked.

I would need to speak to Holmes, since I hadn't yet heard the details of the case from him. But from what Watson had told us, it was, as Beryl said, theoretically possible that Stapleton might have escaped. I could certainly believe it within his character to torture his former wife by sending letters that would leave her in an agony of doubt as to whether he really was still alive. And the tone of the letters, the refusal to accept that Beryl was not his personal property to abuse as he wished—that also accorded with everything I'd heard of the man.

But waiting this long to do it? That part of the scenario didn't make sense to me.

"If the letters really are from Rodger, why did he not object when you married Sir Henry? Surely, that would have been a far more likely time for him to issue threats—and it's not as though your marriage could have been hard for anyone to have heard of, given Sir Henry's position in the neighborhood. If Rodger is alive and has been keeping watch on what has become of you, why only start writing now?"

"I don't know." Beryl was trembling now. She pressed her lips together. "I don't know, but it's been driving me mad with wondering. Everything that you say is true. If Rodger is still alive, why has he not made himself known to me before this? But then I ask myself, what if he fled somewhere abroad, perhaps, and has only just returned to England? That would account for it."

"And you haven't told Sir Henry of these letters?" I asked.

"No." Beryl sank back into her chair as though suddenly exhausted, folding her arms protectively over her middle again. "I've been terrified, you see, that if I did tell Henry and these letters are indeed from Rodger, then he might go out and hunt Rodger down. And then I would lose him." Her voice sank to a whisper. "Either Rodger would kill Henry—he tried once before—or else Henry would kill Rodger and be arrested for the crime."

Before I could answer, the French doors opening onto the terrace flew open, and Becky and Hugo tumbled in, with Prince trotting along behind.

"Mother! Mother!" Hugo charged at Beryl, scattering snow from his boots and mittens all across the carpet. "Becky and me are going to stay up all night so that we can see Father Christmas! And what are all those papers?"

He drew up short, looking at the pile of letters on the arm of Beryl's chair.

"Just boring grown-up things, sweetheart." Beryl still looked white, but she forced a smile. "Nothing for you to bother about."

Becky gave her a frowning look as Beryl crossed swiftly to re-lock the letters in the desk drawer, but Hugo was too young to take the words at anything other than face value.

"We're going to stay up tonight and wait for Father Christmas, and that means I'll be able to see when he comes to deliver my baby brother!"

"Well," Beryl began, "remember, the baby might not come

exactly on Christmas morning. And Father Christmas might … he might decide to deliver a baby sister—"

"No, I asked him to bring me a brother on Christmas morning!" Hugo's small voice was positive, his lower lip thrust out with determination.

"Well…" Beryl looked rather helplessly at her son.

"What about some hot cocoa?" I asked. "Your noses are both as red as cherries. I'm sure you could do with some warming up."

"Perfect." Beryl looked relieved. "I'll ring and ask for some."

Prince curled up on the hearthrug and promptly started snoring, and Becky and Hugo were soon settled in front of the fire, too, with trays of cocoa and ginger biscuits cut into the shapes of animals. From the look Becky gave me, she knew very well that Beryl and I had been discussing something to do with the mystery, and I would have to determine how much to tell her when she inevitably asked. But for the present, she was content to make the gingerbread cats and horses and rabbits hop into the cocoa cups for Hugo's amusement.

"We told him that the new baby would very likely arrive sometime close to Christmas," Beryl said in an undertone, when we'd sat back down in our own chairs. "And somehow he got it firmly into his head that Father Christmas would be bringing him the brother he's been asking for, and now nothing can persuade him otherwise."

She bit her lip, watching her small son noisily slurping his chocolate on the hearthrug and laughing as he offered a biscuit to Prince.

"If only—"

I could read the rest of what she'd been about to say in her expression: If only the worst trouble her family faced was the possibility of Hugo's having to be persuaded a baby sister would be just as much fun.

"We'll find out the truth," I promised. "But if the letters are from Rodger, Sir Vincent's death doesn't fit in. Rodger wouldn't have any reason for killing him, would he?"

"No. Not that I'm aware of. But he might have committed the murder simply for the sake of stirring up the old story of the curse and inciting the locals to panic and make trouble for Henry on that account. He's not ..." Beryl drew a shuddering breath. "When I knew him, he was scarcely sane when it came to acquiring whatever he wanted or punishing those who he considered had done him any kind of a wrong. If he *has* survived this long, and he now believes that I am happy with Henry, then Rodger would be—" She shut her eyes for a moment. "I believe that he would be mad enough to attempt anything that would destroy our lives. Even if he himself were to hang for the crime."

Unfortunately, she was right; an all-too-plausible answer existed to every objection one could raise about Stapleton being the author of the letters. I could hardly claim it was impossible for a man to return from the grave, not when my own father had survived his supposed death at the Reichenbach Falls.

"We will find out—" I started to say again, but before I could finish, the drawing room door burst open and a man in rough workman's clothes staggered in, red-faced and panting as though he was on the point of collapse.

"My lady!" Belatedly, he tugged off his cap and faced Beryl, still breathing hard. "There's been an accident at the mine! One of the tunnels collapsed, and Sir Henry and the gentlemen from London are all trapped down there underground!"

WATSON
CHAPTER 4

THREE HOURS EARLIER

Our carriage arrived at the entrance to the mine about one half-hour before noon. The prisoners were not yet due to arrive, but Holmes had insisted on our arriving early. He had come down to breakfast carrying a rucksack and refused to say what was in it or where he had been the previous night. Jack was with us at Holmes's request; Holmes had said that his presence might be valuable.

When the four of us got out of the carriage, we saw in the distance behind us several other carriages and an omnibus, all approaching the snow-covered hill we had just ascended.

"Mr. Holmes," said Sir Henry, "before the others arrive, perhaps we might know what we are looking for."

"We are looking for anything out of the ordinary. And I should direct your attention to the group of convicts in the omnibus."

"What connection would they have with the deaths of Sir Vincent and his driver? They were in Dartmoor."

"Yet someone may have killed Sir Vincent to prevent their arrival. So, what the convicts do when they have arrived may be worth observation."

"What kept you away from the hall last night?"

"Merely some extremely basic detective work, more close investigation of the two obvious points presented so far by this case. Those points, however, suggested a third, and so it was well after midnight when I returned to the hall."

Sir Henry frowned. "I have no idea what to make of that, Mr. Holmes."

"All will be made clear at the earliest practical opportunity, Sir Henry," Holmes said. He turned to the carriage that had stopped just behind us. The carriage door was just opening. "But here are our friends, the Throckmortons."

Both men were dressed in heavy tweeds against the cold. Both looked at us with flat-eyed curiosity as they got out. "What's in this for a London detective, Mr. Holmes?" said Throckmorton Senior.

"I am representing Sir Henry's interest. Attempts have been made to besmirch the Baskerville name and reputation by the choice of weapon employed during the two killings yesterday. I wish to prevent another occurrence."

"And we are here to protect our interests. It is our mine."

Another coach pulled to a stop just behind the Throckmortons' carriage.

"Here is our coach, with Mr. Merwyn. The driver is Mr. Barret, the most competent of all the company's foremen," said Junior.

"Perhaps he can give us a quick tour before the prisoners arrive."

Barret proved to be a robust, competent-looking fellow. He fairly leaped from the carriage driver's seat. Upon being told we wanted to see around the mine, he gave a nod.

"Fine. I needed to inspect it anyway. But I won't be able to play nursemaid to Merwyn. He's still in the carriage."

"Migraine?" Holmes asked.

"How did you know?"

"He told us yesterday that he suffered from migraine and the mine brought out the ailment," I said.

Holmes flung open the carriage door and peered inside, where Mr. Merwyn sat slumped in the rear seat, hunched over his briefcase, fingertips pressed against his temples, hat on the seat beside him, muffler around his throat.

"Gentlemen," Merwyn said. "Do not let us detain you in any way. This too shall pass, as the good book says. Or is it the poet? At any rate, I shall be better soon and able to walk around. For now, though, I should appreciate being left to myself. The omnibus with the six prisoners should be here very soon, along with the prison chaplain, and three guards."

This last statement seemed to have cost him more energy than he could bear to sustain, and he relapsed into silence, sinking his chin onto his chest, his fingertips still pressed against his temples.

* * *

Holmes brought his rucksack with him as we went with Barret for a brief tour of the mine's snowy exterior. We stopped beside the rumbling diesel generator. For a moment, we watched its acrid smoke puff up from the exhaust pipe and dissipate into the cold winter air.

"This machine supplies electrical energy for the dewatering pumps and the air circulation fans," Barret said. "It also supplies electricity for the hydraulic lift that will take us directly down to the newly opened central chamber. It's there that the men will tackle the next phase of the work, to clear out the rubble left by the explosion."

We saw a maze of wires, running along the snowy ground from the generator to a wooden enclosure just above the mine entrance. "Those also serve the electric lanterns inside the chamber. Better light means better efficiency, which in turn means the rubble is removed sooner," Barret said.

"And time is money," said Throckmorton Senior.

Holmes was kneeling beside the generator, his back to us.

"What have you got there?" asked Barret.

"One of the copper wires has been disconnected from the generator," Holmes said. Still kneeling, he held up the bright metal end of a single wire, the black-taped body of which was bound up with the others in the cables leading to the chamber.

"Impossible," said Barret. "Look here at the panel box. All the connections are marked, and they all have their wires clearly visible."

Holmes shrugged and got to his feet, still holding the wire. "No matter, then," he said. "Ah, I see that the prisoners are getting off the omnibus."

We turned and saw the prisoners step down slowly, side by side, two by two, each man shackled to his fellow. Three guards waited, each with a rifle.

A gray-haired man wearing a clergyman's collar was advancing towards us.

"I am Father John Gill," he said. "Prison chaplain."

We introduced ourselves. At that moment, one of the prisoners, for no reason I could ascertain, punched the man he was chained to. Immediately, a guard stepped forward and clubbed the attacker with the butt of his rifle. The man sank to his hands and knees.

Jack turned to Father Gill. "And this is the sort of man selected to get a second chance?"

"I don't know what could have provoked him," replied the clergyman. "Or what prompted such a harsh response from the guard. But this is, after all, only a trial visit, and in the future, when familiarity on both sides has been achieved, as well as a modicum of trust, perhaps we may be able to relax a bit more."

"How will they wield their picks and shovels in the mine if they are chained like that?" Jack asked.

"Inside the mine, their bonds may be unlocked. The mine itself is a most efficient prison. Walls thicker even than Dartmoor's."

I scanned the line of prisoners, trying to spot which, if any, might look suspicious. Of the six, none stood out, other than the man who had been struck by his companion. He appeared smaller and far less robust than his companions. The men were all clean shaven, from their chins up to the tops of their bald heads, which were hatless against the cold. They wore gray wool sweaters over their gray cotton uniforms and moved with extreme reluctance, forming up into a line, still two abreast.

I realized Holmes was not with us.

"Don't know as I'd be any too eager to go down there myself," said Jack to Father Gill. "What do they get out of it?"

"A day out of their cells is the only sure benefit. Possible good conduct reduction in their sentence, possible reference for a job—"

"So they can say they're good at breaking rocks and shoveling them into a basket?"

"Possibly some other job somewhere."

"Look at them," said Jack. "Standing hunched over and staring at the ground. They don't want to be here."

There came from behind us a familiar voice. "Which presents the question," Holmes said. "Who is forcing them?"

"I have nothing to do with that side of the operation," said Father Gill.

We turned as yet another carriage arrived. The Throckmortons and Barret and Father Gill looked at each other in puzzlement, then at Holmes.

"That would be Chief Constable Penn," said Holmes. "I asked him to bring one or two of his men to provide extra security for the generator."

"You're telling us how to run our business?" said Throckmorton Junior.

"At no cost to the mine," said Holmes.

"Well, that's all right, then," said Throckmorton Senior. "Can't have too much security, I always say."

"Yes, you're right, Pa. Can't have too much security," echoed Junior. "I guess if I were going in there, I'd feel better knowing the constables were watching over the generator."

"You are not going in?" Holmes asked.

"With a bunch of convicts? Not on your life."

"Nor you, Mr. Throckmorton Senior?"

"As it happens, we are constrained by another engagement in town. Our carriage driver is ready to take us there now."

Holmes nodded. "As you wish. I, for one, will go in and see the elevator and the central chamber, and I should like to do so before the prisoners enter the mine."

Holmes took Chief Constable Penn aside for a brief word. The little man nodded. We watched the Throckmortons depart in their carriage.

"Quickly, then," said Holmes.

We went to the entrance, where we were met by the foreman, Barret, who stood beside the controls to the lift.

"What did you say to the chief constable?" asked the foreman.

"I asked to have his men keep watch on the generator, and to immediately arrest anyone who tried to get near it," said Holmes. "Now I should like to go down in the lift immediately."

"Straight down the passageway," Barret said. He pointed to a passageway tunnel carved out of the rocks. "Let me know when you're ready."

Holmes nodded. "The three of you stay here. Do not let the prisoners follow me."

"I'm coming with you," I said.

"And I," said Jack.

"And I," said Sir Henry.

"I haven't time to argue," Holmes said. He set off into the tunnel.

Stubborn, I followed and stepped onto the platform behind him.

"Ready," Holmes called.

The sound of the hydraulic motor below us grew louder as Barret threw the switch. Just as the platform began its descent, Jack and Sir Henry got on as well.

We were moving downwards in a narrow shaft, just big enough to allow the platform to pass freely. Powerful electric lamps illuminated the sparkling ore-laden walls around us and below us. Soon, we had reached the bottom of the shaft, and those walls no longer blocked our view. Some fifty feet away in every direction, more walls glittered in the light of more electric lamps that ringed the edge of a great central chamber. The lamps cast jagged shadows below us around the rubble that nearly filled the void.

"Those rocks down there need to come out first," said Sir Henry. "The miners will break them up and take them out so they can get at the ore."

Holmes was not listening. He was kneeling on the edge of the platform. Without warning, he spun around and was soon over the edge, hanging on by his fingers. His long, lean frame cast an eerie shadow onto the ore-laden walls of the central chamber.

"I see it, Watson!" he cried.

Then he let go.

I knelt on the dusty wooden platform, craning my neck, looking downwards. Then I saw where he had landed and felt a surge of relief.

Holmes was crouching some twenty feet below the descending platform, just a few feet away from where the edge would soon come to rest, getting something out of his rucksack. Moments later, as we drew ever closer, he cried, "I have it!"

Then he was standing on the jagged rubble, triumphant, holding a bundle of dynamite sticks in one hand and a pair of cutting pliers in the other.

"I have cut the wire," he said. He called up, "Barret! Will you please reverse the lift? We wish to come up immediately!"

"Will do," came the answering call from the foreman.

The lift stopped, hung motionless for a long moment, then,

with a whine of the electric pump motor, started upwards just as Holmes clambered up onto the platform. Soon, we were within the narrow confines of the shaft. The walls seemed to move downwards around us as we moved slowly back towards the tunnel that would lead us out of the mine.

"Who would have planted that dynamite?" asked Sir Henry.

Holmes replied, "We will know when we reach the top. Then, if I am not very much mistaken, we shall also have our murderer."

We reached the edge of the tunnel floor and clambered over. I could see natural daylight at the end. But between us and the daylight were the silhouetted figures of men, hunched over and moving in our direction.

"Go back!" Holmes called to the two men. "Get outside now!"

Then came a flash of light and the roar of an explosion, and the grinding crash of rocks coming down amid a blinding, billowing cloud of dust.

There was a moment of silence.

Then we heard a man's shrill cry coming from within the chaos, a scream of fear and agony.

CHAPTER 5

On the drive from the train station, I had understood Uncle John's descriptions of the moor's wild, untamed magic. Now I could sympathize with the local superstitions and fears surrounding the place. The sun had nearly set as we drove towards the mine, and the moorland seemed filled with an almost sinister menace. Shadows pooled beneath the gnarled cairns and tors. Freezing cold gusts of wind tore at our carriage and rattled the branches of the few scrawny trees that clung to the granite-studded hills.

A road had been cut through in the last year so supplies could be transported both in and out of the mine, but the surface was still rough and uneven, setting the carriage to jolting and swaying, and the pace set by Sir Henry's sturdy pair of horses felt unbearably slow.

Becky and I were seated on one side of the carriage seats, with Beryl opposite. Her face was white and strained, and she winced every time the carriage jounced over a rut in the track, but she had refused categorically to be left behind. I couldn't argue with her; no force on Earth could have prevented my going out to the mine either. Hugo at least was too young to understand fully what had happened and was back at Baskerville Hall, being kept amused by the nursery maid.

I'd meant to leave Prince behind at the hall as well, but he'd howled as we set off and refused to be left. Now he sat on the carriage seat, with his nose halfway out the window and all the ruff of hair around his wrinkled neck raised and bristling.

Becky was pressed close against my side, her hands tightly locked together in her lap. She kept asking the same questions. "They can't be dead, can they? The miner who came running to tell Lady Baskerville would have said if anyone had been killed, wouldn't he? They'll be able to dig Jack and Mr. Holmes and Dr. Watson and Sir Henry out again?"

I would have given practically anything to be able to reassure her, but the workman who had come to give us the news had left directly after the tunnel's collapse and hadn't been able to give us many details. All I could say to Becky, over and over again, was, "I hope so. I don't know."

The trip seemed to last an eternity, but at last we came within sight of the two forty-foot high water wheels that were used for pumping water away from the underground tunnels. Becky and I scrambled out of the carriage, and the coachman came around to help Beryl alight more slowly.

My heart skipped a beat as I saw the entrance to the mine. What once had been a tunnel that led straight into the rocky hill and from there down underground was now a mound of rubble and splintered wood. The support beams and columns must have snapped like matchsticks when the earth and rock caved in.

Mr. Merwyn, who was looking white and shaken in the light of the lanterns that had been set all around, came to greet us, with his hands outstretched.

"Lady Baskerville, surely you ought not to be here. I would be happy to escort you back—"

"I'm perfectly well." Beryl's lips were pressed tightly together, but she waved aside Mr. Merwyn's offer.

"This is a terrible business—terrible!" Despite the cold, Mr. Merwyn mopped his forehead with a handkerchief.

Near the mine entrance stood a small stone building that housed machinery I assumed must be used in processing the tin hauled from the mine. A group of men were clustered around what I thought was an air-compressing engine, talking and gesticulating. Several of them, I noticed, were also casting uneasy glances off into the darkened moor that stretched beyond the circle cast by their lamplight.

Word of Sir Vincent's death must have reached them, and now they were all uneasily keeping watch for spectral hounds, although they probably wouldn't be willing to admit it out loud.

"I cannot think how such a dreadful accident can have occurred," Mr. Merwyn went on.

A sturdy-looking man in a tin miner's hat turned around. "I'll tell you one thing. It weren't no accident."

"This is Mr. Barret, our foreman," Mr. Merwyn said to me in an aside, then frowned at the other man. "But what do you mean that it was not an accident? Surely, a cave-in of this nature, while dreadful, cannot be other than—"

Mr. Barret interrupted, jabbing a dirt-stained finger for emphasis. "I've been working in mines these thirty years and more, both above ground and under. And my old dad was a miner before me. I know what I know, and this"—he waved at the mine entrance behind him—"was no accident. There was an explosion, just before the cave-in. Heard it with my own ears. I let two of the prisoners in, and one of them must have had a charge of dynamite with him. He must have set it off, trying to bring the whole tunnel crashing down." He cast a dark look at Mr. Merwyn. "This is what comes of hiring a lot of thieves and murderers to do honest men's jobs." He glanced belatedly at Beryl. "Begging your pardon, my lady."

"Oh, surely not … that is, we must not make assumptions… a dreadful business, to be sure, but once the facts are known—" Mr. Merwyn mopped his face again, looking decidedly nervous—as well he might, considering the idea to employ convicts had been championed by him.

At the moment, though, I cared less about who was responsible than about Jack, Holmes, and Uncle John, who were trapped somewhere beyond that wall of rock and dirt—and it was taking every ounce of my self-control to demand why no one was trying to dig them out yet.

"Does anyone know if the men trapped inside the tunnel are alive?"

Beryl stiffened. I held my breath. Becky was holding on to Prince's leash with one hand and clinging to me with the other, and I felt her fingers tighten around mine.

Mr. Barret shook his head. "We're trying to work out how to get a speaking tube past the cave-in so we can find out. But it's a tricky business. Shift something in that lot"—he nodded at the mountain of rubble—"and we risk triggering another collapse. Well, come on." He handed a shovel to Mr. Merwyn. "We can get started shifting the outer layer if we're careful."

If I'd been in the mood for humor, I would have found Mr. Merwyn's expression funny. He looked at the shovel as though Mr. Barret had just put a live and venomous snake into his hands. "But surely … that is, I don't know the first thing about—"

"We're short-handed, what with it being so near Christmas," Mr. Barret interrupted. "We'll need every pair of hands if we're going to stand a chance of mounting a rescue."

Still looking highly dubious, Mr. Merwyn followed Mr. Barret towards the collapsed tunnel entrance.

Beryl was white and shaking, her gaze fixed on the mound of rocky dirt and crushed wood. "Do you think … do you think Roger can have done this?" Her voice was a ragged whisper.

"I don't know. We'll have to find out whether any strangers have been seen around here today."

I couldn't make myself move to approach any of the men or start asking questions, though. My entire attention was fixed on the spot where Mr. Barret and his men were clearing a few of the smaller rocks from outside the collapsed tunnel. The progress seemed interminably slow, but one of the men working suddenly raised his head.

"I hear something! There's someone banging on one of the rocks inside."

An instant hush fell over the crowd. It was hard to hear above the drone of the engines and creak of the waterwheels, but straining, I could hear it, too: a rhythmic thumping coming from beyond the collapsed earth that blocked the mine entrance.

Jack? Holmes? Sir Henry? Any of them could be the one knocking. Or any of them could be already dead, crushed somewhere under that mountain of rock.

"Someone's alive in there, anyway!" Mr. Barret set down his own shovel and straightened. "Let's get that speaking tube through, lads! Easy does it."

My heart seemed to stand still all the time the men were working. Mr. Barret and the rest of his crew had to stop and start a dozen times, trying different spots, then giving up when they were blocked by solid rock. Finally, I heard one of the men shout, "We're through!"

They'd thrust the pipe through at an angle, starting up at around eye-level and angling downwards and into the mine.

Mr. Barret bent to put his mouth close and called out. "Hello! Hello, can you hear me?"

I heard Beryl draw in a sharp breath and murmur something that sounded like, *Please* under her breath.

There was another near-endless pause, then another voice, muffled and distorted by the metal, called back. "I can hear you."

Becky had been leaning up against me, but at that she jolted bolt upright. "That's Jack!"

It was. Even muffled, I knew his voice, and the cold, clenched knot inside me relaxed at least a tiny fraction. Prince's ears pricked up, and he gave a high, anxious whine. Becky was already flying towards the mine tunnel entrance, shouting.

"Jack! Jack!"

"Careful." I caught hold of her hand before she could get too close to the rock pile. "We don't want to cause any more cave-ins."

The three of us, Beryl, Becky, and I, approached more slowly, just as Mr. Barret asked through the tube, "How are the others in there?"

I heard Jack cough, then answer, "Sir Henry's arm got hit by a falling rock. Dr. Watson thinks it's only a sprain, but it might be broken. And Mr. Holmes took a nasty blow to the head that knocked him out. Two of the prisoners got the worst of it. One of them has a broken leg, and the other still hasn't woken up.

But they're both alive."

I exhaled a long, slow breath. Beryl pressed her eyes shut a moment, swaying.

"Can we talk to him?" I asked Mr. Barret. "That's my husband, and Becky's brother."

Mr. Barret hesitated, then stepped aside. "Only for a minute, mind. I'll need him to tell me everything he can about how things stand in there so we can decide how best to dig them out."

"Jack!" Becky stood up on tip-toe so she could better reach the end of the pipe. "Jack, are you really all right?"

"I'm all right, Beck. Just a bit dusty, that's all."

I strained to listen, trying to decide from his tone of voice whether Jack was telling the truth. He wouldn't tell Becky if he'd been hurt by the falling rocks, too.

"Is Lucy out there with you?"

"I'm here." I bent closer to the pipe.

Jack coughed again. "Hello there, Trouble."

I swallowed hard, waiting until I could trust my voice. "You're the one who's trapped in a collapsed mining tunnel, and *I'm* trouble? Where are Uncle John and my father? Are they there with you?"

"They're back a ways further into the tunnel. This part I'm in's too narrow after the cave-in for anyone to stand up in. You can only crawl, so I volunteered to get as far towards the entrance as I could to try and let everyone on the outside know we're here."

Jack had volunteered. Of course he had. And right now he was probably lying flat in some small crevice formed by the fallen rocks and wooden beams. With thousands of tons more rock and earth above him, just waiting to bury him in an instant if there was another collapse.

Mr. Barret stepped forwards. "I'll need you to move back when we're done here, and move everyone else as far back as you possibly can away from the entrance. We'll try to dig our way through, but we may need to blast if that doesn't work."

"All right, will do," Jack said. "And Lucy?"

"I'm still here."

Jack coughed again. The quality of the air in there had to be terrible. "Be careful, all right?"

I blinked a hot prickle away from my eyes. "Again, I think you're confused as to which one of us is in greater danger right now."

"I know you. You're going to find out who's responsible for this." Jack's muffled voice came through the pipe. "So just be careful."

"I will be."

"Since I can't see you, I can't tell—did you have a hard time keeping a straight face while you said that?"

I hiccupped an uneven laugh. "You take care, too. Tell my father and Uncle John we'll see them soon. And tell Sir Henry that Beryl is all right." I would like to have said so much more. Actually, I would have been glad for any excuse just to keep talking so I could hear Jack's voice. But Mr. Barret was clearing his throat with obvious impatience beside me, and even without any knowledge of mining, I could see time was our enemy just now.

Becky stood on tiptoe again. "I love you, Jack! Don't forget you promised to take me for a toboggan ride sometime while we're visiting down here!"

"How could I forget that? I love you, too, Beck."

Becky almost never cried, but I could see her lip trembling as we both turned away and let Mr. Barret take our place. I put an arm around her.

"Sir Henry is alive, too," I told Beryl. "You heard that?"

Beryl nodded. "But he's hurt—"

"Dr. Watson will take care of him!" Becky said. "Don't worry, he's a very good doctor."

Mr. Merwyn had been hanging back, but now he came forward to meet us, looking grave. He opened his mouth. He probably meant well, but if he commented on what a dreadful business this was one more time, I was going to scream.

"How long do you think it will take them to dig through the caved-in area?" I asked.

Mr. Merwyn shook his head. "I am hardly an expert, you understand. But I should say several hours, at least. There have been other cases where similar accidents have occurred and it has taken days for the rescue efforts to dig their way through to the men trapped inside, and by that time—" He cut off abruptly, with a suddenly conscious glance at Becky. "That is, I'm sure it will all turn out quite all right in the end."

Again, he was plainly trying, but his false heartiness wouldn't have convinced a two-year-old. Becky glared at him. In the ordinary way, she wasn't rude to well-meaning strangers, but now she wiped her eyes and snapped, "I'm *ten*, not a moron! Those machines"—she gestured to the air-compressing engines—"are supposed to keep fresh air coming into the mine. And those"— she pointed to the water wheels—"keep the mine tunnels from flooding. And if anything goes wrong with them—if anything gets damaged while they're trying to dig and blast their way in—then everyone inside there now could suffocate or drown."

"I … well …" Mr. Merwyn looked discomfited, but he obviously couldn't deny the truth of Becky's words. "Mr. Barret is a first-rate foreman. I'm certain he'll be doing his very best to ensure they all get out safely."

Beryl swayed suddenly and might have fallen if I hadn't caught hold of her arm.

"I'm sorry," she murmured. She rubbed her forehead. "I'm not going to faint. It's just—"

"You must take care, Lady Baskerville." Mr. Merwyn gave her an anxious glance. "If you like, I would be happy to escort you back home. I have my own carriage—"

"No, that's quite all right." Beryl straightened. "We have our own carriage, too, and Mr. Barret said they had need of every able pair of hands. I think—" She put a hand on her middle. "That is, I think I had better return home, but Lucy and Becky, if you'd like to stay—"

Becky answered before I could decide exactly what I wanted. "No, it's all right. We'll come back to Baskerville Hall with you."

I thought Mr. Merwyn looked rather disappointed not to have an excuse to leave the digging efforts. But he tipped his hat and turned back towards the mine.

The coachman helped Beryl climb back inside the carriage, but I hung back a moment to ask Becky, "Is this really what you want?"

I would have been willing to wager a significant amount of money that wild horses wouldn't be able to draw Becky away from the mine until Jack and the others were safely rescued.

Becky's lip trembled again as she shook her head. "No. But Jack is right. You're going to find out who was responsible for this, aren't you?"

"I don't know."

If Mr. Barret was right and an explosion had triggered the cave-in, I doubted one of the prisoners had set it off in the tunnel and somehow failed to get away in time. The most likely scenario was that some other culprit had lit a slow-burning fuse or rigged up a wire detonator, then left to establish an alibi somewhere far away from the mine.

Especially if that culprit was indeed Stapleton.

There was patently nothing at all we could do here to help with the rescue effort either. But every part of me still wanted to be here, just so we would be able to find out the second there was any news. Staying, though, would only offer whomever had done this a greater opportunity to get clean away or destroy any evidence of his or her crime.

"Do you have any ideas?" Becky asked.

"I'm not sure." What I had was less an idea than a single investigative thread on which I could try pulling to see what happened. Better than nothing, but in no way guaranteed to yield definite results. "There's one person I could try speaking to, though."

"I'll stay at Baskerville Hall with Hugo and Beryl if you want me to," Becky said in a small voice.

I blinked, then pretended to cup a hand around my ear as though I hadn't heard properly. "I'm sorry, but did you just offer to stay *out* of an investigation?"

Becky gave me a very small smile, though it was a wan effort. "Only because it's almost Christmas. Besides, Hugo is so little, and he must be afraid about his father. Maybe I can help Beryl cheer him up and take his mind off things."

"I'm sure she'll be glad of it."

"All right, then. Come, Prince."

Becky tugged on Prince's lead, trying to urge him into the carriage. But the big dog planted his paws in the ground and refused to budge.

"Prince, *come*."

She tugged again. Prince put his ears back and growled deep in his throat. Becky's mouth dropped open.

"He's never done that before."

He hadn't. Prince was nearly as big as the spectral hound Uncle John and Holmes had encountered, and he was a champion guard dog, perfectly capable of terrifying anyone he considered a threat. But with Becky, he was as gentle as a mother sheep.

"He must not want to leave Jack and the others," I said. I blinked hard. I was going to start crying, too, if I didn't stop myself, and that would accomplish exactly nothing. "All right, we may as well let him stay. I can speak to Mr. Barret and see if he'll allow it."

Mr. Barret was busy organizing the distribution of picks and shovels when I approached him again, but he made no objection to Prince's staying behind.

"To tell the truth, it might not be a bad thing to have a guard dog about the place tonight." He gave a quick glance out at the jagged tors and boulders of the moor. "It'll make the lads feel less uneasy-like."

"Do you believe in the stories about the hound?" I asked.

Mr. Barret flattened his lips into a grim line and shifted the tin hat further back on his brow. "I believe there's evil in the world; whether it comes from man or beast, I don't know. But something killed Sir Vincent Percival and his coach driver, there's no getting away from it."

"And you think the collapse of the mine tunnel is connected to his death somehow?"

I was already certain in my own mind the two had to be linked, but I wanted to see what Mr. Barret would say.

"Stands to reason. Maybe one of them prisoners Sir Vincent and Mr. Merwyn are so keen on giving second chances to didn't appreciate the idea. But I'll tell you something else, there's a bad feeling in the air tonight, and if you want to leave that dog of yours here to guard against man or beast, I won't argue."

I fought against a shiver and nodded. "Thank you. And you'll send word on to Baskerville Hall if there's any news?"

"We will. Soon as there's anything to report." Mr. Barret stumped away, with Prince—seemingly content now—trotting at his heels.

I let out a breath. In an odd, illogical way, Prince remaining made me a tiny fraction less torn about leaving, as though he could actually keep watch and guard against any fresh disasters.

I looked up at the clock mounted on the wall of the miner's rest house. It felt as though it ought to be nearing midnight, but it was in fact just barely six-thirty in the evening.

Now I just had to drop off Becky and Beryl at the hall. Then I had a call to pay in Coombe Tracey. I urgently needed to speak with Stapleton's former mistress, Mrs. Laura Lyons.

CHAPTER 6

Holmes's face was smudged with dust, his clothing filthy and rumpled in the light of our single lantern. But he straightened as Jack crawled out of the narrow crevice that had allowed him to approach the mine's entrance.

"You succeeded in establishing contact?" Holmes asked.

"I did." Jack wiped the dust and grit away from his own eyes. "Spoke to Lucy and Becky, too." He glanced at Sir Henry, who was sitting propped up against the tunnel's rock-cut wall, holding his injured arm. "They say that Lady Baskerville's all right."

I saw the quick flash of relief, followed by pain, cross Sir Henry's features and knew he would have liked to ask Jack more questions about his wife and family. But Holmes said, "And you gave them the report on our condition, as I instructed?"

Jack nodded. "Told them that you'd been struck unconscious and two of the prisoners were injured as well."

The last was true enough. I had examined one of the men—the prisoner who had struck one of his fellows, as it happened—and determined his tibia was very likely fractured. And another prisoner, an older man, was indeed still unconscious.

"But why—" I began to ask Holmes.

He was contemplating the other members of our group, a line between his brows, but Jack answered in an undertone. "If whoever did this thinks Holmes is unconscious, maybe dying, and some of the prisoners are in bad shape as well, they're less likely to try collapsing the mine again before we can get out of here."

I suppressed a shudder, thinking of the tons of rock and earth all around us. The air felt unpleasantly close and oppressive, and the lantern cast leaping, sinister shadows on the tunnel walls that brought to mind illustrations from Dante's *Inferno*.

"You think this was a deliberate attempt at murder, then?"

"I'd wager that's what *he* thinks." Jack nodded towards Holmes.

Holmes approached the prisoner with the injured leg.

"Your name?"

The man cast a baleful eye on him. "Why should I tell you that?"

Holmes's eyebrows rose a fraction. "You have some other more congenial way of passing the time? Come now, we are all in the same position of being trapped here until a rescue operation can be mounted from outside. I might also point out that those shackles"— he pointed to the chains that still linked the prisoner to the man beside him—"will make it exceedingly difficult for you to maneuver down the tunnel to a more secure location without our assistance, if further blasting with dynamite is required to clear our route to the outside. You might as well tell us what we wish to know."

The man still looked surly but finally grunted, "Owen."

"I see, Mr. Owen. And can you think of anyone who might hold a grudge against you? Anyone who might profit from your demise?"

Owen's face split into an unpleasant leer. "Well, some of me old mates back in London would have good reason for wanting me out of the way. Seeing as how I did them out of their share of our last robbery haul."

"What about in this part of the country? Is there anyone on Dartmoor who might wish you an injury?" Holmes asked.

The prisoner stared, then shook his head. "Nah, how could there be? Only got transferred here a month ago and haven't set foot outside of the prison in all that time."

"I see. Thank you."

Holmes turned to the next shackled man in line, then on to the next after him, always asking the same questions and receiving similar answers. None of the prisoners had any connections to Dartmoor.

At last he came to the last man, the one who had been struck by his fellow prisoner outside the mine, and then knocked unconscious by a falling rock. He was an older man, with a hunched, wizened frame. He lay sprawled on the tunnel floor now, his breathing heavy, but the fluttering of his eyelids suggested he might soon be regaining consciousness.

Holmes frowned over him for a long moment, and I could, I thought, follow at least some of his thought process. If any of the prisoners were, so to speak, the odd man out, it was this one. Older than the rest by at least twenty years, and with patently little to offer in the way of physical strength, there seemed no obvious reason he should have been selected for work in the mine—which made it likely there was another, hidden meaning behind his presence here.

"Who can tell me the name of this man?" Holmes asked.

The other prisoners exchanged glances, then Owen, who

seemed to have elected himself something of the group's spokesman, said, "That's Martin Legrande. Nasty, arrogant old weasel."

"Picks fights, does he?" Jack asked.

"Only when the guard's looking. Be a right shame if he died down here." Owen eyed the unconscious prisoner with a smirk that belied his words. "Only got another month left to serve on his sentence, and then he'd be a free man."

Holmes's expression didn't precisely change, but I had known him for too long to miss the kindling of interest at the back of his gaze.

He turned to me. "Watson, if there is anything you can do to assist Mr. Legrande in recovering consciousness, would you please do so without delay. As for the rest of you," he turned back to Owen and the others, "I shall speak to the prison warden on your behalf in exchange for any information you can give me about Martin Legrande and the reasons for his imprisonment."

LUCY

CHAPTER 7

Uncle John had spoken of Laura Lyons as a woman of remarkable beauty, and I could still see the traces of it in her face. But the ten years since my father's first investigation here hadn't been kind to her. She was now somewhere around forty, and her features had coarsened with age. Her hazel eyes were faintly bloodshot and surrounded by deep pockets of loose skin, and though she had fairly plastered her face with both rouge and powder, it wasn't enough to conceal the network of broken veins across her nose and cheeks.

Laura Lyons was a secret drinker, unless I was very much mistaken.

She was still studying the card I had sent up with the maid when I was shown into her sitting room.

"So you are Sherlock Holmes's daughter."

"I am." I had written as much on the card.

She eyed me with slightly raised eyebrows. "You do realize that your relationship is hardly a reason for me to agree to an interview, given my cause for disliking Mr. Holmes."

Perhaps not, but it was a reason for Mrs. Lyons to be intensely curious about me, which was what I had been aiming for. I'd been afraid she would refuse to see me unless I gave her good reason to want to know why I'd come.

I could also argue that Mrs. Lyons ought to be grateful to Holmes, since by exposing Stapleton as a would-be murderer, he'd saved her from suffering a similar fate as Beryl had at the man's hands. But it wouldn't do any good. In addition to the signs of drink in her face, Laura Lyons had the perpetually discontented look of someone who has a grudge against the entire world for failing to meet up with her demands for happiness. Her troubles would always be someone else's fault and never of her own making.

"Have you been sending hateful anonymous letters to Lady Baskerville?"

I'd also decided at first glance that Laura Lyons wasn't the sort of suspect who could be cajoled into talking with false sympathy and friendliness, and my best chance was to shock her into telling the truth. Which was fortunate, because at the moment my supply of false sympathy and patience was at an approximately zero level.

Mrs. Lyons's hand flew to cover her mouth. "What are you talking about?"

"The words only have the one meaning of which I'm aware. Have you at any time in the past eight years sent Lady Baskerville nasty anonymous letters?"

Mrs. Lyons drew herself up, her expression one of outrage. "Certainly not! How dare you suggest—"

"You're lying." I cut her off; I was in no mood to listen to a long tirade about her injured innocence either.

"What?"

"Again, the words are prone to only one interpretation. You covered your mouth just now, when I asked you whether you'd written anonymously to Lady Baskerville. It's a curious thing, but when people are shocked, they might put a hand to their throat or their heart. But when they're about to lie, they'll frequently cover their mouths—as though they're trying to physically stop a truthful answer from coming out."

"I—I—" Mrs. Lyons stared at me, her mouth opening and closing without any sound coming out.

"Also, you used your own typewriter to type out the addresses on some of them." I gestured to the Remington machine that sat covered in one corner of the room. "Typewriter characteristics are as distinctive as fingerprints."

Which was true, and if Beryl hadn't destroyed the typewritten letters, I might have been able to identify them as having come from Mrs. Lyons's machine. But I doubted she had the presence of mind to demand proof of my accusations. Her eyes were darting from side to side, as though looking for an escape route, and her skin had flushed to an unhealthy mottled red.

"I … very well, I admit it," she finally said. "Writing a few letters isn't a crime. And I only wrote them because she'd refused to help me in any way, even after her marriage to Sir Charles! As rich as he is, you would think that she would have felt duty-bound to give me something! A few hundred pounds a year that she never would have missed, that was all I was asking for. But if you can credit it, she refused categorically to allow me a single penny."

"Yes, it's hard to believe how she could possibly fail to feel duty-bound to assist her abusive former husband's mistress, who, incidentally, was willing to aid and abet him in the attempted murder of her current husband."

Mrs. Lyons blinked at me, sullen resentment in her gaze, then lurched to her feet and turned to a cut-class decanter that stood on the mantle. She sloshed some of what looked like brandy into a glass, downed it in a single gulp, then turned back to me.

"Why have you come? You can't tell me that the great Sherlock Holmes is concerned with a few letters. I didn't even break any laws!"

That point was debatable, but I ignored it and said, "I want to know whether the man you knew as Stapleton survived the affair of the Baskerville Hound and has now come back to Dartmoor."

"*What*?" Mrs. Lyons's eyes went wide, and this time, oddly enough, her hand did come up to rest over her heart. But I wouldn't even have needed that gesture to be sure that her surprise was genuine. Either Laura Lyons was a first-rate actress, or else this was the first she had heard it so much as suggested that Stapleton might be still alive.

"Have you written any letters to Lady Baskerville lately?" I asked.

"I … no. None in … months. Or perhaps even the last year." Mrs. Lyons looked dazed. She shook her head. "Do you really mean to say that Mr. Stapleton might be alive? Who says so? Has he been seen?" I thought there might be an edge of fear in her voice, as well as shock.

"Do you have letters from him?"

"None since years ago, when he went missing."

"May I see those?"

She stood, hesitated and then pulled open the lower right drawer of her writing desk. She reached into the back of the drawer. She pulled out the drawer entirely.

"Empty. It is just as well, for I am ashamed to have kept them."

"Who could have taken them?"

She shook her head in bewilderment. "I had them out late one night not long ago." She glanced at the decanter on the mantel and then continued, "I was alone, and weak. They were memories of a happier time."

"You're certain that you've not tried to communicate with Lady Baskerville in the last few months?"

"No!" Mrs. Lyons's face turned resentful once again. "Not that you'll believe me, but scarcely anyone wants anything typed at all around Christmas time. I've barely even touched my typewriter." She cast a dissatisfied glance at the covered Remington. "The only business I've had in the past two weeks was from Mr. Merwyn. He asked me to type up some contracts to sell his shares of stock in the Grimpen Mine, and to buy option contracts with the proceeds."

My heart sank, because I did in fact believe her. From the moment Beryl had mentioned anonymous letters, I'd marked out Laura Lyons as the most likely author of them. But I honestly didn't believe that she'd had anything to do with the most recent ones claiming to be from Stapleton, which left me no nearer to—

I stopped short in that line of thought, frowning. "Mr. Merwyn wanted to sell his stock shares? Why would he have done that?"

"I don't know." Her voice turned sullen. "He didn't confide his business plans to me; just asked me to type up the sale contracts and the others. 'Put options' were what those were called. He'd probably be shocked to find out that I was capable of understanding anything of what I typed."

"I need to go." I stood abruptly. "Thank you for your time, Mrs. Lyons."

I didn't wait for her to answer. A theory was taking shape in my mind. The details were still hazy, but one fact was terrifyingly clear: I needed to return to the mine without delay.

CHAPTER 8

Never had words been more welcome than that December evening in the Grimpen Mine, when I heard Holmes's voice in that cold, hard tunnel.

"Watson! Sir Henry! The men outside have cleared a passage."

A full moon shone above the snow on the surrounding hills, and we could glimpse it as we clambered over the rocks and timbers that still clogged the base of the tunnel. The silver light seemed to beckon us. Finally, we emerged into freedom and safety.

I was supporting Sir Henry, whose painfully injured arm hung in the sling I had improvised. Just ahead of me was Jack, and leading our procession was Holmes.

I saw Barret, the mining foreman, coming to greet us. Holmes took his proffered hand, though with a distracted air, scanning the surrounding area.

"Those prisoners just pushed past me," Barret said. "I was looking the other way, watching for you, and I didn't see—"

"It's not your fault," said Holmes. "Where is Merwyn?"

"Why—around somewhere."

Then Prince, the Kellys' big mastiff, bounded up, brushing

past Holmes, his big floppy jowls panting and quivering with delight as he leaped up on Jack.

"Here now, Prince," Jack said, though his tone betrayed his relief and happiness. "Down, sir. Down!"

Holmes watched the two of them for a moment, then crouched down, opened his rucksack, and took out something. "Jack," he said. "I believe Prince can help us."

Jack crouched down beside Holmes, holding Prince's collar with one hand. With the other, he placed the object Holmes had given him beneath the dog's quivering muzzle. The great animal gave little cries of anticipation.

Jack then spoke, low and firm, into the big dog's ear. "Prince. Now! You catch him, sir! Now … catch him!"

At a gesture from Holmes, Barret bade the other men move away as Prince raised his huge head and sniffed the air.

"Give him room, lads," the foreman said.

Prince took a few steps away from the entrance, then towards the far side, and then he stopped, motionless, for a long moment. Then with a great baying cry, rearing up in the air on his hind legs like a proud stallion, he bounded forwards. Had I not known it was from Prince, that cry would have struck fear into my heart. Upon hearing it, the other men backed away, watching in awe as the big mastiff bounded off, down the path, past where the prisoners' omnibus had been and heading straight towards the chief constable's carriage.

I saw a shadow moving behind the carriage, then suddenly a man's figure emerged, carrying something in one hand, and scurried like a rat across the pathway. With a mighty leap, the great dog crashed down upon the running man and bore him to the ground.

"Help!" came the cry. "Help!"

I recognized Merwyn's voice.

* * *

A few moments later, we were clustered around a bedraggled Mr. Merwyn, on his hands and knees, cowering behind the growling Prince. The solicitor's clothes were torn, his face was smeared with mud, and his spectacles were nowhere to be found, but he was otherwise unhurt. He squinted at us in the light of our torches.

"Get this hellish creature away from me," he said.

Jack made a gesture with the flat of his hand. Prince immediately trotted to Jack's side and sat, looking up at Jack with adoration as Jack rubbed his ears.

"Mr. Merwyn, you are under arrest," said Chief Inspector Penn, hauling the solicitor to his feet.

Merwyn stood, defiant. "On what charge?"

Penn nodded towards Holmes, who came forward.

"For the murder of Sir Vincent Percival, the murder of his driver, Mr. John Hornsby, and for the murder of the prisoner Martin Legrande."

"Who?"

"Your uncle. He died in the explosion which you caused here at the mine."

An odd look, perhaps even a momentary smile, passed over Merwyn's face. "I deny the allegations. You have no evidence."

Holmes produced a calfskin boot from his rucksack. "There is abundant evidence. To begin with, this is your boot. Your initials are in the lining. Our dog tracked you here, following the scent."

"Why are you showing me my own boot? And where did you get it?"

"It was in a dustbin behind the offices of Percival and Merwyn. There is blood on it. Likely the blood is Sir Vincent's or Mr. Hornsby's, or both."

"I deny any connection. I was in the hospital unconscious in my bed the entire night that those two unfortunate gentlemen were killed."

"We will pass over that issue for the moment and examine your briefcase."

Holmes unbuckled the flap and lifted out a shiny metallic box, from which protruded a metal tube with a wooden handle.

"This is a detonator," Holmes said. "You used it to set off the charge in the tunnel. You did so the moment you saw the prisoners had entered and were far enough inside to be trapped. You would have set off another charge using a wire near the generator, only the generator was guarded by the Chief Constable's men."

"I deny that as well. I merely picked up this metal thing, whatever it is. Someone had left it behind the Chief Constable's carriage. I was going to return it."

From his rucksack, Holmes produced a red knit hat and matching scarf. "These were also in the dustbin, along with the bloodstained mate to that boot."

"If they were, someone else put them there."

"Chief Constable was with me when I found them. You wore them to impersonate John Hornsby, after you had followed Sir Vincent's carriage on your bicycle on the way to Baskerville Hall. You climbed up onto Sir Vincent's carriage when it slowed to make the turn from the main pathway. You struck Mr. Hornsby from behind with a hammer and pushed him from his driver's seat, leaving him dead on the ground." He turned to Sir Henry. "That was the disturbance on the carriage ride to Baskerville Hall that Sir Vincent mentioned to you, Sir Henry."

"By God, it must have been!" said Sir Henry.

"You remained outside during the interview," Holmes continued, addressing Merwyn, "muffled with the red scarf and hat to keep from being recognized. When the interview had concluded, you drove Sir Vincent far enough from the hall to be sure no one was watching. You stopped the coach and lured him out on some pretext or other. You struck him from behind with the same hammer with which you had killed Hornsby. Then you desecrated Sir Vincent's body with a garden rake, in order to awaken the legend of the Baskerville Hound among the local citizens and cloud any official inquiry with superstitious fears. You left his body unattended and returned to where you had left the body of Hornsby, where you used the same garden rake to commit the same atrocity on him. You then left the horse to wander, still with its carriage, into Coombe Tracey. You yourself rode back on your bicycle to your office and disposed of the bloodied boots, hat, and scarf, into a canvas sack in the office dustbin, which you expected would soon be emptied of its incriminating evidence. It would have been, had the Chief Constable and I not gone to your office last night and discovered it. You then cycled to the Coombe Tracey Hospital, where you returned the rake and the hammer to where you had found them in the tool shed. Chief Constable Penn and I found them there last night, and we noted they had been wiped cleaner than the other tools."

"Which proves nothing."

"You then climbed back into the ground floor window of the patients' ward, removed the pillows you had used to give the illusion that you were sleeping in your bed in a drugged state, took off your outer garments and hid them beneath one of the other beds, and crawled beneath the blanket, believing yourself to have successfully committed two separate and undetected murders. The next morning, when you awoke to find that snow had fallen and covered your tracks, you likely felt even more certain that you would not be caught."

Merwyn sneered. "Anyone could have stolen a pair of my boots, and planted them with those articles of clothing in our office dustbin."

"True," said Holmes. "Which is why Chief Commissioner Penn did not arrest you this morning. We needed more evidence, evidence that specifically and incontrovertibly incriminated you. And now we do have more."

"Are you referring to that metal thing in my briefcase? I told you, I found it and picked it up, and you cannot prove otherwise."

Holmes ignored him. "First, there is the matter of the dead plant in the hospital ward, where you disposed of the draught of laudanum that you pretended to take."

"Many plants die indoors."

"Not overnight. And the soil around the base of the plant can be tested for opium or alcohol. There is also the evidence of your quarrel with your senior partner, Sir Vincent. He kept a journal, which I obtained when I visited your office last night. In it he recorded his recent meeting with a stockbroker, one of the firm's clients, and noted that he would have to take action with 'M.' That initial stands for 'Merwyn.'"

"A thousand other names begin with that letter."

From behind us came the clear, firm voice of Lucy James. "But a witness will testify that it was you," she said, then continued. "Begging your pardon, gentlemen. I couldn't help overhearing. I have just come from speaking with Mrs. Laura Lyons."

"What could she possibly know?" Merwyn asked.

"For one thing, you stole letters from her that Stapleton had written years ago. You used them to imitate Stapleton's writing and send threatening letters to Lady Baskerville. You hoped to terrify both her and Sir Henry—perhaps enough that they would withdraw their support of the mine and leave the area."

"Lies!" Merwyn licked his dry lips.

"Mrs. Lyons also typed contracts for you to sell your shares in the Grimpen Mine Company and buy put-options with the proceeds. If the mine had collapsed, you would have made an enormous profit. And if Sir Vincent knew about your dealings with the stockbroker, he was sure to realize the truth and expose you. So he had to die, along with the man who had the misfortune to be his driver."

Merwyn set his jaw in defiance. "More lies. And I was in the hospital!"

"Not while you were killing those two men."

Holmes said, "Thank you, Lucy, for this very helpful information."

He gave a nod to Jack, who moved away to the edge of the little crowd that had assembled. I noticed that both Throckmortons had returned. They appeared fascinated by the drama unfolding before us.

Holmes then turned back to Merwyn.

"But making a profit was not your true motivation to cause

damage to the mine," he said.

"So, having failed to produce any incontrovertible evidence, you now claim to be a mind-reader, Mr. Holmes?" asked Merwyn.

Holmes ignored him. "Your true motivation was to kill your uncle, the convict calling himself Martin Legrande."

"I have no uncle."

"He was due to be released next month and had learned of your association with the Second Chance Society. He had some incriminating information about your past that you could not afford to see made public, and he would have done just that when released, unless you paid him. Which you understandably did not wish to do. Satisfying a blackmailer can be a never-ending business."

"Preposterous. Slanderous. Unsubstantiated and unprovable."

"The list of prisoners being considered for the Second Chance program was in your desk drawer. With ink from your desk pen, you had marked those who had been selected. One of the names, of course, was Martin Legrande. I saw you smile earlier, when I told you that he was dead."

"You said I was arrested for his murder. I smiled only at the preposterous nature of the charge."

"I am inclined to agree with you on that point," said Holmes. "And there is another here who shares that opinion."

Then came another voice, venomous in its tone. "Because I, dear Merwyn, am *not* dead."

The words were from a gaunt, shrunken man, hunched and decrepit, dressed in a prisoner's uniform and sweater. I had watched over him in the tunnel, doing what I could to keep him comfortable and stable until he regained consciousness. Now he stood beside Jack, leaning on him for support.

"Gentlemen and Lucy," said Jack, "let me introduce you to Martin Legrande, soon to be released from Dartmoor Prison."

Merwyn's eyes bulged with horror, then fear, and then rage.

Holmes continued, his voice silken. "I thought you might be less cautious in your responses if you thought that the most important part of your plan had succeeded. Your uncle had some extremely interesting things to say about you when we were together in the tunnel after the explosion."

"And knowing how you tried to bury me alive in that cursed tunnel, nephew," said the hunched, shrunken figure, "I shall soon take pleasure in telling all the world the true nature of your character."

Merwyn lunged forwards, clawing out with curved fingers in a blind, senseless fury. But before he could reach his uncle, Jack stepped forward. His fist caught Merwyn in mid-stride, landing squarely on the point of the murderer's jaw.

Merwyn's legs buckled. He landed, face downward, crying out in pain as his head struck the cold, hard ground.

The two Throckmortons stepped forward, watching Chief Constable Penn handcuff the prostrate solicitor. "You caught a snake, Mr. Holmes," said Throckmorton Senior, shaking his head in wonderment. "We had no idea. We owe you."

"Goes for me as well," said Throckmorton Junior.

Wordlessly, Holmes reached into his rucksack and handed him the bundled sticks of dynamite, still with a short length of bright copper wire attached. "These were at the base of the elevator," he said. "I cut the wire that Merwyn would have used."

"Name your fee," said Throckmorton Senior.

Holmes nodded, giving one of his flickering smiles. "My fee requirements are quite modest. I require only two things."

"Which are?"

"First, that you give Mrs. Laura Lyons an opportunity to perform typing and other secretarial work at your offices."

"Done," said Throckmorton Senior.

"And, second, that you add an annual celebratory bonus to the wages of the men who work for you here at the Grimpen Mine, to commemorate today's fortunate outcome. Ten percent, I believe, would be appropriate. A tithe comports well with the spirit of the season."

* * *

Approaching from our carriage, we could see the great silhouette of Baskerville Hall, still commanding a lonely eminence atop the hill on which workmen from generations past had raised it up centuries ago. But the great stone mansion no longer appeared ominous or foreboding. Its dark and mighty façade was now transformed. Golden illumination from every one of its windows shone brilliantly into the night, as if a palace ball were taking place within. Seated across from Holmes and me, Sir Henry, Lucy, and Jack were also looking outward, eyes shining, as our carriage drove into the circular drive and came alongside the grand spectacle.

"Something good has happened," Lucy said.

"They know we are safe," said Sir Henry. "I sent word from the mine."

The moment our carriage stopped, Jarvis the butler strode down from the portico and was soon alongside, offering dignified assistance as each of us stepped down onto the freshly-swept gravel.

"Plenty of lights, Jarvis," Sir Henry observed. "Are we celebrating Christmas Eve?"

Jarvis had no time to make a reply, for at that moment a small figure dashed towards us from the portico and leaped into Sir Henry's arms.

"Daddy! Daddy!" little Hugo cried. "Father Christmas came early! He brought me a baby brother!"

Beside me, Holmes stood quietly for a long moment, taking in the scene. Then he gave my shoulder a brief pat. We turned and followed Lucy and Jack into the brightly illuminated entryway.

LUCY

CHAPTER 9

"Lucy! Jack!"

I felt as though I had barely closed my eyes before Becky's excited voice awakened me. She was standing in the doorway to our bedroom, still in her nightgown, with her uncombed blonde hair standing out in a halo all around her head that made her look like an extremely untidy angel.

"It's Christmas! It's Christmas morning!"

Beside me, Jack opened one eye. "I think for it to qualify as morning, it has to have stopped being dark outside."

I didn't know what time it was, but not even a small chink of light was filtering around the edges of the bedroom curtains.

Becky ignored that, bouncing on her tiptoes with excitement. "Hugo's baby brother has come, and now we're going downstairs to see what else Father Christmas has brought!"

Remembrance struck me. "Becky—"

But she was gone before I could finish; I heard her clattering down the stairs with Hugo.

Jack and I looked at each other. "Maybe Father Christmas got held up by bad weather?" I suggested.

Between the rescue operation at the mine and the birth of the baby—not to mention Mr. Merwyn's arrest—I hadn't even had time to wrap up the book on anatomy for Becky.

"Or else he didn't have room in his sleigh for anything but Hugo's baby brother on the first trip, so he'll bring gifts on the second round," Jack said.

But Becky was already thundering up the stairs again, this time with Prince on her heels; I could hear his short, happy barks.

"You'll never guess! You'll never guess!" Becky burst through our doorway again, her cheeks flushed and her small frame almost vibrating with eagerness.

Jack sat up. "Since we'll never guess, I suppose you'd better tell us."

"Father Christmas came! There are piles of presents under the Christmas tree! *And ...*" Becky paused dramatically. "Hugo and I *saw* him! He wasn't going up the chimney—I always thought that part of the story was silly, why would he use the chimney when he could just come in through the door? But we saw him through the window; he must have just gone out onto the terrace when we came down. I saw his red velvet suit and his white beard and *everything*! He put his finger to his lips just like this—" Becky demonstrated, "—and then he went 'round the side of the house and disappeared! Now come downstairs!" She was already tugging on both Jack's and my hands. "So we can all open the presents and see what he's brought!"

* * *

A short while later—although not nearly short enough to suit Becky—we were all up and dressed and sitting in the drawing room. Beryl was still upstairs in bed with the new baby, but Sir Henry was there, with his injured arm propped up on cushions. Uncle John dozed in a chair by the fire, while Becky and Hugo disappeared under piles of torn wrapping paper.

"I've got the fingerprint kit!" Becky called out. "*And* the skeleton key, and the lockpicks and rubber cosh! I never even got the chance to mail my list, but Father Christmas knew exactly what to bring all the same!"

Holmes had lit his pipe and sat smoking in one corner, looking on with half-lidded eyes. Anyone might have thought he was mildly bored by the proceedings.

I sat down beside him, while Becky plunged into a demonstration for Jack of how the new fingerprinting brushes and powders worked.

"You've a trace of spirit gum left on your chin," I murmured.

"Ah." Holmes's hand came up to rub his jaw.

And somewhere in his luggage, I would no doubt find a red velvet suit as well, which he had procured and brought down to Dartmoor in expectation of just such a sequence of events as had occurred this morning. Nothing about Sherlock Holmes should have surprised me anymore, but I had to ask.

"I give up. How did you know what to buy for Becky ahead of time?"

Holmes unclamped the stem of his pipe from his mouth and regarded me with a twitch of a smile. "As I have frequently observed to Watson: You know my methods. When one has honed the art of deductive reasoning, applying those skills to deduce the Christmas wishes of a ten-year-old child—albeit an extraordinary ten-year-old child—is really quite … elementary."

A Note of Thanks to Our Readers

Thank you for reading this collection of Sherlock and Lucy short stories. We hope you've enjoyed it.

As you probably know, reviews make a big difference! So, we also hope you'll consider sharing your thoughts!

Here's the link if you'd like to review the whole collection:
amzn.to/2RgxJ8U

and here are links for each of the individual stories:

Flynn's Christmas
amzn.to/2q9lUIh

The Clown on the High Wire
amzn.to/34XxbKk

The Cobra in the Monkey Cage
amzn.to/33M7NXP

A Fancy-Dress Death
amzn.to/33QM15y

The Sons of Helios
amzn.to/32OpVyY

The Vanishing Medium
amzn.to/2XgVFMd

Christmas at Baskerville Hall
amzn.to/2rKlWH4

We really appreciate your responses!

To keep up with our latest escapades, please visit us at www.SherlockandLucy.com

About the Authors

Anna Elliott is the author of the *Twilight of Avalon* trilogy, and *The Pride and Prejudice Chronicles*. She was delighted to lend a hand in giving the character of Lucy James her own voice, firstly because she loves Sherlock Holmes as much as her father, Charles Veley, and second because it almost never happens that someone with a dilemma shouts, "Quick, we need an author of historical fiction!" She lives in Pennsylvania with her husband and four children.

Charles Veley is the author of the first two books in this series of fresh Sherlock Holmes adventures. He is thrilled to be contributing Dr. Watson's chapters for the series, and delighted beyond words to be collaborating with Anna Elliott.

Flynn's Christmas, finds one of the Baker Street Irregulars with nowhere to sleep, but with a life-saving job to do for Mr. Holmes.

The Clown on the High Wire takes readers to the Olympia Theatre in London, where Holmes is called in to solve the bizarre murder of a clown whose killer may be anyone in the big top arena. This crime, and each of the four stories that follow, connects with the murderer who escaped in *Die Again, Mr. Holmes*. The five stories make a "Season One" of adventures for Holmes, Lucy, and Dr. Watson.

In *The Cobra in the Monkey Cage*, a desperate appeal from Dr. Watson's medical school classmate leads to the London Zoo and a night of perilous adventure for Sherlock and Lucy.

A Fancy-Dress Death features Irregular Flynn, and takes the Baker Street team from the rough section of Whitechapel to a posh London mansion for a fancy dress ball. Flynn, of course, doesn't have an invitation. All too soon he discovers that death is also an uninvited guest.

An aristocrat's London estate is the setting of *The Sons of Helios*, where the search for a stolen painting leads Sherlock and Lucy to a mysterious occult organization. Then the case takes a deadly turn.

In *The Vanishing Medium*, Lucy and Jack track down a murderer, but their old adversary from *Die Again* strikes back with a vengeance, leaving Holmes and Lucy with a life-or-death mission to accomplish in the upcoming "Season Two".

Rounding out the collection is *Christmas at Baskerville Hall*, a heartwarming Christmas adventure with a touch of suspense. Sir Henry Baskerville, now happily married, invites Sherlock Holmes to that infamous baronial mansion in darkest Devonshire for a family holiday. But Sir Henry has an ulterior motive and the powers of evil are at work.